The novels of

# Wilhelmina Baird

## CRASHCOURSE

"A PUNGENT, GLEAMY-DARK STREET-FUTURE, illuminated with memorable style, a gratifying sense of humor, and a killer eye for twisted technological detail." —WILLIAM GIBSON

"A NEAT AND NASTY PREMISE . . . an exciting debut performance." —*New York Times Book Review*

"A WELCOME ADDITION to the field . . . Baird has a fine way with a plot, and a sensitivity to character." —*Locus*

"EXTRAORDINARY . . . get ready to enter an exhilarating future . . . Baird has created a captivating, original world and a compelling, suspenseful story." —*Worlds of Wonder*

"A STUNNING DEBUT NOVEL about three characters living in a kind of Cyber-Dystopia . . . an exciting reading experience from cover to cover." —*Northshire Edge* (VT)

## CLIPJOINT

"THE ACTION IS EXPLOSIVE . . . no one can fault her ingenious originality. First-rate entertainment." —*Booklist*

"ANOTHER FRENETIC JOURNEY of discovery through her cyberneticized view of the future . . . Baird is one of the most interesting new writers to recently emerge in the field." —*Science Fiction Chronicle*

## PSYKOSIS

"NARRATOR CASS IS ONE TOUGH WOMAN, and her account of their adventures has both guts and heart. Fast-paced, sassy, sometimes gritty, space opera . . . intelligent fun." —*Locus*

"THINGS PICK UP IMMEDIATELY AND RELENTLESSLY, sweeping along to the book's conclusion. Baird has created an inherently interesting alien race, and reveals the details in and around a well-plotted adventure story." —*Science Fiction Chronicle*

*Ace Books by Wilhelmina Baird*

**CRASHCOURSE**
**CLIPJOINT**
**PSYKOSIS**
**CHAOS COME AGAIN**

# CHAOS COME AGAIN

Wilhelmina Baird

ACE BOOKS, NEW YORK

This Ace Book contains the complete text of the original trade edition. It has been completely reset in a typeface designed for easy reading, and was printed from new film.

CHAOS COME AGAIN

An Ace Book / published by arrangement with the author

PRINTING HISTORY
Ace trade edition / October 1996
Ace mass-market edition / October 1997


Cover art by Bruce Jensen.

For information address: The Berkley Publishing Group, a member of Penguin Putnam Inc., 200 Madison Avenue, New York, NY 10016.

The Putnam Berkley World Wide Web site address is http://www.berkley.com

Make sure to check out *PB Plug*, the science fiction/fantasy newsletter, at http://www.pbplug.com

ISBN: 0-441-00479-2

ACE®
Ace Books are published by The Berkley Publishing Group, a member of Penguin Putnam Inc., 200 Madison Avenue, New York, NY 10016.
ACE and the "A" design are trademarks belonging to Charter Communications, Inc.

PRINTED IN THE UNITED STATES OF AMERICA

10 9 8 7 6 5 4 3 2 1

# Acknowledgments

Thanks to my editor Laura Anne Gilman, for her (as always) hard labor, patience and carefully detailed criticism.

To Matt Bialer for trying (and to Bonnie Obernauer for talking to me).

To Steve for various kinds of postal encouragement he already knows about, much of it decent.

To the printers who have to set this up, and haven't yet killed me (though it could still happen).

And to James, for reading it.

Any book takes more than one person. At least since Aristotle, and even he picked his students' brains in the garden. I take responsibility for the dumbnesses in this one myself; for the gracious help, I am properly grateful.

❖

**ENCYCLOPEDIA COSMOGRAPHICA UNIVERSALIS,** *selection* Solar System, q.v. Sol, *menu choice* Earth, *q.v.* Terra, *subsection* History, *select for period, see sub-menu for area of interest: selection* CHANGE. *Press T for printout, text only, H for download of complete entry.*

(*T entered for text printout.)*

***CHANGE-compiled by J. ABIOLA and M. R. KARALAMBIDES:***

The event known as Change constitutes the greatest evolutionary advance known to modern HoSap. The organism responsible [*holo: amorphous bluish bubbles cramped at the bottom of a crack in bare rock*] was discovered accidentally toward the end of the Fourth Alien War, by a human woman [*holo: young female face with shaggy black hair*] who lost control of her equipment while prospecting the surface of an alien planet [*holo: bare rocky landscape against jungle background*]. (See also under *BLAINE, Cassandra; DELORN INDUSTRIES, family history; ALVIORI, also called GEEKS; NGSC21-433-III; ALIEN WARS, The.* Additional information under *SYMBIOSIS.*)

The familiar organism we now know as a symb, of unknown age and origin, was at that time in stasis, having lost its first host, possibly through shipwreck, in a world whose proteins had proved incompatible with its own [*shot from above of wide volcanic plain rising to a cone, covered with yellow furry mosses against a purplish sky*].

Records suggest the dormant state may have lasted centuries, if not millenia. Since the occupying Alviori (q.v.) [*holo: line of toadstool-like lifeforms with bright-colored caps and sinuous flexible threads*] were unsuitable hosts due to incompatibility of genetic constitution and intellectual functions, the initial traumatic human/symb conjunction awakened the static organism to activity by providing, for the first time since its original loss, a suitable substitute intelligence and genome. The symbiote quickly spread to all the human personnel in the area [*awkwardly grinning group, most in Naval uniform*], and subsequently by infection to their human contacts and thence throughout a large part of the race. Infection of artificial intelligences with human-based brain-cells occurred subsequently by another accident (see under *PLAGUE, the Great, Origin and Development; QUASI-ORGANICS AND THEIR ORIGINS*; ref. RAKKAINEN, Ole, *Cruise of the* **Yardbird**, Heyman & Wye, Hampton-of-Argos; PERELLA, Kimotha, **Mandeville's** *Travels,* Syrtis Major University Press, Mars, In-Solar; NORTHMARK, Garvey, *Building a Dragon*, Northmark Industries Press, Inc., Dekker XIV, Reimann Cluster).

By this means, Humanity acquired its modern capacities for shape-changing (see under *MOLECULAR DISPERSION*), telepathy (q.v.) and personal space-travel by bodily displacement (see also under *PSYCHOKINESIS,* cross-ref. *TELEKINESIS; DISCORPING, Theory and Practice;* and ref. CUELLAR Y MUNOZ, Alfredo: *Molecular Transition States In and Out of Vacuum,* Outbound Publications, Resurrection U.P.; JIANG, Chia-shi: *Warping the Phase,* Humboldt Books Inc., Nyovnyi Mir). Unfortunately for the peace of Earth and her colonies, not all contemporary humans were disposed to accept symbiosis, for a variety of religious, political and cultural reasons, and the current divided state of HoSap into Changes and Norms came about after painful social convulsions [*rioting mob in a variety of clothing, from farm blues to brilliantly ridiculous high-fashion, image partially obscured by a hail of missiles, in an atmosphere of smoke*]. (See also under *SYMBIOTE WARS; JONES, CHURCH OF, History and Culture; NORMAL HUMANITY, Definition and Customs;* and *TRANSPLANETARY COMMERCE, Forced Adaptations.* Supplementary bibliographies will be found under each of these headings.)

While the advancement of Change has profoundly affected our culture and society, in particular our ability to penetrate intergalactic spaces [*smiling naked woman with silver purse slung around her neck, swimming gracefully on a background of stars and leading a small child in a snowsuit by its chubby hand*], limited only by the range of our ships and the extent of our personal ambition, the development, like all great leaps forward, has not taken place without complications . . .

# ONE

## Bounty

The orange holo-sign reading SAM'S USED STARSHIPS spread across the sky at right-angles to the white smear of the Milky Way, its array of orbiting hulks lit intermittently by strobe-lights. The office hung vaguely in mid-space with a crooked sign saying OFFICE not quite parallel to one of the walls.

Most of Sam's customers arrived under their own power, so his parking-lot was minimal. So was their equipment. Mass-energy ratios were what they had always been and clothes equaled energy, which cost money. Money always being in short supply.

Desi, consequently, flipped around the yard stark naked, blue and snarling. The blue was voluntary and the snarl simulated, but then, she was working on a bargain.

"So what is this?" she growled, echoing her voice off the adversary's inner ear for effect and prodding at the brains of the mutated Starmaster with supplementary tailpods that hung in mid-orbit. Her discorporated finger penetrated hardened cerosteel like mist and tickled the meat-computer's outer membrane. The Starmaster giggled, wriggling. "A fricky greenhouse or something?"

The vendor caught up with her a few steps ahead of his breath. He'd been scoping this customer out telepathically with his symb's help for ninety seconds, which came close to touching the regs on civil liability, but Desi was discorping around so fast they kept losing track, particularly since her own symb wasn't even trying to cooperate. Contrariwise, the pair of them seemed to take pleasure in being opaque, which was at the least bad manners. He found some of these Outer types trying.

"A very nice small merchant vessel, creatively customized for high-intensity living, low shift-average, one careful owner . . ."

"Hi, baby," the Starmaster graveled in a rasping contralto. "You wanna try my improvements?"

"Who was also a sex-maniac," Desi completed. "Why'd he sell her?"

The vendor fiddled with his slate. "He—er—migrated elsewhere. The ship's been completely therapied since . . ."

"We could do lunch, sweetheart," the Starmaster proposed huskily. Light dawned in Desi's eyes.

"The lover ate im," she said.

"It was a misunderstanding," the vendor pleaded. "Their relationship became rather intense and she began to—er—feel competivity towards other women. A misdirected mother-complex, according to the therapist. She became over-devoted and . . ."

"Ate im. Next."

"She's been through a full course of treatment with a first-class reactivator," the vendor protested. "I've a certificate guaranteeing her freedom from negative reactions . . ."

He was talking to vacuum. He groaned and set wildly about seeking human life-trace among the AIs. He found her burrowing into the brain-casing of a dull-blue yacht with gilt trim and an impressive nose-array.

"Really, Miz Smeett. I must ask you not to enter into brain-contact with the computers . . ."

"Why, they all cannibals?"

"No, of course not. I mean—uh—it confuses their emotional reactions."

"Good," Desi said. "You know all that garbage up front's cosmetic?"

"Well— The last owner had a passion for tech but not

much money. He liked to look as good as the other guys, if you see what I . . .''

''Inferiority complex. What did he die of?'' Desi drew her head back out of the casing and patted it. The yacht relaxed slightly.

''But Miz Smeett, he didn't . . .''

''He went away and left me,'' the yacht sniveled in a nagging female whine. ''Inherited money and got a lech for a new Shimoon with gen antennae. He didn't care what became of me . . .''

''You got a voice cut-off?'' Desi asked brutally.

''I can change register,'' the yacht whined, shifting to tenor.

Desi grunted. ''Okay,'' she said. ''I gotta have a ship. Mine took a mete-hit right in the braincase when she was thinking about something other than her screens, the stupid bitch. Is what happens when you let em get into philosophy. Now I'm fricky stranded. Since all the others are macho, psycho or mentally disabled I guess I'm gonna have to make do with self-pity. Whadya asking?''

That took another heated twenty minutes. By the time she'd written ''Daisy Smith,'' in careful slow script on the bottom of the contract, signaling an advanced education, and thumbprinted it, the vendor was sweating. He watched her disappear through the yacht's dull-blue hull with something approaching self-pity of his own.

''God protect me from Out-Rim bounty-hunters,'' he muttered. But Desi was off-net.

''Can you reabsorb that junk on your snoot?'' she said to the yacht.

''If I have to. It took a lot of concentration to grow.''

''Great. Get with it. How are you at silence?''

Sulky hiatus.

''Even better,'' Desi appreciated. ''So let's space.''

The yacht waited for its new owner to melt through the hull before it defiantly poked the despised nose-assembly right back out, cosmetic or not.

Installing Desi's professional equipment, which ran to size and was awkward enough to use up her and her symb's combined mental energies plus all her muscle and the ship's full complement of waldos, took three sweaty swearing hours.

"Hey, lamebrain," Desi grumped, "this is plain, common inorganic multifaxing. Like you did every time you ordered the nans for Master's Rice Krispies. My patterns are currently passing the in-membrane faster than your retarded reflexes receive, which is why we got arc-parts all over the hold and every damn one in the wrong order. If we stay way behind, the template's liable to back up, which can torque the print-outs, and then you get reversal of atomic structures. You taken a course in applied quantum mechanics for idiots?"

"No," the ship said, guardedly.

"Uh-huh. You know about reversed atomic structures? Otherwise known as anti-matter. Tell you anything?"

"No," even more guardedly.

"Boom," Desi said, with an expansive gesture. "White flash. Dwindling singularity. As in, you, me and it, goodbye. And in addition, my agency's paying for me to be working. Mucha moola. So if you recycled that antique S-M musculater and cleared me a workspace we'd be through by Christmas."

"The Master worked out in the after hold."

"Well, Mistress is fixing up her operating table, which is why we're building the arc here. Then I can maybe recycle your synapses. Haul the power-cell over."

"I thought you were a bounter."

"Who said? Leave thinking to guys is qualified." Desi grinned like a shark. "Call me Lady Bountiful, but from a different agency. The gear's surgical. I'm a medic."

The yacht shivered as a waldo hefted the cell-case into its seating. "That cell's bracketed into phasespace, I can feel false realities against my backbone."

"So where you want it bracketed, the neighborhood swimming-pool? I use gravitronics. Which are unstable."

"Gravitronics."

"Listen, buttdimple, you heard of a Higgs field, otherwise called phasespace? Virtual particles that skip in and outta reality and create energy as they go? Your main drive uses it."

"Yes," the yacht said, hurt. "I use it to slide around the curve of spacetime when I change location."

"Hallelujah. Well, the continuum, including its quantum

phase, is deformed by extreme gravitational fields such as you find in deep gravity wells, which is why you need to be clear to warp. The torsion's strongest in heavy stellar cores, near black holes and around neutron stars. Where there's maximum flexion of reality and the quanta are warped nearly out of existence."

"I wouldn't know," the yacht said sulkily. "We avoid them. Gravitational distortion twists my warplines."

"It would. That kind of energy's gravitronics. If you went on main drive while you were in there and pushed hard enough with the well's gravity to sling you, it's just possible you'd go right through and come out elsewhen."

"That doesn't mean anything. The continuum's four-dimensional, you can skip around the curve and come back in again. If you overloaded the engines, you'd just blow up."

"Limited vision," Desi sighed. "The multiverse is like chrysanthemum petals, a whole set of closed loops almost touching. Except unlike petals they aint all the same shape and color. Classic chaos theory. A jink near the start and things end up different."

"You're talking about other continuums?"

"Yep. Outside. Loops, nearly touching."

"There's no outside."

"That depend what 'outside' mean. I'm talking multiple sets of dimensions. Besides ours. Elsewhen, which the fricky little quanta flip in and out of. Everything that's possible is possible. We're in this bit. Other petals is what they call outspace. Alternatives. You could go through to them, if you pushed hard enough. Just needs energy."

"In theory," the yacht said.

"Everything's theoretical till you stick a pin in it. I work for Hermes Central, which you won't have heard of. It's the Federal outworld medical agency. Of which I am an agent." Desi leered. "I change things, such as people. Using the arc, since I haven't the power in my bare hands. Hermes *know* elsewhen's real, they've looked. Trust me. Don't ask about it, data's classified. You need a lot of hard gravity. If you're also lunatic it helps, but that's how the human race advances. Loony pioneers kill themselves today, some other guy makes millions from it tomorrow."

"The physics there are different too?" the yacht asked, after a pause.

"I guess the chrysanthemum must be infinite," Desi said, frowning. "Everything that's possible. Lot of variants must have different physics, maybe most. But if the petals are infinite, there must also be a lot of them near enough ours to move through. Hermes thinks maybe you can't get into really unlike ones, you'd be too alien to their local realities to exist there and you'd kinda squirt off them. But there're others you can. Theoretically."

"Theoretically," the yacht echoed. "Suppose we go up in a flash of radiation?"

"That is also possible. You can't make omelets without taking risks."

"I'd rather not."

"Nobody asked you. But in my case the risks is limited, cause I am following a guy. Who already took them, on account of he's crazy. Where he's been, we can go. He's weird but he can't walk on water. That I know of."

"Even if you can change dimensions, it must be illegal. Overwarping's a Grade Four felony."

"Which is your proof. Government doesn't legislate against the impossible. I didn't say my boy was legal, I said he was there. He's crazy but a genius. If water can be walked on, he'll do it tomorrow."

"Your cell's too big," the ship complained. The thick torus of the arc had grown up to fill half the hold, with the operating bench, poised in a stasis-field, exactly centered in its complex coils. The bench was longer and wider than was needed for humans. The cell loomed over it like a menacing spider. "If it slips off-net, we'll discorporate anyway."

"It aint going to. It collects and stores quantum-energy like your batteries, it's just calibrated for extreme conditions. Keeps the grav-field warped, gives power out steadily and goes on doing it. State of the art. I'm the control-mechanism." Desi's face slipped into a natural rounded innocence while she was working, but she kept her wolf grin. She had very good teeth. "Hermes Central's business. Whupping deviated guys back to shape. With this." She slapped the torus. "You'd be surprised how much clout she has when she's powered."

"No, I wouldn't," the ship said positively. "Does it hurt?"

"Them, or you?"

"Me," the yacht whispered. The ducts nervously sucked air and left the cabin smelling stuffy.

"If you get in my way." Desi twitched on the CHARGE lever. "Dunno, now you ask. They yell a bit, but I thought it was fright. She's inclined to spark."

"Um," said the yacht. The hold's inner surface rippled with a quiet flood of macromolecules reinforcing its ceramic. "I had to get an international criminal."

"Your late boss being County Sheriff. Judging by the vid collection I put down the toilet."

"They helped him concentrate."

Desi whinnied. "Uh-huh."

"He did some very trying work."

"One-handed. Did his partners survive?"

Silence.

"You swear you're a Fed?" the ship persisted.

"I am a Fed. Controlled discorporation of other people, plus lube and refit. At the expense of your friendly neighborhood agency, duly funded by the Central Government. On a job, which is why I need you. If guys think I'm a bounter, it's okay as camouflage. Out here they used to bounters, federal agents they dissipate on sight." She craned her neck up at her equipment. "Course, since this works with overwarped gravity on highly-charged quanta with a whole lot of torsion, it is not a good idea to lose concentration. Red snitch there is the bad-idea button, which remind you to switch the arc off before starting into gravitational roller-coasters. It's one powerful transformation device. No knowing what it might transform, overloaded."

Silence.

"Well, gotta work. And catch up with a guy, when I have time. Now we spacing. Switch the fax off before my boss assumes I'm truly incompetent, I'm going forward. How's your cuisine?"

"Ethnic."

"Which ethnos?"

"Early Ukrainian cheeseburger."

"Logical," Desi said bitterly, discorping.

The *Wynkyn de Worde* was as bad as it sounded. The scent-organ was equipped with perspiration-inducer, perspiration-suppressor and Russian Leather. The evil-minded set all three at once. There were also palm trees in the corners. Desi passed through several people on her way to the bar, arousing furious yells, and leaned on the plastic. The barkeep looked her over, saw raw bounter and decided not to even try throwing her out.

"Whatever it is, we aint got it."

She smiled evilly. "Then gimme a beer. Aint what, it who. Broke outta the Special Holding Facility on New Prosperity three months back, still on the lam. I'm paying. Cash. Look like this. Or thereabouts."

The loungers scoped the projection. It was good, for second-hand guardroom recall, but the nose was fuzzy.

"How much?" someone said from along the bar.

"How'd she get out?" a skinny drink with wild hair and hollow eyes asked from her elbow.

"Old-fashioned minicutter, someone too dim to frisk her right. Ten thou for information, twenty the corp. Breathing. If she aint, I lose interest."

The skinny drink whistled. "Unexpectedly bright," he opined. "Even amazing. Who'd have expected wits in that genotype? Where did she hide it?"

"One, the guard who was paid to should've, if he doing his job. It's okay, he enjoying his retirement. Two, don't ask. Hear she's currently working for the outfit who gave her it. Thought she'd exotic appeal, or something. Word is, they're here. Any offers?"

"What did she do?"

"Beat up a blood-bank."

"You mean held up," he offered helpfully.

"I mean beat up, she hasn't the brains to recognize money. Put three nurses and a tech in the hospital. Don't know her own strength. Guess it accidental, she was looking for the restroom. Or so they told me. Anyone?" She looked around.

Silence. Someone played a riff of sweat/unsweat/mute

skunk on the scent-organ and vanished through the wall, howling. It wasn't Desi who did the kicking, the whole room was offended.

"Nah," the barkeep said, turning away. "Beer?"

"You heard."

"When you drunk it you go. We don't appreciate bounters hereways."

"You gonna make that personal?"

"Nah. I'm gonna call the goon squad."

"Coward," Desi said, grinning.

"Hey." The skinny drink edged half a hip on the stool beside her. He was narrow enough not to need more. "Could we maybe get together on this? It sounds interesting. Name's Jones."

"No. What's interesting about that? I was called Jones, I'd keep my lip shut."

"So what are you called?"

"To the bar," Desi said, turning her back. "Get lost."

"I can get you publicity, I work for TV."

"Then you should wash out your neurons. Any bounty on you yet?" She made a show of consulting the files a genuine hunter would carry on wetware. Since she hadn't any wetware her symb faked it. She was interested to see he had none either, which made him a pro. Longrange teeping barehanded was a scarce talent. She smacked a telepathic tentacle out of her head and he discorped reluctantly ten feet backward, looking pathetic.

When she left he was leaning over the scent-organ improvising variations on musk, amber, lemon tea and Russian Leather. She held her nose, but he wasn't looking.

A faceless shadow brushed against her among the bushes that crawled on the steps and whispered. "What does Echelon get me?"

"Five to ten if you messing with a Federal officer," Desi said, putting her heel on an encroaching bush. "What's Echelon?"

"That way," the shadow whispered. "Soon. Try the China House."

"Okay," she said grudgingly. "I'll cred you a thousand, but if you kidding I scoped you."

"I'm straight."

"Then for godssakes put your face on. You're disgusting."

"Aint doing it for you. Watch out at Echelon."

"Eyes in the back of my head." She demonstrated. They were protuberant, luminous and green. Her hair clung stringily across the eyeballs.

"Gross," the shadow said. It retched to prove it. Desi walked on, grinning.

Echelon was what it sounded. Slinking blurs moved through the alleys and faded in and out of walls. Desi notched her bio-detectors around to three-sixty, dispensed with the hind eyes (the hair was making them water anyway) and braced her disruptor. Forcible rearrangement of their matter didn't bother her kind much personally, they'd a disgusting tendency just to reassemble, but it did play hell with their armor.

"Wanna play games, doll?" a silhouette whispered.

"Nah, I gotten too old for Housy. Why'n't you buy yourself a Barbie? I'm straight anyhow. Where's the China House?"

The silhouette sniggered. "Get yourself a sex-change. And then they won't have you, cause they bent. Left three, right. Watch for the doorkeep, she a full-body psycho."

"Fine, I get off on stomping physicals."

"Don't bet. What they do with china's break it. Since it seem you a stranger, how about sharing the take with a friend?"

"Sharing aint my disease, and I got no friends."

She saw the muzzle-flash in time to discorporate and come out behind kicking, but the silhouette had gone. A gamy smell circled the alley and a black streak zigzagged the length of a wall. The rattle of its tailrings faded.

"Dimplebutt," she concluded, reassembling her left boot from somewhere in vacuum. It came back tarnished. "Hope you end frozen in half-tomorrow."

The weed-odor was almost as strong as the smell of snake. The sidewalk underfoot felt like more mobile vegetation. But a frail jangle blew through the towers, a multiple tinkle like hundreds of little porcelain bells. She remade the boot and used it to walk with.

* * *

It was hundreds of little porcelain bells, fringing the eaves of a translucent pagoda. Faint light shone out through the walls and shadows moved beyond. The arched door had a guard. Your basic cube with evil red eyes spaced around the upper edge, a real psycho shape. Desi forked her fingers. The cube grew paws at the corners and lumbered. A mouth flowered in the side nearest. "Want something?"

"Looking for a guy. Any objections?"

"Girl-guys only. Pay at the door."

"You in the wrong file, Sis. I aint a customer."

The cube braked. "What kinda print you carrying?"

"Wouldn't make no difference to you, it written in writing."

"Tough," the cube sneered. "Bounter trash. You maybe think you coming through me."

"No," Desi said peaceably. "Don't think, I know." She was inside the lobby. The cube reversed and displaced after her. Desi re-shifted and came out with the disruptor on freeze. "You like ice?"

The cube took the charge in the focus, reverted abruptly to a thickset woman with graying braids and set in place, her clothes crumbling at the edges.

{No fair,} she complained telepathically, {that illegal. Gonna take me all night to straighten my nuclei.}

"You could have stayed and looked at my print. Carry it with me. Happy straightening."

Desi walked forward into the pagoda. Ambulation was the obvious way to get around since the building had corridors, and the corridors had doors. The partitions were so translucent you could get free kicks by looking if you had the bend, but that wasn't why her stomach was growling. Doors meant the chicks dealt with hume Normals and other aliens, which where she came from was throw-up territory.

"Shut up," she told the growl and kept using her boots.

The lobby opened on a desk womaned by a twinner. Both halves glared at her. "You the bimbo froze Roseanner?"

"That wins you a plastic duck. Wanta try for the big prize and catch pneumonia?"

The halves were currently two-thirds interpenetrated, which

gave them three eyes and four profiles. The middle eye had a double share of temper and broken veins. Their united red/blue sequins shivered and modulated from the middle outward into poison greens. ''Maybe we'd rather call the madam.''

''Nah, that'd be too rational a solution. You two half-lobes haven't the intellect, be too liable to cut down on horseshit. Bet you aint happy without a fight a night.''

''Yeah,'' one half said, single—or at least one half of their mouth moved—''maybe we aint at that. And could be she'd rather sling you out herself.''

Desi shrugged. ''Makes no difference to me, I going through anyhow. I'll tell her hi from you if I see her.''

The combined weight of their reaching psyches leaned on her mindshield and bounced off, frustrated.

{So what the frick?} Right reflected.

{Aint as bount as she looks. Federal officer? Health Department? Some freaking alphabet, anyway,} Left mirrored back. {They all trouble. Let's call Ryka and let em fight.}

{Why'n't we just let the bitch on through and see if someone maybe swallows her?}

{Not with her shield. How'd the Feds do that?}

{Grow em in bottles.}

They wrapped their spare arms around their waist for comfort. ''Test-tube baby!'' they yelled in unison.

Desi didn't listen.

The China House was low-expensive, entrances everywhere and a dozen different species interconnecting. She shoved her head through a couple of partitions and found the meat was as varied as the customers. Once you dispensed with decency anything could go. A lot of it was going much too far. Heads and other organs swiveled in indignation and muddled sonics bounced off the cero. The pagoda was insulated, but the walls sang.

She pulled her upper half free from a particularly revolting combo of blue gel bubbles and platinum Neanderthal and came face to face with the madam's holographic ghost.

{I take it you've a warrant for this intrusion?} the ghost asked, in a cold upper-class telepathic husk.

''Gotta disruptor. On freeze, but that could change.''

{Suppose I pull the fuzz and let them take you?}

"Could try. If you paying enough, and I don't freeze you first."

The disruptor wasn't pointing at the ghost, it was leveled at the office ten steps behind it. Which was doorless and semi-transparent. A flare of rage burned up behind the wall. The madam discorped out into the holo, a flame-haired virago in a smoke-gray bodysuit. "What do you want?"

"Guy who works here."

"Does she have a name?"

"I expect so."

"You mean you don't know it."

"*I* do. Problem is, you likely don't. She may not know it herself."

The virago drew her brows down. "One of those. I suppose you want to go through the personnel."

"You won the prize. Begun to think the outside decoration left you brain-damaged."

The last traces of ghost evaporated and drifted in fumes down the passage. The virago, embodied, bared her teeth. "Now, you wait. You want to search, without knowing whom you're looking for?"

"I'll know her when I see her. Was hoping you'd call up the meat and parade em."

"And you think I'll stand still for it?"

"Bet you stand still for more'n that, every time the Mayor calls," Desi said. "If I just freeze you, it stop being your problem." She eyed the hair. "Been wondering what that do if the temperature drops."

The madam paled. "Which agency did you mention?"

"Didn't. You really want to know?"

"Shit," the virago growled. "Let's try the downshift, then I needn't interrupt anything."

"Doubt you *could* interrupt some of that without a surgeon."

The madam bit on the lower arch of her Cupid's bow and tossed her mane. Flame and smoke poured down the corridor.

"Preferably before you scare off the customers?" Desi considered the coiffure. Vulgar, but went with the decor. The curl of incense that trailed off the back-tress was nicely done. She thought with taste added, she could use it. She filed the thought. The madam caught the edge of the file and the smoke darkened.

"Don't push your luck."

"I aint lucky," Desi said modestly, "I purely skilful. But I'll save you time. If her symb's functional, I don't want her."

The madam nodded briefly.

{Downshift,} she ordered on a telepathic snap. {Non-symbs only. Get your butts down here on the double.}

A chorus of psychic groans answered.

"Come into the parlor," she added bitterly. "I hope you weren't expecting refreshments."

"Here? You're kidding. Couldn't be sure I wasn't drinking a client. Your downshift in bed?"

The madam lifted the edge of her lip. "Bed's where they work. You just broke up the quarter-final of the local-league pingball championships, senior division. We'd a good chance of winning."

"Gee," Desi said. "It's the area Girl-Scout Toadstool. You should put a sign out."

The parlor had as many odd-shaped doors as an educational toy and the decor was so neutral it was almost invisible. The air smelled like distilled water. Gelatinous furniture floated around waiting for butts to shape itself to. The madam fell gracefully into a couch that turned scorch-color when it touched her hair and Desi propped herself on the wall. A wandering davenport nudged her leg and she kicked it away. It retired whining.

The meat drifted down slowly, mincing, scrambling and crawling on its belly. Doors clacked. Some of the girls carried pingball shooters and they all looked ticked off. They summoned furniture and struck attitudes. Desi pinched up her face.

"Jeezle. I knew this wasn't the Truegood Taj Mahal, but the ambience is a record. There a water-shortage?"

"This is a tournament." The madam tossed her flames. "The girls are athletes. Since you think you know your criminal lawfiles, and supposing you aren't some P.I. on the prowl, which I don't want to know because you're trouble already, howabout you ident her, cop her and scoot while the Twinworld Voodans still think it's a time-out?"

"If she's here. Sure hope so, gonna major bore me to take the place down." Desi strolled between lumps of gelatin. "Nice line in crim types you got pinging. They all out of Correctional Facilities? And I wasn't thinking a little light forgery."

"That new?" a bronze-colored slither with diamond eye-paint drawled in a grating contralto. "Does this place look like a ladies' academy? You should see the other side, even I wonder how they got em outta solitary long enough to ping. We were nineteen/twelve last, for nine serious injuries. You buying info?"

"Nah. Not this time. I'll take her."

She slapped a hand on a loose-limbed ape-mutation with orange fur and a dog muzzle. Its forehead sloped sharply up to a point but its tits, contrariwise, might have been inflated with a footpump. The lower scenery, also on display, was also spectacular. The choice brought uproar.

"Hey! That our attack center. You can't have her now, we need her."

"How about coming back after the game?"

"She'll be here," the bronze said cynically. "She aint smart enough to slope. Guy don't know her own way to the bathroom, she has a minder."

"Her country needs her. Try your first reserve, smarts equal speed. Good shooting. Hope to not see you."

"Check, double," the bronze spat, eeling to a door. "Come on, gals, someone call Lucy. We've started needing luck."

The team headed for the exits, leaving the ape-mute behind. Its little brown eyes were bewildered. The madam scowled. "I hope you're satisfied."

The orange shoulder twitched under Desi's hand. The mute dropped its pinger and its fingers spasmed. The fur shriveled and its fuchsia-colored trikini melted to a rag. The deformed skull reshaped to human.

A naked man stood among the gelatin, his skin blue-white, spikes of hair curving like snowfalls over his forehead. He opened clear blue eyes and smiled. Frost furred the furniture and a luckless armchair cracked and fissured. Bits tinkled on the floor. His gaze swiveled and found Desi. Their eyes locked. Electric contact jolted between them.

"That was a great fuck," he said to the air. "The greatest. Bill me. Kill me. Rue me. Try to sue me."

Desi's eyes were misted with rainbows that slid down her cheeks in melting zigzags. "Ice?"

"Long time no see," the man murmured. His long eyelashes fluttered, and stiffened. The face twisted.

The manshape was melting back to narrow-skulled brute, its eyes blank, a rime of frost on its long fur. It bared its gums on yellow incisors and rolled back its eyeballs. The madam's face was hard.

"Who the hell was that?"

Desi blinked. Two cold snail-trails marked her blued skin. "An optical illusion. Pay it no mind. Unless you happen to know the guy's address. His idea of a calling-card but it don't smell recent. I'll just take my meat. Grateful for the cooperation, your community thanks you."

"The frick it does," the madam rasped, but Desi's leash had settled around the mute's neck and they were already evaporating out. "Damned bureaucrats," she concluded, to the air.

The evening telepathic holo was forming everywhere, in heads and homes throughout the Change-human world, as people in from the office or out from the mines slumped into their evening shapechange or out of their workaday utility body, calling up drinks from dispensers if they had them, or getting their symbs to convert surrounding materials to fake alcohol the symbs wouldn't get hives from, if they were currently in space or on desert planets. They ran through the channels and made their choices, and the colors bloomed in the air, invisibly, inside their minds.

⌘

# TP–TV

## *the station of the multiverse*

BRINGING YOU NEWS, VIEWS AND RAVE CLUES FROM OUR OUTSTATION NEWSDESK, WITH ALL YOU WANT TO KNOW ABOUT ALL THAT'S WORTH KNOWING THROUGHOUT THE COSMOS, WITH RARE REVIEWS FROM YOUR FAVE TEEPS, WHEREVER, WHOEVER AND WHATEVER YOU MAY BE—OVER TO OUR SPECIAL CORRESPONDENT IN THE BIG BLACK: —IT'S ALL YOURS, JJ, AND WATCH THAT STATIC, YOU'RE ONLINE—HERE'S JONESY!

❖

[*Fade-in of a square male face with a jaw like Dick Tracy swimming among the station test-patterns, curled scalplock falling on his shoulder. Big white grin. It takes shape and takes over. The nose hesitates a moment before it follows. Voiceover rattles the recorder boomboxes:*]

Hi, fans, here's your brave raver with the latest collects from your raring rovers with the hottest news from Way Out There. The War with the Newts is the day's big story, with the creepy crawlers being driven back from our major bridgehead on Bridecake Station, but heavy fighting's reported around outpost planets Brightside III and V. Just watch those suckers go! We'll be lining on our on-the-spot teeps throughout the day as the situation progresses, so stay tuned for latest news from the front.

And hi, homeguys, pleased to meet so many of you in your private brainstorms back in the cradle of Ourkind, the old steady Milker. We guys here in the wild and wooly outlands where we got the wide universe leaning on our backbones get ant in our pant when we think of you-all fuzzy-warm among the cozy nearstars where you know where you're going, but it's all the day's work for Yours Truly, so here come today's wildest pictures. Roll em!

[*Black modulating to multiple star-patterns, rushing-in effect that hits the eyeballs, and closeup. Small brownish violent woman with purple eyes (some exaggeration around the chest and exact shade of the eyes unlikely) throws a leash around an orange ape-shape with dangling pinger. Woman wears four-inch skirt, eight-inch heels and an aluminum bra. Hint of a bug-eyed face looks curiously over her right shoulder. Smoke and flames well up in the background, surrounded by dancing furniture. Voiceover tones to deep warm rumble, to match the Profile:*]

Rollover II, would you believe, and in the roaring red light district a bootless bountress seizes a prey. Get a load of the monk's tits! Though Bount's the baby for my money. Unless you'd rather have the lady in the background. You come vacationing, spare a thought for the China House, folks, and the commercial's free with your teep's compliments. Unlike the merchandise, which comes expensive. Girlpeople only, men, sorry. Have to keep our eyes on this madam, she got fire, wouldn't you say?

Now let me take you around the scenery, cause this place is worth it. Like the bar of the *Wynkyn de Worde,* get a load of the wildlife. And that's before you taste the liquor! But remember it's real, you gonna need your neutralizer. Keep it in mind next time you're hopping. And a view of the spaceport. Yes, believe it or not, people, they've really got one and it takes passengers—and that gives you an idea of the fun times you have waiting for you here on Your Man's coordinates. Look forward to linking you. Though the Man will have moved on by then, call of duty. This story's worth a follow-up. And now, over to the latest sports results, fresh to you from our teep team at Top-League Headquarters. Be feeling you around, guys—but first—a word from our sponsor!

# TWO

## Business

''I don't *like* that arc,'' the yacht repeated, sniveling, as they came out of phase into reality. ''It's dangerous.''

''Only if you mess with it. So all you gotta do is don't and it's hunky.'' The live Desi wore jungle-camouflage coveralls and fieldboots. Her eyes were basic gray shading slate. They were also furious. The pseudoape flopped, legs and arms waving.

''It needs more shielding.''

''You couldn't carry more shielding. I'm the control when it's online. Just don't break my concentration.''

''What do I do if your control fails?''

''Scream for help and vanish. But it aint going to.''

''How can you know?'' the yacht wailed.

''I'm paid not to let it. So take an end of this beef and get it on the table.''

''If the cell functions on torqued quanta, couldn't power leak over the interface and take us elsewhen?''

''I don't warp and work at the same time,'' Desi said. ''Unhealthy. Which is why we're sublight. One thing at once. How close to my neutron star are we?''

The yacht posted the holochart above the table. The edges shivered.

''Quit playing *Titus Andronicus,* willya? Take us three degrees closer and increase speed, I want right in the well before I switch the arc in."

"It's not safe," the yacht bleated.

"A lot safer than it will be if I get you lobotomized. Shut up and make with the engines."

Silence. An airduct made a wrenching gurgle.

"Without commentaries."

Re-silence. The yacht leaned on her power and the neutron star grew larger in the forward screen, its heavy gravity drawing them in. Ejected material streamed from opposite sides, spreading in the dark like the beams of a lighthouse. Spurting radiation strobed in the plates, blanking them out in an epileptic stutter. Red haze outlined the trailing edges. Desi's symbiosed vision was fixed to register x-ray and gamma-ray emissions but the plate-edges hesitated close to whiteout as the disk expanded.

"I can't hold off so much energy much longer," the yacht blurted. "It's too strong, my outer shields are burning . . ."

". . . Two, one," Desi concluded to herself. "Cut drive to idle, auxiliaries full ahead."

The yacht fell like a stone into the well of the star's gravity, swung around in a descending spiral that browned out the plate, and caught herself into a zipping wheel. She hung on the edge of the torrent of plasma, her power-cells battling the rotating jet, and the engine-note rose to a howl.

Desi, still counting, waited for mark to check her orbit, snapped off the warp-drive and leaned her mind to controlling the cell as it sucked in energy. The arc heated, hummed and began to glow as its coils took up the collected forces. The ape-mute squealed and tried to pull away. The coils brightened as the hum rose. The hold glared with sparks.

"Increase power," Desi yelled, eyes on the meter. The yacht, burning inside and outside, flung all her weight into the engines and whipping gravity carried her outward.

"Keep a hold on your torque, my symb can't handle too many gees while I'm working. Cut acceleration and neut out your timeshift, we want back into normal space in the zone where we started."

"Sublight and falling," the yacht said palely. "Within

original timezone. Clear space all around. I hope you don't do this often.''

The screens blinked and came back online, to a dark sky and sparse starfield milky with gas. The neutron star was invisible somewhere behind. Desi sucked sweat back from under her hair.

''Could be worse for a learner. Let's look at the grav-gauges.'' She did. ''Three quarters. Could also be better. Let's see anyway. And keep your inboard current even, random voltage-jumps play hell with my chemistry when my symb's working. You better learn faster, I could still trade you in.''

The mute was struggling against the inertia-field in the torus, its little brown eyes flickering with fright. Rags of plastic hung off its chest-development and its azure buttocks were naked. It maybe had as much brain as a dog. It showed its teeth and barked. Desi shook her head.

''Real lowclass joint. Gotta good mind to sic the SPA on em.''

{Do that,} said the quiet voice at the back of her brain. {Meantime, shall we do what we're paid for?}

Desi sighed. ''Fricky yacht's right, this stuff's dangerous. I'm really gonna burn all our asses one day. Sure hope you covering the spare angles.''

{I have the okay from Hermes Central,} her symbiote said. {Just hope they have their warplines in order this far out, organics take it hard if you disphase their nuclei into distorted templates.}

''More work for the undertaker. We could fix it ourselves, I've extrapolated bodies back from original genetic trace before,'' Desi said. ''The symb's gotta have a residual memory, once we kick it into functioning.''

{I'd rather not. That's how we came to walk home. Three days, one stellar core and a nervous breakdown each. Could be why the ship copped a meteor, she was worn out too.}

*Yacht* shuddered.

Desi threw the last switch and stood over the bench as a bitter flickering grew around her. Her ears hissed. Half-visible landscapes glowed through her head.

{I have the templates,} her symb reported. {On mark, lining in, and coming into phase—now. Hit it.}

Desi closed her eyes and slapped her two hands on the ape's temples. The ape bellowed, and Desi's own outlines flowed and shimmered as the gravitational forces of the starwell ran and transformed through her incandescent fingers. The arc blazed within its ceramic. There was a snap, and the ship darkened.

"Shit!" she growled, sub-vocal, all her attention on her patient. "What happened?"

{Don't worry. You're still online. Your nervy friend panicked and blew her fuses, I'm going to need a brain-to-brain talk with her.}

"Kick her for me while you're in there. Hey, buttsy, get us engines. I need to see what I'm doing, while I still have a practicable template to work from."

The lightplates jumped and came back to an orange glow.

"You scared me," the yacht said selfrighteously. "All that frying. I thought the cell had overloaded, I was afraid we'd burn up." A small nervous tremor came through the ducts.

"I need you to think, I'll send you a postcard," Desi said savagely. "I'm trying to operate, on telepathic instructions from some guy In-Solar. Hermes has the original genotypes for guys like this who're really out-of-body, and I can't reshape without knowing what they are. So I'm trying to remake from a copy that jiggles anyhow, on account of all the relay teeps it takes to get here, and I do not need my brains screwed around with. Get us some light. The cell's linked with me, and if I burn you'll smell us."

The plates hesitated and rose to normal. A faint scorched odor trailed from the airflow.

"What's that?"

"The galley microtoaster got caught in the flux back in that grav-field. I was fixing breakfast . . ."

"Holy hell," Desi said sourly. "Who asked for breakfast?"

"I was only trying to be helpful," the yacht whimpered.

"Then don't." Desi turned her attention to the corpse on the table. The arc, drained, was fading to darkness, all the lights on the panel green. She switched it out. "Well, wise guy?"

A gangling boy of maybe seventeen sat up slowly, looked around him and began to scream with high, hysterical regularity. "No!" he shrieked. "It's *cold.*"

"What the hell? You," viciously, in the general direction of his forehead, "get your other half under control or I'm gonna hafta trank him. Which in your case could kill at least you, state you're in. Hear me?"

The boy went on screaming, a nerve-shredding obbligato to the drone of the cooling arc. His breath rasped and choked in his throat.

{Take it easy,} her symb said, {we're both trying. He's really screwed up.}

"Ah, shit. He was supposed to have forgotten. Frick, that brute hadn't the brains to remember. It probably enjoyed it."

{That isn't what's wrong with him.}

"Then what the hell is? You saying I fouled up the transfer?"

{No. It's some kind of overhung pre-ape trauma.}

"*Co-o-old,*" the boy shrieked.

{Uh-oh.}

Desi grunted. She put the weight of her shoulder in the slap. The boy's head jerked and his screams cut off. He sat still, fighting for breath, tears streaking his face.

"So you honked up. What's the story?"

He shook a raggedly uncut head. "Him. It was him. The blue guy. Like dying . . . I saw him. Great corpse, but it was so *cold.* I thought he was here."

"Just an illusion. Guy's long gone, it one of his habits. If it's who I was thinking."

A pale ghost shimmered into being between them, an icefall of hair over its forehead, blue eyes hilarious. It twirled like a dancer, shedding snowflakes. The air crackled. The boy cowered. "Yes."

"Then forget him, he aint real."

"I didn't mean to go so far . . ."

"They never do," Desi sighed. "He's ambidextrous. Among other talents. Dad said you'd a girlfriend."

"I had," he said miserably. "We quarreled. Then I met this guy and he told me I could pay her . . ."

"Then he showed you how without giving an estimate. I expect it's illegal."

The boy's reddened eyes squinted around. "He really isn't here?"

"Be surprised if he's even in the same dimension. Ghost was a record outta my head. Handling consequences isn't his bag."

"But it *hurt* . . ."

"Tell me about it. You're lucky to survive, internal frostbite can be fatal. Whose idea was the monk?"

"Mari-Liu called me a dumb ape. We were going to the prom and he suggested, pay her, dress up fancy. But he and I kind of spent time beforehand, he said it would put us in phase . . ."

"I get the picture. Listen, cradlemeat, one, don't get cozy with guys you don't know, they could have funny ideas. Two, a real ape is an actual anthropoid. The higher branches are quite intelligent, IQs better than yours. Cept even the highers' imaginations are limited, so unless you program your symb to snap back you still end in the zoo. A baboon, contrariwise, such as in your wisdom you picked as a model, while extremely repulsive to the human female so I expect it basically did the job, is believe it or not even dumber than you are. And since your symb's just as smart as the brain-power you stick it with, turn into a dog and you'll find yourself barking. In short, Sweetbuns, you made a monkey of yourself."

The boy groaned, cradling his skull. "It was his idea. I didn't think . . ."

"Sure you didn't. Result is I just spent three months running in circles trying to track you. You mammy's having worse hysterics'n you and you daddy's throwing money around like he cared. Come and eat. It's good for hysteria. You still got traveling to do." She snorted quietly. "There's an upside, seems you have a talent for pingball. You could turn professional, would be your salvation. You could also see my Tailormaid and put some pants on."

"I'm not hungry," the boy said piteously.

"Sure you are. Which is lucky, cause the galley fulla burnt

toast. Help yourself. Just don't ask my AI for anything complex like maybe fried eggs, I'm not sure her neural capacity's up to it.''

He stood up, shaky. ''You're sure he's gone?''

''Certain as I could be. On account of, unlike you, I want him. That pretty much guarantees his absence. Relax, if he was here I'd know it.''

{We both would,} her symb agreed. {Nice touch, making the ape female.}

''I keep telling everyone, it was a baboon. Talk to what's supposed to be in charge of him and tell it the difference.''

{I think it got the message.}

''I sure hope so. Doubt if female matters, sexual habits of all baboons equally disgusting. If you ask the galley nicely she maybe make fresh toast,'' she added to the boy. ''Ship can't be totally useless at everything.'' The yacht sighed, deep in its airsystem. ''And you, quit playing martyrs, it's boring.''

The boy smeared a hand over his face. ''My dad's going to be in an all-time snit. And I daren't even think about Mari-Liu.''

''You never know, when women reach puberty they get this brain-shrinkage at the sight of anything pretty and male. Can last twenty years, or even twenty thousand if they live so long. By the time they recover they've made cosmic boners. She could forgive you. Try thataway.'' She jerked a thumb and the boy discorped. Desi teeped him arguing with the galley.

{Not just women,} the voice said dryly. {And it doesn't always stop at twenty years, or even twenty thousand. You think that kid has an identity problem?}

''Whadda you think? Daddy's little boy. Needs advice on his choice of friends.''

{I'll talk to his symb. Maybe he needs a change of peer-group.}

''I shouldn't bother. If the others are like him, the whole pack's barking its way across the cosmos. I won't rescue more of em.'' Desi rubbed the tips of her fingers. ''I hate these big jobs with laying-on of hands, takes me days to remake my nailpolish.''

{A catastrophe. I seem to remember it was you wanted

travel, I'd have settled for life in a warm backwater with insentient vegetation.}

"Now you aint being realistic. You know what you get in warm backwaters with whatever vegetation? Mosquitoes. Take my word for it."

{Mosquitoes. Right. Let's get the kid back to ground-zero and I'll counsel his symb on how to cope with him. I'd rate both of them teenage retarded. Kids survive at his age in general, I'm more concerned about his father. High blood pressure.}

"That your trouble, you a lovin idealist. Better warn Pop, them was formidable hysterics. Kid needs somebody try to be nice to him. Temporarily, anyway."

{As also to me. I'm short on raw materials. How about some protein?}

"Help yourself, I'm entirely made of it. I'd settle for a double whisky. Hey, numb-neurons?"

"Me?" the yacht asked nervously.

"Who else? If the kid in the galley wants something fancy like cheeseburgers and cola with a side-order of rhinohorn, the answer's no way. Breakfast here is cereal and coffee."

Silence. "He's going to be disappointed," the yacht said at last.

"He's tougher than he's been raised to think. Assuming the latter. And he doesn't get thousand-cred running shoes either unless Daddy's paying, we aint a charitable foundation."

{I thought that's exactly what we were,} her symb murmured.

"Not so's I'm going on a diet for other people's feet."

{Oh, I see. The hardware was a business expense.}

"Sure it was. You didn't expect me to buy the arc personal?" Desi was outraged. "What you think I am, a planetary government?"

{I was talking about the disruptor. Nice little tool. Put a real dent in our liquidity. Not actually a surgical instrument, as such things are usually understood.}

"Certainly it was a business expense," Desi said. "You wouldn't want me to confront that madam with my bare fingernails."

{I don't see why not. Your talents are advanced or you wouldn't be here, and I didn't notice her do more than grumble.}

"She might have done anything," Desi said self-righteously.

{I don't see that as the problem. You like gadgets, that's what's wrong with our bank-account.}

"Everyone needs a hobby."

{I just wish yours wasn't military artillery.}

"You rather I took to corping on as a monkey?"

The silence was very marked everywhere.

The boy clung to the bench with his fingernails, the vault of the torus looming above him. "You sure it's okay? I'll end back where I started?"

"Trust me."

"Uh—" He was getting back his cool. "Do I actually have to? I mean, is it true Hermes can change dimensions? Someone told me," he added defensively. "If you kind of left me in a neighboring reality, we could maybe have this not have happened."

"Who would that someone be?" Desi said with irony. "Time we got this damn boat disciplined. Quit thinking until you've developed a brain. One, messing with the multiverse is high-illegal. Two, theory says if you create another reality, apart from causing litter you only double. That means you, here, stay in the trouble you were in when you started. The double maybe avoids the monkey, but considering the time-lapse and your mentality, it could be whatever else you did in the meantime's beyond my range. Or anyone else's. I refuse to be doubled into something I can't handle, assuming doubling happens to be possible, which I don't admit. And three, you can't afford it. You know how much energy it would take? You want to spend your life in two sets of Leavenworth, I'll pass. Don't panic. And don't touch the arc, you'll burn your fingers."

"I'm scared . . ."

"Sure you are. Try thinking about what to say to Mari-Liu. It's only a complicated form of multifaxing, but live organics take big energy. Hang on."

The cell came into phase and the arc brightened. Desi frowned at the dials. "You know where we going?" she asked her symb.

{Hermes' coordinates are clear this time. Give it all you've got, it's a long way. FaxNet's waiting to collect the package.}

Desi fixed her mind and threw the switch. The arc blazed to white, and sizzled. The boy turned a panicked face, wavered like seaweed and went out. Violent lightnings crossed the torus and the ship's lightplates dimmed to twilight.

"Do we gotta have this show always?" Desi complained. She was hanging on the table, her fingertips white. The lights dimmed farther to reddish dusk. "Shit! If the power goes now we'll lose him. Buttsy here cut me off from my grav-field before I'd totally charged up the cell."

{I said we're far out. Getting him back whole if he went wide'll be a problem for someone. Relax, I have the high sign. Hermes received him.}

"I hope the lady's forgiving."

{She probably will be, you weren't entirely wrong. Are you okay?}

"You should know." Desi slumped, her shoulders bent, her face gray under the toughguy makeup."Boy, I hate these edge-of-capacity jobs. I hope Wimpy has charge in her engines or we're gonna be walking again. Vacuum bores me. Hey, snotnose, how's the power?"

The lights brightened tentatively, and came back up wan.

"I think I'm functional," the ship said, muffled. "You almost drained our grav. I've enough engine-power to keep running but that neut's radiation stressed my plates, I need time to regenerate. Don't ask me for more speed. If you have to do this, could you please stop calling me rude names? I'm trying to learn, but upsets muddle my concentration."

{She has a point.}

"What you think she does to mine? Okay, Gorgeous. We'll recharge at the next station, I don't feel like another star-run. I take it you're against Wimpy as a label?"

"I'm registered as *Windrunner*," the ship said primly. "It's painted on my hull, if you hadn't noticed."

"Hadn't. Aint had time to go out there. Okay, you're *Windy*. 'S practically the same."

The ship groaned somewhere, deeply. Desi made for her cabin grinning.

"More steak?"

{Thanks,} her symb said, {but I'm processing all I can handle. Don't take it for granted *Windrunner*'s wrong about the risks. We'd a couple of close calls there.}

"One of them her fault. You're stressed out too. How you think I am?"

{Do I have to answer that?}

Desi licked her fingers and called up the holomirror. It showed her small and stormy, her hair in a mess, her makeup smeared and dark bruises under her eyes. She scowled at it. The problem with a low starting-weight was, it limited your choices.

She drew her corpse out lengthways, colored it black, tilted the eyes towards the temples and experimented with arrangements of braids. As an afterthought she grew her nails half an inch and did her best to glaze them irised. It wasn't any use, her fingertips were flaking. She paraded the result from several angles and poked a thought toward the Tailormaid. That cost her some mental grinding, and produced a nanofabricated scarlet satin gown with thigh-slits. She thought boots to match and lay back, satisfied. The couch hesitated, narrowed and lengthened a foot.

"Better," she approved to the ship. "You're getting the hang of it."

"I've been programming my domestics," *Windrunner* sniffed. "Do you have time now to look at the intruder?"

Desi sat up like a spring. "Intruder?"

"Maybe I should show you the vidnews first." *Windrunner*'s voice had the ghost of self-satisfaction. "Then you'll know."

The station logo flowered and brightened in telepathic colors inside Desi's brain.

⌘

## TP–TV

*the station of the multiverse*

STILL ON-BEAM, TEAM, UP WITH THE DATEST ON THE ALL-THE-CLOCK-AROUND SHOW WITH A FLASH FROM OUR OUTEST AND GREATEST. OVER TO YOU, J-OKAY JONES, AND HERE'S TELLING YOU WE'RE ALL PANTING FOR IT. MAKE WITH THE JUICE, MAN:

❖

[*Fade-in of Dick Tracy, his genial grin splitting the screen and his warm deep voice ringing the contents of the heirloom breakfront:*]

Yo-hello again, folks, here's Jonesy keeping on teeping with the fire and fury you know and love. So where's our beautiful bounter, you're asking, and what's the latest on her putrid prisoner? Well, that's exactly what I'm here to answer. Open your peepers and grab an eyeful, cause this babe's a blockbuster! And take my advice and adjust for light-level, she'll sizzle your eyeballs! Here we go, guys:

[*Fade to a purple-eyed bimbo in rainbow chiffons leveling ultraviolet nails at a terrorized apewoman. A stainless-steel doughnut spits lightning, slightly heraldic, and the ape turns into a handsome athlete with hand-pumped muscles who screams with rage at being recorped without permission. His equipment's awesome. Purple-Eyes overpowers him with her menacing beauty and dominates him out of the room. The spacewaves fill with a scent of amber, based on burnt toast, and a neutron star spins on blued-out screens. The picture whirls into vortex and vanishes. This is related to Desi throwing a beerglass at the control pad.*]

Stick around, people, I'll be seeing you . . .

[*Dick dies out in a sizzling noise.*

* * *

*Rising lava checked on a burp from the subspace radio. Desi took a deep breath, counted to forty and keyed in. The projector lit up to create the holo of a pop-eyed suit with a carmine complexion. "Miss Smeett?"*

"I'm strictly a Miz. Your boy get back damaged?"

"*My son's health has never been better, though I understand that may not be your fault. Apart from nausea, which seems to be the result of rhinohorn for breakfast. And I don't recollect authorizing the purchase of eight-hundred credit running-shoes.*"

"Neither did I. If you're thinking of taking it out of the bill, think again. I gotta lawyer. Your son's legally major and his shoes are his problem, whether you dumb enough to pay for them or not."

"*I was not thinking of taking it out of the bill, Miz Smeett. I was thinking of suing you for breach of privacy and defamation, pursuant to the way in which members of my family have been represented on the vidcasts. I understood your agency to guarantee full correction with discretion. Believe me, Miz Smeett, I too have a lawyer, and I can promise you'll be hearing from him.*"

"I'm thinking of doing some suing myself. Those vids weren't authorized. If anyone's privacy was invaded, it was mine. Anyway," she added by way of comfort, "nobody gonna recognize either one of us. Picture was flattering, if anything. To him."

The suit's complexion deepened to purple. "*That, Miz Smeett, is perfectly irrelevant. The whole program was in the worst of taste and the, shall we say, modifications to my son's anatomy hold my family up to ridicule. None of us has ever appeared in public as a—er—female baboon. It's perfectly clear you were deficient in your duty.*"

"Duty to do what? Stop your son eating disgusting breakfasts, or buying overpriced shoes? Maybe you should try being home sometime, you could set him an example. Unless you prefer him as an orange she-monkey. It could be rearranged."

The suit sputtered. "*I repeat, Miz Smeett, you'll be hearing from us.*"

"Via Medcom Headquarters at Hermes, please. And make

a note to yourself and underline it, next time it happens I leave him where I find him.''

''*We have a minimum figure of fifty billion in mind.*''

''Don't stay awake nights counting it.''

The comm shut down with a petulant snap.

''Shit!'' Desi said with violence. ''Where is that perverted teep? Let me get my claws on him. What the hell's wrong with your proximity alarms?''

''He recorped in while you were working, I thought he was a friend.'' *Windrunner* sniffled a little. ''You've an awfully nasty temper.''

''I'll tell you who my friends are,'' Desi said dangerously. ''Where is he? I'll annihilate him.''

Part of the wall behind her solidified into a wild-eyed drink with stand-up hair. He looked sheepish. ''Hi.''

''Whaddya mean, 'Hi'? You think you're welcome or something? What is this technicolor hogflop?''

''I'm a card-carrying reporter for a major station,'' the drink protested nervously. ''We've a duty to our public, to keep them informed on subjects of general interest. I was in the neighborhood, and you were interesting.''

''Then your station gotta love multibillion cred lawsuits. Such as you are getting tomorrow morning. Listen, frickhead, you are intruding in matters covered by medical privilege. I got professional immunity.''

''I realized that,'' the drink admitted. ''Too late. How was I to know, until you got into bigtime reshaping? You let me think you were a bounter.''

''Why does everyone here keep thinking?'' Desi said, disgusted. ''It a lovin epidemic. You could have found out anytime by looking at my print. I carry ident.''

''You didn't show it. *Everyone* thought you were a bounter.''

''What's that got to do with anything?'' She was exasperated. ''My job involves discretion, Stripe-Pants right that far. 'F I flash my stuff all over the continuum, how discreet I supposed to be? Anyhow, what's with the butt and the warp-trail eyes? Thought a good teep was objective.''

''I can be,'' the drink argued earnestly. ''Truly, I could show you just as you are.'' He took in the scenery with appreciation. "In fact I'd like to. Is this your base form?"

"No," Desi said stonily. "It's the one I wear to hear feeble excuses."

"Dammit, my station appeals to a sense of adventure. People don't like things in ordinary daylight, our entire audience are couch-potatoes. What they want's the excitement and glamor of Out There, without the discomfort. I give them Art."

"Is that what you call it? Won't make no difference, you smeared my good name and you will be hearing. Plus I don't know what you doing lurking in my walls, but you could leave. Now. Before I throw you out personal."

The drink looked slightly hopeful. "Really?"

Desi glared at him. "On second thoughts, no. You'd probably enjoy it. *Windy,* I want this creep evacuated."

"Okay, okay," the drink said, in haste. "I'm going. You know this will cost me my job?"

"Couldn't happen to a more deserving guy," Desi said cordially. "Ciao, nosebag. *Windy,* shut the lock after him."

The drink discorped in a rush of displaced nuclei and a ringing silence. Desi turned back to her mirror and observed she'd lost the beads from her braids.

"Frick," she said. "That retard distuned my molecules. Gimme another beer, Windbreak."

"You promised . . ."

"No, I didn't. But I will. *Windy.* And try using your proximity alarms, you'll find 'em forward alongside the mete sensors."

The domestic slopped the beer on the table. Desi didn't notice. Her eyes were distant.

Jones reoriented himself in void and located the feel of intelligent movement among big bright stars. He reached for it, discorped neatly just off the hull and addressed *Windrunner.*

{Hey. Our deal still on?}

"So long as you show discretion. She has a *terrible* temper."

{Don't worry, babe, I'll keep my head down.}

He drew himself together and slid through the cero. The after hold was full of provisions, plus tubs of matrix nanos for Desi's wardrobe. He cleared himself a corner and laid out his air-mattress.

"A-a-ah. Life on the road. Got anything to eat, honey?"

{Does it occur to you this may not be ethical?} his symb asked acidly.

"Yes. It's not."

{Then why are we doing it?}

"Because this is the most interesting babe I've met since last time, and there could be a scoop in it?"

{You mean there's a gap in your sex-life. Why don't I discuss it with her other half, before you find you're discussing it with the Press Commissioners?}

"What makes you think that? Come on, don't be a drag. Do you think the high-U getup's natural?"

{Experience. And no. There's a law against Peeping Tommery. You got us into this by thinking she was a bounter and maybe illegal. Do you know what the Federal penalties are for messing with a medic in the course of her duties?}

"Doesn't matter, the other look's cute too. Don't you think she's kind of—well, vulnerable?"

{Not in a million years. Did you hear what I said?}

"Sure I did," Jones said. "I'm dying of terror. Wonder what she's doing, out here all alone? The Blue Boy with temperature problems worries me."

{Peeper.}

"Just doing a little teeping . . ."

{Like hell,} his symb said rudely. But it retired into silence.

Jones closed his eyes and looked at the insides of his lids, which got him a Desi-angle on her cabin. The mirror, he saw with regret, was switched off. But the rest of the decor was crystal clear. He was actually a good telepath. He modestly left her private thoughts alone—her symb would have latched onto him anyway—and concentrated on the surroundings.

The cabin shimmered in her narrowed gaze, bulkheads wavering. A liquid shape was slowly materializing, a pale ghost that took on outlines. Of a naked man with frost in his hair, who opened blue eyes in a blue-white face. His lips smiled.

"One hell of a good fuck," he murmured.

"Ice," Desi said softly. Her lips and tongue moved in Jones's mind, giving off a faint taste of beer. "Where the hell *are* you? Come on, baby. Make with coordinates.''

Her concentration tightened, her senses fixed in the image before her. And pictures formed slowly in her head.

{No,} the symb-voice said urgently from behind her brain.

''Yes,'' Desi retorted. The room-temperature had dropped by twenty degrees and her lashes were crusted with rime, a blue tinge under her black satin skin. ''Why do you think I'm here?''

{He's created his own dimension-cycle. If you once move out of the standard continuum we could wander forever.}

''Specially the way he does it,'' Desi agreed. Her teeth snapped together. ''That exactly the reason. Keep a tag on his course for me.''

{I'll do what I can, but in his creation we could end up anywhere. There's no guarantee he's kept standard parameters. What if we reach a paradigm where I can't function?}

''He isn't God,'' Desi said. ''Not even him. He needs help too. His own symb's functional, you can bet on it.''

{I . . . it's under control.}

''I think he's that good. *Windrunner?* Take some coordinates.''

{I hope you read his mind right.}

''So do I, kid. But I've had practice.''

The icy shape drifted, gracefully turning. The pure blue gaze looked through everything, on into worlds all its own.

Jones, in the hold, caught vibes from the edge of its ghost-mind, and shivered.

# THREE

## Reflections

"URGGH," Desi snored. She woke with a jerk and knocked a glass over. It spilled warm beer on the pillow and showered her hair. "Shit. Lights, cookie. How we doing?"

{Near enough,} her symb said. {Do you have to drink beer? You know I can't process the third glass.}

"Tell me about it. I thought my head got this way single-handed." She stared around, dissatisfied, and squinted at a nail. It looked much as she'd expected. "I went back to pink."

{Don't blame me, it's the liquor that does it.}

Desi groped for the floor, found it with difficulty and recognized she'd also shrunk six inches. "I wish you'd hold the templates like other guys' symbs do."

{Anytime. So long as you don't expect me to telepath around the edges of dimensional interfaces and converse with Hermes while I'm doing it.}

"That's the suck of this job," Desi muttered.

{Excuse me for failing to see the relevance. Just whom did you want to stay tall and black for? Especially while working?}

"Forget it, you wouldn't understand."

{The hell I wouldn't.}

They had roughly this conversation every morning, Desi

realized. She called up the mirror and found things were really as bad as they felt. Down to the thigh-slit red satin, where the nans had parted up the front from redistributed pressure. "Jeezle. Lucky I aint on holovision."

{Um.}

"What the frick's 'Um' mean?"

{Um, on the whole.}

"You know something I don't?"

{Have some breakfast. And take a pill with it, I'm sharing your headache. We're half an hour off contact.}

"Shit! Why the hell didn't you say so?"

{I just did,} her symbiote said patiently. {Is it worth repeating that I don't advise this? He could kill you next time.}

But Desi had her head in the closet. "Hey, *Windy*, hustle me some coffee. And keep the toast pale, I'm liable to throw up."

"If I know anything, so am I," *Windrunner* muttered. The galley started pumping.

"Hold course," Desi directed, nose in the local cluster. "Enhance this group for me, willya?"

"Where are we going?"

"That your business?" Desi was grumpy. "We're following a guy. A cold blue guy, who leaves trace behind him. On purpose, by the look of it."

"And changes dimensions?"

"Such is my belief. Spare me the lecture, I already had it."

"Is it legal?"

"We been over that. The group, now."

The holo jumped and stars sprang out thick and violent, their multiplied patterns lensed in gravity, flaring blue. New, hot and piled together, the sucking hole of galactic center bending them visibly. The chart trembled at the edges.

"You got an imaging problem?"

"It's nerves," *Windrunner* quavered.

"Thought your last owner liked sport."

"He was a real sportsman."

"Then you should be used to risks. Gimme a closer look at three-four-seven, twenty minutes."

"Stationary hole," *Windrunner* opined. "Big one. A gulper."

Desi considered the streams of converging star-material with satisfaction. "Aint that right. So take us on into it, fifteen minutes and counting. Mark."

"Mark fifteen minutes," *Windrunner* repeated. "It'll tear us apart as soon as we come out of warp."

"Not at this range. This far out it's a piece of cake. Cut warp at three minutes, I'll cue you."

"Fourteen minutes thirty and counting. Cut warp at three. Isn't that close?"

"Who's doing this? Keep your snoot level."

"Um," *Windrunner* said with abstraction. "I'm too young to die, I'm the late 'thirty-eight model. It's okay for you, you can regenerate . . . Thirteen and counting."

"So can you, hotdammit. Concentrate, willya?"

"I never did before. Twelve minutes thirty."

"Concentrate? Sure don't sound so."

"Twelve. Regenerate. My previous hull was recycled . . ."

"It what?" Desi was startled out of her stargazing. "You mean you're a retread?"

"I guess so," *Windrunner* said gloomily. "They also recycled my memory. Eleven, thirty seconds."

"Sonofabitch!" Desi took time to fume. "Just wait till I get back . . . Keep your nose up, retread. They fool the last owner too?"

"Must have done. Eleven." Gravitational forces tugged them, rippling the continuum. "I've navigational problems, the target isn't stationary . . ."

"Sure it is. Keep your fix and stay on heading, the visual effects are illusory."

"Ten, thirty seconds. If you run in on this one as you did the last, we're going through the middle. I can't hold my hull together in that gravity . . ."

"Nobody's asking. I want speed. Increase warp and hold."

"Increase? We're going faster than I can brake already . . . Ten."

"Don't even try. We take one swing on the edge of the well and rewarp to full power."

"You'll kill us," *Windrunner* moaned. "Nine, thirty."

''No, I won't, baby, we're running the interface. Trust Mama.''

{Urgent call from Hermes Central,} her symb reported. {They want to know what the frick you're doing. And I quote. They innocently believed you were coming back to base to answer the charges from Boyo's daddy.}

''Sorry, can't hear em. Always get static this close to a hole, they oughtta know that.''

''Nine minutes and holding, warp thirteen, rising. Though I'd say that's an underestimate,'' *Windrunner* added. ''We're outrunning the gauges.''

''Sure we are. Normal. Watch your stress-monitors, I don't want to lose hull-pressure.''

''Oddly enough, neither do I. Monitors moving into the red, fifteen and rising, eight forty.''

The black hole was a glory of incandescent gases. Disrupted nuclei hissed in the speakers. Its larger blue partner was flattened to a yoyo, partly distorted by lensed gravity, partly drawn out by tidal forces. Gusts of raw energy spun between them. A broken halo of reflected nebulae defined the singularity.

The image in the tank had gone through blue and was moving to white, rainbow diffraction-rings at the edges, the distant background sullen red. Desi's nose was stuck in the middle.

''Don't get hysterical, you've excess capacity. They build in safety factors . . .''

{In a retread?} her symb murmured.

{I wish you hadn't said that,} Desi teeped back. ''So you got nothing to worry about,'' she concluded aloud. ''How we doing?''

''Eight, twenty-three and counting . . .'' {I heard that,} *Windrunner* added miserably. {I have a symb too and we're both telepathic. Are you really worried about my memory?}

{No,} Desi and her symbiote said in chorus.

{You're both lying.} ''Eight minutes.''

''I might but she wouldn't,'' Desi said firmly. ''Watch your mark. Countdown in seconds from three minutes thirty.''

''In seconds from three, thirty. Seven and a half.''

''I'll give you the mark. I always find the images fairly impressive.''

{So I've noticed,} her symb said dryly. {My personal hope is you won't sit around admiring the scenery.}

"Not the both of you," Desi complained. {Listen, I did the math for this personal. Dontcha trust me?}

{I have no choice. You sometimes forget that I too am an intelligence.}

"You actually get scared?" Desi said incredulously.

{Not entirely, since I've species consciousness to fall back on. Let's say I worry.}

"About what, for hotssakes?"

{You.}

"Seven," said *Windrunner*. The singularity filled the tank, its lensed fire licking the walls, brilliant flashes reflected off the instruments. Disintegrating gas poured down its gravity-slope, tattered photons speeding to nothing. "Stress-index in the red and my skin's pulling. You're about to lose the cabin furniture . . ."

"Tough. Keep going, you've elasticity. Let me know if the engines get too much distortion, but so long's you're snoot-first you only lose your beauty. Until we're closer."

"Thanks. Did you want to know it hurts? Six, thirty and counting."

{Stick with it, you're okay,} Desi's symb advised.

"I trust you, it's her I'm worried about . . ."

{So's everyone. Contrary to appearances, she's fairly reliable. I've been suppressing Hermes, they were getting blasphemous. Should I pass you the news that you're fired?}

"I still can't hear. Ready to cut drive, and warm auxiliary engines. How's your stress-index?"

"Up against the frame," *Windrunner* said. "It'll take me a year to regrow my hide if we ever get out . . . Six. I've had my auxiliaries ticking for five minutes, can't you feel them?"

"Not when I'm calcing. I'd bet on your capacity, but you're the guy who knows. If you feel your skin tearing pull out fast, full auxiliary thrust, and give it all you got, we'll need it. But don't try to fool me."

The main cabin couch stretched out like a licorice bootlace, bulked momentarily through the doorway and tore into segments. Desi, flying from the edge of the tank, was stretched to a tadpole, reinforced skull creaking, her feet vanishing in distance. A bulkhead splintered and the tank rocked, the light itself twisted by gravity. Distressful noises came from behind. *Windrunner*'s voice was reedy.

"Four, descending. Warp twenty and off the scale, skin just holding. Speed helps but there's stress on the engines. Won't we come apart when we reenter . . . ?"

"Not if we're fast enough. Hang in, we need seconds. Start countdown, cut drive on mark at two minutes, stay prepared to switch back in on zero."

"Three, thirty and counting. Three twenty-nine. Twenty-eight. Twenty-seven . . ."

{I think she'll hold, I've been sharing data with her symb. Keep your concentration.}

"Uh."

"Three. Four . . ."

"Set to cut warp, bring up auxiliaries—Mark!"

*Windrunner* screamed back into the continuum, a smoking ghost. Layers of plasma tore off her hide, her armored nose-plates vaporizing as she swung into orbit, tearing gravity stretching her. They spiraled down, an on-and-off flash of lensed stars cutting the screens as they swung into and away from Center's massed starclouds. Desi hung on the panel, mumbling.

"Two, ten. Two, nine . . . Ready for warp, full drive on hold, steady . . . One, three. One, two . . . Don't panic . . . Eight. Seven. Six . . . Wait for my mark . . . Two. One. Mark, and warp."

The ship flicked, glimmered and winked out. Reality melted, and broke on the hull. The tank quivered, dissolved, reformed slowly and burst out in a new pattern of stars. A hot small group hung before them, bunched galaxies, scarves of close-packed young suns. Glass smashed in the galley and the panel warp-gauge cracked. Fluid spilled down the plastic.

■
■
■
▪

"And here we are," Desi concluded. "Not bad, *Windy*."

"Where's here?" *Windrunner* asked, shaky.

"Other side the mirror, where we were heading. Congratulations, you got us to elsewhen."

*Windrunner* made a groaning whistle. "Totally illegal."

"You knew that. Or why would Hermes be making the ruckus? We're here. General stand-down." Desi sank on the remains of the couch, which squelched. She scraped jelly off her coveralls. "Take five, we'll clean up later."

"Thanks," *Windrunner* said sourly. "Can I regrow my skin now?"

"If you want to. I want beer."

{Oh, no,} her symb moaned. {I haven't recovered from your last headache.}

"Don't worry about it," *Windrunner* said. "By the time I get around to rebuilding the galley, you're both going to be entirely sober."

Desi started to snarl, but the speakers had shut down. The yacht was working on her skin.

"Frick," Jones said, uncoiling from wrecked cases and clawing packaging out of his hair. Pools of spilled nans crawled around looking for something to alter and he hastily stepped over them. "Does she do this often?"

"Looks like it," *Windrunner* said. "Would you like some beer? I'm regenerating, but I could stand you breakfast."

"Rather have coffee. If the wild woman's files include it."

"Mine do." The bulkhead by his elbow re-formed as a dispenser with spigot, with a cup beneath. "And croissants?"

"Great. Am I sharing them with Missy?"

"Not while I'm working," *Windrunner* said distantly. "I need my energy for essential repairs."

"I believe you're sexist."

"Only Des-ist. Though my previous owner *was* a gentleman."

"Um," Jones said through a mouthful of croissant. He dipped the tail in his coffee. "I suppose we've doubled."

"I don't think so. It feels cut off here, no-one to double with. A nonrelated continuum."

"With reasonable laws of physics?"

"Must have, I'm still traveling."

"Thank God, that lets us off with thirty years to life if we ever get back to major reality. What's she want here?''

''Don't ask. She mentioned blue guys. She probably means to upset the natives.''

He shook his head. ''Sexist. Boy Blue's dangerous.''

''Like everything she does,'' *Windrunner* said.

The coffee was good. He pitched his vision through the forward sensors onto a vista of hot near stars, young galaxies, strong redshifts. The whole was compressed, in violent expansion. The plasma crackled with colliding nuclei. ''Uh. Young here, that's big banging, looks recent. Hope your field can take it.''

''So do I. Radiation doesn't do my genes any good.''

''Check. What's the nebula ahead?''

''Planetary system with half-condensed gases. Couple of stable knots in the middle.'' *Windrunner* was cold. ''I believe Miz Smeett wants to explore it.''

''Naturally. Enterprising lady. Why? Uh-oh.''

A blue-white ghost with frosted hair walked slowly through the rear of the hold and drifted across it, stepping on air. A wave of Arctic wind expanded outwards and icicles formed under the heat-ducts. The coffee scummed over with a web of crystals and the mug abruptly cracked and dumped its contents in Jones's lap. He yelped as the liquid froze through his pants. ''Holy frick! Who *is* that guy?''

{Incorrect assignation, I'd say,} his symb said with irony. {Watch it, there are more.}

There were. A procession. Their half-visible shapes, faintly phosphorescent, drifted through like a chain of beads under dimming light-plates, their blue eyes spearing the dark. The pooled nans shrank, congealed and shattered to spilled sugar.

''Hots!'' Jones chattered. ''You gotta get rid of him, I'm dying of frostbite.''

''You think I want him? He's freezing my conduits, I've red lights all over the engine-room. He's materializing out somewhere inside. Tried to shut him out and he cryoed my systems.'' *Windrunner* was outraged. ''He's a projection, hence the multiple images, but I never met a holo that could freeze the heatplant. They're walking right through and out by the nose-plates.''

"Has to be telepathic, in that case. Heavy teeping. Another of Miz Smeett's entertainments?"

"You should hear her language. The source is below and we're headed right into it. I think this image zeroes on intelligence. The display started when she asked for a fix on the planet ahead."

Jones scraped frozen coffee off his jeans. "Gimme another look."

*Windrunner* obligingly switched back the scanner, browned-out by the lack of current in her frozen generators. Black sky was scarved with gases, centered on a glare that dazzled vision. Darker pock-marks mottled the disk's surface like an antique looking-glass, the night-limb edged with atmospheric rainbows. A blue sun beyond spurted violet-white, its flaring corona killing the stars.

"Holy hell. Are those icefields? Can't be, can they? It's too close in. Must be hotter than Hades. Shit—"

He was outside the hull, in space, falling. Enveloping brilliance swallowed him up.

***"He-e-elp . . ."***

■
■
■
▪

"What was that?" Desi asked vaguely, squinting in the scanner. She ignored an Arctic image walking through her. "Did somebody speak?"

{Your friend's passenger jumped ship. The short way.}

"What?" Desi looked up with annoyance. "What's with this ship? How can I concentrate with people yelling and guys walking around? Aint got no passengers."

{You haven't now. He fell through the hull.}

"He didn't fall," *Windrunner* said. She sounded upset. "Something pulled him. Right out of my hold. He was there, then he was gone. I couldn't stop it."

"Yeah?" Desi growled, letting the scanner go. "You got some explanation how he came to be there?"

{I noticed a presence in mid-jump,} her symb murmured.

{Didn't seem the moment to raise the subject. But the explanation isn't difficult . . . }

Another bright burst opened on her retinas.

⌘

# TP–TV

*the station of the multiverse*

HEY THERE, RAVERS, WE'RE STILL WITH YOU, THOUGH HAVING A FEW SMALL PROBLEMS WITH THE IMAGE. NOT TO WORRY, OUR GUYS CAN HANDLE IT, DON'T ADJUST YOUR MINDSETS. AND HERE WE GO WITH THE NEWEST HEW-UPS, INTO FRESH DIMENSIONS WITH OUR MAN ON THE SPOT. IT'S ALL YOURS, JJ:

❖

[*Fade in-and-out—the image is wavering. Dick's still with us, probably a station artefact, but his mouth and voice aren't quite under control. His scalp-lock waves wildly. The recording boomboxes squeal and settle:*]

Oops, sorry, friends, I got interference. You ever fell through a black hole?

[*Image good under the circumstances, baroque around the edges. It's possible their correspondent was travelsick. Stripped electrons spit in the holo with an authentic rattle. Distant sound of ringing phones as the first complaints start to pour in from nervous parents.*]

So where do we go from here, you ask? Outbound, kiddies, lost in the flower-garden, as you might say. I mean what you're looking at's another dimension, yes, I mean it, and I'm right there for you. Just keep your peepers open and share the shivers of your dauntless newshound as he threads the continuums, out in the weird theoretical multiverse, always on the lookout for new thrills to keep you guessing. Here we go for the ride of your lives, and hold onto your hats, folks! Yee-ee-a-ay!

*[The screen dissolves in whirling circles and comes back up to different stars in odd perspectives. Hot gases spin in spirals. Dick Tracy re-forms, sweating slightly, waving clasped fists over his head, and the phones start to ring again as the kids call in wanting to see it over. A loud clear cop-siren draws nearer and the image dissolves in a splutter of static.]*

Desi was luminous with rage. ''What the frick's this? I threw that hotshot out once . . .''

{That, alas, was last time,} her symb said. {He just left again, and not under his own steam. Did you mean to go down?}

She glared into the tank. ''Was thinking it over. Suppose that now we aint got the choice.''

{My conclusion exactly. I shared the opinion it might be smarter not to.}

''Oh, shit.'' Desi brushed a ghost aside and narrowed her eyes around the wreck of the cabin. ''Get the visual litter out, *Windy*, and when I got time I gonna ask how this happened. Maybe you better start preparing your answers, we're having a test on it. ***You.***'' Directed with all her force straight downward. ''Knock the clever imaging hot off, whoever you are, I getting hayfever. Okay. Let's get down. It's registering over three hundred degrees in upper atmosphere, but I got a suspicion the lover's kidding. Oddly enough, it's high oxy. Aint *that* an interesting thought, at the temp? Ready for transfer.''

''What about me?'' *Windrunner* called miserably.

{Clean the lovin cabin and work on your answers,} a trailing thought streamered. She sighed deeply and started putting the couch back together.

''Does anyone mind if I fix my DNA in my spare time?'' she asked the universe. It didn't reply.

{Don't try to land here—Dammit.}

They were drifting slowly down through atmosphere, which was nowhere near three hundred degrees. The planet's surface shone like liquid metal, reflecting sunlight. Watered-silk patterns rose in it, swirled and were absorbed. The movements could have been convection but their slow lazy shifts had a kind of deliberation, oily trails running behind them. The rest of the disk stayed faceless.

"Dammit?"

Desi's symbiote wasn't given to profanity, particularly since it didn't mean anything in its private terms. In moments of stress it could catch the habit.

{There's some kind of landmass up ahead. This isn't water.}

"Never thought it was. Too viscous. Is it metallic?"

{Nothing so simple-minded. I'm looking for molecular boundaries, and I haven't found any.}

"What does that mean?"

{In principle, the whole mass is a single complex molecular lattice.}

"Stretching right around the planet?"

{As far as I can tell. There are interpolations of solid material, but the liquid's continuous.}

"And that movement in it isn't convection?"

{Doesn't act like it. There should be regular patterns reflecting rotation, likewise pole-equatorial temperature differentials. Not to mention the effects of bottom-structures.}

"It must be cooler at the poles. Aint it?"

{No.}

"That's nutty."

{Doubtless. It's also true, I've been feeling out temperatures. Can't tell you why because the layer's impermeable, but I'd guess at temperature-exchanges under the surface. Temperature's stable, within slight variations, all over.}

"It's impermeable to *you*?" Desi said incredulously.

{That's what I said.}

"And there is a rotation?"

{Slowish but steady, thirty-eight hours more or less, axis nearly vertical to the plane of the ecliptic which simplifies things, but the surface is inert. Or rather, not. I mean it ought to be circulating with the core but it isn't.}

"How's that again?"

{The planet's turning,} her symb said patiently. {There's a solid core, probably rocky, which sticks up here and there like the landmass I see, and it's turning. But the liquid isn't. If you like, it has a tidal action equal and opposite to the rate of rotation so any given part faces permanently in the same direction. And if you hadn't noticed, there's no satellite.}

"Hoo-boy. That combination has to have interesting effects on the orbit."

{In spite of which, it shows every sign of having been at more or less the same distance from its primary for a lot of billennia, unless the star itself has unexpected habits.}

"It probably has rhinohorn for breakfast," Desi said bitterly. "Did you say a landmass?"

{I did. Right here.}

"Don't suppose you've nosed out our teep while we're down here? Or the original of ghost?"

{Neither one, positively or negatively. As I said, I don't get response from under the surface.}

"You mean the teep fell in and sank."

{I mean I've no evidence he exists at all. That any living person exists. Your ghost pretty certainly isn't here, the image smelled of time.}

"This charmer *dissolved* Teepy?"

{I couldn't say. There aren't even traces. No elements, no personality. He could never have existed.}

"Would you know?"

{Yes. He was a powerful telepath and he left psychic imprints. Which faded out in the outer atmosphere. And he wore modern clothing, meaning nano-fabrication. They don't digest easily and the memory-molecules are strictly artificial. I can't detect anything that isn't natural.}

"No organics?"

{Organics everywhere. Not-human. No traces I recognize.}

Desi landed to her ankles in slush and screwed her nose up. "Jazz place. Is that smell ozone?"

{As people use the expression for organic decay.}

"Organic decay's what I'd have said myself. Extensive."

{The whole continent's covered with this stuff. Or something like it.}

Desi kicked at the slush with her boot. It parted easily, like boiled spinach, and oozed back just as quickly to fill in the grooves. Dark gleaming rock showed below.

"Then it isn't sentient. Primitive slime-molds? Rock's strictly igneous, basalt and granite. Solidified magma. Plus the stuff out there."

{Yes. Confirm no sediments, at least in the neighborhood, organics are primitive and non-intelligent. They're also mutating like crazy. That's what the smell is.}

"Mutation?"

{Death. And incredibly rapid breakdown and decay. For re-use, by the feel. It's the same basic protein all over the continent but the forms don't stay stable as long as five minutes. There are forms up to eight feet high inland. Same stuff, but heaped in agglutinations. Signs of leaching in the interior rocks, as if the newer forms were looking for skeletons.}

"Calcareous?"

{Silicate. Would be normal here.}

"Good word, I love it. That's what this place is, hellangone normal."

The quicksilver sky hung above like a cup, superheated cloudbanks reflecting the sea. The temperature below should have been hotter than an oven. It wasn't. The atmosphere should have been poisonous. It wasn't. Desi was recycling her airflow, if only against the smell, but her sensors denied the existence of micro-organisms.

"How does the veg rot without bacteria?"

{I'm not sure it's vegetation. It's organic, it moves, it contains chlorophyll. It doesn't exactly rot, it takes itself apart and rebuilds differently. The process releases free radicals. The forms aren't entirely individual.}

"A lovin group-mind?"

{I doubt the existence of sexual processes. 'Mind' would be putting it too strongly.}

Desi swore. A green column was climbing her boot and putting out pseudopods like antennae as it mounted. She kicked it off and it relapsed into slush.

{Spiteful. A nice hopeful little mutation.}

"Excuse me for holding up the march of progress."

{Don't let it worry you, the next will be taller.}

"Yech. Where's my intruder? They're going to charge me

with murder if I don't bring him back clean and shiny. Sucker can't have vanished into the atmosphere."

{The signs are he did. Hold on, there's something moving.}

Desi's eyes tracked the horizon. The dark currents drifted, black spots on old mercury, but from ground-level the material looked less metallic and more organic. Something not quite transparent that caught the light and broke it up like the clear iris of a pale eye, faint mauve in the depths, almost iridescent. The watered patterns moved inshore and something with them, distant and uncertain as a shiver in the air. Skimming the surface with lightning speed. She narrowed her eyes and squinted.

"Oh, boy."

The point glinted in the even light, spinning out reflections. Point, exclamation, shadow. Solid, upright, mirrored. A bubble the shape of a man that slid over the curved horizon like a burning teardrop and fell, glistening, in on the shore. And stopped at her feet.

"Well, hi, Des. Long time no see."

Ice stepped gently onto land, his shape and face taking on definition. The shiny surface had flowed away as if his feet were repelling magnets and his planted silver boots scarcely imprinted the carpet of jelly. But his face was as it had always been, blued, smiling, frozen locks curving over his forehead and candid blue eyes that looked through her.

Cold-effects like his took plenty of energy. Desi used her personal temperature-field in extreme conditions and it drained her metabolism. Ice used his twenty-four hours a day. Or had. Maybe he let go when he was alone. If that ever happened. She'd never seen it, all the time she'd known him. He kept it under permanent, perfect control, never missing. Part of his charm. And danger.

"Hi," she said coolly. "Your choice, I think."

"Mine?" He looked pained. "Come on, Des. You forgotten we're married?"

"No. I never forget that."

"Then try looking pleased to see me."

"I am. You don't know how pleased. Among other things, I wanted to talk to you about the kid."

His smooth brow creased. "Kid?"

"Baboon. Oversized. Orange." Desi gave him the benefit of her vision. "And for some reason female. You remember the one?"

"Oh, *that* one." Rueful smile. "I loved the trikini."

"You don't surprise me. You didn't have to leave him in a screaming trauma, or in a brothel either, however mind-bending the chuckles were. Did they pay you for him, or did you pass him on for kicks? The restoration was also hilarious, as was his Daddy's face when he saw the vidshow. As a matter of fact he's suing me for fifty billion credits. Am I still on your wavelength?"

"Aw, come on, Des. I did the whole thing entirely free of charge, and the kid asked for it. It can't have been that bad. Fifty billion?" Another crease in the perfect brow. "Isn't that excessive?"

"Only if it's coming out of your own bank account. When it's someone else's, the zeros are optional."

He made a casual planing motion with his hand. "Give Daddy time and he'll simmer down. What about you and me, Des?"

"Just the question I wanted to ask you. Where are you hanging, these days? And on roughly the same topic, what you done with my intruder?"

"Intruder?"

"Male, human. More or less this size." Desi leveled a hand above her head. "And skinny with it. Got a bone to pick with him, preferably his skull."

"You've found someone else," Ice said with gentle reproach.

"Dammit, I've had time to find twenty. But in his case you're off-net, the only relationship I want with him's murderess and murderee. Where is he?"

He shook his head and a few snowflakes drifted, melting, onto the slime-molds. "Don't know a thing. Should I?"

"You don't know much about anything here, do you?" Desi said. "Aint like you."

{He doesn't scope out right,} her symbiote said quietly. {I'm not registering brain-activity.}

{Don't let it get to you,} Desi teeped back. {You know my boy, his brain-activity's off the register and he's never sounded like other people.} Her telepathic tone, strictly shielded, was sad. {That was why I liked him.}

{His metabolic implants disturb his brain-patterns, I'm used to that. But I'm not getting patterns here at all. Or rather, I am but they're not his.}

{If you know what his ought to be you're a better guy than I am. I always thought I got special treatment. Most of the time.}

{You undoubtedly did. You don't follow. This shape isn't thinking.}

{Then who is? I take it I'm talking to someone?}

{I don't even swear to that. Ask him something only he could answer.}

{I already have,} Desi said. {He evaded, but that isn't new.}

{Try something personal, a long way back. Some small detail.}

Desi kicked absently at a ghost-urchin the size of a tennis-ball rolling around in the jelly. Its irregular spines enclosed gelid threads. "This lover has an exoskeleton."

{I said they mutated fast. Keep him talking.}

"Pretty," Ice said with appreciation. He put his foot on the urchin and crushed it. Green ooze froze and flaked off his boot. The spines looked sharp but they'd broken like glass. Desi looked down at it.

"Still having hot times in the bayou? Still got your passion for high-spice cookery?"

"Still got my taste for everything, baby."

"Uh-huh. The memory man. Remember the nightgown you bought me on honeymoon? The one I never wore cause we didn't have a fire?"

Ice's face smoothed over. His blue eyes gazed at the far horizon. "I don't ever remember a nightgown."

"Sure. Cause I kept it for the fire-department but they never came. Not even when you put hot sauce in my Mary and scorched my tongue off and I threatened to break the glass in the corridor. You haven't always been frigid."

"Never with you, babe."

The blue eyes were still fixed on the horizon.

{It's as I thought, he doesn't understand you. There's no echo. Just a blank kind of question.}

{Not surprising, I made it all up. He really shoulda scoped me. What's going on?}

{Touch him.}

{He'll freeze my skin off and my field with it,} Desi protested. {I hope you're ready for fast repairs.}

{Oddly enough, I don't expect to need them. The ambient temperature's too high.}

"For what?" Desi asked, putting her hand out. The figure in front of her rippled, changed and melted. A smear of sparkling stuff, neither jelly nor crystal, stayed fraying on her fingers, then peeled off and dropped back into the ocean. She was alone. Another ghost-urchin, spinier than the first, rolled in from the interior and made a faint attack on her ankles.

{For the ice to be real. I knew it was faking.}

"It, who?" Desi stared around, her neckhair rising. "He didn't really know me, did he?"

{There wasn't any 'he'. It was another phantom, like the ones on the ship. Backed up with local material, I'd say formed out of the sea. If that's what this is. But only an appearance, no human personality.}

"He managed to talk to me."

{He's been here. Or touched it, enough to leave his traces. But he's not here himself.}

"So who am I talking to?" Desi stared aggressively around her. "Hey, meatbrain? Where you put my vidsquid?"

The air stood still. The little ghost-urchin tired of her boots and wandered away, leaving prickmarks in the ooze. The sun shone down on the viscid ocean.

***I?*** don't ***know*** what ***your?*** ***speech*** ***means***. A voice without breath. ***You?*** ***speak*** beyond ***me?***. ***He?*** ***spoke*** beyond ***me?*** also but ***he?*** showed ***pictures*** so that ***I?*** ***knew*** ***you?***. ***He?*** said that ***you?*** would ***wish*** to ***know*** ***him?***.

The voice ran up and down the scale with crystalline inflections, the words ringing together in minor scales as if spoken inside a glass chamber.

{Oh, boy. Does that mean what I think it means?}

{It has no concept of the meaning of pronouns,} her symb agreed. {It repeats its lessons.}

{Ice was always a lousy teacher.} Desi gazed around her thoughtfully. "Where are you?"

*All* *where*. *I?* am *alone*.

The mirror ocean glimmered and shifted, dark patterns welling up in front of her and running inshore. The waves made no splash when they reached the granite but curled back, almost as if the rock repelled them.

*Alone* is *large*. *I?* am *in* *it?*.

The patterns welled and died. Other, wider stains rose and spread seawards, darkening the horizon.

"Jeez," said Desi.

{It's always possible he might have answers. While you're waiting, I'd advise you to think for yourself.}

"Thanks a lot," Desi said nastily. "How do you communicate? Can you recognize pictures?"

*You?* are in *my?* *alone*. There *is* *therefore* *outside?* *alone*. *I?* cannot *know* it. *I?* can *see* *your?* *pictures* but *I?* cannot *know* *them*. If *you?* make *me?* *see* as *you?* *see* *yourself?* *I?* try to *know?*. *My?* *knowing* is *partial* and *incorrect*. *I?* *can* do no *other*. For *me?* there is only *alone*.

"But you know Ice."

The *picture* *I?* showed *you?* is *all* that *I?* *know* of *outside* *alone*. *You?* *I?* have *seen* in *his?* *mind*. Therefore *I?* *know* it. *I?* *believed* that the *picture* was *you?*. *I?* was mistaken. There is *much* that *I?* do not *know* about *outside*. If there *is* *outside*. *I?* *believed* *he?* was another *alone* like *myself?*. Now *I?* am *puzzled*. *I?* *understand* *nothing*.

"That's my boy," Desi said, with resignation. "So, great. What the hell are we dealing with?"

{Just what you suspect.}

"A big baby."

{A misjudgment. I'd say the mind's ancient. It's defined itself. It lacks experience, so understanding. You're its second human. You could try to make a good impression.}

"You're wrong, I'm its third. It swallowed the last. Or something. You, what happened to the guy?"

*You?* are *speaking* of *the one?* that *thinks*?

"It's possible. I've been thought to think myself."

{But not by everyone. Your little friend's a professional telepath. Does it occur he could be painful to the innocent?}

"No problem, he's painful to me. I'm sure he'd stop thinking if you asked him nicely. If you're in process of digestion he's probably panicking. When you digest teeps, panic makes them noisy."

*Your?* *thought* once more *surpasses* *me?*. Do *you?* *wish* *me?* to *return* *the thinker* to this *dimension*? *Digestion-process* *I?* do not *understand*. Does *one* *intelligence* *digest* *another*?

"In principle, no. Don't let's discuss it, it's an unhappy subject. In answer to your question, yes, I should on the whole be pleased if you would return the guy to this dimension. Provided there was air in the last, naturally. I prefer alive guys, even teeps."

*I?* have great *difficulty* in following *your?* *thought*. Would *I?* place an *intelligence* in an *environment* that would *cause* its *extinction*?

"I don't know, that's why I asking. Bring him back and we'll talk about it."

⌘

## TP–TV

*the station of the multiverse*

HEY THERE, WILDPEOPLE, SCUSE US FOR WAKING YOU BUT WE HAVE A FRESH NEWSFLASH HOT IN FROM OUR DAUNTLESS TEEP-ON-THE-SPOT, JONES THE JUICE, KEEPING YOU SHAKERS ROCKING AND ROLLING. FASTEN YOUR SEATBELTS AND HANG ON YOUR HAIR, HERE'S JJ!

❖

[*Fade-in of Dick Tracy, scalplock twirled into a pyramid, wearing cloth-of-gold pyjamas. His eyes are pink but undaunted. The playback speakers quiver:*]

Here I am again guys, bigger and uglier than ever. Though the question of the moment for your hyper-hero's where that is. Take a look at the scenery, and I'm offering prizes to anyone can show JJ the way to go home.

[*Opalescent light from no particular direction. General impression of a milky sphere with what could be a distorted foot in an oily sneaker somewhere forward. A long way forward. A waving pinkness sorts into fingers, which seem to be groping. Creased jeans wrinkle between. The whole looks as if it's turning slowly, though the gravitational effects are so distorted it's hard to tell. The background diffuses panic, bravely suppressed:*]

So wherever here is, your man is too, and take my advice and enjoy it quietly, this kinda place gotta be rare. Sure hope so. How I got here's another story. Which I hope to unfold as soon's I locate my right ear. Just joking, your fall-guy fell out of a spaceship, and that's gospel. Anybody wants to say it was careless, I'm not about to argue. Being spherical's an interesting experience and if anyone would like to change places, my space is available. I'll keep you up-to-date with the news as it happens, trust Jonesy. **He-e-e-elp! . . .**

[*Abrupt break-up of image in diminishing spirals that draw to a point, and whiteout.*]

Desi looked down at the knot of arms and legs that had discorped at her feet, collecting green guck on its jeans as it struggled.

"Thank you," she said distantly. "Are you by any chance broadcasting?" To Jones.

"I was," he said with apology, trying out an innocent boyish smile. "It's my job. Seemed preferable to screaming. Was kinda cramped there."

"Then knock it off, you scaring Blinky. She aint used to guys who shout in her ear."

"Sorry," he said, getting up stickily. He looked at his jeans. "Uh-huh. You got interesting friends. Believe it or not, she scared the shit out of me."

"Oh. Thought it just slime."

They looked at each other with hostility.

{Wasn't his fault,} her symb intervened. {*Windy* told you it hooked him.}

"So nobody asked him to come. Nobody asked you to come," she said to Jones.

"I guess not. But I lost my job, only chance of keeping it's sticking with you. I gotta do something."

"Why not do it somewhere else? I just been fired too, and sued on top. For fifty billion credits."

"Aint no such number. He's kidding you, sweetheart. Anyhow, network'll take it out of my hide."

Desi looked him up and down. "You ask me, there aint fifty cents in it. Not even if you showered."

He examined the guck on his palm. "What is this stuff?"

"Slime-mold. I'm told it's mutating."

"Yeah, guess it must be." The guck curled up in a string and dripped ropily toward the ground. "What's *that?*"

"Blinky," Desi said, following his eyes across the translucent ocean. "Aint sure it a that. Maybe a who."

"Jeez," said Jones.

"Not very likely."

Shining figures were rising from under the surface, taking on color and body in the air. A man and a woman, horizontal and bucking. Their faces were intent, mindless. The man thrust with more and more violence and the woman began to scream. Her flesh cracked open and split at the belly, a widening fissure like cracked china that climbed her chest between the breasts and split her skull in two like a doll's. A scarlet fountain spouted from the wreckage and a homunculus rose up, rampant, arrogantly staring. Both the larger figures had fallen into shards, fragments of china daubed with paint.

The tableau dissolved in abstract writhings and bred four men around a grassy square who dealt silver blanks imprinted with hieroglyphs. A heap of glitter was piled between them, random linkages of chain jumbled among cups and circles, soldered into lumps with misshapen cylinders. One of the men threw his hand down and raked the heap toward him. The other three stood, palms opening into spreading razors, and sliced the first to pieces. The dismembered joints jerked away with caterpillar motion. The razorhands caught them and threw them on the heap and the bleeding chunks fell as circlets of gold. The survivors calmly resumed their seats and tossed their blanks together, crimson to the shoulders.

Faceless gingerbread figures spun with the rigid movements of wind-up toys. Two, narrowlegs, caught an arm each of a bellbottomed glider with a gilded face. Bellbottom resisted and the others pulled. It jogged around as if trying to disengage, but its substance had melded with the two automata. They pulled harder and Bellbottom, with a tinny screech, tore down the middle and the halves fell apart. Human intestines spilled on the ground. The narrowlegs let it drop and turned indifferently away. Thick red stains spread across the ocean and sank in drowning rings.

''Loving thing's psycho,'' Jones said palely, watching what looked like the start of a space-battle. ''Where does it get this filth?''

''I can guess,'' Desi said. ''But it hasn't understood. Look. Screwing her brains out. Why? It's how you have a small one. You play for gold and divide the winnings. People meet on the dance-floor, two guys want the same woman, if she won't have them they let her drop. It's trying out ideas it doesn't understand. Someone else's.''

''Drowned in blood.''

''But it hasn't any itself.'' She turned him a weary eye. ''It asked how I could think it would destroy another intelligence. You, for instance.''

He shook his head. ''That's nice, but I still say it's psycho.''

''We're alien. Solid little people with blood inside. Maybe it finds that distasteful. Empty it out and the people get dead. Except those didn't. Did you notice? They were dummies.''

''Dummies that bled.''

''Dummies with red stuff in them. Was it blood? I don't

know if it understands dead. How old do you think it is, at a guess?''

{No way to say,} her symb answered. {This is a young universe. We haven't doubled because we aren't here, we haven't evolved yet. If we ever will, here. But it's been in existence as long as the planet's been solid. It remembers hot rain, meteor-hits from the sky. But then it was young, without understanding. Now it's aware of the continuum around it. It senses the stars, the movements of gravity. It tracks the planets of its own system. It considers. Not less than a billion years old. Could be older. It has no sense of time. It has no concept for tomorrow.}

''When was Ice here?'' Desi asked.

*I?* do not *know* *your?* *speech*. *You?* find *my?* *thoughts* *unacceptable*. But *I?* have *read* these *things* in *his?* *mind*. *The thinker?* who is beside *you?* *burns* *me?* with *his?* *sensation* and *I?* *quiver*. Why does *he?* *burn* *me?* with *strong* *thoughts*? This is *all* *outside?* *me?* *Your?* *thoughts* *fly* *away* from *me?* like the small *organisms* that build on the shore. *They* *flow* *away* from *me?* into *newness?* before *I?* have *time?* to grasp *them?*. So *you?* too *flow* *away* into the *outside?*, *burning* *me?* but leaving *me?* in *negativity*. *He?* too *burned* *me?*. *He?* showed *me?* these *pictures* of *beings?* that are *multiple?*. *I?* have become *aware* that *I?* am *not* *multiple?*. Why do *you?* so *burn* *me?*? *I?* *look* at *your?* *fragility* and *I?* have *sensations*. They are *like* the *red?* that flows from *your* *bodies*, the *clear?* that flows from *your?* *eyes*. *Sensation* *burns* *me?*. Why do *you?* do *this*? *I?* cannot follow *your?* *thought*. How can a *thinker* interrupt the *being?* of *another*? *I?* am *burned* with *ununderstanding*.

''It's saying we hurt it?'' Jones said with incredulity.

''It's specifically saying *you* hurt it. Bloody teep.''

{I don't think it has a concept of 'hurt'. It has sensations it can't analyse. It reads them as something like blood and tears, without knowing what those signify. So it shows you blood-and-tears pictures. Because you give it that sensation.}

"Shit," Jones muttered.

"You mean it's lonely. It had no comprehension of multiple people, but now it knows about them, it's become aware it isn't one. It's learned that communication's possible, but there's no-one to communicate with. It can't exchange its thoughts, and it wishes it could."

{I think that might cover it. It's been alone for a billion years. I imagine there's no intelligent life close enough, if there's any yet anywhere. Then Ice came. And showed it pictures of life and passion that were completely alien but suggested a mindlife it had never conceived. Now it knows it's alone. It doesn't understand the mindlife, but it knows it had a companion and lost him. It wants company.}

"Uh," Jones said uneasily. "How does that add, exactly?"

{It could mean it won't want you to go,} his own symb said. {Until you've spent time talking to it.}

"Time?"

{Like the rest of your life. Weren't you listening? It's basically immortal.}

"I'm iffy on that. I was figuring to go home someday. Preferably today. You may not have noticed, but I'm getting hungry."

{You may not have noticed, but so am I.}

"Great. Help yourself to slime-mold."

"When you guys have finished," Desi said. "This isn't a joke. It had Ice, it let him go and he didn't come back. That's my boy. I agree with your partner, we've a little local difficulty. I doubt if it wants an hour's social conversation. On the other hand . . ." She turned back to the ocean. "My friend and I hafta go to our ship, we need to eat. Take in energy? We'll consider your problem while we're doing it."

***You?* *wish*** to ***abandon?* *me?*.**

"No, we don't. We aren't your solution whichever way you cut it, we'd only live long enough to talk for five minutes. Your time. You'll finish both of us and get shit out of it. Let me think, it's what I'm paid for."

"I'm paid for it too," Jones said wistfully.

"Then earn your pay," Desi said. "We'll be back."

* * *

"Any future in taking a fast run while its attention's distracted?" Jones asked hopefully, forking up salad.

"No. For one thing, its attention aint distracted. It has plenty of spare neurons to keep an eye on us."

"It hasn't any eyes. Has it?"

"That what I mean. It don't look like it has, but it sees pictures. And on top of that you hurt it more than I do. Ergo, lover's mucho telepathico. Nope. When in doubt, the male of the species twists hard and breaks his key. The female, being weaker, has to fiddle the lock until it turns. So eat your nice prote and I'll consider how to actually sort this out. Never forget, I was built to raise kittens."

"What does that mean?"

"I've a highly-developed sense of survival."

"I'm pacified," Jones said, without enthusiasm.

"Hey, Blinky?"

?

"We're going to wander around. See you later." Desi looked in the mirror and twined her hair into arches to match willowy fairness and floating chiffons. She had another try at her nails but they were still flaky. "You guys ready?"

"As much as we'll ever be," *Windrunner* sighed. "What if this thing keeps us forever? I'm too young to waste the best years of my life."

"Quit whining. You've the run of this universe, it just aint entertaining. Anyhow, even if it tries to keep us, all it gets is a nice line in corpses. Sooner or later. And anyone who even thinks about new Eve gets his eye blacked."

"Didn't cross my mind," Jones said hastily.

"No need to be insulting," Desi retorted. "Let's go."

"Why do you always pick long and skinny?"

"Black holes. They stretch you. Gives me the practice. Except—" with a spiteful look at her chest, the nearest she could reach to her symb, "when I fall asleep and she lets go. Then I spoil my gowns."

{And she's also discontented with her basic genotype,} the symb added in counterpoint.

"Looked okay to me," Jones said. "Cuddly."

The symb gave a mental groan and Desi turned him a molten look. ''From the man of proven bad taste. Somebody find me an asteroid.''

*Windrunner* put herself into phase. ''What flavor?''

''Big, lotta volume, stony for preference. Map me what's available.''

The system came up in the tank, gas-giants swimming in dustclouds, smaller rocks in eccentric orbits. Uncertain lines traced extrapolations. ''Lot of small stuff, minor knobs of nickel-iron, loose cometary material. Mining country. It's still agglommerating. Not many big lithites, unless you're interested in the outer sats.''

''Could be,'' Desi said. ''Cept they heavy to handle. How about that monster with rings? Must have eleven.''

''Thirteen,'' *Windrunner* corrected. ''The four biggest are all volcanic.''

''Active?''

''Three of them. The fourth's quiescent.''

''Which mean it blows up tomorrow. What's that fat boulder with three orbiters on high eccentric?''

*Windrunner* enlarged it. An unevenly battered hulk with circling rocks, accelerating in from out-system. ''A disaster. Due to plunge into the sun next run, it's losing its track. Conflicting gravities, not to mention the dust. I've considerable skin-friction. If you're staying here long, I'll have to divert drive-function into the cooling plant.''

''Transcendental,'' Jones muttered.

Desi ignored him. ''I'd rather you diverted it into your tractors. I want that rock.''

''Tractors?'' *Windrunner* squealed. ''You want me to *haul* that?''

''You got it. Shouldn't need much, it's headed inward. Lean on it a bit.''

''Where are we putting it?''

''It's a present for Blinky. I want it next her in a nice stable orbit.''

{Mmn,} her symb considered. {Possible, but problematic. Is it big enough?}

''We can't handle a moon, haven't the pull. She can enlarge it later, must be what she done for herself. You notice her orbit runs through dustclouds?''

{I'd had the thought.}

"But she hasn't slowed enough to fall inward. Looks like maybe she sweeps up material. And uses it somehow."

"That, I don't follow," Jones said, leaning over the tank.

"Blinky," Desi said. "The billenial thinker? The drag should have modified her orbit enough to drop her in the sun, if she wasn't keeping herself out some way."

{That, or her climate's varied a lot over the ages. Which doesn't seem likely, with that brain's degree of organization. Besides, her constitution's typical of a fixed inner planet. There are others out there still agglommerating.}

"Which makes it look as if she formed out-system and drifted in," Desi concluded. "In her young youth, maybe? Started out a comet, something like that, and built a planet under her as her own volume increased?"

{Anything's possible. You're going to need atmosphere. That rock isn't big enough to hold it on its own.}

"Let's hit on that problem when we get there. How're your tractors, *Windy?*"

"I've the stone on leash. It's going to be difficult, there's a lot of mass. Do we have a black hole or something you can charge from? My batteries are low."

{Not that I can detect,} Desi's symb said, after a pause. {It's a small, young continuum, it probably has micro-singularities but nothing big enough in the area to give us impetus. You still have power in your engines.}

"I was hoping to use that to get us out of here," *Windrunner* muttered.

"Forget it," Desi said. "If we don't solve Blinky, we aint going anywhere. One problem at a time."

*Windrunner* sighed gustily. "Batteries online. If I give this thing a bit more pull . . ."

{So long as you can brake it at the far end. We don't want more acceleration than we can hold.}

{Shit! That exactly what the dumb bitch hoping for.} "Listen, lamebrain, Blinky can look after herself. Get over-smart and she may eliminate you. Which could be embarrassing. So no bright ideas. Just haul the damned rock, and let me try to work out the next bit."

*Windrunner* subsided into sulky breathing.

"What are we doing?" Jones asked nervously.

"Protecting our asses. Windy, keep the rock on track, and if I were you I'd start braking."

An orange line drew out in the tank, pulling the boulder toward the sun, curving it toward the green ellipse that marked the planet's projected path.

"Battery-power dropping into the yellow," *Windrunner* reported. "Are you sure you want to do this?"

"Yes. Keep moving."

"The final braking's going to be a problem."

"Um," Desi said. "Can we tailor this orbit closer?"

"I'm doing what I can. But there's a lot of friction, and I said complex gravity. If my reserves fall too low it'll go on past, and it's no use yelling at me."

{Batteries are batteries,} her symb added. {She's heading into red and I'm not sure we have the pull between us. Get your minds online. All hands to the pumps, the tractors are slipping.}

"Oh, shit," Desi said.

The mirrored globe swelled below them. *Windrunner* was pulling back on her tractors, the orange trace accelerating as the asteroid swung in. The cabin lights did their familiar flicker and the tank winked out and in again. Lightplates and tank came back dulled, the holo-image fuzzy. The converter whined and the air took on a chemical taint. Jones began to cough.

"I'm . . . doing . . . what I . . . can," *Windrunner* gasped. "Batteries in the . . . red. Switching my engine-power . . . into . . . traction . . ."

"Do that. Hang in, babe."

". . . but I . . . don't . . . answer . . . for the . . . consequences."

{And I suggest everyone adjust for vacuum,} Desi's symb said. {It's going to be close.}

The trace swept in toward the globe, the acceleration-gauge reddening as the batteries faded until it glowed dully like a runnel of lava. The rock went on picking up speed.

"It's . . . getting . . . away from me," *Windrunner* said, thin and high. "Severe . . . strain . . . on all . . . systems. I hope you're all . . . ready . . . for space . . ."

"Listen . . ." Jones began.

And the lights went out.

⌘

# TP–TV

*the station of the multiverse*

STOP THE PRESSES! HERE AGAIN WITH THE LATEST FLASH FROM THE WILD SPACES OF THE MULTICOLORED MULTIVARIOUS MULTIVERSE—FROM OUR SPECIAL CORRESPONDENT, JONES THE JUMPER! OVER TO YOU, JJ!

❖

[*Jones appears in wavering distortion, his scalp-lock shading blue, his jawline ditto. Image pauses, hesitates and comes back up, a shade too healthy. His voice alternately fades and rumbles. The boomboxes shudder:*]

Well, got out of that one, and can't say I'm sorry. It's a big relief to be back in my old-fashioned skin, however worn. But hey, guys, no trouble's too much for you. Have a gander at the newest sensation, and bet you never seen anything like it!

[*A small, sulky-blue ship with the stubby remains of a once-proud bow array hangs laboring in red-tinged dust, sparks burning off her skin, her fading tractors hauling valiantly on an irregular rock that dwarfs her completely. She vibrates with effort, her tail glowing with the heat of overstressed engines.*

*A quicksilver teardrop swelling below shines in the light of a hot young star. The hurtling rock curves toward it, headed for a slingshot orbit that will throw it into the sun—or speed it farther, right through the system. Its track abruptly curls inward, and mirror glitter reflects from its sides. One of its satellite rocks loses contact and skims into space.*

*The ship staggers with the sudden loss of reaction and its tractors grope feebly. It catches itself, switches out the power and takes hold of its failing engines. The captured asteroid swings into equatorial orbit around the planet, heaves on its axis, steadies and stabilizes. The image settles, as if the satellite had been there forever.*]

Will you load that in? And all done with mirrors. Nothing up my sleeves, folks, what you see is what you get. Panting for the next shivering installment? Well, stick around cause I'm sure it's coming. But meanwhile, a word from our sponsor . . .

"We did it!" Desi yelled. "Blinky got the idea, she pulled the lover in herself. I knew she could help if she tried."

She flopped on the couch as *Windrunner*'s lights came hesitantly up. "Back there for a minute I was almost worried."

"You were?" Jones said. He was shaking. "I was hoping you weren't."

A pale figure materialized in the cabin as the lights settled and laid its briefcase on the chart-table.

*"Miz Smeett? I am empowered by the Civil Court of Truegood to serve you with this subpoena . . ."*

"No!" yelled Desi, leaning with the full weight of her telepathic fury. The figure disappeared in a whiff of ozone.

It left the subpoena behind.

# FOUR

## Pangs

*You?* have brought *me?* a *rock*. *I?* supposed *you?* had a *purpose*, since it cost *you?* *pain?*. What do *you?* *wish* *me?* to *do* with it?

"You helped by grabbing. Don't think _Windy_ could have held much longer. Can you keep the orbit stable?"

Its *path* is secure. *I?* can *retain* *my?* *own?* *environment*. What are *your?* *intentions*?

"I need some brain."

*You?* make *me?* *afraid?*. What is *your?* *purpose*?

Jones scratched his neck. "She's jittery, I wouldn't like to scoop her brain-tissue. If that's what you're thinking. Not sure I'd like my own scooped, either."

"Will you shut up?"

"Seriously. This is a complex organism which you know nothing about. How can you tell what damage you're doing?"

*Damage*?

"Don't listen, guy don't know which way to put his pants on. I need a few neurons, general-purpose, like you use for thinking. Can you fabricate spares?"

Cautious pause. *My?* *thought-functions* are *myself?*. How can *I?* *fabricate?* *my?* *own?* substance?

"You gotta do it already. You develop."

That *thought* *I?* do not *know*.

"Sure you do," Desi insisted. "Or you couldn't grow. You must replace cells and enlarge your consciousness." {Doesn't she?} she added dubiously.

{I'd suppose so. Ask if it remembers being smaller. Covering less of the planetary surface, or having a smaller surface to cover. If it's survived meteor bombardment, it must have replaced tissue in the past.}

{Has it? Survived metes and all?}

{It must have, since it exists.}

"That's what I thought. So how about it. Do you?"

Another pause, longer. *Your?* *thoughts* *confuse* *me?*. *You?* speak in *many* *voices*. As *he?* did. Are *you?* *legion?*?

"No, just symbiosed. My partner's intelligent and we share our talents. Within limits. It won't keep me alive if we're both annihilated. All my people have two voices because we're all two. Some people's symbs rarely speak at all. Mine yacks a lot because I need its advice."

{Which you never take.}

{I take it all the time.}

{I wish you'd taken it over last night's beer.}

"That's what I said. Yackety-yackety." {I don't suppose you could project your own material into the ocean here and help Blinky out?}

{No. For one thing, it would take me a century to invest so much mass, my kind developed in medium-weight animals. For another, if this organism mutates it may be dangerous for all of us. This is a god in its way. Do you want to offer a god my powers? I very strongly advise against. It could destroy us.}

*Your?* *thought* travels far *beyond* *my?* *understanding?*. *I?* do not *know* *your?* *speech?*. How could *I?* *threaten* to *destroy?* *you?*? *You?* make *me?* *afraid*. *I?* see the *end?* of *universes?* in *your?* *other?*'s *thought*. That is not *myself?*, *I?* do not *destroy?* *thinkers*.

Desi sighed. "She don't mean you do, she means plus her you could, even if you didn't mean it. You're very powerful.

You can change matter, you're strongly telepathic. None of us could do those things before we symbed. I was born with this partner and she gave me her talents. I'm a shapechanger and a telepath because of her. Symbs are a group mind, all the same organism. It gives us the power to teep. Or something."

"You have to be one of the world's great communicators," Jones said. "Blinky, what she's trying to say is, her symbiote can't help you, though it helps us, because you're too big. Since all symbs are the same organism, if you owned too much of its mind you could become so powerful you'd rule the whole of it. Including us. Even across realities, since it seems they can teep through dimensional boundaries. You could destroy us all."

{Because you lack experience. You don't know your own strength. But listen,} the inward voice added to Desi. {You haven't scoped the problem. It isn't conscious of its own cell-structure, it probably grows at a purely organic level, like you when you metabolize. As all your people did all their lives before they had us. It doesn't know which parts of itself you can skim harmlessly.}

"Theoretical, and disagree," Desi snapped. "If she had no control she'd have overgrown the planet. Listen, Blinky. Do you remember being smaller?"

***I?*** have ***considered*** the ***question*. *I?*** have a ***time?*** in ***my?* *has-been*** when ***all*** was ***distant?*.** And ***you?*** speak of ***bombardments*. *I?*** have ***knowledge*** of ***distress?*, *knowledge*** of ***has-been* *sensations*** like the ***red?*** that came from the ***people-shapes?*.** When the ***red?*** came from the ***people-shapes?*, *he?* *transmitted* *strange* *sensations*. *My?* *sensations*** were ***strange*** also, ***strange*** and ***red?*. *I?*** am ***now?*** in ***tranquility*.** As ***I?*** speak ***I?*** am in ***tranquility*. *Tranquility*** is ***not-red?*. *I?*** cannot give ***you?*** the ***meaning*** of ***my?* *thought*.**

"It's okay, Blink, I get it. The brief answer's yes, she's been smaller, she was bombarded. Okay. What about the other question? Can you control your expansion? Is this as big as you get, or only as big as you *have* got? Will you grow on out over the continents?"

*I?* occupy *now* *all* of *my?* *space*. It has been *so* now while the *stars* *changed*. *I?* *choose* not to *overgrow* the *continents*, to do so *would?* bring about the *injury* of *my?* *movers*. The *movers* are not to *be?* *injured*. The *movers* are the *seeds?* of *thinkers*. The *destruction?* of *thinkers* is *red?*. But *I?* *eat?* the dust from *outside* to *remake* *my?* *substance* when it grows *less*. And if *my?* *continents* become too *small*, *I?* shall *eat?* more and *enlarge* *them?*. When *I?* *eat?* dust *my?* *thought* grows *larger?*.

"Gotcha. She can control her growth when she wants but you're right, she don't really know she's doing it. I need something, Blink. Overgrow me a piece of yourself. This big." She showed the tip of her finger. "Or smaller. It won't hurt your slime-molds, trust me. Then hop it out on this saucer."

"Won't it hurt her?" Jones looked unhappy. "She's quick on the trigger. And when I think of it, how can you tell it's she?"

"I can't," Desi said crossly. "Lover's neuter, unless it have tricks I aint found out yet. No sexual activity among the slime-molds, strictly cell-division. It also a person. I supposed to call a person 'it'? Why'n't you stick to your nasty trade and teep dancing-boys hotting or something? If Blinky's used to being blasted, a little cut won't hurt her. Go ahead, babe, grow me some brain. On this little saucer."

⌘

## TP–TV

*the station of the multiverse*

STILL BRINGING YOU ROARING REDHOTS FROM THE TOP OF THE NEWSLIST, THE ALL-STAR STATION FROM THE SUNSTUDDED OUTBLACK. DON'T FORGET, PEOPLE, TOP OF THE NEWS, TOP OF THE BLUES, TOP OF THE LIST OF THE PRIZE-WINNING CUES—TEEP-TV, THE PEOPLE

WHO KEEP THE HITS COMING. SO LET'S BURN IT UP WITH THE LATEST NEWS-FLASH—WAIT FOR IT, WEAVERS—HERE'S JONESY!

❖

[*Dick flings his scalp-lock, tries to organize his jaw which has gotten into a melting moment and pulls his face together like india-rubber. He bares his teeth. A mouthful of rolling stones, all mossy, fall into place and turn to ivory. The boom-boxes grumble:*]

Hi once again, my heavenly hearties, and we sure gotten you some great grinds coming. Screw in your eardrums and bolt on your corneas, and I hope you've lined in your recorders, cause I'm only teeping it once. Action!

[*Gelatinous shoreline in iridescent tones of black-green putrescence, this week's fanciest fashion-shade, with a sturdy small shape planted blockily in the middle. (The template slipped again while Desi's symb was busy.) It glances up, scowls like a blastfurnace and gets hastily mutated to a diaphanous blonde with momentous mammaries. It bares thoroughly competent fangs and we have a brief glimpse of Dick looking desperate. The blonde settles for sullen discontentment and offers a Petri dish to the ocean. Which hesitates, shrinks, and lifts a dainty pseudopod. It dips the extreme tip in the dish.*]

BLONDE, CONTRALTO: So, cut it.

OCEAN, LOW DIAPASON: ***Aa-a-aah!***

[*The tip of the mass drops into the saucer, which is discorped out of the picture. The sea-surface breaks up right to the horizon in heaving flashes of mold and silver. The sky turns black and rains lightnings, through which the blonde can be heard yelling.*]

BLONDE: Okay, it's over! Don't be so dumboid, anybody think I cut you leg off, what a wet-neck!

[*The scene slowly settles and the sky dies back to rancid ultramarine with viridian striations.*]

DICK: Whew, that was a close one!

[*His smile comes back to full candlepower and the boomboxes stop screaming. Distant listeners take out mental earplugs:*]

Well, fans, there you have it. Never say I don't risk my life for you! Back soon with the next brim-full installment—if I live that long. So—all you happy hoppers, take real good care, and once again, from those beautiful people who brought you **Bluelips** + ™—back to the studio . . .

"Kind of imaginative, aintya?" Desi growled, recorped to the cabin with her dish carefully balanced in stasis.

"How's that?"

"Thunder and lightning."

"Seemed to me your friend was upset."

"Bullshit. Was psychosomatic, ask your symb. She read someone's mind—probably yours—and made what you thought were appropriate reactions. Brain tissue's insensitive, hasn't any nerve-ends. Like cutting her toenails."

"Maybe its isn't. And it doesn't have toes."

"Stand outta my way." She strode past on her way to the arc and paused to glare evilly over her shoulder. "What's the big-tit thing? You perverted?"

"It's the net housestyle. The marks like it."

"Your marks is perverted."

The door slammed behind her.

"Yeah, guess some of em have to be," Jones sighed. "*Bluelips* + ™?"

{Have you seen the holo that goes with it?} his symb inquired. {I'd say she's right about the reaction, it pulled it right out of somebody's mind. It's experimenting with emotions. Having none of its own.}

"You sure about that?"

{It's intelligent, it's fully organic, it has limited experience. Learned from the boyfriend that games were expected, thinks humans like them. It's trying to figure out how they work.}

"Worked fine with me, I was scared shitless."

{Not while I'm looking after your tail. But you undoubtedly expanded its knowledge.}

"You mean I taught it how to scream."

{I'd call your reactions a little edgy. Do you still find the lady vulnerable?}

"I think she's going to kill us. But okay, it was my idea."

{I only hope you can finish what you've started.}

"So do I."

{Have we thought any farther about the satellite's atmo?} Desi's symb asked.

"Did cross my mind Blinky might help." Desi scraped a sample from the Petri dish onto a slide and put it under *Windrunner*'s scanner. "She maintains her own, and this material's part of her."

{I didn't see manufacture as the problem, we could set up a mechanical conversion program. The problem's the gravity to keep it when we have it.}

"And I was born stupid. Don't it seem to you Blink's own atmo's rich and thick, considering her base-rock aint that dense and her biosynthesis is in its early stages?"

{The gravity here's naturally high.}

"Not enough to change the laws of physics, as last seen. She has some kinda forcescreen, check it out."

{I did notice a hitch, coming through.}

"Which was because she decided to admit us. *Windy*?"

"Here," *Windrunner* rasped. "But I'm getting asthma. It's lowered resistance, I'm not used to all this stress. That, or an allergic reaction to alien dust. Possibly both."

"You're breaking my heart. Blow your nose, or whatever you're using, and scope the upper atmosphere."

"I heard your conversation and the answer's affirmative, there is a forcefield. I was aware of it when you first went down."

"Were you," Desi said dangerously. "Next time maybe you'd share your insights. We may live longer."

"I'll try to remember that," *Windrunner* said.

"And if you think your skinny buddy can take you home, forget it. Couldn't navigate his way out of a shithouse, hasn't the training. He's a fricky teep. Much like a stud-bull, they know what to do but they can't explain it."

{And that warning I'd take seriously,} her symb added.

A snuffling sound of seriously-taken warning.

{Though she really has an allergy.}

"Frick. All we need." Desi squinted at her readouts. "This'll work, I can whip up the growth-nutri. It's complicated but within our capacity. But I've a minimum cloning-time of fourteen hours, with all the accelerated growth we can pressure. *Windy*'s right, that's a damn big asteroid. How long before Blink wants her Christmas present *now?*"

"If you were telling the truth it doesn't matter," *Windrunner* snuffled. "There's no way out."

"I was telling the truth. I'm not anxious to spend eternity here, either. Can we fix a desensitization prog to stop Madam sniffling?"

{If we'd the energy and time,} her symb said. {We've multiple problems. Dust filtered through her field when we lost power and the contamination got into her ducts. If she can keep up her field-strength the attack should wear off as she metabolizes, but all of us have lowered resistance. And the batteries are weak. She's holding the shield against high grav-levels while we need extra energy to clone. This will be a big piece of tissue.}

"Shoot, I wasn't figuring a full-size cover, we'd wave it like a flag. It can develop after it's planted."

{That's what I thought you thought. But I also imagined your thinker needed gratification.}

"Or she might want us to stick around."

{It might find that logical while it has nothing better. As I keep reminding you, it has no time-sense.}

"And my field-strength's declining," *Windrunner* said thickly. "The cloning-tank's a big drain, especially accelerated. We need to recharge."

"We need too damn many things."

{That's what I was saying.}

Desi glared into the depths of the tank, where crystal threads had begun to swell and spiral. "So can we or can't we hold for fourteen hours?"

{We can, just.}

"But it isn't going to be easy," *Windrunner* husked. A drip of clear fluid ran out of the air-duct.

Desi regarded it with revulsion. "Life never is."

"Fine," Desi panted. "Can you keep on hauling? Get the lattice right over the horizon. I'm breaking my back on this damn converter."

"Doing what I can." Jones was panting too. The asteroid's gravity was just high enough to keep them on its surface, insufficiently high to make walking easy. He'd dug the nodes of one end of the field-generator in along the terminator line and was trying to spread the rest as far as possible over the satellite's sunward surface. "Be easier if it wasn't turning end-over-end."

"Be a whole lot easier if I'd a terraform company in my kanga. Which aint being so, gotta do what we can. Figure this the favored side, net could spend nearly sixty percent of its time in sunlight. That should power it enough to keep it running."

"Won't be as much as that. Sat's going to be occulted by the planet every revolution."

"It's a high-emission star. Do you have to be so damned optimistic?"

Jones paused in the dark to wipe his brow and sneer at his distant companion. Sweat was trickling down his back. "If I'd known you wanted advanced manual labor, I'd have brought working jeans."

"Order yourself something outta my Tailormaid. *Windy* can recycle the nans."

"Not the way she is right now."

"Well, boyo, if we don't get her outta here before she gets worse, you won't need pants. And to do that, we hafta finish. Try working."

He stamped nodes vindictively into the rock. The sky beyond was tinged with red, the stars too big and too close. A steady hiss of invisible dust ran past his eardrums and roughened his skin. He could feel his nose itch. "Way we're going, we'll all get asthma."

"I'll brew you antihistamine," Desi said, and sneezed.

"Gesundheit. Need help with the converter?"

"No." Her voice was muffled. "It's coming online, watch the exhaust. Ah, shit. Ice spent my life telling me I'd end up dead, but I never did. At least, not before."

Jones discorped hastily over the terminator. The rock was twenty miles across so the move was athletic.

"Hey." He reached for her hand. "Tough woman. What got under your skin enough to make you cry? Does the guy mean that much?"

Desi sniffed defiantly, jerking the hand away. "All I got under my skin's hay fever. Wish you'd keep your nose out, no-one asked you to come."

"That's right, they didn't."

"I'll solve this problem. *Windy* can hold out if she'd control her emotions, these fricky organics are built resistant. She's hypochondriac. We can help Blinky, it's a question of time. All it may take is a coupla centuries. Or maybe millenia. Can't extrapolate her growth-rate, she's too alien."

"You'll get bored, if you don't get terminally accidented. And maybe hungry, unless you eat slime-mold, and the planet seems to value them. I bother you. Sorry. Would it be better if I stayed in the hold?"

Desi sniffled. "Transporting sentients through dimensional interfaces happens to be illegal."

"You only just noticed?"

"Don't be dumb," she yelled. "I could make a case for myself as being on a humanitarian mission, which I am. Even if Hermes squawks, I could end by clearing it, except for you. *You* are what will cost me my license."

"I'm a big boy. I stowed away under my own power. And I too am licensed to break my neck in pursuance of my trade, if circumstances require it."

"Well, you don't hottin need to do it on my ship."

"Unluckily, she's currently the only one around."

Desi took another big sniffle. "I haven't time for this. Gotta cook antihistamines. How's the field?"

Jones hooked an arm around her waist. "Holding. Do you consent to having my arm around your waist?"

"No."

"Do you mean to file a formal protest?"

"I'm trying to think, dammit."

"That's okay, then."

They hunkered together on the edge of the net to watch the oxygen-carbon dioxide mixture hiss from the vents as the converter dug itself into the rock. A steady stream of dust was sucked through the field into the intake and a growing plume of powdery exhaust streamed out along the orbit behind.

"Couldn't we recycle that to augment sat volume?" Jones said. "And how about plantings?"

"Both good ideas, can't use em," Desi mumbled. "Our batteries are in the red. Could do something if I carried dirt-programs but I'm not into agrichemicals. Rock's bare, no biologics, I'd have to program my own nans and train *Windy* to make em. If we'd time to enrich I could try cuttings, but the converter's at full stretch making oxy for the brainstuff. Couldn't use my own houseplants anyway, they're extra-dimensional. Might disagree with Blinky's metabolism."

"It won't be eating them."

"Not the problem. Physical touch of alien proteins can be enough. Like this fricky dust that giving us allergies. I can't stick her with a contagious sat, that would really eat my license. I've a legitimate profession, we got rules."

"So bring up slime-molds. It can spare them."

Desi paused. "My symb has a theory Blinky and her flora maybe linked together. If it is flora. Could alter her ecology by messing with it."

"Maybe," Jones said. "The molds must contribute to its own atmosphere."

"We wondering if they also do something else. Like you said, she cares. My symb wonders if they could be actual continuations of Blinky. Like independent sense-organs?"

He considered, watching the bubble of field that would protect the growing atmosphere rise, glistening. "I'm agnostic. No telling what you'll find here."

"Yeah. You thought of trying *National Cosmographic* rather than that garbage-recycling plant you work for?"

"Sure. I freelance on the side. Strange as it may seem, even I have ethical doubts."

"You've what?"

"Doubts. Ethical. Like the possible effects on this planet

of large enthusiastic cosmological expeditions arriving with heavy equipment.''

''Jeremiah. Don't even think it.''

''I'm trying not to. But the damned thing's unique.''

''Aint a thing, it a person,'' snapped Desi.

''That's what I mean, doll. A unique personality. Which, farther, is capable of resenting it. How about we try out a sheet of organic? The field and the atmo are coming nicely. Then perhaps we should commune with Blinky. On the subject of its external sense-organs.''

''She won't understand. Her grasp of language is limited.''

''Not as limited as you think. That thing's playing something close to its chest, take the word of a pro teep. Come on. We both asked for it, but neither of us actually filed requisitions. *Per ardua ad astra*, which my Pop translated, it's a rocky road to Dublin.''

Desi stood, dusting her pants. She turned her hair experimental green, and let it fade. ''Shit, I'm beat. I was hoping to clone at least four sheets and spread em around. Give em a chance to make some ground-cover. Wish to hell we'd a spare battery.''

''Charged, naturally.''

''Right. We'd manage if we'd a charge on the ones we got. You are also right about the sunlight, it won't keep the field going forever. Not with this mass to cover. Hope I aint made a real, serious miscalculation.''

''You rate marks for trying. Let's corp this sheet out.''

The air of the planet was vibrant with electricity. St Elmo's fire played around the rocks and the taller slime-molds, rising into pylons on silicious skeletons, sparked at the tips. Heavy low clouds hung over the shore.

''You there, Blink?''

Lowering pause. A chain of lightning ran along the belly of the cloud-layer, trailing a sulfurous smell.

***I?*** have ***awaited?* *you?*.**

''Not what you'd call enthusiastic,'' Jones muttered.

{It's nervous,} his symb said. {What you cloned and laid out up there is itself.}

''We noticed,'' Desi said. ''*Windy's* having a nervous

breakdown. I'm not happy about the converter myself. And I'd have liked more spread on that clone-tissue.''

{It's lucky it got three whole colonies in the end,} her symb retorted, {*Windrunner's* flat. Had you noticed she's having respiratory difficulties?}

''How couldn't we? We're sharing em. Haven't smelled air like that since the dog died. Listen, Blink. We done what we can, it's your turn. Stuff up there's growing. You won't get reaction for a while cause the area's too small, but if the sheets we've planted live to unite, you oughtta end with an echo.''

''What if the clone turns out idiot?'' Jones whispered uneasily.

''Will you quit thinking?'' Desi hissed. ''Blink, we need help. Can't do any more, my ship's outta energy. That tissue needs maintenance. You gotta tend it. The atmospheric converter's battery has a limited half-life and the strength of the forcefield depends on sunlight. Its duration's limited, in terms of your lifespan. Sat's gravity's too low to hold atmosphere itself. If we could add plantlife it would help the oxygen, which means slime-molds. You hafta agree, we don't understand them. And there no guarantees this'll work. We need you.''

The dark clouds spread, casting shadows on the ocean. Agitated patterns rose in the swells and sank, roiling. Another blast of sulfurous lightning slashed the clouds and the air around stirred with static.

What am ***I?*** to do?

''Try to talk to your brain on the sat.''

***Talk?***?

''Telepath. Set up a connection. Whatever you do to establish communication,'' Jones said impatiently.

''Don't rush her,'' Desi said. ''Feel it out, Blink. Touch it, see if anything comes back.''

More silence. Electrical activity stuttered through the vapor with a noise like tearing silk. Something tall and glistening stilted awkwardly across the slope behind them, a string of smaller copies staggering in its wake. The pause drew out.

''Shit,'' Desi whispered. ''Tissue can't have grown enough

to reflect. Less something wrong. We maybe should've fixed heavier UV shielding . . ."

The ocean welled in a flurry of pattern and the clouds split in a slash of light.

"What?" Desi asked urgently.

Jones's hands were over his ears, his face screwed with pain.

***I?*** heard ***myself?*** ***cry***.

"We get our slime-molds?" Jones asked. He was lying on Desi's bunk eating protein sandwich. He was suppressing the thought it was lousy protein. *Windrunner* was still in the throes of asthma and he was doing the cooking on a camp-nanoconverter.

"Phe-eww," Desi groaned. "We do, if I transport em. Which I have undertaken to do. After dinner. Dial me another, huh?"

"We're on the camper. *Windy* doesn't feel good."

"Tastes like shit. Dial me one anyhow. If the tank pings, switch the culture into her airsystem. She sound like a herd of whales dying."

"Where is it?"

"Second growth-tank. Try the main air-pump. And throw me that sandwich."

Jones located a red-lit tank and *Windrunner* posted him a systems printout. He recorped the vaccine into the main pump and the wheezing diminished.

"Thank God for that," Desi said. "I may have tasted worse prote, but I can't recall where. How's your skin-rash?"

"I could survive. Blinky helping us on atmosphere?"

He'd discorped back to the ship to cook when Desi, her symb and the planet got into their second hour of complex biological discussion. Desi made a face.

"Humpty-toity and mind our own business. She's gone possessive since the lover squeaked. You could look. If I don't sleep, I gonna die."

"Me too. What do I say if I don't like what I see?"

"Keep it belted. Don't you know about proud parents? Tomorrow I'm looking, see if we can't get *Windy* some power.

Place aint exactly boring, but I could leave without agony."
"Amen," said Jones.

⌘

## TP–TV

*the station of the multiverse*

*FLASH*FLASH*FLASH*FLASH*FLASH*FLASH*FLASH*

❖

[*Colored babble. Dick firms up out of it wearing a pineapple in place of his scalplock. After a moment it corrects itself, wavers, and turns to a pumpkin. He's not sure what's wrong but looks embarrassed. His voice takes a moment to stop wobbling. The listeners reach for their earplugs:*]

Sorry, folks, interdimensional interference, the outer galaxies are frisky this a.m. Or whatever glad hour you're currently enjoying. Did I promise you excitement? Let's hear the Lost Boys clapping, and the Lost Girls too, put some shoulder in it, we need you guys to believe in us. All together! And glim in on this. Tell me if your guy's a genius or what!

TECHIE VOICEOVER FROM SOMEONE'S HEADSET: What's with the hotting vegetation?

DICK, EXASPERATED: So how about you fix it? Aint that what you're paid for?

[*A badtempered swirl melts the image. His head quivers, vanishes and returns, in a coonskin cap. Dick, martyred:*]

As I was saying—get your teeth in this!

[*Quicksilver planet, mostly in darkness, reflects dully through roiling atmosphere. A brilliant droplet hangs off its flank. Amoeboid pools patch the surface. They grow pseudopods that meld at the boundaries. Thick air fuzzes the stars at its edges and a line of sunlight bright as a cutting-laser burns at the limb. The droplet is visibly losing its facets, rounding out as it enlarges. The view pans into the black patchwork among the metal where lumpen jelly heaves and wobbles. More mold discorps into being and globs over the rock.*

*A smudge of cloud on the darkside discharges a miniature flash of lightning. Its vast parent spawns a storm-system over its equator and replies with chained electricity. Vivid discharges link them together. The satellite drifts around the planet's limb into full sunlight and a last flash of fire whites out the vidscreens. Dick, jubilant:*]

That's my baby!

"Looks like Blinky taking it serious," Desi noted.

"You've no idea. Want a closer look?"

"Thanks, saw your last. Loved the pumpkin."

Jones reddened. "Interdi interference," he repeated defensively. "This one's for your eyes only."

"I'm looking. Thought of making the jaw more authentic?"

"House style. All I do is report news. Concentrate, dammit."

The shoreline where they'd stood was deep in mutating jelly, mostly ambulant. Larger and smaller spiny spheres rolled around clicking. The towers on the edge of sightline were higher than pylons, their silicon armatures massive as mammoth-bones.

The silver ocean boiled with patterns, wave after wave of welling complexity. Dark clouds shaded the sky, pulsing with continuous electrical activity. A bulge heaved out of the crystal, shedding silver, and slowly formed a group. Linked bulbs grew heads and limbs and firmed into two hunched figures, tied by the taller one's arm.

The lumpy platform they grew out of could have been anything, but part looked like a rough cube. The faceless bulges were slumped together, heads and arms running into one. The smaller and blockier sprouted a sudden and startling grass-green mat, which faded to red-brown and darkened to crimson. Blood ran down in gelatinous strings and dripped off the bulb's lower curve. Before it could drip the mat snapped back, withdrew to the top and turned yellow-brown. The small hump melted into the larger.

"I never," Desi said with indignation.

"You did too, babe. You were too tired to notice."

The group paused, frozen, dewed with crystals. It stayed quiescent for a long moment. Then the jerky motion began again. The tall hump reached a lethargic tentacle, caught the small one's head-bulb and twisted. The bulb tore free, its blank curve reflecting the ocean. A scarlet river spouted from the severed edges.

"I sure as hell didn't do that."

"Was too tired to notice."

Jones was pained. "Me? I don't even carry hardware. I'm a lovin pacifist."

The tentacle drifted down to re-link the pair and the severed bulb drew out to a teardrop that elongated into the body and united. The red fountain guttered and died.

The figures joined tentacles and melted together in a single lump. The whole show sank quietly into the sea.

"It's been repeating that image, or something like it, over and over, for maybe three hours to my knowledge," Jones concluded, shutting down his vision. "The blood never reaches the surface."

"What's with it?" Desi was blank.

{I'd say it's trying to absorb you,} her symb offered. {Mentally. A new phenomenon.}

"Then it's doing badly. Neither of us hot on sado-maso. Less *he* Jack the Ripper in his spare time." She looked at Jones accusingly.

"Haven't a rip in me. All I want's a few quiet zees."

{That's its problem. It saw humans as competitive and bloody. Neither of you fits, and it's confused.}

"Tough," Desi growled. "Excuse *me*, I'm an accredited medic. You know, one of the caring professions."

{Or at least, you hope so.}

"They can't fire me, aint had my trial yet."

"But I'd also say it was trying to swallow us. And we seem to be sticking in its gullet."

"Giving it bellyache. Why do those things have blank faces? Some of Ice's projections were quite detailed."

{It's possible it comprehends you two as mental beings. Or doesn't comprehend you at all. It's never met paired people before, not in the flesh.}

"Poor little Blinky," Desi said.

{You could treat it as an adult with unknown potential. The thing's a god. In its way.}

"If I gotta call it Ms. God, Sir, I can't talk to it. My experience of talking to gods is limited. Does it say it minds?"

{How could it? It doesn't understand language.}

"Then nobody gotten hurt. Since things improving, find me a heavy star. A real, hot, stinking bummer."

"I don't think I can," *Windrunner* said feebly. "I haven't the strength for ignition. Asthma takes it out of you. Even if we'd battery-power."

A lengthening silence. Jones rubbed his ear. It wasn't a bad ear, though forested over with wild hair that grew wilder with effort and lack of sleep.

"Well—" he began.

Two pulsating phantoms walked through the bulkheads from opposite directions and collided in the middle with a few polite sparks. They paused to recover their ghostly dignity and turned on Desi as one.

"*Miz Smeett*," said one.

"*Defendant*," said the other.

"*I am empowered to inform you . . .*"

"*. . . on behalf of the Federation Medical Agency, Hermes . . .*"

"*that your non-compliance with the subpoena legally served upon you last week . . .*"

"Oh, shit," said Desi. "We're on a non-congruent time-path. That's gonna be a bastard."

"*. . . has resulted in formal termination of your contract . . .*"

"*. . . and your professional association will reconsider your standing as a competent physician . . .*"

"*plus indictment for contempt of court . . .*"

"*for which purpose I hereby serve . . .*"

"*. . . and in pursuance of which, I formally leave you with . . .*"

"*this writ, duly issued by the court . . .*"

*"... a summons to appear before an adjudicating committee ..."*

*"non-compliance with which will lay you open to prosecution."*

*"And, Miz Smeett,"* said the first severely, *"I advise you to give this matter your most serious attention."*

*"As you rarely do,"* the other added.

Two legal envelopes thunked on the chart-table. The ghosts exchanged a friendly nod and left through the hull.

"Are you nuts?" Desi shouted after them. "We're stuck in a fricky parallel timeline."

"Forget it," Jones said. "They've gone. Have another sandwich."

"Rather have a beer," Desi said. Her symb groaned.

*I?* *face* *not-I?*. The *other?* *appeared* to *me?* as a *red?* *dream?*. *My?* *not-I?*, *flesh?* of *my?* *flesh?*, reflects *my?* *thought* to *me?*. *All?* is *changed?*. The *stars* still *sing?*, the *blue?* *wind?* still *blows* out of the *wide?* *places?*. But *my?* *not?-I* *shares?* *my?* *being?*, *we?* *sing?* in *harmony*.

"They say two heads is better than one."

Maybe the song wasn't meant for Desi. It maybe wasn't meant for anyone. The planet broadcast its thoughts to the universe as if it was joyously alone. Perhaps in the end all of them, Desi, Jones, *Windrunner*, were invisible to it, too small to notice.

The ocean was calm, patterned with tranquility, a blue-violet sky burning off it. Mounded slime-molds as high as houses bundled uneven rocks on the beach and pushed them laboriously into pyramids. An occasional sphere as big as a football bounced over the landscape, rolling on its spines.

"You guys okay?" Desi was supposing it could pick up her thoughts. "Can you handle the atmo?"

Purely formal question. The developing globe in equatorial orbit had doubled in size, pulling in dust and meteoric debris. Its gravity increased every moment. Its amoebic spread of brain silvered the rubble, drawn out thin to cover the rock.

The converter might still be working below but the field-generator was redundant already. The exchanges of lightning and charged particles between prime and satellite had created a forcefield around the nascent atmosphere. The silver skin pooled in crevices and grew thicker, reflecting sunlight. Maybe the planet really was a god. It didn't answer.

"Obstetrics was never my thing," Desi muttered. "Hey, Blink, we need a star. Preferably collapsed, preferably heavy. If there aint a black hole yet. Unless you want permanent fleas."

***Fleas*?**

"Minor parasite, archaic but itchy. Causes lumps. Like you had in the sea lately. Scratch-yourself country. Jonesy wouldn't tear off my head if I let him, we sharing a ship. Sex-games is the least of our worries. Our batteries are flat."

***Batteries*?**

"Gravitronic storage. Where my ship keeps her power. We ran em dry towing in your baby. Don't bother to blame yourself, we hadn't the power for jump anyway."

***Blame*?**

"Forget it. It strike you your slime-molds getting out of hand?"

***I?*** have ***accelerated?*** ***my?*** ***nascent?*** ***thinkers*.** ***I?*** was in ***haste?*** to ***know*** ***their?*** ***thoughts*.**

"Aint convinced you oughtta push, wild mutation makes monsters. Let em evolve. Less it monsters you want. You think it ethical to use thinkers as laboratory animals?"

***I?*** do not ***understand*** ***your?*** ***thought*.** It is ***red?*** to ***accelerate?*** the ***thinkers***?

"Yeah, I guess. Red to use em. If red's bad. Let em develop, results could be more interesting."

***They?*** are in ***part*** ***myself?*.**

"We'd figured. Could still be more interesting to let em develop. You might surprise yourself."

***Surprise*** is what ***I?*** ***continually*** ***experience*** with ***you?*.**

"Could be."

***You?*** ***wish?*** to ***leave?*** this ***space-time?***?

"You got it. I'm looking for the cold guy who was here.

He's gone, so there's a way. But we need power. Gravitational energy to charge our batteries. Dig?"

*You?* follow the *track* of the *cold* *thinker?*?

"That's what we do."

*Protect?* *yourselves?*.

"What?"

But they were off-net. The glimmering surface blackened with patterns as if the planet had clenched like a fist. The lights reddened and dimmed.

"***A-a-a-ah-h!***" screamed *Windrunner*.

The universe went black.

# FIVE

## The Reivers

The darkness flashed with half-seen lightnings and smelled dusty. *Windrunner* was whimpering in her ducts. Desi clung to the panel and Jones grabbed her hand in the dark.

"Can't help till we come out," he said mildly. "We're between continuums. Nothing to sight on."

"At least we aint on vid."

"Missed, this time," he agreed with regret.

"So, wise guy,"—small defiance out of big darkness—"how do you teep across a time-break?"

"I don't know," Jones admitted. "Guess because teeping's a mental activity. Compared with ghosts, which are electrical. Especially when they leave documents. Must have been sent by gravitronic transmitter. Odd things must happen at dimensional boundaries. I send on a narrow band and the station's receiver clarifies the signal. They're probably getting multiple images and she's picking out the ones that make sense."

"Could have fooled me."

"I expect the others made even less."

"Then why haven't we multiple ghosts?"

"It could happen. We're only assuming the last were contemporary."

"*Assuming?*"

"Fraid so. They may have been sent out three weeks back."

"Shit," said Desi.

"Uh-huh." The hand slid to her waist. "I'll drink to the thought, if you have more beer."

She slapped absently. "Not till we've light. Can't see the damned icebox."

Light came back in a flood of overcharged plates. *Windrunner* squeaked, took hold of her power and leveled down the lumens.

"I have full charge on all batteries. Stand by, testing engines."

Desi squeezed her eyes on blinded tears, located Jones's hand and detached it daintily. "Well, bedammit."

"Your planetary friend must have listened."

"Depend where she's put us. *Windy*, gimme a reading."

"Position uncertain." Cautious. "Environment stable, power-reserves optimal, my skin's fine. Asthma's passed off. Minor mess from our last transfer, I'll get the mice on it. All systems functional. We're in a galaxy with normal parameters. Dust, no more than I can handle, heated gases, I'd say a nebula. Several stars in near proximity, but closing with a medium yellow dwarf. Homey. Seems familiar but isn't. If you know what I mean."

"I sincerely hope I don't," Desi said grimly. "What *do* you mean?"

"Everything in sight's on my current chart-system."

"Shit in spades."

Jones looked careful. "Uh?"

"Sounds like a close parallel. Aint the real thing, we're still moving away from our baseline. Can tell that myself, my nose says so."

"Is that bad?"

Desi was irritated. "Do newshounds learn anything except how to be obnoxious? What you get in close parallels is . . ."

The trans crackled and spat a callsign. A voice like a meat-grinder rebounded off the walls.

"You! Heave to and strike your ensign or I'll blow you to eternity. Prepare to be boarded."

"Is?" he asked politely.

She shrugged. "What you left at home, only nicer. Just as sweet as cotton candy. That, bub, is a pirate. What turns up in sandbanks where you come from?"

"Nightcrawlers and pirates. Can we outrun him?"

"No," Desi and *Windrunner* said simultaneously.

"Do you *want* a hole in your skin?" Desi asked solo.

*Windrunner* slowed. The writs fell off the chart-table with a rustle. Desi stamped them into the flooring, which digested them. The screens lightened on fluorescing gases and a black ship with frigate outlines, bristling gunports and a skull-and-crossbones on the forward quarter. It was swelling fast astern. They sighed in unison.

"Post a blue cross," Jones suggested.

"You nuts? They'll torture us for interesting chemicals. Anyone asks, I'm a roving bounter. Practically their sister. If you've sense, you are too."

The black ship loomed in the plates, a swelling mass that wiped out the stars.

"Boarding," the metal voice scratched. "Resistance will be dealt with. I advise you to surrender."

"Been hoping for bounty all my life," Jones said with resignation.

Mating airlocks clanged together. Desi slid her disruptor from the drawer and clamped it out of sight under the panel. "Step in, brother," she shouted cordially. "You're totally welcome."

The trans laughed like stripping gears.

The squad marched lockstep three abreast, with a ring of matched boots. They had a cute air of enforced discipline, like the Hitler Youth with Navy blasters. Cropped skulls glistened under their vizors. The rearguard was armed with rocket-cannon and one in front toted a flamethrower. Their officer went with the country, cropped, shaven and much too cleancut, like the ninth green of an expensive golf-course. His clear cold eye hinted a degree in advanced sadism. He looked Jones and Desi up and down, did a double-take, looked at them again and reddened slowly.

"Your pardon, Ma'am. Bringing in a prisoner? If you'd given the callsign . . ."

Desi held her face in and swallowed saliva. Jones's mind tweaked her.

{Answer the man, hotssakes,} his thought whispered.

{Jeezle, what is this?} Desi thought back. "Testing your efficiency," she said rapidly. "At ease, men. Lead the way, Commander, I'm in control."

The squad wheeled smartly and left, saluting. Jones wiped his brow.

{Amazing,} her symb said.

"I'm amazed too," Desi confirmed.

{A complete corps of peergroup clones?}

"Piracy as a whole's illegal."

{I'm being shocked.} It sounded shocked.

"I suppose they're symbed?"

{You suppose correctly,} her symb agreed. {Radio silence. Hots knows what genetic abnormalities they have down there.}

"Including our own." Desi glanced at Jones. "You listening, prisoner?"

"With attention," he said unhappily. "I've cut down emissions. Why am I the prisoner?"

{Don't ask,} his symb advised. {Place is a snakepit.}

"Cut em completely, you still read like a top-class teep. I'm Ma'am. Let's hope it helps us."

"Transcendental. Unless . . ."

"Yeah," Desi said. "Unless."

"Radio silence," he said.

Their symbs closed down and the air went dead.

The planet was small, black, rocky, and lit dimly by its small yellow sun. Frozen atmosphere lay on the rocks and luminous gas-clouds banded the sky. Rare stars burned redly through.

The frigate dropped inward with *Windrunner* behind and they drew up together in geosynchronous orbit a couple of miles apart. Desi listened.

"They've gone down. Ship's empty except for the watch. Hang loose, *Windy*. Let's join the party."

The surface was dark, prickles of starlight sparkling off

boulders. The view was black on blacker. Desi felt around.

"Let me scope, they know I'm symbed but they'll detect you at one peep. Life-sign below, base underneath."

"Surprise me," Jones muttered.

A wide valley stretched in front, almost flat enough to be a plain, scarred with worn ringwalls. They discorped closer and found a crack splitting it end to end that fell away into nether darkness. Faint red light at the bottom suggested volcanic activity in the depths.

{I think you'd better all three trust me,} Desi's symb husked in a bare whisper.

{Trust, hell, we've felt it out for you,} Jones's retorted. {Just hang on our tail.}

"Shut it, any teep in lightyears could hear you guys sneeze. Jonesy stinks of overgrown talents. Head in. And if I come out inside ten miles of basalt, someone gonna pay."

Silence. Desi closed her eyes and felt the environment. Space. Space enclosed by rock. Rock. A moment of suffocation, and her discorped molecules slid through a wall and came together in air, falling.

She controlled her outline, found a floor and lowered her toes to it. On reflection she also tinted her skin blue, her eyes green, and grew seven fingers. Her long black hair twisted up in a braid, but her nailpolish stayed flaky. She scowled. Jones corped out beside her with unexpected delicacy and smoothed his hair. It made no difference.

"At ease, Commander," she said. "Out-systems bounter, picked him up in passing but his ship died of it. Seems he aint best friends with the government."

The head clone laughed politely. "Not many of us are. You'll introduce him to the Captain yourself?"

Desi produced a cute tinkly trill. "A pleasure."

"In his quarters, Ma'am. He's anxious to see you."

Desi ran an eye around the vault of the guardhouse. No doors, so all the crew was symbiosed. But it had windows, arches over far green landscapes. Glassless. The sky shone limpid turquoise on woods and fields threaded with silver, where tiny distant laboring people did something rural with extinct animals.

{Jeez,} Desi's symb murmured small. {An Italian primitive.}

{Thank you, Ma'am,} Jones's whispered back. {We're actually cultured. There's a bad smell here. Watch out.}

Jones was mute, his face wooden. The guards' bunks were crude modern steel against the fine-veined marble. The pillars were textured smooth and soapy, clear across the room. Girly posters had been stuck on the decor and beerglasses stood in their blood on the table. The commander caught Desi's look and braced.

"You men! Get this mess cleared. Who's on duty? If the Captain sees it, you're on extra watches."

Several Youth frowned and vanished the glasses. Another dissolved puddles. The girly posters stayed.

{Pity about the genes,} Desi reflected, {they'd be cute if there was only one of them.}

{If you like psychotics,} Jones agreed.

Puffy white clouds processed quietly across the sky. Miniature yells from the miniature plowmen drifted in on a grass-scented breeze. A spare thought blew through Desi's inner ear.

{I hate this fricky decor. Gives you the willies.}

She thought the Commander. A chorus of muted but heartfelt agreement rippled the pillars. He reddened slightly and gave her the nearest to a good-dog grin a Hitler Youth face could manage.

"Don't worry about the bounter, Ma'am. We'll hold him for you till you're through with the Captain."

"You do that." {Now where?} she asked silently.

{This way, I think,} her symb opined.

Baroque ceiling-paintings and more turquoise. A seascape this time, with silk-sailed ships bucketing over a green ocean. Its neatly-patterned waves foamed white without ever moving out of their places. Dolphins heaved up and down in the crests as the whole panorama filed slowly east-west.

A man stood in the archway with his back to the room, his outline cut on the sky. As Desi corped in he turned to face her.

Blue-white skin, frosted hair, his clothes lightly powdered with sparkling crystals.

"Yo, Des, I've waited a thousand years."

She took a breath.

"Ice."

He re-corped into her arms, his cheek on hers and their ribs jammed tight in a bone-breaking hug. "Can we go to bed now?"

Desi made automatic and half-forgotten adjustments to her body-temperature and tried not to yell. His face was cold enough to take her skin off and his hands burned through her coverall.

"Sure, boy. Can't wait."

The mind she registered was definitely different. He was flesh and blood, and they were still married.

Jones looked around the guardroom and cautiously picked a stool. "Bother anyone if I park my butt?"

"Okay, if it stays there."

He raised defensive hands. "I'm cool. Just a rambling wreck from the Inner Systems. Interesting concept you got."

"It stinks," a Hitler Youth said, dropping on his bunk. "You oughtta see its night cycle."

"The one with the Rembrandt virgin."

"Stands on the moon and squints," a clone confirmed.

"Shut it," the commander said wearily, shedding hardware. "You want the boss in? This month's flavor," he told Jones. "He's reading art books."

"Was worse when he was into ancient literature, kept having Yog-Sothoth swoop down in iridescent bubbles. Or something disgusting. Gave everyone nightmares."

"Worst of it is, the bitch enjoys it."

"She hasn't much else to enjoy," the commander grunted. "Stops her smashing crockery."

That got sounds of agreement. Someone opened a marble refrigerator and got out beer and someone else uncovered half-visible touchpads and began dialing burgers. They took off their uniforms and threw them on the furniture.

"Interesting work?" Jones suggested.

"Shithouse boring, apart from the raids," the commander said, down to his undershirt, dropping onto the stool opposite. "Don't know you didn't do better as a bounter."

"Yeah," a clone agreed lazily, scratching bared skin. "Captain has a taste for it, flunkies fall in line and take the leavings."

"Standard pirate country," Jones said.

"Not entirely. Captain has this artistic hangup. This week we're the Ruritanian Army, no hair, real wool uniforms that itch like hell. Last, it was loud silks and cutlasses in our boots."

"Hotting cut myself."

"Might as well have stayed on the stage," a brother confirmed.

"We thought of it. Maybe as a troupe of tumblers."

"We'd have been hell on wheels on the road."

"Until the Patrol got a read-out on our genetic profiles." The commander was getting set for a wellworn story. They probably told it to each other with every change of costume, by way of comfort. "Ancestor wanted tissue in case of accidents. According to his lawyer."

"When we tracked him."

"So the lover cloned himself twenty times over and froze the lot of us."

"Then he smashed himself definitively into a neutron star, someone found a roomful of cute little babies and was fool enough to de-cry them all."

"Without checking out our gene-status. The whole family's illegal."

"By which time Lawyer had disappeared in the bushes."

"*With* the old guy's fortune."

"The bastard."

"We got along fine as a specialty dance-act," the commander said mournfully.

"Finest corps-de-ballet Truegood ever had."

"Till they went on tour and we were genechecked for passports."

"How could we know?" another said bitterly. "We thought maybe we were cousins or something."

"And that was the end. Pig-ignorant and slated for regeneration."

"So we located Lawyer and he didn't give shit. Like, sorry,

guys, you're twenty years too late. Should have asked for an opinion before you got born."

"And we ended in jail."

"You weren't symbed?" Jones asked, startled.

"Not back then. Or they couldn't have jailed us."

"Old families have conservative traditions," the commander explained.

"I heard," Jones said.

"Ours is real old."

"But while we were languishing without a competent attorney, the Captain corped in, passed us his symbiotic infection and invited us here as his personal guard."

"Couldn't refuse."

"Might be worse, apart from the artwork," the commander said with a sigh.

"But we do regret the corps-de-ballet. We were *good*."

"You're not his basic fighting group, then?"

That raised their eyebrows. "You should know. Des commands em, she's a spitfire. Was expecting em behind you. Weren't they with her?"

"The lady was alone," Jones said truthfully. "They must be operating someplace else."

Snickers.

"Operating's the word."

"Without anesthetics."

"These are *bad* hombres. And Madam sure leads em."

"But they bring home bacon. Wait till you see it."

A wave of brightness went around the circle and somebody passed him a burger. "We get to share."

"Girls."

"And boys, and aliens."

"Things to be said for it," the commander acknowledged.

"I can see it might have," Jones agreed. "What brings the Captain here? Environment looks hostile."

More snickers. "He's a hostile guy. You could call it a vocation."

"Nah," the commander defined. "He just likes to be himself."

''Problem's with the self he likes to be.''

''Tends to reduce the population. So he got sort of invited to leave inhabited areas.''

''But it's okay, he likes it that way.''

''Government likes it that way, too. If he's far enough out.''

''Far-out covers it.''

''Ain't so hot for other people, though. They keep freezing to death.''

Laughter.

''He's kind of special,'' the commander said cautiously. ''Word of advice. Don't cross him.''

''I hear you.''

A heavy sigh from the back of the room. ''I still liked it in the chorus.''

''Have some beer,'' the commander said. His eyes were growing teary. ''You look okay.''

''Sympathetic.''

''We knew a lot of sympathetic people once.''

''Before they thought of checking out our gene-status.''

They all sighed in chorus.

''Whoa,'' Desi said, fighting her biology. ''Let's think about this.''

''Why?'' Ice asked, tugging at his shirt. It shed a pile of snow on the floor. ''Come straight, Des, you've been a career-woman. You know you promised we'd get around to the baby.''

{Uh-oh,} her symb whispered.

''Sure we will, honey,'' Desi said soothingly, running her fingers through his hair. Not actually snapping it off took practice. She'd once had plenty. Her metabolism was getting the habit back uncommonly fast. ''Have you had that genetic checkout? Just to be sure?''

''We've been through this, babe. One, if you want a doc I'll have to kidnap one, I'm not letting Bones get his skeleton hands on my genes, or yours either. And the Patrol's edgy. We agreed on nothing showy until it was over. And two, it's pointless because we both know we're healthy. Let's just do it.''

''Okay, but let's just not do it tonight, it's too early in my cycle. And I don't want my kid got while she's looking."

Ice was pushing her back on the bed, lips nibbling at her ear, his hands feeling for her front zippers. His degree of physical control had always been abnormal. Desi gasped and tried not to arch back. She clasped him around the neck and pulled his head down on her breasts, burning her lips on his glacial nape.

"Ouch! Let me get my boots off. And get her outta here."

"Des, we've this routine every time. She can't see us. And she wouldn't if she could. She's asexual. She's furniture. How the hell does this unfasten?"

Desi wriggled and lost the coverall. She was mostly what it had been covering. He held her wrists and grinned down at her, his cold weight generating heat in her belly. "Don't tell me you've come over modest."

"That one thing I never tried to tell anyone."

And if she didn't loosen his belt they were in for explanations. She and Ice had had explanations before, he always won and that was mostly how she'd gotten pregnant last time. With the same guy in another world. She felt her way around his pants' band, his tense muscularity moving beneath.

The brown woman stared ahead, brown hair, brown skin, brown dress. Her dull brown eyes were fixed as pebbles, repellently dry like the eyes of a corpse, something mummified that had been propped in that corner so long dust had drifted in and filled them. She was cross-legged on the carpet, hands in her lap, her vacant stare pointing nowhere. Or maybe at someplace that wasn't there. She'd as much living presence as one of the stools. But her psychic charge was strong and dangerous. A stool she wasn't.

"Look at me, baby." Ice's breath stirred hot in her ear. "You're breaking me up, woman. You know I can't stand it when you do that. I'm ticklish."

She let the belt fall to the floor and ran her fingers the length of his spine, the smooth ridged column like melted icicles, his hot breath scalding her neck as it steamed from his zero lips.

The decor swam and melted, marble bleaching into white plaster with a dark heavy crucifix above the bed, half-shuttered windows that let in sunlight patterned with dust.

Tropical-looking flowers hung like shutters over the blue, and a faint stir of air moved them in perfumed drifts. The room was dim, striped with sharp zones of sun and shadow. A scale of string-notes outside ran up and down in half a tune. The flowers panted, weighted with heat. Angular dark wooden furniture pressed down the floor. The towering bedhead rose above her, its corner-posts carved into grim-faced angels.

"Uh," gasped Desi. Her head hit the pillow and tipped backward. The bare plaster had a single glass, and it covered the ceiling. She could see Ice's back with its hard muscles, the line of his hips, his crumpled pants lying on the boards, his shirt hanging off a straight-backed chair. His white head was bent to her throat as if to suck her blood. Her own face, drunk and blind, stared back at her with lips parted, her teeth gleaming.

She'd lost the upswept braid and fancy colors. Her skin was pearl-pink, sweating slightly. Her hair was spread on an embroidered cover that could have come from a church, scarlet encrusted with gold, twined with human figures and interlaced foliage, the scratchy surface lightly lacerating her nerve-endings. A scent of incense lingered in the folds. The slate-gray eyes that gazed up looked semi-conscious, dazed with perfume, blind with desire.

The brown woman was still propped in the corner. Her pebble eyes were brown and shiny with a slight glaze, as if the surface had absorbed its dust and extruded intelligence. The mind behind was wholly hostile. Desi found Ice's teeth biting softly at the base of her neck, and tried to keep hold of her senses.

The squares of sunlight crept like molasses over waxed planking, flower and incense odors heavy as smoke, dragging almost visible scarves of mist. The room smelled of sacrifice, a hot sharp blood-smell mixed with the fumes.

Ice tensed, gasping. Desi moaned.

The pebble eyes sharpened like knives. Desi, drunk and drifting, watched the dust-woman in the mirror drink the sacrifice of Desi.

The guardroom darkened abruptly as turquoise toned to sapphire and began to break up. The merry plowman choked on a note and made a noise like a faraway death-rattle. The sun fell, and faded. Black clouds chased the light, a stroke of lightning cut the sky in two and the neat little clumps of trees lost their outlines as if swept by a hurricane. Or more like *The Last Supper* sliding ineluctably off its canvas. The panorama had grown shabby. Something like rock showed through the veining. Jones sat up in alarm.

So did the commander and most of the guard.

"Uh-oh. She's having another, watch your butt. Try the table, it's better than nothing."

Jones looked at the spreading areas of rock, which were dark, grainy and peeling off in sheets, and took a dive along a floor that wasn't marble. The burned sheen said industrial laser. He stared out from between the table-legs. "Another what?"

"Jeez knows. Hey, Tom, sling me my helmet." The commander and two of his clones were on their bellies beside him, hands protecting their skulls, and they didn't look even slightly ashamed. "Another crisis. Could be anything. Sometimes it's the food. Sometimes I think she just bores easy. She's a topgrade P-manipulator, and someone told me none of them are stable."

"And this one got herself kicked out of the Academy." Gruesome chuckle from under a bunk. "They're Liberal Arts over there—very. *You* guess what she did to collect an expulsion."

"That's why she's here," the commander agreed. "If you ask me, she has a crush on the Captain."

"Nothing so fricky simple," a clone opined. "Throws a dingdong every time he and Madam get together. I think watching them gets her rocks off. Can anyone reach the top half of my body-armor?"

"Could be." The commander jammed on the helmet and slid Jones a lewd wink. "Captain has hobbies. Isn't just Madam, she does it when he's questioning prisoners, too."

"The kind of answers you can hear through the walls. But the stuff she throws with Madam's the worst."

"Those two got something has her really yodeling."

A section of ceiling fell with a crash just north of the table, filling the air with plaster and rock-dust.

Jones coughed, trying to keep his breathing shallow. ''He lays his wife in front of another woman?''

''You're tooting he does. Maybe switches *him* on.''

''What about her?''

''Madam?'' Thoughtful pause. ''She's private. Maybe that's what lights Bitch's fire. Seeing the boss's lady get what's coming even when she's politely said no.''

''Wouldn't surprise me. Ceiling only falls with women prisoners. Maybe she likes to feel the cute ones begging and pleading and getting it anyway.''

''And fricky liking it,'' the commander added. ''She sees they do.''

''But you oughtta hear em sobbing afterwards.''

''Specially when their husbands are looking,'' the commander said.

''The guys prefer couples.''

''That way, you hear em both screaming.''

''Captain likes that, too, I guess.''

''But she likes the rest of the game as well.''

''Takes her meat rare. But Madam's the picky kind.'' He winked. ''Must be as good as a two-way mirror. Better, maybe. She sits so still you can forget she's there. But she finds a way to let you know. After.''

''Done it to all of us, one time or another.''

''Makes you feel sticky. But Madam's top number.''

Jones unstuck his shirt cautiously from a clammy back. The air had grown perceptibly colder and his hair and clothes were full of grit, but a line of sweat was fingering his spine.

''Meat in there ever get raw?''

''You can bet it does. Seeing the gear the Cap takes in with him.''

''Lady's been gone for a while.''

''Madam? She'll be gone a whole lot longer.''

''A *whole* lot.''

Choked guffaws.

''Interesting guy, the Captain.''

Jones shifted in the settling powder and froze as another plaster bomb exploded on the corner of the table. Another choking cloud billowed up and fragments of stone bit his legs through his jeans. The guards who could reach had struggled back into pieces of their armor. Leg-guards and helmets covered random bits of body.

"Jeezle!" When he'd air to speak. "Isn't this dangerous?"

"Said watch your butt," the commander said. "She's telekinetic too, but don't shit your pants, it's superficial. We've five miles of rock over us."

"If that crazy bitch doesn't lose control and cave it in one of these days."

"Hell, even she can't be *that* crazy."

Jones, face in the dirt, shivered. A real top psychic manipulator with high TK powers could do exactly that, and the only reason the Academy was likely to expel her was advanced psychosis of herself or her symb, probably both. And if she'd gotten this far without being lobotomized somebody had gotten her out of the hospital, and no-one took that sort of risk without an advanced psychological imbalance of their own.

"You guys thought *seriously* about life on the road? Lot of places Rimward never heard of Truegood."

"Every time she has a crisis," the commander husked, spitting rock-dust. "But it's easier to get in here than out."

"That's what I figured."

Desi was missing and the roof-falls came oftener and harder. She was surface-tough, looked like she could take care of herself, but she'd that vulnerable streak . . .

A truck-sized chunk of ceiling broke free and crashed onto a stack of bunks. The reinforced frames buckled, and kicks and curses came from the debris. The room froze.

"Hots." The commander sounded shaken. "Captain must be having a ball."

"Get many funerals?"

"It'll stop when they're through."

"There *was* the time Gip was in the bathroom . . ."

"Twisted bastard." The commander wiped his mouth on his hand. "Don't remember anyone crying."

"Still hard to be brained with your pants down."

Jones tried to see through the murk. The table was sagging and the bunks trashed. His neighbor mopped a cut cheek. The room had been lasered out of baserock and the bared walls had gouge-marks like the scars of old wounds, overlaid with new holes, the dust from which was clogging his lungs. A severed cable sputtered sparks. Everyone was under cover and those in reach were risking limbs for armor.

A rush of air eddied the dust and set it swirling.

"What is it this time?"

Desi corped out in the ruin and Jones relaxed with a sigh. She was in one of her drawn-out modes, splendidly purple, dark-blue hair bound in a stalk with spiraled silver wire. Fuchsia draperies thrashed her legs in the draft from what was left of the window. A businesslike blaster was strapped to her thigh. He lifted his head again, suddenly wary.

"Well? I suppose someone has an explanation?" Her lips were drawn back from carnivorous teeth, her eyes glittering. "Or nothing I'd care to hear, maybe?"

The bright silks of a functional fighting-crew materialized around her. The clutter bristled with guns. This lot looked like *bad* hombres. Desi's etiolated shape had a hard resolution under chiffon, filmed with icy glaze, talons shining with new paint. He could feel musk and blood-smell steaming off her. Vulnerable as a cobra.

Talons. Desi'd spoiled her polish operating the ape, she complained about it. Days to come right. The guard-commander looked confused. Jones focused his mind and beamed it into rock.

**{Desi! Corp out, now!}**

The walls wavered.

The frozen woman stood astride him, a spindle heel poised on his knuckles. Cold lightnings played in her hair, and the roof began to decay in earnest.

Desi's eyes widened in the mirror. Ice's cold thighs were between her feet and his cool glassy rod, thrusting and sliding, filled her center. She arched under him, opening wider to take him in. The dark crucifix leaned, a menacing black sword, the defiled altarcloth printing embroideries into her back at every grind. She moaned as his cold ribs dug her breasts, driving twin icicles in like nails. The incense smell dazed her senses. Chill bands circled her wrists, holding her down.

* * *

{Look up.}

An image stared back at her, snapping her back from the edge of orgasm and opening a shivering crack in her mind. The brown eyes of the brown woman burned, red in their depths, alive with inner light. Her face had changed. Not mummified, not wooden, but carved in a feral grin of triumph. The hot eyes taunted.

{Wake up, because *I* call you. *My* will holds you pinned to this bed with the cross of shame watching your sin. *I* put it there to show you what you are. *I* chose the mood and the decor, *I* brought you here to serve me. *My* need opens your legs and loosens your womb. The child you'll bear will be *my* fruit, and the less you want it the more you'll have it so that you'll know your mistress. *My* desire drives him on, and I'm going to make him hurt you. You'll beg and scream and he won't hear you, because *I'll* possess him. And it'll be like that tomorrow and tomorrow, as long as you live, and every day you'll come back and be hurt again, because *I* say so. Look at me and know me, because after it's over I'll make you forget—until next time. And then you'll look in this same mirror and see me smiling, and you'll remember and know. Poor queen, so showy and proud, ruling nothing. *I* rule here. Look at me and feel it. And struggle, yes, I like that. Fight me. It makes my pleasure sweeter.}

Her violent will pinned Desi to the bed. Ice moaned, thrusting harder. His face was blank, his eyes lost. The hard loins moved like oiled machinery, divorced from will. Desi controlled panic, trying to discorporate, to stay relaxed. Ice had never hurt her, his control was too good. She looked in his face and saw emptiness. Her muscles tightened. He would hurt her this time.

His thrusts grew faster, moving to frenzy. He grunted for breath. The rhythmic shift of his weight drove the air from Desi's lungs. She choked on a whimper.

A line of light cut her head like the beam of a lighthouse and the room tore across. The rhythm broke. And the face in the mirror contorted into crude frustrated ugliness. The sinister beauties of the Garden of Delights faded to the dust of a cheap brothel, and the brown woman's will fell apart with her illusion. Desi came out of nightmare to the surface, the common reality of a common Desi in the wrong bed.

{**. . . corp out now!**} She knew the voice.

The brown woman's face was demonic. Her mind reached out to grab Desi's throat and fling her backward, trying to force her into the mattress against scratchy needlework, choke her with scented smoke, jerk her closing thighs wider. Desi sprawled for a moment racked between states, her neck-muscles straining.

Ice saved her. He looked up, confused, blue eyes startled, his prick slackening as he lost his erection. The white hair, half-melted, hung on his brow in a cascade of ice-curtains. His face was groping, half-awake. She wrapped her arms around his neck in a vigorous hug, melting him further with her own heat.

"Ice, baby, you're the best. I've always loved you. Always."

And discorped, knocking aside the brown woman's rage, the pain of loss, Ice's reaching hands.

She hung for a moment in swaying polarities of will, half-in and half-out of two realities until an urgent hand reached out of chaos and fixed on her wrist. She closed hers around it. The two teeps were locked in combat, the woman's eyes volcanic, her face distorted to an inhuman mask, Jones ignoring a frozen spike heel, his mind lit like an arc-lamp. A huge block swayed above the guardroom table, trying to fall. His spare arm jerked Desi out of her half-world and crushed her to his chest. Different ribs, different hair, same loss of breath. She saw him in closeup, dirt-smeared, his clear eyes intent in a camouflage face, his mind bent on the jittering rock that the brown woman's will pressed.

"I wasn't expelled from the Academy," he said with absent friendliness.

Desi tried her freedom, found it intact, and re-formed in the bedroom long enough to plant a solid foot in the woman's chest. She recorped back to add her symb's weight to the fight. The manipulator, preoccupied with Jones's mind, lost her balance. She went sprawling in the corner and the pressure slewed with her, spinning the rock away. It crashed harmlessly on top of the refrigerator.

As they melted out into open space Desi heard Ice shout from behind her. "Des! Don't leave me!"

And they were in vacuum, her tears boiling off into the void, stars winking bleakly through hydrogen veils.

"Close," Jones panted, recorping into *Windrunner*'s cabin and scrubbing at the grit in his nose and mouth.

"You don't know how close," Desi gasped. "Thanks. I just missed getting royally screwed."

"Missed it. Uh-huh."

"Not *that*, dorko. Been there before, but without the trimmings. Aint important, except kind of a pity we didn't get to finish. I meant *screwed*."

"The P-man."

"Boy, was she. Sickest bitch I ever come across. Shit over ears and rolling in it. You dig that stuff?"

"No."

"Me neither. Wake up, *Windy,* this is a rat's-nest. Get us out, like now."

Silence.

"*Windy?*"

Snivel.

"Move, dumbo. What's wrong now? Place be fuller of pirates than a fur rug with fleas in less than two minutes and they will be shooting. Engines, dammit!"

"I saw him."

"Tell me about it," Desi said, exasperated. She smeared a bare wrist across her nose. "Who?"

Another snivel, low and broken like a hurt dog. "Him. They blew him to powder back in the Coalsack, and I saw him alive here again today and he was with *her*."

"*Who* her?"

Jones groaned. "The other *Windrunner*. *Windy*'s met herself, and her old boss with her. It's a risk in close parallels, you said so. They're like home. The planet sent us to your boyfriend, and the rest followed. Meeting yourself's traumatic."

"Jeezle! We haven't time for a nervous breakdown or we

facing the trauma of a cannon up the ass. Engines!'' Desi scowled. ''Mr. Meathead was a pirate?''

''You have that in common.''

''In my day Ice was only a genius. Insane, but only. She said he was a gentleman. So where are *you?*''

''I can't have risen to it,'' Jones said modestly. ''Haven't much initiative. *Windy*, it's serious.''

''Hanging out with a common yellow tramp, with fake antennae all over her nose . . .''

''*Windy,* if you aint outta here in the next five seconds I'm lighting a fire inside your braincase.'' Desi unclipped the disruptor and set it on HEAT. ''This is a firelighter. I am about to corp aft now, carrying it.''

''*Windy,* she means it.''

A long liquid snuffle.

''You don't have to get nasty,'' *Windrunner* said. ''I'm going.''

The engines hummed, caught and began to murmur. Stars and gas-scarves jumped in the plates and suddenly moved backward. Jones ran gritty hands through his hair. Desi put the disruptor down.

''Thank you, *Windy,*'' she said sweetly.

*Windrunner* went on sniveling.

''Where are we going?''

''Anyplace but here. Maintain acceleration, and warp soonest. Try Galactic Center, I want a grav-source.''

''Too late.'' Jones had his eyes on the screen. ''Here they come.''

A pair of phantom pinstripes passed through the bulkheads on crossing diagonals, met in the middle, bowed to each other and converged on Desi.

*''Miz Smeett.''*

*''I am duly authorized by the Court . . .''*

*''. . . to inform you that . . .''*

*''. . . in view of . . .''*

*''. . . your stubborn refusal to comply with requests for legal confrontation . . .''*

*''. . . the Patrol may be warned of your outlaw status . . .''*

*''. . . my client feels compelled to raise his estimated dam-*

*ages to seventy-five billion credits, which will if necessary be charged against your salary . . .''*

*''. . . and you may be posted as a fugitive.''*

''Put em over there,'' Desi said, jerking her thumb at the recycler. ''You won't have noticed, but I'm busy.''

*''Good day, Miz Smeett.''*

*''Have a nice day.''*

Both ghosts evaporated. The recycler snapped shut on paper.

''Do you earn seventy-five billion credits?''

''You crazy? He can ask. Hell, he could double it, won't make any difference.''

''Hostile fire incoming,'' *Windrunner* said. She gave a noisy sniff. ''Shall I take steps?''

''If you know any. Hotshot! This a medship, we're unarmed.''

''So it is,'' Jones said unhappily, fielding a fresh trio of lawyers. ''Go away, we're busy.''

*''Miz Smeett . . .''*

*''Miz Smeett . . .''*

*''Miz Smeett . . .''*

⌘

## TP–TV

*the station of the multiverse*

ONLINE AS ALWAYS WITH THE NEWEST, FRESHEST, RAVINGEST RIOTS FROM THE ROARING OUTBLACK, BROUGHT TO YOU AT RISK TO PERSONAL LIFE AND LIMB BY OUR OWN CORRESPONDENT—IT'S THE JONES BOY!

❖

[*Red-scarved space with brighter patches, dim close stars. Silver locusts stream up from a dim yellow dwarf and swell into multiform ships acned with gunports. The leader is a primrose-colored yacht with imposing nose-array, skull-and-crossbones on her port quarter, boring forward with vibrating fury. Her field sparkles red and blue as she squirts violet flashes of heatseeking missiles. A smaller, humbler blue version runs for its life ahead, defiantly flaunting a big blue cross outlined in neon. The missiles zoom into closeup, a rosette of glittering warheads. Brief glimpse of the pilot, an imposing block of bleached muscle, lounging in his couch with a paw on the panel. He idly scratches the bulge of belly that overhangs his pants' band, matted with pale curled hair. He pats the console. Glimpse of Dick Tracy looking nervous:*]

PIRATE: Go it, *Runner*, blast em to eternity!

*WINDRUNNER,* SQUEAKY WITH OUTRAGE: Ooh!

DESI, IRONIC (SHE'S CROSSLEGGED ON TOP OF HER CHART-TABLE, STARING INTENTLY INTO HER TANK): Don't look like he recalls your face.

*WINDRUNNER,* A DESPAIRING WAIL: He's stopped loving me!

DESI, STICKING HER NOSE IN THE DEPTHS OF THE HOLO AT SOMETHING THAT LOOKS HOPEFUL: That's guys for you.

*WINDRUNNER,* HER SQUEAK RUNNING UP OFF THE SCALE: The brute. And with a tramp like that!

[*Dick Tracy, uneasy:*]

This one's close.

[*The missiles swell in pitiless detail. Their armed noses smirk smugly. The blue ship absorbs her neon cross, shakes, and sprouts a set of businesslike torpedo-tubes. A shower of anti-missile-missiles spreads behind her and the sky breaks up in a festival of light. The cabin shudders and the lightplates brown out. A breathless pause. Even Desi looks startled. Dick Tracy lets out an audible gulp.*]

DESI, SEVERELY: That's against the Geneva Convention. I said we're a medship.

*WINDRUNNER,* TEARFUL: That'll show her. I took the cross in first.

DESI AND DICK, SIMULTANEOUSLY: *Windy!* No!

[Windrunner *has grown a heavy-duty cannon above her tail-unit and the engines hesitate as she shifts power into its firing-batteries. Just in time, the yellow nose-array's closing. A blinding flash shivers her field and plunges the cabin into darkness.*]

*WINDRUNNER,* MIXTURE OF PAIN AND FURY: *Oww!*

[*The pirate ship evaporates in a silent explosion that ripples outward and flings* Windrunner *up and down on its shock-wave. Desi falls blasphemously off the chart-table.]*

DESI, FEELINGLY: Shit.

[*Dick Tracy: (several expletives deleted):* ***Beep! Beep! Beep!***]

*WINDRUNNER,* VICTORIOUS: That'll show him! (SHE BREAKS DOWN IN AGONIZED WEEPING.)

[*A mighty force out of the multiverse picks them up bodily and flings them into outer darkness.*

*The picture breaks up in confusion.*]

Desi and Jones kicked around the darkened cabin in a tangle of arms, legs, mixed bits of recorporated people, equipment and furniture. The panel smelled of burning. *Windrunner* shook with heartbroken sobs. Salty glaze ran out of her airducts.

"Hey," Desi said. "The guy wasn't worth it."

Gulp. "I was faithful to *him.*"

"Aren't we all? And they were only duplicates, he wasn't *your* guy. You'd have hated him if you knew him."

Another gulp, and a hiccup. "Do you think so?"

"Sure."

The sobs lessened. "I saw mine die, back in the Coalsack. They blew him to atoms."

"He had it coming, with his taste in nose-arrays. You leveled the score. Brought the parallels into harmony."

"If he hadn't shot at me . . ."

"Catch hold of that, babe. He fired first."

"Does anyone know what's going on?" Jones asked painfully from the floor.

*I?* was *mistaken*. *I?* *regret?* *my?* *fault?*. *I?* *believed* *I?* had located *your?* *other?* in a *neighboring* *continuum?*. It was not the case. *I* *fear* that *I?* have *caused?* *you?* *distress?*. This *other?* was *different*.

The telepathic boom resonated in the bulkheads.

"Blinky? You still tied to us? You got sidetracked into a parallel. Ice wouldn't be so dumb, he doesn't want two of him either. Wherever he is, it's someplace new."

*I?* have *realized?* *that*. This *time?* *I?* have located the *correct* *sequence?*.

"I hope so," Desi muttered, as dimensional stresses tugged at their fabric. "Wouldn't like to go through that again. Want to go home yet, teep?"

"I paid for the whole ride."

"As you like."

" 'Like' is an exaggeration."

*Good* *luck*.

"Love your friend's sense of humor," Jones said sourly. His voice cracked, dropped to a slow deep drone and screeched back to falsetto. "What the hell?"

The lights browned back on.

"Oh, Jeezle."

Desi's voice emerged as a parrot shriek from a mess of parrot color. She appeared to be melting like a candle, her head spindling to the upper plates and her arms stretching. Her skin-color shifted from green to yellow. The screech was upper registers of blue macaw.

"Desi? You'll hurt yourself . . ."

She laughed from distant caverns. Jones glanced down at a block of coal with shovel hands unaccountably doubled. He checked and found a second set of eyes. He blinked all four and tried to focus.

{Don't bother,} his symb said, {I can't do a thing.}

"What's happening?"

{Ask *her,* maybe she knows.}

{Not responsible,} Desi's symb said. {It's gravitational overload, we ran into something too heavy to handle at the dimensional interface. The arc's got switched on in the rumble, maybe with vibration, and that's what's causing the random shapechanges, it's programmed for reinforced change. I can't help, this mess is outside my capacities. Hope the cell doesn't blow, we're overheating.}

"Help!" screamed *Windrunner.*

The bulkheads and fittings were distorted beyond recognition. The deformed dials showed wildly tracking needles, most swinging well in the red.

"*Windy*, dump grav," Desi's eldritch shriek came from overhead. Her neck had grown so long she had to bend double to stay in the cabin. "Bleed it off into the nearest well or just blast, but shed power. We're about to lose environment."

"I can't," *Windrunner* wailed. "The gravity outside's wild already, there's more energy than I can contain. And it's getting worse. Have you seen the plates?"

Jones concentrated all four eyes on a wilderness of roiling, twisting light. Desi's screech was too high to signal emotion, but it had a quiver.

"Biggest gravitational lens I ever saw, it's reflecting and re-reflecting a whole wall of galaxies . . ."

{Or maybe just this one,} her symb said. {It looks to me . . .}

"Hotso, everything in sight's imploding. Like water into an outlet-hole . . ."

A twisted lawyer walked through the wall and presented Jones with something puffy.

*"Miz Smeett? The Court takes a serious view of your behaviour. A very serious view indeed . . ."*

Jones, stunned, accepted the object, which melted and folded over his hands. Several projectiles exploded out of it like live pigeons. They blundered and flustered around the cabin, cooing with terror and dropping birdlime. Jones shook one off his coal shoulder and it burst and disappeared in a puff of feathers.

The lawyer had been making an inaudible speech in a voice

above hearing, and now unrolled a Japanese sunshade with a haughty snap and disappeared into the converter. His squeaking bat-tones hurt their ears even after he'd gone.

"You were saying?" Jones asked morosely, brushing away another pigeon and looking down purple jeans. His legs dwindled in abrupt perspectives that vanished to infinity. He wiggled his toes, and quavering wave-motions drifted up like bubbles and broke into small upwellings of light.

{I was saying, I think we've come out in the path of . . . }

# SIX

# A Piece of String

{ . . . a piece of string.}

''Help.''

Desi exerted her will and twisted. She spiraled down to mere overtall and doubled to peer in the tank.

''It really is,'' her diminished voice said, far and wee.

''What?''

''The leading front of a string. Jeezle. Lover's still halfway from redout or we'd be gone already, but it's coming up blue as the lost horizon. How would you like to just dissolve into photons?''

''I'm against it.'' Jones batted a pigeon. ''Can't we do something?''

''Die?'' Desi quavered. ''*Windy*, have you pull in the main drive at all?''

''No.'' *Windrunner* was too demoralized to whimper. She sounded drained. ''Can't make warp against the gravity and the front's spreading the full width of the tank, I can't even see how far it stretches. It's eating galaxies. We're right on the forward edge of its grav-field and there's a fold in spacetime that's squeezing the locality down to pure energy. And that's only its advance shockwave. It's drawing all the neighboring matter into it. I can't even discorp, my molecules are liable to fly apart. It's all I can do just to hold together.''

{Likewise,} Desi's symb whispered.

{So let's do something,} his own proposed.

"Me?" Jones said. His hands were coal-colored but his voice was pale. "Can go down broadcasting, if it helps. I thought strings moved over millennia."

"They do. But we're already in its field, and millennia we do not have. The laws of spacetime break down at the boundary. Vanishing could look like millennia from outside, but you won't know the difference. We are going to snark. You could make just one intelligent broadcast, maybe."

"Would it listen if I tried?"

{Convince it it got us here,} his symb proposed.

"If you mean Blinky, I don't believe she meant to," Desi said.

{Is that relevant?} her symb asked.

"That makes three to one," Jones sighed.

"Four," said *Windrunner*.

He gathered himself. Pigeons flapped by his head. The cabin was misty as if reality were wavering at the edges. Desi crouched against the roof, her color graying as the lower wavelengths of light collapsed.

**{BLINKY!}**

The cabin was shrinking, farther-away objects losing their outlines, the lights dimming to blue. The straight edges of bulkheads and panel had a visible and increasing curve.

**{HELP!}**

The yell echoed across dimensions: {**. . . ELP!** . . . ELP! **. . . ELP!** . . . ELP! . . . **elp!** . . . elp!}

"She's sent us to the wrong epoch," Desi said. "This stuff's primitive. We're almost back to the local Big Bang."

**{IT'S THE WRONG EPOCH. WE DON'T BELONG HERE.}**

{. . . **ERE!** . . . ERE! . . . **ERE!** . . . ERE! . . . **ere!** . . . ere!} sang the echoes, jostling each others' heels.

An endless stasis. Across continua puzzled heads lifted, cocked, waited, and called the Society for Psychical Research. Distant slime-molds paused in their construction of complex lattices and multiple ghost-stars stopped rolling.

The continuum shuddered, and the environment deformed like a pressured balloon. Jones was knotted as his head lost contact with his guts. The lights strobed. He could see the table through his chest, and something between that clenched and pounded.

"Could someone hold my hand?" a small disconsolate voice asked from the vortex. "I never died before."

"Neither did we," Desi whistled. "You don't have a hand." But she gripped the panel with a skinny paw anyway. "Poor little *Windy*."

The pigeons melted to luminous bats, swelled, shrank and drifted away. Time snapped like a rubber band and *Windrunner*, moaning, shot like a squeezed orange-pip back into space.

The world halted, and the cabin filled with falling paper.

"Jeez," Desi gasped. Her voice was up half an octave to match a stretched eight-foot frame and her skin was blue-transparent. Heart and lungs pulsed mistily beneath. But she was within human limits and reasonably solid. "That was *really* close."

"You look like a holo from a medical edvid."

"Speak for yourself," she retorted. "Thanks, Blinky."

***I?*** am to ***blame?***. ***I?*** ***see?*** that ***I?*** am ***inexperienced?***. ***I?*** had ***hoped?*** to ***help*** ***you?***.

"You did. Dimension-changing's always a risk. My symb generally takes soundings first. Gives us a chance to adjust to emergencies."

Silence.

***I?*** ***believe*** ***I?*** ***begin*** to ***comprehend*** ***soundings***. ***This*** ***feels?*** like the ***epoch?*** ***you?*** ***need***.

"Long's it understands emergencies," Jones muttered.

***That*** also ***I?*** ***believe*** ***I?*** have ***begun?*** to ***comprehend?***.

Desi glared from four feet above him. "Sure you do, Blink. You understand as well's you can. Guy's upset."

"Upset? I think my guts leaked outta my mouth."

"That was your brains. Your guts I can see and they fully functional. How are you, *Windy?*"

Careful pause.

"I've changed shape," *Windrunner* said. "Like you. And I can't change back."

"Then I sure hope you resorbed them gunports, or we gonna scare everyone soon as they sight us."

{She hadn't,} her symb said.

"How did I know?"

{We're suffering gravitational overload. I said the arc had gotten mixed in our local continuum. It made its own connections in the flux. Looks as if it's been working on environment all this time.}

"Like pigeons." Jones wiped guano out of his hair.

"There aint any pigeons. Just floating bits of writ, or whatever that guy was throwing around."

{The arc-effects must have been hallucinatory,} his symb supported. {I saw pigeons too.}

"More likely *his* LSD. Hope the arc finally switched out."

{Worse,} her symb said. {Burned out. That last surge finished it.}

"Thank God," Jones said. "It can't do more damage."

{And how do you imagine we're getting our shapes back?} his symb inquired.

"I don't believe this. We can't return to normal?"

{In a word, yes.}

"Shit," Desi fluted. "Got no tools, I'm not an arc-mechanic. How long this shape gonna last? Aint my choice of Saturday-night look either."

{Can't say,} his symb sighed. {Our own molecules are stressed. My recreative powers aren't functioning.}

"What's that mean?" Jones asked, scratching through ripped jeans. His skin felt funny.

"Don't go out without a spacesuit," Desi rasped. "Better still, don't go out."

"We're stuck like this?"

The cabin was a pyramid with etiolated furniture and *Windrunner's* insides were on show too, a compressor working deep in her airducts, a mess of optic fiber speckled with nanocircuitry behind the panel. Fuzzy starlight shone through the bulkheads. Her gunports had melted to greenhouse-shaped bulges.

{For the moment.} His symb sounded weary as its owner.

"When does it wear off?" He was still coal-colored, hammered to a chunk with bulldozer paws. "I look like *King Solomon's Mines* sung in German."

No answer.

"Hey," with increasing alarm. "You can't mean it won't."

"He ain't saying," Desi said. She sat on the edge of an overstretched chair. "Neither of em are."

{We can't make a forecast,} hers said wanly. {We're as stuck as you, we can't imagine being confined to one form. But our molecular structures were pulled so far out of shape we've no elasticity. Normally we're highly mutative, it lets us keep up with altering environments. This genetic state's outside our experience.}

{We should tend to adjust,} his said.

"When?" Jones rasped.

Another silence.

"They don't know."

"As in, maybe millennia?"

{We don't know,} his symb confirmed.

"You can always report trends. Longterm weather-records. Plate tectonics. Me," Desi added with gloom, "changing's my business. This gonna crimp my life permanent."

"You think the marks want to watch rocks creep?" Jones was yelling. "I'm supposed to make news."

"That what I thought," Desi said spitefully. "So try making something creative."

"When I'm like this?"

"Your brain shrunk too? They don't see you. Thought Dick Tracy was a network invention."

"They don't have to see *me*, but I have to touch *them*. I can barely reach *you* when you're standing next to me, and to create anything interesting I need to travel."

"You gonna have to go by spaceline. Like everyone."

"I can't afford to be everyone."

"None of us can. Thank Blinky you weren't compressed to a wrinkle."

"Thank you," Jones said bitterly. "I always wanted a stable life. I'd rather have picked the details, we look like racially integrated shrimp."

Desi peered through her belly. "You do got pants. You needn't watch yourself peristalting."

"You could put clothes on."

"Like which? Nothing fit me."

{You're being childish. What's important is whether *Windrunner*'s navigational systems are functional,} Desi's symb said severely.

"Yes," *Windrunner* confirmed, shaky. "A lot of my nav gear's mechanical. It's changed shape but it's still in ratio. Needs recalibrating, but I think I can do that."

"Then do it and let's go," Desi said. "We been here."

"Are we still in the same dimension?" Jones asked, staring in a short fat plate.

"Feels like it. Would say the opposite end."

The sky was almost dark. A smear of gases cut across the tank, a thin disk with bright center seen sideways. Scanty stars spiraled outward and a rhythmic hiss of static spat from the speakers. Pale blotches in the void behind might have been galaxies very far away.

"Let's have a chart," Desi said. "Recognize this, *Windy?*"

"No," *Windrunner* said, subdued. "Everything's so sparse it has to be old."

Desi grunted. "Yeah, lot of stuff over the event horizon. Galaxy's old, too. Old, shrunk, scattered."

{The center's almost eaten it up,} her symb whispered. {I'd say these were the last of the spiral arms. Most of the dense material's gone. You can hear the flare as the central hole cycles. There's still gas, and a lot of radiation. Systems here have lost their protection, the inner clouds are thin. Even the arms won't last forever. The continuum's ancient.}

"Huh?" Jones said. "Say she's kidding."

"She's talking longer than you got, jerkhead. By the time the black hole there eats all the gas this sun's archives. Radiation, conversely, could be a nuisance."

"Then I'm the right color. Pass the sunscreen."

"Let's hope it works."

"Thanks."

{We could all need things we never needed before,} Desi's symb said. {We've never been inactive.}

"Yeah, that's right," Desi agreed. "You never have."

"Neither have we," Jones complained.

{Good,} his said sardonically. {You've a new experience coming. You get to learn how to use your legs.}

"Huh?"

"We can't discorp, guy. Gotta do it all physical. Like Norms do."

"Jeez," Jones groaned. "Can I just die?"

"Be my guest," Desi said politely.

The planet was worn, smallish and heavily clouded. Traffic outside the junkbelt was thin, its one outstation loaded with shielding. The signal from ground was wary.

"*Skrwddlbk . . . ?*"

Desi rammed a translator-bead into her ear.

"*. . . business?*"

She glanced around. "Uh . . ."

{Try the truth,} her symb suggested. {You're a traveling medicine-woman.}

"What am I curing with, laying on of faith?"

"I'm going to love being the freak-show," Jones grumped. "How do I record? Can't feel my relays."

{Bad news, Bub, I'm not just too weak to amplify, I think we've also outlived our origins,} his symb said.

He snarled, a faultline in the coal-seams.

"*I don't recognize your configuration,*" Ground said suspiciously.

"Ship's customized, we're a medicine-show."

*Windrunner* sighed, deep in her ducts.

"Well, aren't we?"

The echoing sigh was even deeper.

Desi doubled in the mirror and tried to twist her neck over her shoulder. "How's the middle of my back? Can't see it."

"Sunscreen smells like guano," Jones said, squeezing up his nostrils.

"All aliens stink, they'll think it's species-normal. We gonna need it. Place is crawling with UVs."

"Does it *have* to be green?"

"Can make you purple, or maybe yellow, but the yellow's chromy."

*Windrunner* searched her guts and produced a lighter. "I

never bargained for this, it's as bad as childbirth. I suppose you want me to find an airlock?''

''Unless you'd rather we cut our way out.''

''I haven't used one this incarnation. Maybe never. I'm not sure how they work.''

''Don't worry about it, I'll show you.''

''It's very inconvenient.''

''Uh-huh,'' Desi said. ''How your lattices?''

''Aft locker,'' *Windrunner* whined. ''I didn't order them.''

''Uh-huh,'' Desi said again.

Jones looked at his foreshortened muscles. ''Any hope they've mutated?''

''Anything's possible.''

She laid them on the deckplates. They'd mutated. She hunched her knees, hitched her elbows and the gloves dangled. The long oval headpiece flattened her nose.

''Your hair has airspace.''

''Got in the habit of breathing with my lungs,'' she said, muffled.

His was wide all over with a saucer-shaped helmet that flattened his skull. The gloves bulged dangerously over the knuckles. ''Hope the trip's short.''

''Short's I can make it, just hope we don't go through the landing-strip.''

''You mind if I pray?''

*Windrunner*'s whimper followed them down. ''Ow-w-w!''

Parked traffic was sparse, a few dust-scored freighters and one longhaul liner with unreadable logo. Nothing moved but automatic maintenance crawlers and a couple of chugging intership longboats that looked robotic. The descent was bumpy. The instrument panel read like a sundial and the drive-regulators were approximate.

''Sorry,'' Desi said. ''Aint done this since last time, and then I'd an altimeter.''

''Don't mention it,'' Jones said morosely. ''I like dying. Especially with you.''

The planet was blotchy, mired and cratered. Dark patches of atmospheric pollution smeared the dayside and the night glimmered with sparse lights.

"Frick. Where *are* they?" Desi said.

"Probably aren't many. Mined out, lost their ozone, stripped the outer planets. Those pockmarks are grown-over stripmines. Likely power-shortage. Maybe burning wood."

"What wood? They're probably recycling the last of their fusionables without actually beginning on the magma. Some of those mines look in business to me. What would grow over them without ozone? Poison ivy?"

"Even poison ivy's picky."

"I'd bet it's poison, anyhow."

"So what are we looking for?"

"Traces. Blinky must have seen something."

"Of what?" He turned awkwardly. "Why do you want this guy so badly?"

"That's between him and me. Didn't ask you to come."

The lighter bucketed into atmosphere, skipped, shuddered and secreted an onboard computer with rusty groans. It cleared its screen with an electronic sputter and began to run columns of green numbers.

"Hey," Desi said. "Last owner had backup. Never seen anything this old before, he musta been a collector."

"It better work, or you and I will be a hole in the tarmac." Jones inspected his hands. They were still like shovels. An orange glare blazed picturesquely from the forward screens. "Would you say we're overheating?"

"Not sure," Desi said cautiously. "Long time since I did this." The screen burped and developed a whine. The lighter's nose swung, and steadied. "You can stop eating fingernail, we picked up a beacon. And Baby responds."

"Must be because they're from the same era," Jones said sourly.

The glow died and the streaming green numbers dwindled. The planetary curve blanked out the sky, and flattened. Ground rushed up. The lighter bonked on something hard, took a couple of hops, squealed a little and shut itself down. The lock creaked.

"See?" Desi said. She reached for the wallhanging she'd brought with her and slung it on her arm. "Let's go talk."

Their passage through the terminal was short and disruptive. Since they'd no legal papers Desi offered the Portmaster a couple of spare subpoenas, which he turned several ways to peer at the seals, finally stamping them with a red marker. His few exposed parts were smeared with mauve sunscreen, and his pale blue irises ran into darker sclera. He'd too many fingers. He rattled Desi's duffel and looked suspicious. "Snake-oil vendor?"

"Herbalist," she squeaked. "With diploma."

"Watch it in the street, they string someone up now and then for variety. Not much happens here."

Jones tried to look invisible. The spindled, scrawny figure ignored him.

"Rimworld, huh?"

"Thataway." Vague thumb-jerk.

"Are you bioengineered?" His pale irises tried to look through her, but her symb was part of herself. Her guts churned behind the field of the lattice.

{Uh-oh,} her symb beamed. {Been synthing around. These people are Normals.}

{Then it's lucky you guys aint operational,} Desi thought. {Infecting Norms without their consent's less legal than usual.} She led the way out.

{You think the air's breathable?} Jones's symb whispered.

Jones set his teeth and unsnapped his field-control. The lattice collapsed to nodes, gloves and faceplate. He took a breath. The air smelled of concrete, dust and burned hydrocarbons. A touristy couple in baggy coveralls heading for the liner sneaked a glance, pirouetted and scuttled backward. Their tagged baggage wheezed after. Desi halted.

"What you do that for? You're sforza scary."

"So you wouldn't do it first. If we're going to drop dead, it happens later."

"Coulda told you. Basic metabolism's a lot like ours, except they're Normal. Place is nearly healthy, apart from radiation." She dropped her own lattice and slung the wall-hanging over a shoulder. "Let's try the town."

Jones squinted. Strings of beads fell intermittently to her thighs. Underneath was ultramarine with visible pulsing. Her hair stood on end. "Awesome," he commented.

"Huh?" Desi was striding out, trying not to wince as her bare feet hit hot flooring.

"Come greet this homicidal population."

"And remember the doors hit you in the face," she said.

"So they do," he agreed, rubbing his cheekbone.

"They say it's good for you."

"Bruises?"

"Exercise."

"I never noticed the lack."

{That's because I've always looked after your metabolism,} his symb told him. {Now it's your job. Watch what you eat, if you poison us we both die.}

"Terrific," Jones muttered.

The street hit them like a fist in the chest. The terminal's shield cut off at the doorway and bleared automatic doors opened on a wall of noise. The sidewalk writhed with bodies like live bait in a bucket.

{This silence is scary,} Jones's symb commented.

{Like being alone in the universe,} Desi's agreed.

Desi stuck a finger in her ear and wiggled it. "Not where I am."

{We've gone deaf,} her symb whispered.

{Except to each other,} his agreed. {It feels terrible.}

Jones hunched his shoulders. "Why are they all wearing headsets?"

"And using extract of cement-mixer for music?"

{Relieves psychic pressures,} her symb said. {It must be hard to live piled together on tarmac. I suppose those teepees and cooking-pots are permanent?}

"But you just said they're telepathically deaf."

{As posts. Doesn't stop them needing wire-space.}

{?} Desi thought.

{Like birds on a wire,} Jones's explained. {They get murderous from having no room to escape.}

The live bait was ragged, dun-colored and lumpy, with sparse black teeth and slow clotted movements. A double river of aluminum triangles flowed beyond the forest of ragged humpies. Greasy smoke smudged above them. Colored shapes skittered in the distance.

Desi looked around, shivering. "*This* is where I gotta spend my life? How in hell do you get through the corpses?"

"Do as they do," Jones said. "Tromp."

He planted a foot and the crowd shrank away. Fingerless hands pawed their clothes and drooling mouths sucked. Somebody tugged at Desi's hanging and beads scattered from a broken string. She jerked it free and grabbed Jones's arm.

"Norms *do* this?"

"They must develop survival techniques," he said, pushing, knocking away fingers that crawled up his thigh. He lunged out squatly onto the curb.

A sluggish current of traffic ran between banks of human wreckage. High masts drifted on invisible winds, aluminum triangles tacking up and down in reflective flashes. Runners and skaters slid between them wrapped in layers of staring glitter. Everyone was muffled, sunscreened and most of them misshapen. A leaden smog hung overhead.

"Sailshaw, mister?"

A triangle had drawn up alongside, thirty feet of aluminum sheeting making thunder-machine noises. A gob of spit hit Jones's thigh and ran slowly down. "Anything at all, so long as you're leaving."

The plank was maybe eight feet long, with two battered bucketseats in-line behind and bare room for the driver before the mast. Desi folded her legs and was nearly decapitated by a passing bedstead on a recumbent bicycle. "See why they wanta string people up."

"Could turn out catching," Jones said grimly.

The driver hauled his sail out at right angles and headed into the stream. The plank darted forward in jerky rushes. He turned a shaven head smeared eau-de-nil. He had double pupils. "Tourists?"

"Umm—Can you suggest a hotel?"

"Downtown," he diagnosed, and shot around a skater. They exchanged obscenities. The plank was barely wide enough for the seats and maybe six inches deep. It floated a couple of feet above the roadway, heaving up and down on the flaws in the paving. The sail pulled in spurts. The wind, a hot fetid draft, was against them, blowing puréed tomcat stench in their faces.

"Ow," Desi said, bouncing on the splintered plastic of her seat. "My butt wasn't made for this."

{Elderly grav-lift with an uncertain battery,} Jones's symb analysed. {Sail's a light-wing, it pauses whenever it crosses a shadow. The dome isn't very transparent. I'd say rival drivers don't like each other, they twist the sails to reflect light back and jerk the other guy around. Upsets the opposition.}

{But good for the insurance industry,} Desi's said.

"Thanks," Desi said. "I needed encouragement."

"Anyone thought how we pay?" Jones asked.

{Try a bead,} Desi's symb advised.

"A what?"

"Compressed carbon with chemical impurities," Desi explained. "A boyfriend gave me a How-To-Do and I did it. Some societies use em as currency."

{Lucky this is one,} her symb observed.

"Oh." Jones inspected the hanging closer. "Hope they aint *really* valuable, you can lose skin over em."

The driver swung his wing suddenly all the way over and the plank canted. His passengers clung to their buckets, and honks and screeches blasted around them.

"What—?"

A windowless vehicle like a heavyweight slug was slewed across the highway, blocking the junction. The traffic-flow washed against its flanks and ran back again. A gridlock was spreading behind. Horns and shrieks expanded, red-shifting into distance, muffled by smog.

Two red-and-yellow flunkeys clung precariously to the slug's rear and a couple more up front. A tough-looking uniform with a big blaster rode herd from a scooter, making a production of using his wrist-comm.

He turned slowly, targeted the sailshaw in his blank faceplate and standed the scoot. The roadway was ankle-deep in dead organics. He waded through to push his scowl at Desi. "You the rimworld quack?"

"Herbalist," she squeaked, indignant. "With diploma."

"Get in." The uniform jerked his head at the slug. Its featureless pointed head and tail close to the ground seemed to slither, and the gray outer casing had an oiled leaden gleam. It looked as if it left a trail of slime behind it.

"If you're going my way," Desi cooed.

The uniform snarled. His boots were smeared with basic fertilizer. ''Just get in.''

She detached a random bead for the driver and his double eyes bugged. But it was maybe herself, the hanging had slipped.

The shape on the dais might have been a woman. Or a suit of armor, or any domestic robot of the early anthropomorphic period. It was encased in aluminum, the diabolo-shaped torso painful to look at. The chromed joints shone and a rigid peacock-tail sticking up behind was bedewed with brilliants.

A long horse-tail plume sprang from the top of the helmet and fell in rippling waves to the hips. It was possible it might be human hair. A skin-fitting mask sketched features, the eyes veiled behind diamond disks and a cupid's-bow grid of gold mesh at the mouth.

Two attendants sat on stools behind, backs as rigid as if they were wired. Heavy cloths with huge appliquéed eyes and mouths hid their faces, their own eyes gleaming like dull glass below. Their skirts trailed over black-stockinged legs, in spike-heeled boots that dug pits in the carpet. They were utterly silent.

The slug was transparent from the inside, floored in cloth-of-gold, and the spread buttocks of fore-and-aft flunkeys pressed on the roof. Motorized uniforms swam like pilot-fish silently alongside. Its shielding was so heavy the grav-units labored. They could have walked faster. Nose-tubes ahead of the driver promised aerial torpedos. A tidal wave of sailshaws and windbikes piled on its tail unnoticed.

The statue stirred, and the mask turned its golden rosebud grille maybe a quarter of an inch nearer Desi. The voice it strained was a tired old woman's. ''Help my daughter.''

The words were squeezed to a metallic echo, scratchy with pain.

''What's she got?''

The answer was too complex for the grille to cope with. It came out mangled. ''Ee-cat-it. Onc.''

{Catatonic?} Desi thought. {And she wants a herbalist? She's lying. Desperate, but lying. There's something here she's afraid to say.} ''I'll look,'' she said.

The aluminum figure sat back a little. "Thank you," the grille whispered, as if the metal itself spoke. The women remained immobile. The men above them in silk and velvet swayed lightly to the grinding movement. Desi balanced in the middle of the carpet, naked in her hanging, with her ultramarine gut making patterns behind the beads.

The long streets had become deserted. Grim buildings stood shoulder to shoulder, their high façades faced with lead and hung with gun-turrets. The street-level doors were as low as dungeons.

The slug paused while the driver muttered into his commlink and a door split, barely enough to let the slug through. It swung around in a courtyard and stopped with a jerk. The heavy engine died.

{Hmm,} Jones telepathed. {As exercise-yards go, I've seen worse.}

{You must have frequented a low class of prison,} Desi thought back. {I expect hoops, we played ballgames.}

{I took a master's in journalism,} he retorted. {Why did I believe Norms used windows?}

{These got remainders of high technology, plus they're all psycho. Something's really wrong, though,} she concluded.

The walls rose blind to a lead-glass inner dome that turned the place gray. A low arch each end was built for siege. The slug sank on its skirts and its doors slurred open. Uniforms and flunkeys evaporated, leaving the vehicle dead.

The statue sat. Time passed. The nearer wall-arch slit grudgingly, enough to squeeze out a fat soft cylinder, which unspooled clumsily into red carpet. The end was probably aimed at the slug but the nans were defective, because it misjudged its target by all of three feet. It came up with a flap on the plates and lay there, leading nowhere.

The statue creaked not quite upright, bent a little forward by the fit of the torso. The headpiece was too rigid to look any way but forward, but the two dumb waiting-women put their weight on the elbows to guide it down the steps to the yard. The process was painful as a surgical operation. Each step looked like its last. When the aluminum heels clanked finally on stone the erection swayed, and had to be steadied onto the carpet.

As soon as its weight settled, the carpet rolled back to the house carrying it, leaving the visitors to trudge over pavement. The yard was cold, dank and muddy underfoot. Just before the carpet rolled into the tunnel, the statue turned with an awkward rotation of its whole body and moved a stiff glove in the sketch of a wave, then the door had swallowed the three frozen dolls and slammed on their heels. A few minutes later it parted a slit again, even more grudgingly, less than enough to let Jones and Desi in. They sucked their bellies and forced their own unyielding ribcages through.

{Phew,} Jones thought. {Norms have to do this *all the time?*}

{Guess they must. No wonder they have complexes.}

There was no-one inside. A corridor opened straight ahead, lined with closed doors. Closed and locked, with the bolts outside. The decor was icily geometrical, shiny glazed walls inlaid with gold and steel plaques that constantly changed places with a stiff mechanical grinding. The roof was a maze of crystal stalactites that looked as if a breath would bring them down.

A mechanical whisper came out of a grille set into a doorpost. ''Please come in, I'm sorry about the machinery. When we're on edge it catches our anxiety, it's over-psychosensitive.''

{And seriously short of a good repairman,} Jones thought, limping.

{Didn't you diagnose shortage of everything?} Desi thought.

{I expected better of the upper classes.}

{And you're also worried about your neckwear.}

{Seriously. I'm allergic to hemp.}

''Third door ahead, on the right,'' the grille whispered, as if it was keeping in a terrible secret. ''If you swing the wheel it should open, the night-combination hasn't been set yet.''

The narrow mosspile carpet down the middle of the passage had nan-trouble too, its green invaded by withered patches. Long outliers crawled like tentacles up the walls, where they were caught and macerated by the grinding machinery. Humps of crushed moss fell slowly to decay among the splendor.

The third door had as many wheels and dials as a bank vault. Desi leaned on them, hurt her hands and looked at Jones reproachfully. ''Aint this what guys have muscles for?''

''Sorry,'' he said, grabbing the wheel with coal-colored paws. It creaked, resisting.

{Moses on a bicycle,} Desi breathed. {Where do they *get* this? I mean the clothes and locks and everything?}

{You're culturally ignorant,} he thought. {You don't recognize early fashion-show SM raised to an artform. Has it occurred to you the women may be consenting?}

{Yes, but not many or often. But I'm just the product of a second-rate medschool.}

{That would explain it.}

{Too uneducated in cultural superiority to aspire to being a TV correspondent,} she continued. {Even a *TP-TV* correspondent.}

Jones backed off, hurt.

The inside of the vault was a Hollywood torture-chamber. It was big enough for baseball, if anyone who lived there ever wanted to play it. The white-lacquered walls set off arched iron furniture with points sharp enough to draw blood. The mathematically placed etchings were Gordian studies in complex pornography.

The room was windowless, but iron hanging lamps lowered from the ceiling. Icy tiles were carpeted with white glass rushes, and the temperature would have been average for an industrial meatlocker. A row of blue and pink china kittens stood nervously on a shelf above a sketchy white fireplace, looking as if they hoped for an early summer.

''Yech,'' Desi said. ''Could go catatonic myself here.''

''You fill the space where other people keep their culture with body-templates in overfancy genotypes. This is *schloss* neo-modern straight from a vidshow. I doubt if it's anything to do with the kid. Pure presentation. I'd diagnose a system of daughters-as-capital.''

''So would I,'' Desi said. ''I don't hold with it.''

{But you'll stay anyhow,} her symb retorted. {For the sake of the catatonic young lady.}

''Who aint catatonic.''

{Let's go and look at her.}

A glass bed near home plate was spiked like an icefall and heaped with feather mattresses and down pillows, edged with lace, cold and white as snow. They'd left the door to the corridor open and a patter of steps arrived in the doorway along with a man in a black velvet tunic and pot-belly. He paraded jangling silver chains, the belly swaying. "And who's this? Have we been passed by House Security?" His evil green eye squinted backward. "They do not look like persons one knows."

"Don't be stuffy, Manfred," the door-grille whispered. "I brought them myself."

"But has Your Ladyship authority?" The belly swung as black-velvet-and-chains turned both eyes. The other was yellow. "Has one the Master's permission?"

"He knows they're here. George is Io's father, he *cares*."

"It's possible. The Master makes these mistakes."

"That isn't your business," the grille hissed. "This conversation is being recorded."

"All House conversations are recorded," the belly said, with a careful rounding of tone.

"Not in the women's quarters," the grille said without breath. "You know that. *I* am recording this one."

The belly looked them over, making an inventory. "We'll see," he muttered. "Oh, yes, we'll see." But for the moment he slippered away, velvet soles pattering on the floortiles.

Desi stooped by the bed. The girl was wrapped in cream satin furred with swansdown, gaping over an ivory bosom before falling in volutes to meld with the spread. A lot of swans had died to make that.

The girl could be one of them. She hung a foot in the air and she'd no toes or fingers. Pieces lay under her in a glassy litter, like broken bottles. Big Gothic rings stuck up among them, winking evilly in the hanging iron icicles that threatened her bare throat.

{Those lamps are bad, they've unshielded power-units,} Jones's symb remarked. {Emission-levels are too high everywhere, they're one cause of the household's difficulties. A simple lightplate . . . }

"Why don't you shut up?" Desi fingered a sheaf of gilt braids scattered on the linen, and the scalp they'd come from.

All the girl's hair was cropped off harshly at the skull, fragments of skin clinging to the ends of the twisted tresses. Cold air puffed in her face and turned her own breath to falling crystals. Frosted skin scaled off her cheeks and powdered down lightly. "She's frozen stiff. I suppose the bits broke under their own weight."

{Helped by too much rocky jewelry. And someone being fool enough to dress her later,} her symb said.

"You noticed. Yes, that broke the hair off."

"Huh?" Jones said. Desi pointed.

"Shreds of swansdown from the cuffs on the stubs of her fingers, and the robe won't close because her elbows are bent. She was bare when they found her." She grinned, bitterly. "What did you expect?"

The door-grille sighed on a whispering sob. "It was my fault. I couldn't have anyone know, Manfred spies on us. We're arranging a marriage, and he's kind as well as wealthy. They mustn't think she might not be . . ." Breath. "Perfect. We're running out of excuses for the matchmaker. If you can't help, Io's ruined whether she lives or dies. But she's my daughter." If it could have sobbed it would. It breathed in pain.

Desi nodded. "How long's it been?"

The grille paused, drizzling vapor. "I lose count. Months. A year. She doesn't change. But she crumbles away . . ."

"Jeezle. She's dead, Des."

"Just in cryo. It's lucky they kept the pieces."

"You also got Wonder-Glue in your duffel?"

"Wiseass," she snarled. "If you my dimplebutt assistant, assist me. With the fingers and toes."

"Hottest!"

"Gimme the big bit with the ruby. Why haven't men any common sense? 'Course, it's always so obvious after we've finished."

Jones poked in the tinkling litter, his face squeezed up. Desi snatched the joint impatiently. "And the piece that matches. It's a test of intelligence, you fit em together. *Go!*"

The finger was broken in two at the knuckle and he turned the chunks over trying planes. The pieces were like marble but so cold they froze the skin from his fingers, and they tended to cling. He shook his hand loose with a sickened jerk.

"*Gently,*" Desi said with fury. "They're brittle, if you break em up smaller I can't put em back. Try the curved one."

She turned cracked bits of knuckle to the light and exhaled on them, warming them at her mouth with her damp living breath. The marble furred with rime. Broken surfaces dulled from ruby to mere human meat and started to seep. A drop of blood collected on the edge and fell in the swansdown, staining it pink. She pulled off a huge emerald set in gold, threw it aside, and pressed the clean re-melted halves together. They stuck and melded. She laid the whole finger back on the spread.

"They're frozen so hard we can freeze em together and back into place. At this temperature they ought to hold. Need to do it for all the fingers and toes, and lay em out in order so I get em on right. Blinky was right on-target here, this my cold-hearted lover in his own sweet person. Mr. Cryo, Disincorporated. The low-temp field he's left around her's limited, I'd say to a cube that takes in herself and her immediate space. Probably some nano-shit centered in her body in case they moved her. The braids that slid off have thawed. It's lucky her fingers and toes dropped straight down. Anything that rolls out the field'll go putrid."

Jones swallowed. "This is going to take all day."

" 'S only time." Desi breathed warmth on the next finger. "She lost her feet cause people interfered. It's been going a while, the nans must be close to decay. If she wakes up now, she wakes up sans digits. Keep praying. But don't stop finding me bits of jigsaw. Then we lay on hands. Specifically, mine."

Girl-puzzles needed big concentration. Jones straightened to stretch, his eyes tearful from reflecting facets, his hands raw. Desi had never stopped. Her ultramarine brow was dripping and her hanging had slid into the glass rushes, which tried to digest it. The concentrated carbon disagreed with them and after a while they spat it back out. The white stems fissured, petrified and fell apart into silicate splinters.

Her transparent stomach was tight and empty. Jones rescued the hanging, was growled at and let it drop. He went back to matching bits of toe. Another layer of his own meat froze, stuck to a joint and flaked off. Daughters-as-capital. Worth less in pieces, unlike gold. Desi stopped suddenly with half a thumb and looked up frowning.

"Can't reach the other hand. Doesn't figure, I got there last time."

Jones wiped his forehead with a bloody hand. "I know, I've been watching. You're shrinking lengthways. And getting wider with it."

Desi blinked the salt off her lashes and looked at her arms. They'd grown shorter and thicker and her spine had drawn in. Her color had faded from blue to near-mauve. The pulsing organs under her ribs were striped with bone and misted with muscle. She measured him with a red eye. "And you're taller and slatey. I was a long way above you, now we're almost even. Would you say we'd begun to get our old shapes back?"

He blinked, tired. "Hope so. You're still out of kilter. And I feel odd."

She sniffed herself carefully and sighed. "Yeah, if it coming, it coming slowly. I feel funny too."

He cleared his throat. "Notice anything special?"

Desi stared, started and listened hard. "It's too quiet. Jeezle. My symb's gone. How couldn't I notice? She been with me all my life. It's—like really, truly going deaf." She stared at him, panic-stricken.

"I noticed a while back," Jones said steadily. "Was hoping it might only be tiredness. I'm almost TP-dead. Can just hear you, because I know you. And even you're faint. All the other noise is outside. I can hear the air rustle and the carpet growing."

"You think they maybe *died?*" Desi was pale. "That would be the end. No way back at all, ever. I don't know how to function without her." She looked at the thumb she was holding and a bright blood-drop spread on her fingers. She hauled on a sniff. "Let's do this."

"Okay." He laid his arm around her shoulder, and jerked it away. "Your skin's peeling." His palm was dusted with a floury deposit.

"I know, but this thumb's started to ripen." Desi blinked water that turned to ice and tinkled in the swansdown. "I'd seen it myself. It doesn't matter. Pass me a chair."

He brought one across. "Careful, if you break your ankle there's no-one left to fix it. I'll hold it."

She spread bare feet across wrought-iron flourishes and leaned over the bed, bending double. She swayed, mauvish, her guts writhing, her knees sagged and her butt in the air, salty slush turning solid on her cheeks in the cell of frosted air.

"Des?"

"Uh?"

"You're cute."

She stared at him blankly.

Toes were harder to sort than fingers and the light was fading. The light from the candelabras had reddened and their voltage was faltering.

"You think this is what they do evenings, or have they a power-plant problem?" Jones asked.

Desi sighed, locating a matching surface and pressing on a toe. "Who cares? I hate them and I hate their society. Do the lamps turn up?"

Jones pulled up another iron maiden, mounted precariously and rubbed her neck while he was in range. His legs were still stubby and the angle was dangerous. Her back was damp and more pale powder smeared off on his hands.

"Can't see controls, it must be central. Do you think the local radiation's affecting us because we don't have natural immunity? We've always had symbs to fix our health. Hey! Have you seen this?" His voice rose.

"Making toes," Desi mumbled. She was blue-lipped, her fingertips flaking with frost. But the azure patches that blotched her arms and were slowly blooming on the rest of her body weren't caused by cold. Rosy aureoles spread from their centers, rough shining sandbars tipped with glitter that powdered off at a touch.

"Is this how radiation-poisoning looks?"

She glanced, wearily. "Not that I know. But I never had it. We're both the same, our symbs solved the problems."

Jones examined his own hand, shrunk to a trowel and lightened to granite, and found a blue stain between thumb and finger. Another, larger, spread over the back. He pulled up his sleeve on an arm furred with rough rosettes. The thready tips were swollen in the larger areas, into fronds terminating in nodules. His symbiote was a blind space like a missing heart.

Desi had her nose in her work. A glassy fringe edged her lashes. Her symbiote too was a humming void.

"Do we try the hair?" he asked, passing the last toe.

She huffed out breath one more time, turned the toe around to get it right and pressed it home in the final space. She rubbed her nape. "Don't think we'll get there. The temperature's rising, I been having to work faster and faster as she melted. Was scared she might even come around before I'd done. Hold that a minute, don't want it coming loose when she thaws . . ."

A low laugh of quiet enjoyment lifted Jones's hair. Their heads jerked up.

"My own true love, the blue-eyed Daisy. Truly flourishing. Primaveric. A young girl in flower. My personal Flora."

The ice-colored ghost was sitting on one of the iron chairs, a pornographic painting visible through his shoulder, spikes of glass bedstead cutting his ribs. His smile widened, lips peeling back for a full-throated laugh. Clear and young with the sound of music. Jones snarled. "How does he do that?"

"More nano-trash, at a guess. He gotta leave a power-cell with sensor in places he's been to, triggered on me. Damn thing homes on my genome, it has a timer and when it goes off I'd say it phones home. The ghosts are projections, but he's using real power to get the chill-effects. Except with Blinky, hers was her own memory. Too far-out for him. Or maybe he didn't expect me to go there. Girl began melting after I got here, though her nans must really be near their due-date. He leaves me presents and time to enjoy them, then he calls me back to make it personal."

"Real thoughtful guy," Jones said.

"You've no idea."

"He's expecting you to follow him."

"Sure. Wouldn't be fun if I didn't, would it? Ice is a boy who likes his amusements. Great sense of humor."

"I'd noticed."

"Course it's easier for him, he has a functional symb."

The floating girl spasmed, dropped, snatched her foot out of Desi's hands and sat. Her eyes snapped open, blue and wide as a baby-doll's, ringed with white around the iris. Her pale hands, jigsawed with lines of new repair, fluttered to her head. She stared in front of her, eyelashes batting, while exploring fingers walked around her scalp. Then her small cat mouth opened wide.

"What have you done to my hair?" Her head flicked, the doll eyes staring. "My hair's all gone. It hurts. Rape! Rape!"

Icy beads squeezed from the ghost's eye-corners and bounded off his facial planes and down the smooth muscles of his chest and thighs. They pattered on the chair and the floor around him. Crystals formed under his narrowed lashes, crackling ice-trails glistening on his ribs. The trailing icicles at the bedhead broke off in his polar breath and their cutting fragments stabbed the rushes. The floor writhed.

"Rape!" he gasped, choking. "Des, you put that small toe on backwards. Too late to change it now, she'll have to live with it. Maybe her fiancé won't mind, it's different. And what *have* you done to her hair? Rape, rape, most definitely rape! Help! Wake the household!"

He began to fade until only his frosted lips remained, a long cloud of vapor blowing out, the rushes cracking to shards under it, the furred swansdown crisped with rime. His mouth paled to nothing as the girl shrieked and the lamps jingled, laughing and laughing.

# SEVEN

## Flower-Show

The grille gasped.

"'S okay," Desi said, desolately astride maiming iron. "Just hysteria. You want me slap her face?"

"No. She'll recover." It sighed. "We have to. Io, darling."

Io darling shrieked, a mixture of rage and reaction to the laughter that still shook the chains. The grille breathed, bitterly enough to corrode metal.

Desi quavered back to ground level, noticed like Eve that she was naked and groped for her hanging. A handful of beads was scattered in the rushes. They hadn't managed to digest the carbon but they'd gotten to the nans that held it together. The cell of cold had leaked into air as the cryo-field died and the ambient temperature was close to zero. She was blue and chittering.

Jones fingered his shirt regretfully, stripped it off and draped it over her. Then he began to shiver himself. It was short and wide. Desi tied the sleeves around her waist, sagged to the floor and leaned on the spikes supporting the bed, where the floor began to digest her skin. She tore up a handful and cracked stems spitefully. The rest retreated.

"Hair was too complex. You could try a wig, or maybe make repairs with a hand-regenerator. Better than nothing."

The grille choked on metallic hope. "Our family surgeon."

Io took a hitch to think about it before her next shriek.

{Maybe,} Desi thought into the void. {If it's as decrepit as everything else . . . }

{Might do hair,} Jones sent from a vast mental distance, like someone shouting over wide seas. His thoughts were almost lost in the sound of air-molecules rebounding from her eardrums. {That's their problem, mine's urgent. We need heat or we're losing our own hands and feet.}

The silky blue patches were still spreading and he shoved his hands defensively under his armpits. It was warmer there anyway.

The pot-belly in black velvet pattered back in, the green and the yellow eye gleaming. "Is there something the Master should know? We're being noisy."

Io's voice cut as if she'd been guillotined. She pulled the satin across her breasts and shriveled. Her naked head patched with raw skin looked purely indecent and her ribs and belly hitched with sobs, but her mouth might have been fastened with tape. Tears bounded silently down her cheeks. Her control was as painful as her mother's corset.

The grille had also recovered its cool. "Manfred, I must ask you to leave. Your presence in Miss's room is improper, the Master will be displeased. You may tell him the herbalist has cured our daughter."

"Has she. The person lacks talent with hair-tonic," the chamberlain said. He stepped nearer the bed. "Did I hear the word 'rape'? We possibly need a more intimate investigation."

That turned the situation around.

Io shrank into her swansdown and began to wail, a pitiful little-girl whimper. Her cold eye said she could do it to order, and meant to.

"Rape, rape," the grille shrieked, suddenly finding its full voice. "The chamberlain's assaulting my daughter! Guards! Maids! Anyone! Help!"

The rushes, balked of Desi, found the belly's shoes and started to digest his feet. He howled and skipped in the air. A pair of silent maids appeared in the doorway.

"Witnesses, witnesses!" the grille screamed. "Save my poor child!"

"Time to go," Jones muttered. "I'm not just freezing my buns off, this smells like an in-house power-struggle, the sort bystanders don't survive. People have this need for scapegoats. Do you remember the way to the door?"

Desi unfolded and wavered after him. "Turn right. And hope someone friendly can access the gate-codes."

"The lady with no face has her own brew of competence. Let's make street, before Powernut calls out the guard."

The courtyard was as bare as the moon. Even the slug was gone, though a slurred mark showed where the carpet had crawled up to it. The gate was unlocked. They limped out into a long empty road.

"Could do with a sailshaw," Jones said, looking up and down its featureless length. The sky was dark and the buildings folded in slate-colored smog smeared with rare lamps. There was no-one in sight. The town could have died.

"Not at this time," Desi said. "Symb figured it for a lightwing. It's all they can do to move in daylight."

Jones glanced at her. "You look like a dying lighthouse."

"I'm screwed."

"We'd better walk. If we stop I'll seize up."

She drooped. "Norms sure use energy. My feet got no skin left." She massaged a sole and shivered. "Aint warm."

"You aren't dressed." He stopped. "What happened to the carbon?"

"Carbon? You mean my beads? Fricky rushes ate em . . ." She stopped too. "Shit. That was our cash. Forgot entirely, we left in a hurry. Is it bad?"

"Bad enough. Could use some now, wouldn't mind dinner."

Desi sagged against the wall. "My stomach thinks I died."

"Ditto. I'd sell my birthright for a mess of pottage, if I had either one." He sagged beside her. They drooped together, black, blue, half-transparent and wholly dispirited.

"Keep trucking," Desi said at last, pushing off. "We can't stand here, we need a client . . ." She jerked. "Jonesy?"

"Uh?"

"I'm stuck."

"What you mean, stuck?" He used a shovel hand to lever,

and came up short. His back and shoulders, plus the hand, were cemented immovably. "Holy Jeek!"

Desi dropped back with stooping shoulders. The shirt had slipped around her hips. "Shoulda known, they're paranoid. Guess the lower classes don't get to lean on battlements."

He exerted his muscles, and cemented one calf and the second hand. "Now what do we do?"

"I guess we wait for the morning collection."

"Or starve to death. That might amuse them."

"Sorry," Desi said. "No skeletons in the decor. 'Sides, if you listen you can hear the guard coming."

A distant hooting pounded over the wall, and the clank of metal-soled feet in rhythm. The gate down the road grated. Jones slumped. "Anybody tell you being right's boring?"

They went on standing. Like flies in amber. Like ants in butter. While the metal bootsoles marched out, left-wheeled smartly, clinked fifty yards and unstuck them with a field-projector. These were velveted blue and yellow, but they didn't look like summer butterflies.

{Now, this is what I *really* call boring. Get the feeling you been here before?}

{Yeah,} Jones thought sourly, small and distant. {It's called déjà-vu.}

{I call it bad taste,} Desi said. Four uniforms had her by the arms and legs and were hauling her bumping into the compound. She kicked feebly. It didn't impress them, but she did lose what was left of the shirt. The butt they dumped on the boss's carpet was bare and blue with extra bruises.

The man at the desk, inevitably, was on the phone. He wore black velvet like his predecessor's servant, but with upper-class dignity and silver piping. He possibly also wore a corset himself, though not the wasp kind. He was starkly thin with the dead pallor of something raised in a cellar.

Desi assessed him, sussed out the room and unfolded. An antique-looking white silk scroll hung above a carved table. Art. She jerked, and measured it against her skin. "Esthetic," she remarked, giving a twist to hold it. "I like the contrast."

Jones tried not to look. {Des, you can't discorp,} he pleaded.

{Tell me about it. If decent women have to be covered, I'm conforming to custom by showing decency. It's written in my contract. His phone's on a landline. Could be old fiberoptic, but definitely a landline.}

{I'm fascinated,} his shrunken thought said. {I was worrying about your health.}

{Then save yourself trouble, it's counterproductive. What do you call the boy-half of a harem culture?}

{The Grande Porte. It kills you.}

{Cause this is it,} she said. {We are finally among *serious* people.}

The man with the phone looked harried. Someone yelled tinnily on the other end. A fine distant shrilling disturbed the air from several rooms off. He laid down the receiver and passed a hand over his eyes. "You're the Outworld healers."

"Could be," Desi said. "Got a sandwich?"

Jones shuddered.

"Cause I'm entering my belly in the next sculp exy as a study in void."

The deskman looked at the inner arrangements above and below silk and grew more harried. He did a double-take, recognized the hanging and gave up on it. "My great-grandfather's. Ninth-century recreation of an Edo original."

"Granddaddy's dead. You have a daughter."

His weary eyes sharpened. "How do you know?"

"I can hear her Momma yelling," Desi said equably. "Learned the routine last time, didn't they tell you on the phone?"

"We've tried breathing on her," the deskman said. He sounded infinitely tired. "It doesn't work."

"Wouldn't for you, the sensor's set to annoy me. Driving guy-people crazy don't switch the boy on."

He shook his head, frustrated. "It doesn't make sense. An hour ago she was at her piano lesson."

"Then you hit the jackpot, wouldn't you rather leave well alone? Okay, you aint musical. You could be lucky, her hair may not have fallen off yet."

His eyes looked hurt. "She's a beautiful girl."

"Of course. They all are, boy got taste."

"I don't understand."

"Hang onto that," Desi said. "Cost you one shirt, one steak sandwich. Each. Don't suppose you've tried it, but great-grandaddy's scroll's scratchy."

"Cheap at the price, if you can come through," the deskman opined. It was automatic, he hadn't really noticed he'd said it. He was quite nice-looking in spite of dark sclera and mushroom pallor. Desi nodded.

"My Foundation's non-profit, but they do let me eat."

{You were fired,} Jones noted.

{Weren't you hungry?}

He pulled his belly in.

"Didn't ask the last lot for a thing," she told the deskman. "Didn't they say?"

"George said basically, you left in a hurry."

"You met their Official Eunuch? Guy needs a therapist."

A faint spark gleamed through the harry. "The chamberlain. Eustace. Our paths have crossed."

"That explains it, she called him Manfred. Always helps if you get their names right. He wanta fillet you too?"

"You could make a donation to charity," Jones intervened.

"So you could. So could George, don't want him to feel slighted." Desi looked winning. "Shirts and sandwiches, steak. Plus donation."

"We've real cheese."

"Cheapskate."

"We haven't any steak." He was pained. "You must come from a decadent culture. Possession's illegal. I mean," hastily, "the idea's repulsive."

"We clone ours. But okay, I respect your religion."

{Be reasonable, Des,} Jones pleaded, {they've bits of daughter all over the bedroom. It affects men's stomachs.}

{Bet he hasn't seen her without armor in years. When he says beautiful, he means she used to be a cute baby. Her mama's probably the one who feels bad. I do this for a living and in my professional opinion, my blood-sugars aint what they should be.}

Deskman was wrestling with natural suspicion versus the shrilling at the end of the corridor. He might have been good-tempered when he wasn't harried. "Agreed," he said. "Shirts, sandwiches and a million to charity."

"No twilight homes for decayed torturers."

The eyes were hurt again. "I chair a committee on radiation research. We run a hospital. A shirt for you will pose a problem, you're an odd shape. *Please* will you help?"

"Sure," Desi said. "Right away. Send the sandwiches after us, I can eat on the job."

This girl was even younger than Io and it was obvious how the latter had lost her toes. The white body floated like a skinned fish above an embroidered spread while masked maids tried to force a lace nightie over it.

"No!" Desi said in a tone of command. "Not! Nenni!"

The maids flinched and dropped her. Father had stopped at the courtyard door as if it were a wall and mercifully, kept the butler with him. When they last saw him he was talking earnestly into a pocket tape-recorder.

These maids wore midnight-blue satin over soaring whalebone, and tufts of obviously false yellow hair flowed from their turbans. High platform shoes limited their movements. The door-grille was shrilling like a crazed fire-siren.

It cut off suddenly when Desi came in, on a hostile silence. The effect might have been related to lack of corset and an exclusive resort-shirt with patched-on pineapples and designer label that almost covered her gluteus maximus. It looked new. If it had been bought for the screaming lady, Desi was ready to sell herself for dogfood.

"You did this," the grille spat. "I knew it. It's mere publicity. First you rig it, then fake a cure. It'll wear off if we leave her alone. Henry's a fool."

"It may, but don't hold your breath. Last one was stiff for a year, and when the nans decay your daughter could get gangrene. You gonna fasten her fingers back with paste, or you share the surgeon with the marvelous machine?"

The grille paused. It had learned something. "It's some kind of trick. Euphemia told me about Io's hair."

"You surprise me. Thought she'd keep the details private."

"She tried to cover up," the grille said viciously. "But I know her. A year? Really? I hadn't guessed."

"She's a friend, I take it."

"She called, or at least she had George call Henry, as soon as she heard." The grille sniggered. "Euphemia's so kind. She must have been laughing fit to cry."

"Nice-looking guy, yours," Desi said, neutral. The grille made a noise like a spitting cat.

The girl's hair was black and had been frizzed. It might once have flowed to her waist. Now it was scattered like shining straw. Her scalp was as bare as Io's. Desi bit on her sandwich.

"If you wanta help, phone around, or get Hank to. There could be more. Anyone finds their kid floating, leave her alone. Cut her hair or fasten it up while she's still on her feet. No heavy jewelry. And send me a postcard if anyone gets chills."

"Whom shall I call first?" the grille asked, with a sneer. "Who do you have listed?"

"You dumb bitch!" Desi yelled, waving the stub of a finger and flattening her mouth against the mesh. "How should I know? Got in last night and I aint slept yet. My clothes were eaten by a hotdam floor and my loot to date is one cheese sandwich. Tell *all* of em. You know who did this?" She shoved the finger into the lens of the surveillance-unit over her head. "*You* did, messing, and now *I* gotta put it back. You know how hard it is matching nerve-ends? You gonna ask him to phone, or what?"

The grille shrieked in her ear. "You may have made a monkey of my husband, which isn't difficult, but you aren't making one of me. Phone? And tell everyone we have troubles? You think I'm a fool."

"No," Desi said tiredly. "I know it. Clear out your scrubwomen and let me work."

The maids stomped leaving, but maybe with their soles they couldn't help it.

"That shirt may have been a mistake," Jones said mildly. "I'm not sure she knew Henry had it around."

"Course not. Bimbos like her don't get em. Hank flubbed there, but guy's upset. She-people bite in societies like this, they've nothing else to occupy their minds." Desi stuffed down the crust and stood. "And a betrothal in question over in household #1. Bet this dame was hay-making while Io crumbled. Let's get started while I'm still conscious. Sandwich wasn't bad for *real* cheese, a bit gamey but Dad means well. Problem's the wall-to-wall carpet, these floors are dangerous. If you fell asleep you could wake up a skeleton."

"That isn't funny."

"But Mama would laugh like a drain." She yawned. "Wonder how many more are waiting."

"Aren't two enough?"

"It would surprise me. Ice suffers from abounding energy. Really gets off on making me mad."

"At children's expense?"

"Don't ask questions, just believe it. It won't, however, last forever, his attention-span's limited. He'll quit when he's bored, or runs outta power. Whichever."

"Io dated from a year back. He's had time to re-charge."

"He couldn't be sure I'd be here a year back, he's living in realtime too. He sows a few grains here and there, in case. If they sprout, he harvests. *His* symb's functional. He's dipping in and out of the continuum now, which is also why his powersupply won't last forever. This one aint so deeply frozen, she still got most of her fingers. She may not be the latest. Little corpse someplace aint been reported. Maybe her Mom don't know Euphemia. She'll hear now, though. Give the maids time to get to market."

"They must order by computer, even here," Jones protested.

"You think hired help can't hack the system, in or outta corsets? Landlines, yet. They'd communicate by Morse if they had to."

"I bet Dad would phone if you asked him. It's the original Oedipal family."

"You mean Mama's jealous of Baby." Desi peered into the little frosted face. "Eyes are too close, but she aint my daughter. Thank heat for a bed with no tanktraps."

"Emperor-of-the-Universe size."

"You gotta allow for natural paranoia in the ruling classes." Desi hauled herself onto the mattress and wearily began to breathe on fingers. "Don't touch the tresses, I'll try them later."

"Put it back hair by hair," Jones said. "Since you've fallen for Henry. Shouldn't take longer than a century or so."

"You're jealous," Desi said, pleased.

He slumped on a silk damask chair and chewed sandwich. The floral ceiling odorously dropped holographic rosepetals into the cheese. Desi stuck phalanges together grimly, virtual lilies in her sweaty hair.

"There's another bit of scalp missing. You got a piece like a hexagon with wiggles?"

Jones fished among the haystack. "No. Got two or three shreds you could put together."

She sighed and flopped. The bed undulated. "Nah, they grow as well with chemical regenerant. She'll end up cropped either way. You're getting taller again."

He looked at his hand. "Could be. You're normalizing, too. And paling. Almost like a nuclear sunrise."

"My dream of me. Pale purple with blue fur." She dragged her sleeve over a patch like a rampant powder-puff. "Are we through here?"

Their eyes were almost level and his skin had muted to gray. Blue patches met on the backs of his hands. He rubbed them. "What's the smear? I don't like it."

"Aint wild for it myself, but it's only powdered skin. It's the globules that worry me."

He narrowed swollen lids. The central fronds were minuscule but growing. They looked riper. "Shouldn't it hurt, if it's skin we're losing?"

Desi rubbed her eyes, one elbow on the corpse's belly. "You'd think," she said vaguely. "I'm croaked." She sat up suddenly, rocking the body on its axis. "What did you say?"

"I said . . ."

"I heard you. Jeezle, I'm stupid. It's doing jigsaws, they shrink your I.Q." She set her jaw for a telepathic yell. {**HEY!** Where are you?}

Stubborn silence.

She looked around. "Have we a lamp with an unshielded unit? Pass me a chair, I want up there."

"They should pull down for cleaning," Jones said, fiddling with a silver-gilt dove. "Got it. Careful, they're mutative as hell."

"You don't say. Stand clear."

"Smeett! What are you doing?"

She pulled the lamp to head-height and stretched bare hands to the unshielded unit. "Reasoning with a friend."

{*NO!*} her symb-voice screamed.

She drew the hands back. "You see? Aint dead, just foxing. Now I want to know why. Tell Mama, or I burn us both down."

The silence radiated misery. {You won't like it.}

"Sure I won't. Why else are we playing games? I don't like anything here. Tell."

{It was the radiation, must be,} Jones's said. It didn't sound any happier.

"What was?" Jones asked in a voice of stone.

{What you can see,} it answered.

"What *do* we see?" Desi asked politely. "It's been intriguing us."

Another silence. She moved her hand toward the lamp.

{*Please*, no,} her symb begged.

"So, what's happening?"

The air smelled of reluctance and shame.

{We're in flower,} Jones's symb said. It sounded close to tears.

"You're *what*?"

{Flowering,} her own said. {It's never happened. To our knowledge. Our species reproduces by division, always with the host's consent. Well, almost always.}

{In our race-memory they've always been willing,} Jones's agreed.

{Except one or two.}

{Who scarcely counted.}

"Not like maybe the whole human race?" Desi asked dangerously.

{You've never complained,} hers protested.

{A lot of people wanted us,} his said. {From the beginning. For what we could do.}

"Why does this smell of self-justification?" Jones asked.

"Because that's what it is. They're *flowering*. And they didn't want to be around to answer questions when the flowers matured. Which I assume they haven't. Yet."

"You sound sure."

"They're still swelling. But getting riper. Aren't you?"

Another shamed pause.

{We can't help it,} hers said humbly.

{Why do you think we didn't want to talk?} his added.

"Because you knew you were pulling a fast one?" Desi suggested.

{We don't have the choice,} it pleaded. {It's just happening.}

{It makes us ashamed,} hers said. {To revert back to plants. Losing control of . . . }

"Of what?" Jones asked harshly, into their hesitation.

{Our sexual nature,} his inner voice sighed.

"What does *that* mean?" Desi asked.

{We're reproducing,} her symb said. {Willy-nilly.}

"As clones?" Desi's voice was grim. Another pause.

{Seeds,} his whispered. {Spores, rather. We aren't sure.}

"But not as plain copies? You're going to be something genetically different?"

{This hasn't happened within our memory,} her symb said. {But our kind's very old. Centuries back our common ancestor was dormant for eons. She survived by contracting her faculties to their minimum, a bare awareness. She lost a lot of long-term memory.}

"She, female?"

{We're neuter in stasis,} Jones's said. {But she found a female host, and that determined her new identity.}

{It does with all of us. We take on the sex of our host. If it has one.}

"So right now, one of you's he and the other's she," he deduced.

{It's a way of seeing it,} his symb agreed.

{It's never been important. We're basic neuter, but we take on the host's characteristics. We normally divide when the host reproduces.}

{And take on the sex of the new host.}

"You're normally clones."

"But this time you're not," Desi growled. "How did that happen?"

{Your hands touched,} his said. {Back in the ship. When

the arc was going crazy. We merged for a moment. We couldn't know this was going to happen.}

{It power-surged just before it burned out. It affected our genes.}

{We became sexual. And now . . . }

{We're reproducing. Sexually.}

{And there will be genetic mutation,} his symb whimpered. {We didn't ask, it . . . }

"Just happened," Desi finished. "Have you reflected on what happens when your spores ripen?"

Intimidated silence.

"It'll spread?" Jones suggested. He sounded doubtful.

"Oh, it'll spread," she agreed. "Among a Norm population with no defenses. And since they've mutated and their memory doesn't include sexual reproduction, they can't even guess at the results. It's an atavism. Who knows what they may achieve? Look at us, now. It'll be a real hoot."

Jones was pale. "But it's illegal. And unethical. They've got to stop."

"That's the joke, they can't."

"Then they'd better get serious."

{We are serious,} Desi's symb said. {We know what this means, we're *you*. But it's a biological imperative. Beyond our control.}

"This thing's bigger than both of them," Desi intoned, with irony.

{Yes,} his said defensively.

"What are they saying?" Jones asked wildly. "They're dying? We're going to end up Normal? Without symbs? Non-telepathic for all time?"

Desi sighed. "They've mated. We'll have symbs. What we don't know's what kind, because they don't know themselves. Something mutated, may be even monstrous. They've no way of telling. We're going to end up as whatever they are. What powers the mutation may have, if any, is anyone's guess. I hope you like novelty." She slumped to the carpet. "So we better get practical. How long before you ripen?"

{Twenty-four to forty-eight hours, estimate,} her symb said. {Your metabolisms are speeding up as you revert, and the ripening may speed up with them.}

"You mean we're returning to normal as you predicted, and as soon as that happens, and it's coming on fast, you two blow."

{Something like that,} his said.

"You might have warned us," Jones said, with quiet bitterness.

"They might. But mine knows me."

"You have ideas?" he asked hopefully.

"I've always ideas," Desi said. Her voice was flat. "And biological imperatives of my own. Hermes picks its students."

{She means an atomic furnace,} his symb told him.

"It would be one solution. If I'd access to space I'd prefer a black hole."

A total silence. Jones's back slumped. "I'd hoped to live to win a Teepee."

"Tell me about it," Desi said. "This kid's finished. We could do one other. The one we've missed, with any luck. Watch our skins and let me know if the mess turns desperate."

He sighed. "Okay. It'll pass the time."

"Check. Uh-oh. All aboard the ghost-train."

Blue glass transparency was shaping in the curtains, its icy head poised in a helpless amusement. "Des, Des, you're slipping, you skipped one. And she's lost her titties, vulgar habits with jewelry. But I do believe Mommy's called for you already. Better run, babe. Wonder if this one'll howl like the last? Whoops, thar she blows! Sorry, kids, I'm over-sensitive. Just can't bear to hear a woman cry. Be seeing you."

The girl sat, bumped down to embroidery, felt her bleeding scalp and began to scream. The ghost, still transparent, bent over choked with laughter, and did his fading act. His last wisp vanished as maids thudded in.

The grille clicked on a shriek of fury. "Foreign filth! You call that healing? Look at her hair! You'll pay for your tricks, I promise. I'll see you do."

"Let's split," Desi muttered, as the maids tedded hopelessly among the straw. "Cheese aint enough compensation for Momma."

They sneaked to the door.

Deskman was in the courtyard, a couple of tones grayer. He grounded his recorder. "Is she okay?"

"Bald. Dumb pups tried to put on her nightie. It'll grow, don't worry. Your wife ask you to call around?"

"Yes," he said. "I've done it. Everyone I know. The city's full of ugly rumors. But if she's safe, I'm grateful."

"Check with your doctor. My biology's different from yours and I don't know what nans were used to freeze her." She yawned enormously. "Heard anything new?"

He hesitated. "One, close by. But you're tired."

Desi grinned like a skull. "I got eternity to play with." She gestured lavishly and nearly fell over. The hem of the shirt was below her knees and the cuffs had fallen over her knuckles, she'd shrunk again. Now the lady it had been meant for was the taller. "Or twenty-four hours of it. My metabolism's speeding. Why don't we look?"

He flinched, a film of sweat on his brow. "As you like. I owe you. If you're a shapechanger, I don't want to know." He looked at Jones, whose over-wide pants were bunched around his hipbones. "Take my car. There's a crowd outside. It's growing, it's violent and it could be dangerous."

"Par for the course."

"Can I offer more clean clothes?"

Desi unstuck the sweaty clinging shirt. "Bring them on. I've forgotten what they taste like."

The gates opened on a compact group of deformed citizens with useful-looking clubs. Their open mouths wagged obscenely. The slug's pointed nose forced them aside and bats and chunks of paving glanced off its plates. Its force-shield threw them back.

"What's that about?" Desi asked, bewildered.

Jones shook his head. He was wearing Deskman's shirt and a pair of workpants borrowed from the gardener. "Guy called us shapechangers. Maybe the locals don't like abnormality."

"They don't?" Desi turned the question over. "No, with their genetics they might be picky."

"He's overlooking it because of Daughter."

"Nice of him."

The slug was crawling through another gate, leading into

another courtyard. Another mother was running to meet them. Alone and unsupported. In pants, uncorseted, without benefit of carpet. She shook out hair like a green-dyed waterfall, spilling into haggard red eyes.

"You look like people, Hank made you sound first cousins to the Werewolf. He's scared for me. I'm scared for myself. My baby's high. Maybe a foot, and frozen with it. High I'm used to, frozen not. He also thinks you're the Angel Gabriel. Are you any good at thawing people?"

Her dark sclera were an ugly crimson that gave her irises a neon glare. Her facepaint was smeared and her flip manner had a brittle overlay. She had to be the shirt-owner, she would be pretty when she wasn't crying. Desi's pale-blue skin was gritty and her own eyes would have looked good in a brazier. They measured each other. "Hank the boyfriend?"

"Don't even ask. What do you expect from arranged marriages? I'm not respectable. No decent person would touch me with a pole, but I don't give a shit and I love my daughter. Have you met Hank's wife?"

"We've exchanged insults. This daughter his, too?"

"My only child's legally parthenogenetic," the woman said ironically. "Unless you'd rather believe with my neighbors she was fathered by the Devil. All either of us has is an education. Hank paid for it, but don't ever say so. You need slack someplace in this kind of system. Merrylin would love to see me at her table. Baked, with an apple in my mouth. Come in. I sent the servants for a month in the country last week when it happened, so nobody knows yet. Come look at Bonnie. I'm earnestly trying not to scream."

"Scream if you like," Desi said kindly, "it's free."

"If I did I mightn't be able to stop. In here."

The holos were stars and desert, with flowering cacti. A pool of mirage turned out to be real water that wet them to the ankles. The bed, under a trompe-l'oeil cover imitating a travois, was modest and bare. Its owner hung above it like a hieratic goddess with silver pube-fringes dripping on the spread. Desi looked at her in silence.

"That frozen bastard told the truth, for once," she said at last.

"He was probably legally legitimate. Most of them are, they're almost all elder sons."

"Not this one, I know him. I think his Mama ran him up between sermons, she was a preacher for the Monstrous Regiment. Does everyone do it?"

"Run up sons between sermons?"

"Have carnal knowledge at sixteen with Mom's approval. As three young ladies here to date have, on the evidence."

"Their Moms usually keep their mouths shut, it avoids questions. I think Bonnie's young to be over-experienced, but I can't lose her confidence by being hard on her. She's going to be stuck with a certain lifestyle, and she and I basically have each other. We have to live with that. Other people have to live with other things. That's hard too."

"But you're not exactly walking the street. You have a married boyfriend, and you don't like corsets."

"That makes me a hetaira. Genuinely one of the oldest professions. Hank's my favorite guy and Bonnie's his favorite daughter. For the record, I expect her to grow out of the jewelry."

"Always found it uncomfortable," Desi said. "You can start screaming now, it won't matter. I can fix her titties. You're the first that's saved the hair."

"She picks her own styles." The woman sat abruptly on a rock-shaped hassock and hicupped into her hands. Her shoulders shook.

"Leave her be," Desi growled at Jones as he hesitated, "she'd rather cry alone. You gonna have to hold these tits while I put the nipples back. Spare hand under her braids, pin's loose. Hotssakes, you seen girls before."

Jones laid a nervous paw on the girl's chest and another under her piled hair. They were both cold and hard. Drifts of vapor rose from the contact-points and his skin cracked again. Desi squinted at the mutilated breasts from every angle as she breathed on a nipple with a heavy ring through it, making sure it matched. When the flesh was soft she threw the ring aside and laid the nipple fastidiously in place. The skin ran together. The girl's face twitched.

"She's waking!" Jones yipped, panicked.

"Jeezle, that boy's sense of humor'll be the death of one

of us, preferably him. Hold her still, I need to do this quickly.''

But her steady hands didn't hurry. She went on breathing warm lung-moisture on the next fragment, feeling for the moment when the ring would come free. The girl moaned and lifted a hand. Jones grabbed it. Desi laid the nipple smoothly in place and held it down. The breast yielded and the girl heaved in protest, her lips parting over her teeth. Desi ignored her. A thin line of red oozed under her fingers, and evaporated off. The skin sealed. She jerked her hand away, pulling Jones's wrist, and the girl's eyes opened.

''Shit!'' she said. ''That hurt. Where *is* that bastard?''

Desi inspected the repair narrowly, frowned, and relaxed. ''Made it. Kid needs a bath. I'd say we all do. Her estimate of him seems the same as mine.''

The ghost leaned blue and pale on a holo-cactus, with a white polar grin. The cactus froze and faded to nothing in dwindling electricity. ''Congratulations, you're still too fast for me. You always were, Des, you bitch. Get you next time. Incidentally, you know your symb helped you?''

And he evaporated on a gust of laughter.

''He's lying,'' Desi said coolly. ''Come on, honey, try hot water. And forget that one, he aint human.''

''You're *telling* me?'' the girl said, sliding her legs off the travois. She looked regretful. ''It was his main attraction.''

''I know,'' Desi agreed. ''It always has been.''

They regarded each other with sympathy.

Mother's wrist beeped as she was helping her daughter into a bathrobe, and she knotted the belt in a hurry and fled. Bonnie limped to the shower herself. She was shivering, but her chest looked normal. Her mother came back to splashing, apologetic.

''You look like death, but you're having no peace in the grave. Another friend of one of Hank's friends. They found his kid five minutes back when her maid took in coffee. Horrible brat, it's hardly light yet.''

''Bet she's been up all night,'' Bonnie yelled from the shower.

''Remind me to talk to you about your jewelry,'' her

mother yelled back. "She called Euphemia, who called Hank, who directed her here. You see the smalltown society we have. They think it must be very recent, she was all right at midnight when the maid left her."

{Thought you said it was going to die out?} Jones grumbled. He was gray too, though the skin-tone showing through was almost normal. His telepathic voice had gained volume.

{I said *soon,*} Desi corrected. {Aint soon yet. But the ghost's manifestations are getting shorter.}

{What a performer. He does that *as well as* changing dimensions?}

{Stick with it, we're wearing him down.}

{Not as fast as he's wearing me. This can't go on, Des, if your symb's really functional they're close to explosion, and we can't be here when they blow.}

{She may have tried to push a little,} Desi said. {Functional she aint, he was trying to scare you. But I aint arguing, I can feel her stirring. Let's go.}

"Hank's car's still in the courtyard," the woman said, watching them narrowly. "You'll need it, there's a really hostile crowd. You truly are shapechangers, aren't you?"

"Uh . . ."

"He's grown six inches in the last thirty minutes and you've shrunk four. And changed color, you're both paler. And don't think I don't see the blue blotches." She looked at them earnestly. "I'm grateful to you, Hank and I'll help all we can. But don't you know about the Shapechanger Riots?"

Desi was blank. "We got here yesterday."

"It was all so long ago it's practically a legend, but the upheaval reshaped everything. Did you notice coming in that our fourth planet's missing, nothing left of it but orbiting rubble? There are smashed-up systems all over the sector. They'd a plague of—well, they called it shapechanging. Half the population stopped being human, if you believe the history-tapes. Shapechanging, levitation, telepathy, molecular dispersion. I know it's unbelievable, but that's the story."

Jones winced. "Unbelievable."

"I know you talk to each other without speaking. Hank noticed, and I bet Merrylin did too. She isn't dumb. So the humans that were left formed the Church of Pure Humanity, to wipe them out before they killed everyone. It was bloody. Like most crusades. Those here were driven out to Four and the Navy blew up the planet. The Argoid system chased theirs into the sun, and they say the shapechangers made it go nova.''

''I don't think they could do that,'' Desi murmured.

''I said it's a legend. If they were as smart as all that, I'd think they'd have gotten away.''

''They could have been in their early stages.''

Green-hair turned them red-green eyes. ''Maybe. I'm sure a lot of innocent people died. But everyone learns the story in school. Our ancestors thought they *had* to kill them or stop being human. There's so much random mutation now, we're frightened. People are terrified it might happen again. I've heard of children being stoned as shapechangers who were probably quite ordinary, only a bit strange.''

''Ordinary guys develop wild ESP talents,'' Desi said. ''Clairvoyance, maybe. Minor levitation. Especially when you've heavy natural mutation.''

{How do *you* know?} Jones asked.

{It's in the textbooks,} Desi sent back. Her voice was growing stronger, too. {I've sometimes had to fix em. It's rarely serious but it upsets the neighbors. If the neighborhood's Hume.}

{And I thought we were civilized.}

{Well, we aint.}

''Watch out,'' the woman said, leaning into the slug. ''Di's father's Deputy Governor. He's standing for re-election.'' And she slammed the door.

The crowd was hostile, and larger. They didn't just beat on the slug with shillelaghs, they threw things that splashed and some that exploded. The attacks didn't bother the slug, though the driver uttered blasphemies about his coachwork, but the attendants slid off and ran back through the gate and the outriders fled into neighboring sidestreets and didn't come back. Rocks hailed after them, and the gate slammed shut.

''Hum,'' Desi said.

{? } Jones inquired.

"I was thinking we mightn't need a power-station."

He groaned. "Think again. If they tear us to pieces the spores'll spread everywhere."

Desi's forehead wrinkled. "It's a problem." She gazed at a silky blue blossom. It had widened to cover most of her forearm. The globules' swollen tips breathed in and out with a slow pulsation. She pulled the sleeve of her robe over it. The copilot's eyes shifted nervously in his rear mirror. "Let's hope it's a quickie."

"Amen," Jones agreed.

Outside the Deputy Governor's the crowd was even bigger, hooting and thumping rhythmically in silent motion. The slug swerved through them and the gates slitted just enough to let it in. A small wave of rioters curled forward, and fell back flailing as the driver ran current over the hull. The gates closed, snapping shillelaghs in their steel jaws.

They heard the booming when the slug's doors cracked, a regular thud of clubs on metal. Voices pierced the shield, shrill with hysteria. The maids were invisible under aluminum carapaces but their shells vibrated with terrified shivers. They stood well away, arms folded on the bulge of their chestplates.

"Where?" Desi snapped. A metal arm pointed. They picked their own way across the courtyard to the women's-side passage, where the doors stood open. Metal feet scuttered. There was no-one inside, but the doors banged to as if closing forever.

"Friendly," Jones said. "I believe they mean to use us and throw us to the wolves."

"Hope they aren't planning a private bonfire."

"Depriving their friends of our valuable services?"

"And winning the election. Hell, if he makes a good job of it he could unseat the boss."

Jones glanced sideways, decided she wasn't joking and followed her silently into the bedroom.

The cryo-power was obviously diminishing. The girl here swayed a bare inch above the mattress on rumpled sheets, her body sheathed in a thin glaze of ice. She was unconscious, but the glaze steamed already and a slow drip out of her hair soaked the pillow.

"Uh-oh." Desi scratched her arm. "We've maybe ten minutes."

"It's going to stretch you."

"Oh?" Her knees were shaking and her hands trembled. She circled the body. "Damn, some idiot broke her foot off. Now I got blood-vessels to match. And nerve-ends."

Wet drops fell from the stump to form a widening pinkish ring on the foot of the bed.

"You're finished," Jones said. "Let them send for a doctor."

"And have her bleed to death? I said we've ten minutes."

{I can possibly help.} Her symb's voice was shaky. {If *he*'ll hold the dyke for both of us.}

Jones's partner gave a silent nod.

"Can I trust you?" Desi was too limp to be quarrelsome.

{You always have before. I'm you.}

"How long's it going to take?"

{Five minutes,} the symb said. {If we work fast. After that . . . }

"I get the picture. You, save energy, keep still. Just beam us any strength you have."

Jones closed his eyes. A faint shimmer around his body said a clenched symbiote being inert. Desi blinked, picked up the severed foot and fitted it in place, her fingers a blur of disciplined motion. She breathed warmth systematically as she went and the blood-drops dripped faster.

"Is this all the damage?"

{Nothing else but hair. And the tip of an earlobe. We can do that quickly.}

"We'd better."

{Three minutes down,} Jones's symb reported. {Two to go.}

"Keep counting."

The intricate bones of the ankle drew together under Desi's touch. She started on nerve-ends.

{One-fifteen.}

{We've got to go faster,} her own said. {She's melting too quickly, she'll come around. Can we . . . ?}

"Trust me."

Desi took hold of her internal machinery and dialed it

down. Her pulse slowed. The breath through her lips cooled, steamed and blew out as ice.

''Jonesy. Cool off. Slow your metabolism. Your symb can do it. Get static. We need two more minutes.''

He bit down. His face blued and froze. Desi breathed stasis into bleeding arteries, and her fingers melted into the flesh, disincorporated.

{One minute,} his symb said like breaking ice.

The blood at the edge of the wound had frozen and Desi worked through skin and tissue, matching severed veins. Her hands drifted like smoke. The girl stirred, her eyelids twitching, and she tried to work faster.

{Ten seconds,} Jones's symb reported. {You're going into overtime.}

The blossoms under their clothes fluttered, their silk lightly frosted with rime. Rhythmic booming shook the house, a steady accompaniment to their slowed breath. The floor vibrated.

{Done it,} her symb gasped. {Now the earlobe.}

''Ring as big as a bangle, of course. Don't they ever listen?'' Desi tore at the fastening, which slipped. Her hands were covered in iced sweat. ''Oh, *shit.*''

{Minus thirty seconds. I can't hold much longer.}

''We're nearly through.''

***You?*** have no more ***time?***. ***You?*** must ***leave*** ***now?*** or it will be ***too*** ***late?*.** The ***ghost?*** is ***gone***. ***Your?*** ship is ***waiting?***. ***She?*** can ***take*** ***you?*** ***away***. Do not ***wait?*** or this ***world?*** will ***die?*** with ***you?***. ***I?*** should ***regret*** it. ***Save*** ***yourselves?*.**

''Okay, Blink, gimme ten seconds.'' Desi threw down the bent earring and delicately fitted the lobe to its place. Thawing flesh dripped thick blood on the girl's neck. ''Stick, damn you.''

{Minus ninety,} Jones's symb said. {Sorry, I'm giving, I can't . . . }

{Done!} Desi's own symbiote was back in full possession, expanding exuberantly through her cell-structure. A wave of undirected cold crackled off the body into the air. {They're coming. Let's go.}

A pale thread of ghost in the curtains clapped in derisive

applause as they seized the memory of control and discorped into space. The mob burst in on a naked girl, alone, trying to pull up her sheets, and a frail echo of laughter followed them as the planet fell away.

"Jeez," Desi gasped, dropping into a pilot's couch that more or less fitted her. "How are ya, *Windy?* Got drive?"

"I think so. I've almost regained functions and my shape's nearly normal. But . . ."

A random criss-cross of wandering ghosts drifted through the chartroom, wavering in and out of the panel.

*"My clients insist upon an immediate answer . . ."*

*". . . or we shall be obliged . . ."*

*". . . to take severest action, and . . ."*

*". . . pursue you with the full vigor of the law . . ."*

*". . . under Paragraph III, Section 97 . . ."*

"It's been going on for hours," *Windrunner* sniveled. "I can't get rid of them. And have you seen—?"

"Yes," Desi said, kicking. The flightdeck was knee-deep in paper. "Jonesy, lend me your mind."

"Been doing nothing else for a million years," he sighed, reaching for a couch. "Now what?"

"Still got bad vibes in your genome?"

"A remnant." He inspected his hand. "I remind myself slightly of a fire-shovel. Strictly in places."

"Only places?"

"You're becoming predictable."

"It's fatigue, I'll work on it. One heave and shed energy."

"You're on."

They spread mental muscles in parallel and ghosts and paper vanished, fluttering, into space. The cabin flexed and settled.

"Home," Desi sighed.

The cabin hesitated, breathed in and out and came into balance. Her pilot's chair reshaped to fit. "Okay, *Windy,* a course. Galactic Center. I want warp soonest."

"You always do," *Windrunner* muttered.

{You'd better do it,} Desi's symb said. {I'm doing what I can, but we're both cracking.}

"We can't change dimensions, the cell's burned out."

"Don't need it, initial problem was gravitronic overload. And there's always Blinky." Desi turned to the holotank, and froze. Her eyes were fixed on a sprawling discoloration. "What's this? You cultivating lichen?" She rubbed it with her fingers, which came away blue. "*Windy?*"

Jones stiffened and did the same. Then he turned to scan the cabin.

{Don't waste your time,} his symb said tiredly. {It's what you think.}

"I can't help it," *Windrunner* pleaded. "I'm a person. I'm symbiosed too."

"Person's discutable, but not the symbiosis. And her central meatlocker's pure brain-tissue. It's gotta be budding like a lovin June moon."

"They don't," Jones said absently. He sniffed his fingers.

"What?"

"Bud. You're thinking of something else."

The bulkheads and furnishings were patched with mold, fungoid stains on every surface. A fine haze of powder drifted from the airducts.

"Terrific moment, let's talk poetry," Desi snarled. "If *Windy* blows here she'll corrupt the whole galaxy, the spores'll go straight outward on the solar wind. Plus that central hole radiation, it's spurting every which way. Get me warp, and don't bother with the running norms, they aint important. Just get it."

Jones's face, which had gone back to tan over an exhausted pallor, grayed out again. "I thought we'd skipped that."

"So did I. Ever figure I can be mistaken? In here we're contained, all we can contaminate is us and we can decontam before we hit the next place. But *Windy* isn't, her skin's involved and it's out in free space."

"She has a forcefield."

"I doubt if she'll be able to keep it. The symbs have a biological need to make spores, hers included. She'll try to hold and it'll crack wide open. As ours were about to."

{You don't think our material could help this continuum?} her symb suggested. {Their radiation damage is desperate. We could repair it.}

Desi hesitated, lip in teeth.

***No*. *They?*** are ***misled?*** by ***their?* *needs?*. *They?* *want*** to save ***you?*** and ***breed?*** as well. But this ***environment?* *is* *unstable*.** There ***is*** no way to ***know*** what ***future?* *forms* *they?*** may take, or ***impose*** on ***you?*.** The ***people?*** here ***fought?*** a bloody ***war?*** to ***avoid*** this. ***They?*** have the ***right?*** to ***choose*.** Run away, ***now***, as ***fast?*** as ***you?* *can?*. *It* *is* *correct?*. *You?* *showed* *me?*** how to ***be* *correct?*. *I?* *recall?*** it to ***you?*.**

''So you do, Blinky. And so spoke Zarathustra. Warp, *Windy*, and quit complaining or I'll kick your butt again.'' The cheesy panel vibrated.

''Course?'' *Windrunner* fluted miserably.

''Galactic Center, and give it muscle. We need more grav.''

''I thought we'd played that,'' Jones said.

''This I can handle. I think. Make space.''

The planetary system winked out. *Windrunner* quivered between dimensions. Desi yelped as a pepper of stinging eruptions tore her skin open, the blooms exploding in a haze of dust and bursting silk threads.

Jones winced inside his shirt and a great cloud of spores filled the cabin, the airsystem, the vents of the recycler, choking up the life-support which paused for a beat, setting both of them coughing. *Windy* hung in the frozen cloud of her own emissions, her plates blanked out by sheets of powder.

''Vent it,'' wheezed Desi between sneezes.

*Windrunner* was sneezing herself. ''I'm doing my best. But I have allergies . . .''

''We know, we've heard. I said vent it. Before we all get em. And put me back in lovin realspace.''

Jones stripped grimly and stuffed his clothes into the recycler, letting his skin get rid of its blossom. Desi scratched a healing armpit and concluded he was right. Her shirt was too long again anyway. The outlets labored. The atmosphere grew dewy with silent grief.

''Jeezle! You guys don't *do* this, spare me. You'd have a lot more to cry for if you'd polluted a dimension and ended cashiered. Plus taking me with you. Where's reality, *Windy*?''

It burst back in a flare of radiation, the circling spatter from a furnace the size of the sky. Their screens were distorted by loose energy until the hole seemed to surround them, a vortex of mass. Gravitational swirls threw them forward at just under warpspeed, clinging to the edge of existence. The hole swallowed everything, invisible behind a veil of disintegration, the long traces of dismembered stars smearing like snail-trails into its well.

Superheated gases seared *Windrunner*'s hull and sucked the vented spores inward. She whimpered, but stopped sneezing. Rivers of gravity dragged their bones.

Jones clung to his seatbelt. ''Have you any bright ideas or do I embrace you and discorp forever?''

''Relax. If we discorping, we'll do it hyper. *Windy,* full thrust and acceleration, we're taking a run. Ready to skip. Don't bother with a countdown, it's seat-of-the-pants territory. Warp out when I tell you. Go!''

''Pants?'' Jones repeated. *Windrunner* gathered herself, engines whining. The cabin shook hard enough to tear its bolts out.

Desi shrugged. ''Sane guys don't do this. We haven't the choice. *Windy,* on mark. Ready? Jump.''

Burning gas-clouds streamed along with them, random radiation deforming the images. The instruments stuttered, and went blank. The computer died in a wink of darkness. They dived into infinity.

# EIGHT

## Dump

Serene starclouds hung around them, lightly streaked with fluorescent gas. A faint background crackle cycled over *Windrunner*'s speakers. Jones flopped in his couch.

"Don't let's do that again."

"Systems normal." *Windrunner* sounded as if her nose was still blocked. "Course, Captain?"

"Back where we came from," Desi said, stretching. Her joints cracked. "Want a bacon sandwich?"

Jones shuddered. "Peanut butter. Take it slow, *Windy,* I don't want to die till tomorrow."

{I feel funny,} his symb complained.

"That's me," he said. "You're part of a group organism with interrelated awareness."

{What would you know?}

Desi paused in mid-stretch. A pale shell in striped pants lay sideways on top of a cabinet. "What in hell's *that*?"

"Ghost of a ghost," *Windrunner* snuffled. "They collect stray particles in high gravitation. Probably got caught when we fell in the hole. There could be more."

It was thin as cheesecloth and almost weightless. Desi folded it small and stuffed it in the recycler.

"Are they radioactive?" Jones asked nervously.

"No more than background. It's only a few molecules thick, carby-hydro. Stays inflated by electrical tension. You could eat it, if it had a taste."

"I'm off meat, especially long pig. Peanut butter."

Desi yawned. "I feel funny too. I'll have bacon in bed."

The commlink beeped, flared and spired up a holo. All the needles flickered. A warning whine shook the bulkheads.

⌘

TP–TV

*the station of the multiverse*

"Oh, God," Desi said. "I hoped they'd died."

Jones found a ghost-shell under the couch, folded it small and took a bite. "You're right," he said. "They taste of yeast."

BACK AGAIN WITH ALL THE NEWS YOU'VE ALL BEEN WAITING FOR, FRESH FROM OUR INTREPID EVER-POPULAR CROSSTIME CORRESPONDENT, OUT AMONG THE INTERTEMPORAL TRIBAL TROUPERS AND THEIR TRAGIC TROUBLES. IN WITH THE LATEST, OUR TRIM AND TIMELY TEEPER—IT'S THE JONES BOY!

❖

[*Dick Tracy makes an uncertain appearance, pauses to collect his grin and toss his scalp-lock, checks his pants with a time-honored movement and gets a Bronx cheer from somewhere out of sight:*]

VOICE OFF: Hey, cretin, you're on-camera.

[*Dick jerks guiltily, squinches a hunted look around the set and fishes The Grin from the lower depths. He takes a deep breath. The pants episode never happened:*]

Hi there again, guys, and here we go. Take a lick—excuse me, a look—at our gorgeous intergalactic frozen popsies. Got yourself a preference? Well, don't ask me, folks, I aint the matchmaker, but you can always file applications with all-time family fixers, Interdimensional Datelines, Incorporated.

No, seriously, only kidding, what we have here's all the news that's fit for the family and these dillious dollies are Tots in Trouble. Aint their fault they look frigid, they were waiting for a wake-up signal. A kiss from Prince Charming? No, guys, a hiss from Cinderella—and here she is, our doll-house doc, Delicious Desi, personality Gal of the Month for next December, don't forget your free calendar from our joy-fully generous Promotions Penthouse, and a stamped self-addressed spacecard, please, with all orders.

[*A curvaceous creature with mauve skin undulates insinuatingly, with an air of having sex with herself by osmosis. She pouts at the camera and slicks swelling thighs under a gauze sheath. The floating beachgirl with a teeny tip missing from her fairylike finger drifts in a froth of fluffed tulle which accidentally covers her pubic jewelry. Waves of flowing hair ripple on her pillow in a perfumed breeze. The perfume, Guerlain, washes around the cabin. Jones is proud of it, not many longrange teeps do odors.*

*The goddess flicks the popsy with a puff of scented steam—St. Laurent—and runs a pointed tongue over her pout. She re-slicks her thighs. The popsy starts, rises like Venus from the tulle with a tantalizing glimpse of pube-chains and finds, ravished, her finger re-attached. She sensuously kisses her saviour, smearing both their lipstick. The goddess slicks her own breasts and has a visible and perceptible orgasm, another Jones special. The audience-approval meter, on display by the side, goes up roughly four hundred percent (male) and three percent (female) respectively.*]

DESI, OFF-CAMERA: They pay you for inventing this hog-flop? You been told you got a mind like a used armpit?

JONES, OFF-CAMERA, RESIGNED: Yeah. By you. All the time.

DESI, OFF-CAMERA: This is a *family* program?

JONES, DITTO, (RATHER UNCOMFORTABLE): We cater to liberated families.

DESI, DITTO: (*Beep. Beep. Beep.* Several more beeps at increasing volume.) And if you really want, I'm willing to expand on it. Why don't you show em some irradiated kids?

[*The network becomes aware of the glitch and cuts the sound. Technical snickers stop abruptly. The audience-approval meter registers a three hundred percent rise (female) and a thirty percent drop (male).*

*Dick can be seen wiping his forehead as the image fades. His scalp-lock's drooping. For a moment a disagreeably detailed picture of an irradiated child is superimposed, before the network regains control.*]

"I'm going to bed," Desi said, nauseated. "Have another ghost-sandwich, they aint actually bad for you."

"The last was repulsive."

"That's why I thought of you."

The airduct yawned. "I think I'll take a nap too. Jumping black holes is exhausting, I'm sure I'll feel fresher tomorrow."

"*Windy,*" Desi yelped. "You're a *ship*. Ships don't take naps, that's how my last bimbo got her brain meted. Make like a lovin fish and float. Another mete-hit halfway outta hyper'll kill us."

"If you insist," *Windrunner* said sulkily. "Isn't there an organization for the rights of sentient mechanisms? My last owner sometimes *stopped.*"

"While he screwed you with some other dame," Desi sneered. "A Society for Sent-mech Rights is all we need. Drive on."

"It isn't fair," *Windrunner* muttered. She beamed her speakers at Jones. "Would you like to play gin rummy?"

"Sorry, I'm going to bed too."

"**SPASM**," *Windrunner* murmured thoughtfully.

"Not another one."

"I was meditating." With dignity. "On the **S**ociety for the **P**rotection and **A**id of **S**entient **M**echanisms."

"I like it," Desi appreciated. "If we ever get back, remind

me to help you set it up. Before I buy a non-Union ship. While you're waiting, truck.''

She went to her cabin and slammed the iris. It closed with a pained whistle.

{I'm you,} the voice said. {Tell me what you need.}

Desi woke suddenly, soaked in sweat. ''What?''

{I'm sorry I'm slow, but I'm having to search for my mother's memories. I may do better now you're awake.}

Desi sat up among damp sheets. Her spine cracked sharply. She raised a hand, short and stubby in the half-dark, and willed it long, slender and blue. It twitched once and shriveled slightly. The nails got ragged.

''Who are you?''

{I can see it's upsetting, but my parents didn't know the consequences of reproduction. We're like salmon.}

''Salmon,'' Desi said.

{We die after spawning. We hadn't done it for so long we'd forgotten. I'm new. I may grow quite quickly.}

''That's nice.'' Desi's voice wobbled and her hands were chilly. Her joints ached. ''A new clone?''

{A new organism, from a sexual union. I'm the same species, but my genetic qualities may be different.}

Desi bit on the thought she'd feared as much. ''Can a pair of clones produce new genomes?''

Pause. {The sex and proclivities of the host affect us,} the little voice said, with apology.

''So you're half him. Terrific. What are your parameters?''

{I'll have to find out. I'm newly born. We've no idea of the results.}

''Perfect,'' Desi muttered. ''And our teep genius is the same.''

{His symb's new too, yes. They'll have to experiment. And then there's the ship . . . }

Desi jerked. Her spine cracked again. ''Say what?''

{She's a sentient organism, she has a symb too. Her sentience may even be greater, he's very intelligent . . . }

''What do you—'' Desi stopped. ''Don't tell me. There has to be an ordinance.''

{Several, it's very irregular. It's not quite her fault, her early experiences left her susceptible, and their bodies were in contact . . . }

"I'm half-sister to a *sentient mechanism?*"

{If you want to put it that way. Certainly *I* am . . . }

"I'm gonna commit suicide." She swung her legs out onto the floor and looked blankly at chalky knees and wriggling veins. Her toes were knotted.

{That really isn't practical. We've a dimension problem.}

"What's wrong with it this time?" Desi asked dangerously. Her voice was coarse and squeaky. A short pause.

{It doesn't fit my templates,} the little voice said. {Something happened while we were re-forming and I think we're off-course. We don't know where. But the biosphere's supportable . . . }

"My appearance isn't. Can you do anything with it?"

Silence.

"That's what I figured," she said. "So I'm gonna have to nan my lovin clothes again. I aint used to this, I hurt all over." She switched in the holo-mirror, and froze. She was looking into the wrinkled mask of a very old woman, the spine curved, the eyes watery, wisps of thin hair over bare pink scalp. "Are you ever likely to get back into phase?" She was keeping her voice under control.

{I hope so.}

Desi gazed at herself steadily and a weak salt drop gathered in her eye-corner. It hung there, hesitating, and rolled. There was a gully waiting to channel it. The stream widened, found a withered dewlap and dripped in her neckline. Her shriveled lips trembled. She took a rheumy snuffle like a very old dog, pulled liquid snot up her nose and let a handful of low-backed lace drop.

She dialed a long hooded robe. Her joints creaked as she dragged it over her head and the silky stuff caught on her rough knuckles. She made sensible shoes and considered breakfast. She wasn't hungry.

**Blink**

**. . . hear me? . . . you need to know. Please . . .**

A swirl of air blinked white and vanished. The cabin lights were dim and a bent hippy with sparse bristles and sagging sweater drooped over pooled tea islanded with crumbs. "What was that?"

Desi ignored him. "You looked at the plates lately? We still in hyper?"

"No," he mumbled around burned toast. "But we seem to be in a planetary system. Should make someplace on our auxiliary engines. You did say you'd a space license?" There was a misshapen pink plastic seashell in his ear and scraggly whiskers around his jaw.

"Yeah," Desi said. "Where's *Windy?* We don't need bad light, there's nothing I know of wrong with her batteries."

"Can't raise her, that's why the toast's burnt. We're doing it all manual. Guess she's traumatized."

"I'm traumatized. You're traumatized. Or you haven't shaved. What's so fricky special about her?"

"I'm traumatized. I *also* haven't shaved, because I leave that to my symb, which forgot how. Since I never knew, I could cut my throat. Des, if you look like that long you'll need a style-change. Your vocabulary's kind of young."

"Frick that," Desi said. Her voice cracked into a squawk and her cheek ran fresh glaze. "Why should I grow old gracefully?" She winced. "Knee's arthritic."

"Yeah," he said sadly. "I got up, I nanned a hearing-aid. A professional telepath."

They looked at each other, and their eyes dropped. Desi fiddled with the toaster. The bread came out soggy.

**Blink . . . can if you try. It's important. Please to . . .**

The white blink winked out. Desi glanced around, saw nothing and went back to her dials.

"Good thing the auxiliary engines are mechanical," Jones said, rubbing his back. Sunblind brows hung over washed-out eyes. The bristles at his mouth and yellowed teeth made him look like a walrus. Desi peered in the plates.

"Designed for possible symbiotic failure. I don't know if they're adequately shielded, nobody thought I'd fail too. They figured someone would be in charge."

"Or thought we'd die quietly."

Desi neighed. "Wanta know where we are." She pushed at her hair. "This ticks me off, I *control* my life."

Jones sighed down her neck. "I suppose the new symbs will develop in time?"

"I don't suppose anything. Don't seem to know doodly. We'll have to wait and see."

"What's the environment down there?"

"I'm told supportable, in the unsupported opinion of a part-grown symb with no qualifications. Can look, can't lose much."

The forward plate showed big icecaps, forest, subequatorial deserts, a lot of sea. Wide land-masses, well spread out. Lazy cloud-swirls, white grained black. The atmosphere otherwise was deep and clear. Nightside cloud caught the light with an internal sparkle.

"Something there I don't like," Desi said.

Jones squinted. "Forcefield effects? You think we ought to go?"

"We haven't much choice. We're not going far on mechanical engines and I need *Windy*'s meatcircuits to warp. The continuum parameters shift too fast for human minds in big gravity, her brain's mutated to cope. Dumb bimbo. Is she still sulking?"

"She hasn't spoken. Maybe she's trying to master her meatcircuits."

"Would help if she even mastered the toaster."

The ghost of a sigh came over the commlink.

"I think she's breathing."

"Jeez, it must be Christmas. That don't look like a forcefield. This dimension feels funny, there's a damn sharp event-horizon just out of sight. You could probably go around and come out where you started in a couple of years using mech engines. That's a teeny little bubble, it aint natural. See the black rim around the icecaps?"

He peered dimly. "It must be wide if it's visible here. Think it's linked to the cloud-formations?"

"No telling. I think you and me get to look."

The landscape below was boiling jungle, but the plates showed smudges that magnified to settlements. The images had a fluid uncertainty, but one owned a spaceport.

Desi grunted. ''Back to the lighter. This time, at least I had practice.''

''Do we have one? We left the last with a lynch-mob.''

''Had a check from the lighter-bay. *Windy*'s symb was functional, like ours, or we'd be hanging now. Took them a couple of hours to die. So she picked up her property before she cleared station, standard practice. We have a lighter. What we haven't is access to her memory of airlocks, we'll be opening them manual.''

''Again.''

''Exercise is good for you.''

''Says the good doctor. So why are you groaning?''

The wheel was as stiff as if it were welded. Jones leaned on the rim and his shoulders popped. Desi found a prybar in the toolkit and wedged it through the spokes. The wheel spun abruptly and smoothly to its limit and kicked her elbow. She swore and ground a sensible shoe in the deck. It hurt her heel, but the deck winced. The inner hatch opened without orders.

''She aint dead yet. Encouraged?''

She limped across the bay and dragged herself painfully up the lighter's companionway. Jones lent a bony hand from behind and pulled himself after. He was breathing hard. She dropped in her couch and slammed the hatch. He winced and turned the hearing-aid down. *Windrunner* dwindled into the dark as they screamed toward atmosphere.

''No sats,'' Desi noted.

''Would they need outstations in a space this small?''

''I've known people want privacy. And they're jump-offs for mining. Looks plain backward.''

She hit stratosphere on a trail of fire and shrieked across nightside. A shaggy rug leapt at them and the dawn flashed past in rose-colored glory, streaked with sparkle. Jones peered out. ''Remember your reflexes aren't what they used to be.''

''Don't recall what they used to be, memory's failing.''

She dropped the lighter into sunlight, saw a strip and cut the engines. The lighter bounced, regained its balance in a series of springs and drew up with its nose in the terminal window. The terminal window jerked to concave, like half a soap-bubble. The tarmac behind heaved up and down with a shrugging motion. Jones stared into the aft plate. ''Am I wrong, or has that surface autonomy of movement?''

''Probably,'' Desi said. ''Local mechs probably founder-members of SPASM. Looking around, it's possible they get mutation.''

The tarmac drew away as she stepped off the ladder, leaving her foot hanging over a hole. The lighter shifted, and the terminal hunched and retreated six feet, leaving an area of exposed foundations in jungle dirt.

The dirt gave off a sharp smell of leafmold and rich rotting things and started filling with water. The terminal reconsidered, put out a pseudopod and prudently re-covered it. Desi sighed and lowered herself the rest of the way, chalky claws slipping as she dangled from the ladder. Her tendons cracked and she fell in the hole. It immediately got deeper.

''Okay,'' she yelled, from the bottom of an eight-foot well with mushrooms breaking through the walls. ''Come down, it aint really hostile, just nervous.''

''How do you tell?'' Jones swung, joints cracking, and let go. The landing jolted him, in spite of a surface like warm taffy. It clung to his hands and clothes for a moment and dropped away. The well began to heave up to ground-level and he and Desi fell over each other. The lighter hung ominously over their heads. The agile surface hauled it a couple of ship's lengths away and the terminal window flattened out with a snap.

''What *is* this?''

Desi looked bleak. ''Mutation.''

''Aren't the constructs mechanical?''

''All modern building-constructs are mechanical. They're all also either sentient, semi-sentient or nanoed. Alive, or as good as. How else would they eat up your dirt or renew themselves from environment when they started to wear? Old-fashioned guys had to live with their garbage. Our mechs are engineered to self-recycle.''

''But they're *mechanisms.*''

''*Windy's* a mechanism and she just invented SPASM. They mutate like people. You want advice, watch your hind end. Let's go look at the city.''

''You think there is one?''

''Is that a trick question?''

The terminal was small and severely hexagonal with big picture windows. The glass was so densely polarized, outside was invisible and inside was lit like the depths of an aquarium. The only door was the one they'd come through.

A freeform counter ran the length of the hangar with a stationary baggage-carousel. Close up, it was decorative with no moving parts except the chute-flaps, which breathed damp air in and out. The whole was shaped from a single cast in preformed blue plastic. They stood, scuffing their feet.

"There isn't . . ." Jones began. Desi's rheumy eyes flashed among her wrinkles and he bit on his tongue. The terminal was mechanical humor, molecular discorpers didn't need it. The port furnishings were a joke. The humorists didn't seem high on compassion.

One corner of the building began to deform slowly. The blue faltered, turned muddy and faded to brown and the window lost its shape. The polarized glass slumped, cleared and melted. A fresher, sharper jungle breath blew in as the ex-window puddled the floor.

A shaft of bright sunlight shone behind it and the whole area shrank. Another marshy pool grew in the hollow. After a moment green buttons formed and swelled rapidly into cattail rushes. They shaped, bushed out and burst. Seeds filled the air and Desi sneezed.

"Photophobic," she said, fishing for a tissue. "Thought so outside. Didn't like the reflections off our hull-plates."

"Thought it didn't like our nose in its window."

"Our nose wasn't in the window when we landed. Terminal moved twenty paces to sniff and got sunburned."

The decomposition of the corner speeded and the brown contagion spread. The freeform counter began to droop. The baggage-chute's breathing wheezed as rush-seeds penetrated the system, and the carousel had a convulsion.

Fresh structure was rising from floor-level to fill the gaps. The new wall was a high transparent crystal that reduplicated into grouped organ-pipes. Its only relation to the original was that the pipes stayed hexagonal. The floor cracked and began to reshape, hardening to glass. Desi grabbed Jones's sleeve.

"Come on," she yelled into his hearing-aid. "New form may not be friendly. Move flesh."

The swaying floor had a spilled-sugar texture and the hole was filling with clear-brown angles that reached for the sky. By the time they were outside, the terminal was a tower of pipes with hard sharp edges. It still had no doors. Jones halted. "Mutation?"

"Runaway," Desi agreed. "Use feet."

A roadway led from a parody parking-lot with spiked pavement toward grouped towers.

"I guess the air counts as open," she said. "Watch your head."

He glanced up in time to collect a yellow splash from a passing butterfly with eight-foot wingspan. He wiped his cheek and identified pollen. "Weird."

"The advice was general. Watch your head *permanent.*"

"What's happening?"

"Change," Desi said. "Everything's mutating."

"I can see that. You expecting population, apart from mechanicals? Could anyone survive here?"

"Guess it's okay if you belong. I mean, the regular death-rate's probably pretty steady, once you're used to it. Organisms are adaptive. Course, some adaptations won't fit with others, that's where the trouble starts."

They hopped spikes to the road. She caught him as he turned automatically toward a moving beltway rattling toward the city center. "Wouldn't touch that. Look ahead and you'll see she take a hike over roofs."

"It's an overhead bypass. My feet hurt."

The beltway stopped dead, reversed direction and shook itself into humps like a roller-coaster, complete with big loop. Something metallic in the distance fell off. Echoes scooted among the buildings.

A small zippy vehicle heading for them put on speed and zoomed crazily over the humps. The beltway threw an eight-foot mesh fence across the track and the little car hit it at full speed, flung several bodies in the air and somersaulted with a meaty thunk. Wet chunks scattered.

"See?" Desi said. "Need to know what you're doing."

Jones had paled. "Does anyone survive?"

"Practically everyone, I expect. Shouldn't think those guys are hurt bad, their symbs probably have powers you never heard of. Pity about the cars, second's a write-off. Didn't see the first close enough to say. Depends on its organization. If it a colony animal, nan-mesh or a group of pseudocells, most of em likely get up and start over. If it had a higher hierarchy-level like *Windy,* a complex organism with meatbrain, I guess it's done for. Unless it *very* adaptive."

"On second thoughts," Jones said, "I'll walk."

"I'd call that prudent. Until we reorganize."

"Assuming we're going to."

"Let's assume."

Another white blink.

**. . . Hey. Please will you listen, it's very . . .**

Desi glanced around, but the blink had gone. She shook her head. Harsh light made her eyes water and burned her skin. The blue-white sun was an invitation to sunstroke. The jungle cowered.

At ground-level the roadway became a track edged with growth. Fleshy orange and purple blooms hung over it, dripping thick juices. Some hit the ground and left gummy puddles, some volatilized in mid-air. The roadbed twitched uneasily as though the puddles itched. Desi looked at the foliage thoughtfully.

A loop of creeper fell in her face, had a convulsion and budded to pouches that flung out blossoms big as paper hoops. Jones saw one pucker in time to pull her wrist. The paper snapped like knife-blades where she had been and relaxed, disappointed.

"Interesting," she said.

"I'd like it better if we could discorp. I'm not used to shoes. Didn't mean to make walking a habit."

"You notice none of em's the same?"

"I'm not into botany, I'm a professional network teep. Was," he amended. "They look the same to me."

"Well, they aint," Desi said, batting a questing branch aside. "This one has needles and its neighbor has fur. Little brother behind has spines. And different mobility. Look close, you see the whole grove's related but none's identical."

"Gives a new meaning to the phrase 'writhing jungle'." Jones set his foot on something squelchy. Raw liverish leaves made a rude noise and burst, squirting glop on his boot. The plastic smoked and thinned visibly.

"I wouldn't do that often," Desi offered. "Next might be using sulfuric acid." He looked at her darkly. The roadbed burped and sucked up the wreckage.

A gray frontage among the trees looked like a roadhouse buried in jungle. The building maybe started as rustic logs sealed in plastic, but the plastic had put out leaves and stems with frail plastic flowers and hanging bunches of glassy bubbles. A bower of growth hid door and windows. Desi sighed. "We gotta talk to somebody sometime."

Bubbles burst on her shoulders as she pushed through, with a rotten-egg smell. Jones pinched his nose and bulled after.

She was standing in a long narrow room. He stopped beside her. It had been a long narrow room. Traces of kitchens remained behind, a bar at the side. An upper floor hung in swaybacked sags. The house was a façade. The back melted into stinking swampland that extended to forest. The hardwood boards had decomposed to mush.

"Bad smell," she said.

"Nng."

"I mean *bad.* A black smell, can't explain. Out of shape."

He wrinkled his nose. The swamp smelled swampy, the rot smelled rotten. Grouped lumps that had been chairs and tables had slumped to oatmeal. The floor gave slowly in boot-shaped indentations that seeped fluid. Drifts of black dust hung above it, stirred by currents, and the updrafts made him cough. He pulled his feet loose with a gluey sucking and took a few slodging steps to the rear.

"Careful, it's degenerating fast."

"Yeah."

The mushy stuff merged into the marsh, dumplinged with lumps. The swathe of bog stretched a couple of acres, the smell reeking up in visible clouds. The trees edging it were dissolving too, their branches dripping as they bent into mold. The same black dust drifted across it, rising in the air on damp thermals.

Smaller dumplings scattered the ruins, irregular lumps of organic decay. Desi prodded one with the toe of her shoe and it rolled in an ivory scatter and grinned up at her with gapped teeth, the nearest of a supper-party of human skulls. The bone scummed with jelly as the air touched it and wilted to nothing. A pattern of dust spread on the oatmeal.

"I think," Desi said, "I'd like some fresh air."

Jones held back the vines.

A small chuffing car was standing in the road when they stumbled out. The track had taken a twist since they paused and now led out of sight around a bend. The surface had dimpled and was turning to cobbles. A couple in staring clothes bared their teeth and the little chimney on the car's snout chuffed smoke-signals of pink steam.

At second glance the look was cosmetic. The car was powered by a businesslike cold-fusion cell below and the boiler in the hood was the size of a samovar. The nearer of the couple raised his cap. It was mauve-and-rose plaid to match his suit, which had overstuffed shoulders. "You seem to be walking."

"These things happen," Desi said, halting.

"All the time. We brought our own transport."

"Cute." Her lizard face was expressionless but watchful. "In from the west? We saw the shuttle."

"Something like that."

The man's skull was heavy-boned above the eyes and the woman nestled in a ruff of floral voile. Maybe she was pregnant. Gold sausage curls framed her face. The car was luster ceramic with a neat teapot handle sticking out the trunk. They both had very white teeth. A leaden flatness tainted the air, and the landscape wavered in smoky mirages. A sense of nightmare fell over the forest and the sky darkened. Desi stiffened.

Jones bent, felt among vines and selected a branch. It shifted slightly, but let him select it. He hefted it, adjusted his swing for rheumatic elbows and slugged the plaid-capped man on the side of the head. The mirages vanished.

The man slumped, an impressive pair of ram's horns springing out above his eyebrows. The branch opened turquoise eyes and blinked slowly, passing a swift tongue over barky lips. Jones let go. The woman stood up in her seat and unwound.

She must have been sitting in a coil like a spring because

her spine above neat, well-formed legs was nine feet long in its frilled voile tube. The plump face hollowed and the sausage curls unrolled like sunflower petals as her sucking lips homed on his throat.

Desi stabbed at the eyes with stiff fingers and the face retired. Silky rosettes bloomed on the woman's flesh as the coil drew in, and the air filled with spores. The man's hands and face were already flowering. The little car hopped forward, still chuffing, and bustled on toward the spaceport, bouncing on the cobbles. The spores circled and dispersed. Desi coughed.

Jones tapped his hearing-aid. ''I'm deaf, but not that deaf. They stank of TP.''

''Sure stinks,'' Desi agreed. ''Let's leave, I don't like the neighborhood.''

''Me neither.''

''Thanks, guy,'' she added.

''My line of work,'' Jones said modestly. ''What is this, Des? Mutation like this can't be natural.''

''No. It's too neat. Place feels like an artificial dimension.''

''Another of your guy's private hidey-holes?''

She shook her head. ''My half-grown friend said we'd gotten sidetracked. It vibes out like Hermes. They're Government. That could be a problem when we want to leave.''

''Hermes?'' Jones said, bewildered. ''That's your outfit. Why would they bring us here?''

Desi pleated her wrinkles. ''I knew they'd access to the multiverse, told you I didn't know why, data was classified. You ever hear of a symb *flowering?*''

He shook his head. ''None of us had.''

''My old symb mentioned vague race-memories, she'd nothing more. Those two guys flowered in the middle of the road and they didn't even blink. You know about genetic slippage?''

''It happens with Norms, like the deformed guys who wanted to lynch us. And Changes can mute if they're seriously irradiated. But our symbs control our genetic material. Not letting it slip's part of what they do.''

''What would happen if *their* genes slipped?''

He slid a nervous eyes sideways. "Could they?"

"I think it's logically got to be possible. They're genetically flexible, or they couldn't adapt. Anyone's genome can get out of control if things go wrong."

"Wouldn't they know and fix it?"

"Maybe not. If they were taken over suddenly by some really resistant, bad-ass mutation—"

"Is that what happened to *us?*"

"Maybe someone thought so."

"But we haven't *done* anything."

"We flowered."

Jones swallowed. "And that turns us into rogue Changes? As far as I know, we can't change at all."

"That is a drawback," Desi said. "But you gotta agree it's bigtime abnormal."

"Of course it's abnormal. It's going to kill us. Hell, Des." He turned her a drained face, his eyes pink among the whiskers. "We haven't *hurt* anyone."

"Maybe lepers always say that. You think we could maybe be infectious?"

"*Infectious?*"

"Our symbs, if we have any, grew from sexual reproduction. Which symbs don't. Neither of the originals had even *heard* of it. None of us know what gonna happen next, but that couple back there knew."

The wind blew a flurry of spores in their faces and choked them.

"Normal symbs are clones, so you know the next generation's as stable as the last. Here . . ."

"You think everyone just keeps on changing?"

"Look at what we've seen."

{It's true here's different,} the little voice of his symb said. {It's a flower-garden. Everyone exchanges genes all the time.}

"Could get nasty. Don't know who you'll be tomorrow. I shoulda known a colony like this existed." She scrunched her mouth. "I never expected to land in it."

"With the rest of the trash."

"Hello, dump. Let's hope us garbage adapts quickly."

{Not too quickly,} her symb whispered. {You breathed diseased spores. If I were sexually active, I'd be fertilized and flower.}

{But luckily we aren't, we aren't old enough. Yet,} his added.

{So we have until we're mature to think.}

"How long will *that* take?"

{We don't know.}

"And you can't function till you're grown-up, either?"

{No.} The Jones-voice.

"Terrific," its owner concluded bitterly. "We can't recorp until they're mature, and as soon as they are we get contaminated."

"Interesting way to live," Desi said. A single tear ran over the edge of her eye and dropped in the runnel.

Jones put a rheumatic arm around her. "Baby. I think you're a great-looking woman for three hundred."

She kicked his ankle. And burst into ragged sobs on his shoulder.

Down the road the vegetation thinned and buildings rose out of the brush. Everything was tentative and maybe portable: shacks, a scatter of repairshops, prefabricated manufacturing facilities.

"All of this could be a teep invention," Desi diagnosed, wiping her eyes.

"Could be."

"Teapot car."

"Maybe."

"Dame with a nine-foot spine."

"I don't really believe in her. The guy was a heavyweight teep. I could tell that even without ears."

"Did she really eat people?"

"Maybe again. She did want to scare us."

White blink.

**I have really and truly got to talk to you. We can't go on like this, it's very important. Do you think you could try to listen?**

Jones stopped. "Did you hear something?"

"For a minute. Kind of buzz. Like a mosquito. It's off and on."

"Could it be a mosquito?"

**I'm having communication problems. But I have to talk to you. Will you try to concentrate?**

Blink.

Desi rubbed her ear. "Gone again. Damn. What were you saying?"

{The roadhouse was real,} her symb said. {And the rot and the skulls. I tried to warn you about those people, but I can't get through when you're frightened.}

"I'm never frightened," Desi croaked.

"Maybe you were just a little disturbed."

She choked. "Scared to death. I can't stand being deaf and paralyzed and—*stuck.* I hate arthritis and wrinkles. I want to discorp. Why are we *walking?*"

"Because the beltway's too dangerous. Unless that was an illusion, too?"

{It wasn't,} his symb said. {The problem here's telling what's true from what people think. They get confused themselves.}

"They must, with rogue teeps loose."

Desi ground the heels of her hands in her eyes. "I don't think most of it's deliberate, they're just like us. Including the mechanicals. They don't know what they can do or how long. Must make them nervous. Maybe the beltway don't *mean* to kill people, it just wake up suddenly as a rollercoaster. By the time it's remembered it's really a beltway, they picking bits of car out the street."

{I don't think the flowering woman *wanted* to flower,} her symb said.

{We were bred to protect our hosts,} his supplemented. {We do it any way we can. Confused symbs are dangerous, we don't expect to die.}

Blink.

**Which you will if I can't get to you. You have to help me. Us. Both of us. We can . . .**

White blink. The world paused, and began again.

"Can *you* hear it?" Desi asked.

"Yes. A buzz. I'm not sure if it's real. My symb can't, but he's very young."

{I'm trying to work into your central nervous system. It's

complex. There was a blink, I couldn't hear what it said.}

{The race-memories of symbs here have to be like bits of broken mirror,} Desi's contributed. {If we'd been mature enough to be sexually infected, we'd have no time for memory at all.}

"Sounds like a recipe for psychosis."

"I'm starting to get neurotic myself," Jones said. "You still want to talk to people?"

"Got to. That a car-rental?"

"We've still no money. If we're stuck, one of us has to look for a job."

"Like who? You're null on botany, place is crawling with intermittent teeps, and you don't know if you can still teep or not." He flinched. "You good at nano-engineering, or plastics technology?"

He ridged his forehead. "Lot of people here must spend a lot of time clearing rubble. If I could grow muscles."

"I mend things," Desi said vaguely. "Can feel a couple that need fixing."

She turned off the road into an office lightly built in native wood. The front wasn't coated, and the twigs lengthening between planks were local, with pale leaves that unfurled in sprays. A small android with a chainsaw was barbering them. One of its arms was shorter than the other and its legs had run together to the ankle, obliging it to toddle. It buzzed anxiously.

"Hi," said the chainsaw, nearly taking the android's face off. It bared its teeth. The android banged it against the wall and jerked the string. It looked harried. The chainsaw sputtered and went back to chewing. The android toddled after it around the corner out of sight.

The chainlink fence surrounding the lot was writhing and sparking, the hollow masks of ghost invaders apparently trying to force a way through. Since the gates were wide open it hardly seemed worth it. Jones scowled.

"Something?" asked Desi.

He passed a finger around the neck of his sweater. "Old age. Muddle annoys me."

"Pray for quick change, you could get real unhappy."

The owner sprawled in an armchair, asleep. His clothes were routine car-rental salesman but his skin was rainbowed with chameleon colors. He twitched in time to the tides of pigment that swirled across his face. As Desi stepped in he snored, grunted and wakened. A green flush widened on his cheekbones and the fence outside sizzled and shorted out.

"Shit," he said. His chair woke up too and ran experimental armrests, pinching his fingers. He kicked it.

"Bad dreams?" Desi asked. His color streaked through red and purple and settled to peacock that clashed with his necktie. He shook a woozy head.

"Worse than usual," he said, reaching for water. The carafe skipped nimbly out of reach and sneered from a distance. He groaned and smeared his hair. "Gotta be the weather. But you're right, I got to stop watching horror-vids, third time this week I shorted the fence. Was *The Great Warpsaw Cutup,* last night's Late Great Gold Oldies show. You seen it?"

"Vid, yeah. Show, no. They always give you nightmares?"

"Wasn't the vid exactly, a lot was the beer." He made a snatch and caught the carafe. He poured himself water that turned coffee-colored on its way down, and went a healthier shade of peacock. His eyes among the artwork were full of red veins but perfectly human.

"Often wonder how that film ends *really,* seen it four times and every time different. Told Marty he should use old equipment, more recent it is the more creative it gets, but he has this new relay and he wanta show-off it. Alky levels were variable too, aint sure the third wasn't pure vodka. Ever swallowed a whole can of Stolichnaya before you knew it?"

"I see the problem," Desi said. "How's your symb coping?"

He smacked himself hard across the side of the head, staggered and winced. "Out like a light. Would you kick that desk?"

The desk had been edging toward the door and was drawing its belly in for a run. Jones grabbed it by a drawer as it passed and it squeaked and collapsed on his foot. Its owner unfolded shakily and kicked it several times in the side-panels. It straightened its legs, sulking, and limped back to its place. The car-dealer shook his head.

"Really gotta be the weather, furniture been dancing the

Blue Danube all morning. Looking for a rental?''

''You accept credit-cards?''

''Sure. If you take out insurance to cover my losses when your bank cleans you out. Happened three times last week, two guys ended with a balance of less than four cents and the third copped suddenly for fifteen million. Plays hell with the accounts.''

''Surprised you manage to function at all,'' Desi said.

''Off-again on-again. Been working a dealership fifteen months now, though what I deal changes. Furniture last month, electrics before that. If I get a major symb-change we pack up our gear and move elsewhere. Been a farmer for a while. Was once President, for three days, but I flowered before I could get my pet bill passed.''

''Frustrating.''

''Yeah, well, same thing happens to the opposition. Nothing basic changes much around here, no-one ever stays in office long enough.''

''It's got to be disruptive.''

''Road-upkeep and transportation are the worst, though we've a general agreement anyone who's capable uses their TK power to discipline the beltways. Our vidnet's most fun, someone different works it every day or so and you get a lot of variety in the programs. Horror's Marty's thing, we had a straight run for nearly two months. Guy before him ran a porn-net from his garage, until the cits got together and scragged him.''

''Outrage?''

''Boredom. Right now my symb's functional when it aint unconscious, and I don't think I'm due to flower for a day or two, so I can fix you up if you want.''

''What you got?''

He squinted at her, disillusioned. ''You gotta be joking. We can go look.''

The car-lot was a graveled polygon hacked from the jungle. The perimeter had the soap-bubble glimmer of a force-screen, functional in patches. The patches shifted as the polygon wriggled. The gravel raked itself several times in the first three minutes then relapsed into chaos. Its owner ignored it.

''Lessee. Seem to have a nice Ubanga, fourwheel drive at

the moment, if you don't hang around it could get you where you're going."

"Three miles on the clock?" Jones asked, leaning in.

"All things are possible. Wouldn't rely on it."

The panel shook itself and registered three light-years. Its owner gave it another exasperated kick. "Now, that's a flat lie. Last year's model, maybe fifteen trips. Short rents, naturally. Say twelve thousand. It's reliable, as they go. Only had one complaint of it changing in the middle of a journey. Gets jinky in parking-lots, secret's don't leave it standing."

"Glide-capacity only," Jones noted.

"Hey, come on, my outfit's carhire. You wanta live dangerously, guy down the road rents out hoppers. Don't like to badmouth my neighbors but I gotta warn you, he'd four casualties last week."

"Fatal?"

The dealer's eyes shifted and his complexion, which had been settling to bronze, took another fit of streaks and speckles. "Uh—Not exactly *fatal,* no, but . . ."

"Modestly mortal?" Desi proposed. "What happened?"

"Worst one absorbed its jets at fifty thousand feet and forgot it had gliding capacity. They're manufactured with failsafes but they do self-modify. Total writeoff."

"Musta been dumb, even for a hopper."

"A goner all the way. Compulsory recyclage, even if it had survived." He rubbed his head. "Aint sure the full rigor of the law always best, when they know they're for the highjump they've no incentive to pull out."

"What's this?" Jones asked, with his head in the window of a handsome red pickup.

"Sorry, that's mine and I don't rent it. We've what you'd call an understanding." He looked apologetic. "You get the best service when they've one owner they trust. Can't exactly blame em."

"Pity," Jones said. "Nice-looking truck."

Desi was staring fixedly beyond. "What's that?"

Their heads swiveled. The trees at the edge of the polygon had begun to sag and their thinning foliage let through glimpses of gray swampland stretching into distance. Oatmealy mush crept between their roots and the melting branches dripped on the fence. Where the forcefield was functional it fizzled into evil smoke. In the gaps, viscous liquid dripped on the gravel, which dissolved in puddles. Black dust blew across it.

The dealer's face had become a study in white on white, like currents in water. He made a vague throat-sound and backed away, his hands making motions of denial. "Oh, shit . . ."

"What *is* that?" Desi asked.

He grabbed their arms and hustled them to the pickup. "Get in. Jinks?"

The little android poked its head around the corner. "Uh?"

It caught sight of the ruin and goggled. "Uh-uh." Its voice was a panicked squeak. It dropped the chainsaw, which frantically pulled its own string and pinwheeled away across the gravel, and hopped wildly on joined feet to the truck. The owner grabbed the longer of its arms and hauled it in. He slammed the door.

"Jeezle. . . ." There were tears in his red-veined eyes. "This all I had. We gotta get outta here . . ."

White blink.

**We would advise it. The situation's getting out of hand . . .**

White blink.

Desi blinked too. So did the dealer, but he was too busy driving to make any comment. As they cleared the lot in a screech of tires the desk, two chairs and the carpet wedged together in the cabin doorway, struggling wildly. A glass coffee-machine clinging to a waste-basket rolled up over them and fell on the forecourt. The coffee-machine looked the worse for it, but the wastebasket kept going.

As they rattled around the bend, the whole contents burst free with a snap and started bounding and crawling down the road. Their owner leaned on the accelerator.

"Aint you gonna pick up your stuff?"

"They're probably infected. Just hope we made it."

He kept on driving.

"Stick around," Desi said. "What's going on?"

"Rot," the dealer said. His eyes were red all over. The

pickup bounced on the cobbles. "Lovin wet rot. Started with plants but it spreading to people. Vid report say it hatched in the Arctic under the ice and spread to the tundra. Well, who cared, nobody live there. Then wind must've carried it, cause next it's gotten to the mainland. Spores. Black dust. Blows in your window and you wake up rotting. Didn't know it was so near . . ."

Blink.

**LISTEN. WE!** have to tell **YOU**. This time it's **URGENT. YOU** have to act. Only **WE!** can help, **WE!**'ve been trying to contact **YOU.** Call **US!.** You need **US!.**

Blink.

Desi sat up. "Am I dumb," she said. "Sure we do. But lemme see straight first. Can we look at the ice?"

"Someone you know trying to talk to you?" the dealer asked. "We get a lot of weird static around here, with symbs changing and all. Real strong aura, that. Ice? I dunno. You mean like polar? Could be kinda dangerous . . ."

The pickup revved defiantly and re-formed its snout. The cabin jerked and narrowed. Stubby wings spread from the doors. A white flare began to lengthen behind.

"Hey," its owner howled. "You're all I have left. Let's be reasonable."

"Maybe it is being reasonable," Desi said. "It *is* all that's left. It's picking up from you, and you're scared shitless. Maybe it hates that."

The dealer sagged. "I am scared shitless. Your friend with the aura don't reassure me, didn't catch the message but it came over serious. If we're going someplace, I'd rather it was someplace else."

"That aint going to help in the long run, the wind blows everywhere. This damn black stuff is liable to follow you around till there noplace else left. Me and my friend just got dumped here, so we just started to worry too. I want to see that ice, and look at this infection. Infections are my business."

"Used to be," Jones sighed. She glared at him with much the same expression as the pickup.

"Is. My friend with the aura thinks I should do something,

I think so too. Your truck caught the aura and it thinks so. Are we going?''

''Don't look like I have much choice. You really think you can *do* something with that?''

''Dunno,'' Desi said. ''Gotta look. Then I gotta consult with my friend.''

''Okay, I guess.'' He nodded wearily and the jet-whine grew louder. The pickup gained height and turned northward, reconfiguring as it went.

The jungle wore to brush and then to tundra. The pickup had gained speed and pressurized her cabin but her owner sat tight-jawed at the controls. His colors had settled red and white, eyes like coals in a plaster face.

''Nerves bad?'' Desi said.

He didn't answer. The little android squeaked and drew an umbrella from under the seat. It jerked it open, a cone of bare wire.

''You mean, no parachutes?''

It nodded.

''Don't worry,'' Desi said. She patted the truck's panel. Jones, under her, wriggled in his seat and scratched at his neckline. His knees cracked.

The air was cold and ice had begun to plate the windows. The cabin heater worked on it, but it was made for a pickup. Jones clawed a patch clear and looked down at a landscape spattered with rot. Gray blotches spread slowly and ran together. There was no animal life. White streaks intersected the gray and a distant halo reflected from the cloud-cover. Coming up on ice. Desi leaned forward.

The pickup's engine-note deepened as it staggered, buffeted by air-currents.

''We're icing up,'' the owner said. He sounded as if he was hurting. Black dust streamed past.

Blink. Blink.

**Keep going.**

**YOU** have to keep on. **WE!** will give what help **WE!** can.

Blink.

The dealer frowned. Desi's face was screwed with concentration.

"We're in the middle of a dust-cloud . . ."

"Wind's carrying it past." Her voice was tight. "Keep driving."

"Truck's never been so far without changing before."

"Then let's keep hoping." Desi scraped back her hair. Brown streaks had spread through it, and the pink scalp was covered. Her eyes glinted between their wrinkled lids. The fingers on the panel had grown pink nails. Jones sighed and shifted his knees. The sweater was giving him a rash and his raspy beard grated on his collar.

{They need help,} his symb said. {You hold Desi and we'll do the rest.}

{You've grown.} It had been silent for a while. The voice in his head rang with confident resonance.

{It was time.}

{And when you're adult, you breed.}

{Keep hold and don't let go.}

{You've only to ask, use me. What else am I for? Don't suppose you can fix my knees?}

No answer. He scratched again under his collar and tightened his hands on Desi's narrowing waist.

A white, blue-shaded wilderness blinded them, starkly cut with black. The clouds above were speckled with ice-drops, a dense swarm of polluted crystal.

The pickup shuddered and its wings vibrated, almost losing configuration. It pulled on its engine and got them back to shape. The jet hesitated, and re-caught. The truck staggered, dropped, and headed into the wind. Its skin was puckered with metallic goose-bumps.

Desi's fingertips whitened. Her hair had grown out to a brown shag over tense cheeks. The pack-ice below humped and ground together, dust frozen into it, graying the slabs in abstract patterns. Crevasses were dark wells of collected deposits. Towering glaciers shone like ebony, lacquered black, and their calving icebergs splashed into water that pullulated with diseased motion.

The dealer's jaw was stark. Jones wiped sweat from his forehead and ran a hand over tearing eyes. His knuckles were still stiff and chalky. "Des, it's hopeless. Even if we still had control of our change, there's too much here for one person to deal with. It's visible from space. This strip must be a hundred miles across, and you don't have an arc."

Desi ignored him. "Mutation," she growled. "One mutation in the microorganisms is all it would take. Notice something wrong about this stuff?"

"Everything."

"Just one. Here, on this planet, it shouldn't happen. Everything else changes every five minutes. Bad things like bloodsucker vines aint desperate, cause they change too fast to do much harm. But the rot's stable."

The pickup shuddered and wriggled again, and Desi's fingers dug deeper in its panel. The android moaned. The truck heaved but its shape held steady. Down on the ice a spark flickered. Desi screwed the windshield to top magnification. A wandering ghost turned up its face with an expression of transparent boyish rue. It waved and shrugged.

Blink. Blink.

**THAT** was obvious.

**He's lost control. It changes too fast. Even for him.**

True. **WE!** find **OURSELVES!** in ***difficulty***. **HERMES** ***took*** **YOU** out of **OUR!!** ***control***. **HE** was ***already*** ***aware*** of this ***dimension***, **HE** was ***expecting*** **YOU.** **HE** has ***altered*** **IT.**

**But we're going to think.**

There must be a ***solution***. **WE!** shall ***reflect.***

**Seriously. We'll be back.**

Blink.

Something below snapped like a whip and a continuum sublevel shrank to a point. It imploded in a swirl of disturbed snow and the currents dissipated in widening spirals. The ghost-grin winked out. Only the wind blew below, raising black and white devils of drifting dust.

"Might have known," Desi said. "It's artificial. What you guys haven't noticed is I'm not alone, I still have my friend with the strong aura. You were right again, Blinky, we're still on-track. Now help me, I'm listening."

Blink. BLINK.

**WE! We have a lot to say.** Later.

Blink. Blink.

"Okay," Desi said. "Let's go home."

The pickup U-turned gratefully and headed south over the ruin, its weary wings trembling. Desi patted its panel.

"Good boy. Cute pickup." It wriggled.

She flopped heavily around Jones's neck. He stiffened his knees and restrained his groan.

# NINE

## Bonefire

Bright clear blink. BLINK.

**I got through to you. We're channeling through me now.**

This continuum is so *small*. I could feel IT *beyond* ME like a *bead* in MY *mind*, with YOUR *spark* inside IT. But I could not make MYSELF *small* enough to enter. IT is *artificial*. I do not understand that. I feel *danger*, and YOUR inability to leave. I was to *blame* that YOU have been placed in this *situation*. I am *concerned*. I feel *pain*.

Blink. Blink.

"Not your fault, Blink. Hermes created the place, like you said. Pain's what you get when you catch ethics, trick's not to suffer when it wasn't you did it. We don't blame you. You didn't send us here on purpose."

Muted blink.

I feel *responsibility*. WE! wish to help YOU. That is why WE! are here. YOU were *snatched* from US! It has taken US! *time* to *find* YOU. And then I could not *enter*.

**You woke me up. If it hadn't been for you, I'd still be sleeping. Being awake's exciting. This is a big multiverse. I'm looking forward to exploring it. After we've helped**

**you. I feel pain too. It's very disagreeable. But making plans is fun. We've made great plans.**

"I'm sorry I woke you before you were ready."

YOU do not have to be *sorry*. I was ONE. WE! are TWO!. WE! think TOGETHER!. Through YOU I know *grief*. It has opened MY *comprehension*. I begin to know *worlds* within *worlds*. *Infinity* is before US!. WE! are *grateful*.

**And I got to wake up and look for you. It was an adventure. I think I'm going to like adventures.**

"Horrible brat," Desi said. "You must be proud of her, Blinky, you made her."

YOU showed the way. But I am *grieved* YOU find MY OTHER! *horrible*.

"Manner of speaking. She's a kid and kids like adventures. It's normal. She's come through terrific. You both did."

I think perhaps I shall *like* *adventures* too. But I do not *wish* YOU to *pay* for them.

"This wasn't your fault. You saved our lives."

I mistook the *era*.

"And put it right. You do your best, Blink. You just aren't used to an outside world yet."

I must learn *faster*. It is not *correct* for YOU to *suffer* for MY *errors*. What is a KID?

"Your Other's a kid. She aint grown up yet."

Perhaps *neither* of US! is *grown* *up* yet. I see so much *before* US!.

"In your terms, maybe not," Desi said. "You seem adult enough to me. Your Other doesn't talk like you."

**I was one of two before I was aware. So I'm different from my First, who grew up alone. We're getting used to thinking together. It's nice. We can tell each other things.**

But YOU are in great *danger*. WE! must help YOU. It was MY OTHER! who *tasted* the *plague* spreading around YOU. If WE! had not had that *trace* to follow, WE! might have *lost* YOU. The *multiverse* is *infinite*, and YOU had gone *far* out of OUR! knowledge.

"I think Hermes diverted us here because our symbs had mutated. That wasn't your fault. But that means the Agency won't help me anymore. This plague's killing everyone and

I'm pretty useless, my operating arc's burned out.''

Does **HERMES *know* THAT?**

''They can't know about the plague or they'd try to fix it. But this bubble's so small they may have trouble keeping up. They'd expect mutation, it's local normal. I can't contact them till my symb's online, but as soon as she grows enough to do it she mutates. It's a problem.''

**WE!** are ***thinking***. **WE!** owe **YOU** help. **YOU** ***opened*** the ***way*** for **US!**. **YOU** made **US!** understand about being ***correct***.

**What you really need's an arc.**

**WE!** are not good at ***mechanical*** things. **OUR!** way of ***thought*** is ***biological***. But perhaps **YOU** could build a ***biological* *arc*.**

Desi frowned. ''It's certainly a biological planet, Hermes seems to use it as a dump for defective sentients. But I'd need to analyse cell-samples, then tailor a reagent. Another micro-organism, maybe antibiotic. I need to go into the plague-zone to collect material, and the dust destroys organics it touches. So I need a non-reactive suit, and I've met shuck here that's inert. Hermes would have answers if I could raise em, but it may take longer than we have. Don't know the time-difference but there must be one, this dimension's double-plus skewed.''

**WE!** judge this ***bubble*** is a ***fast* *reactor*** because of **ITS** very small diameter. It is therefore probable that **HERMES *reacts*** more ***slowly*** than **YOU** do. That would explain why **THEY** have ***failed*** to notice **YOUR** problem. **THEIR** actions seem to **ME *incorrect***. **THEY *ought*** to adjust **THEIR** parameters.

''That's what I was afraid of. No argument, we just have to live long enough to tell em they're bastards.''

Jones scratched scanty hair. ''What's the composition of the gray stuff? The sludge?''

''Scuse?''

''Isn't it what's left when things finish dissolving? It's not my subject, but everything alive here's either sentient or nanoed. Is the sludge still active? If it's a residue, haven't the organic cells been eaten out?''

''I guess so. That's what kills em.''

"I was thinking about *Windy*. She's a sentient mechanism. And she's a molecular manipulator like the rest of us when she's normal, being symbed, but she doesn't reshape flesh as we do, a lot of her molecules are metal and glass. Ceramic alloys. Or is her skin organic in itself?"

"Only in a sense. It's basic ceroalloy, but it also has organic components and she controls it. It's true she's another damn shapeshifter. Her symb must be inactive now too. You keep on telling me she's a person."

"But she's in space, she's never been in atmosphere, and no atmosphere's been in her, because we haven't been back. Consequently, unless the spores can cross space, she's plague-free. Uncontaminated. And her reserves of metal and silicates aren't contaminated either. Plus, the sludge may be inert and it's the spores that do the damage. So you could maybe walk in the sludge without dissolving. It wouldn't be fun, but it might be safe so long as you avoided contact with spores. You need a way to deflect spores, which means a suit in inert materials, and *Windy* must have some which aren't contaminated."

Desi scratched her head too. Her hair was thick and brown and her skin was smooth. She hadn't noticed. "If the dust's the active principle I do have to collect it, but I'd have to sample both to be sure. It is an idea. Problem would be reaching *Windy* without taking contamination with us. The dust's into everything."

**We could talk to** *Windy*.

**WE!** could even ***transfer*** material.

**Why don't we go ask?**

Blink. Blink. Silence.

The dealer put the pickup down in a small public park and fell out on the grass. The android scuttled after and started to rub up the coachwork. The pickup had reshaped back to a truck. It and its owner steamed sweat together.

Desi knocked a wandering bench cold and sat on it. Its neighbors took the hint and froze. Her hooded gown trailed like a train and her sensible shoes slopped at the heel. She kicked them off, put her feet up and wiggled her toes. Jones, scratching, sighed heavily. The two men settled on a bench apiece.

"Solved anything with your friends?" the dealer asked lugubriously.

"Maybe," Desi said.

He nodded sadly. "Damn heavy auras. Got no teep-talents this time around but I can feel the vibration."

"Heavy," Jones corroborated.

"Uh-huh." The dealer looked the pickup over like a grieving parent. "Lotta dust back there in the ice."

"Yeah."

"Hate to lose her. Was a good relationship."

The pickup drooped.

"Hope on," Desi said. "My symb's almost grown, and turns out she has a talent for holding stuff together. We were both working on it, back there. Been waiting to find out her parameters. Seems those among them. Mom was scientific."

The dealer grunted, but didn't look happier. The pickup sighed down its tailpipe. Desi patted its hood. The office furniture came humping and draggling down the road, the smaller pieces trailing. The suite perked up when it saw him and the desk led the way into the park. He glared at it. "Heel, you lot, you're in quarantine."

The furniture slumped and huddled under a tree, which bent away from it. The coffeemaker was trying to re-form a damaged funnel. The pickup rolled off to join them and they crawled and scrambled into the back, where they clung together with an air of depression. The little android hopped after, still rubbing. A sign saying ED'S RENTALS sat on top with bowed corners.

"You Ed?" Desi asked.

"Yah-huh."

"Great. You got elected an arc. Biological."

"Huh?"

"Stick around and we'll show you."

A pile of steel sheeting materialized with a clatter in a neighboring flowerbed, followed by some ceroalloy plates and a mound of glassware, most of it broken. Desi winced.

Blink. BLINK.

**She wasn't very nice about it.**

Until **WE!** explained.

"You mean she was nice *then?*" Desi asked with disbelief. She looked Jones over. "Must be love." He scowled.

**SHE *likes* YOU** too.

"Then I'd hate her to hate me. What did this used to be?"

**Most of the forward bulkheads.**

And **YOUR *beerglass*** collection.

"Kind of her." Desi looked at the pile, jaundiced. "It aint picking up contamination there?"

**WE!** have put a ***force-screen*** around **IT**.

"Thanks, guys. Ed here's the arc."

Ed looked alarmed.

Feasible. But **HE** is not ***currently* *telepathic***.

**He's due to change. We can probably fix it.**

**JONES** is ***telepathic*. WE!!** could ***use* HIS *talents*** in ***addition***.

"Is that ethical?" Jones asked. Ed scratched under his armpit and examined his fingernails uneasily. He looked as if he'd rather be somewhere else.

**WE!** can help **ED** to ***change* *later***, if **HIS *state*** does not ***please* HIM.**

"Fine, then it's perfectly ethical. Will you fit me into this? A suit's gonna need heavy shaping."

"Fit *us* in," Jones croaked.

"What's that mean?"

"I'm coming too. You're not going to fricky dissolve by yourself."

"No, you aint," Desi said. "I need you here to watch my ass. And hang onto the arc. Ed, I mean. He needs experienced guidance."

"When did experienced guidance become me?"

"You're the only guy beside me who's met Blinky and knows her capacities, you're the only other guy seen an arc in action, and also Ed's fixing to run. We better use him while he still got the moxy, he has formidable shaping powers. Did you see the mesh he was shaping in his sleep? Plus the modifications to the pickup, you don't believe they grow wings naturally? Hey, Ed, make me some armor."

Ed sighed. "Is this gonna kill me?"

"Shouldn't think so, Blinky's careful. What'll kill you for

sure is dust-infection. Shape me a coverall with faceplate, then stick around. It'll be an experience.''

Jones scowled. ''I still think I should come. You aren't responsible.''

''I was responsible for centuries before I met you. Make with the suit and do what Blink tells you.''

''Ed and I are really going to enjoy this.''

''You and Ed aint here to enjoy it. You're saving the world.''

''Oh, is that all?'' Jones said gloomily.

The road was long and the suit was scratchy. Desi wiggled her shoulders, blowing windows in the haze of condensation that beaded her faceplate. Her feet hurt, as usual.

The melted jungle behind Ed's had swallowed the area and panicked people and their disconsolate furniture were straggling out. They looked at Desi curiously. Sun heated the metal mesh of her coverall and scorched her back. She blew a bigger window, took a deep breath and walked into the sludge.

''One,'' she counted, scraping porridge into a jar and fumbling clumsily with zippers. ''Never worked in a suit, you can't feel your fingers.''

{Keep walking,} her symb said. The voice had subtly changed, softer and deeper. {We need samples farther in. I can feel growth out there I don't like at all.}

''Glad to hear it. If I fall in, we can found a colony. Desi, Incorporated. Here a cell, there a cell. A real riot.''

She stopped again to trap dust and filed the jar. Gluey mold clung to her legs, rising higher as she walked through ragged trees. ''Look dumb if I end in mud over my head.''

{You'd need to fall in a swamphole. This is only residue so it can't be deeper than the original structure.}

''You have any soundings on swampholes? Swallowing this guck is contrary to my system of philosophy.''

{I'll warn you. Collect tree-bark, a nice melted sample there.}

Desi squelched into fields of mold, like walking through glue. She pulled her boot free with a wet sucking at every step and the porridge closed behind. The bark turned to shredded gelatin in her glove.

"We're wasting our time. It all ends the same, different scoops of identical mush."

{You're mistaken. Try wood.}

"That's wood?" But she tore off semi-liquid fragments, labeled and filed them.

{Keep moving.}

The jungle was a mass of decay, steaming vapors veiling distance. Silence lay over it. A shapeless chunk fell past her face and flumped in the ooze. The surface heaved slowly. A glimpse of bone shone as it sank. Prints of feathers lay on the oatmeal like a delicate fossil, and smoothed to nothing. A green moiré butterfly looped down and its dusty wings left a trace of green-gold like dying sequins that tarnished to black.

Desi took more samples, wrote labels with clumsy gloves and slodged on. Her faceplate dewed again with sweat and vapor. As she went deeper into forest the dust grew so thick the sky was hidden in sullen twilight.

She stood still. "Jieronymus."

{I could feel this.}

She'd been meeting sea-anemone growths on rotted tree-trunks, clear lumps tufted with fruiting tendrils. The smallest were the size of a thumbnail, their frilled crowns stirring vaguely. Whole areas were pimpled with them. She'd supposed more variant vegetation with a little more resistance, the jungle's adjustment. She was wrong.

{This planet had multiple lifeforms.}

"Before the plague."

{It's about to have just one.}

Feathered trunks eighty feet high loomed in the dusk, with clumps of eight-to ten-foot saplings bunched around them. Fresh groups of pimples pushed out of the mush.

The tallest stems were translucent, mineral colors gliding in a slow circulation. Their tufted crowns were acned with boils that spurted and burst as the tips searched for living space. Suppurating pops filled the atmosphere with dark snuff that eddied on the wind.

{This one.}

Desi tipped her head back. Her steamed faceplate obscured detail but the surface of the columns stirred, a continuous grainy motion as if the skin itself was crawling. "The dust becomes *this*?"

{It must be the adult form. When there's enough it becomes a colony animal, aggregations of microcellular organisms with their own specialties. There are precedents. It probably cannibalizes the original vegetation for cellulose to brace it.}

"So the height depends on how much cellulose is around to cannibalize."

{Maybe to start with. Later it possibly recycles, or learns to synthesize.}

"You mean once it's started it can go on and on."

{I don't see why not.}

Desi shivered. "Wish I'd a good powered arc, right now."

{It would have to be good. Imagine spores getting a foothold on another inhabited planet.}

"Hermes needs to know."

{Seriously. But don't think you'll be welcome home. You could carry contamination. In your clothes. In your lungs. In the creases of your skin. The old leper colonies had the same idea. Shut them in and leave them alone, someplace distant where they couldn't do any harm.}

"We're civilized now."

{People have said that from your racial beginnings.}

Desi's faceplate was crusted opaque. She scrubbed it and abraded her fingers. A hot breeze crawled under her armpits and mold squelched between her toes. Her lungs wheezed and her eyes stung. The crust abruptly sharded and broke. The tip of a bluish tentacle covered with boils was almost in her mouth. She backed away, over squirting lumps. Warm sticky liquid burst on her thighs.

"Moses in a chariot!"

The grove was collapsing. The group swayed and fell in, the tallest stems slumping onto those below. Dust smoked from the crowns. The breathing forest created its own wind and gusts of powder stung like hail. She'd no right to feel this, her suit was protecting her . . .

She hadn't one. Metal rags ran down her chest like mercury and smoked off in vapor. Her faceplate was a sugary wisp. Gray porridge crawled over her feet and licked at her legs.

{I'm afraid the suit-failure's partly my fault, I ought to

have known materials from a sentient organism would be too nano-loaded, the spores have dissolved out the organic linkages. I suppose it was inevitable . . . }

Desi stepped back, hands to her eyes, coughing dust. A cold draft spread down her back. The ghost was misty, shrouded in vapor, its ice volatilizing faster than it could talk, snow in its hair.

"Sorry, Des, an accident. Experiment, since the place was here anyway? Didn't mean to hurt you, but Hermes fell for my powers of attraction, and bingo, I got here. Perfect setting. I thought you'd enjoy my cute new organism. Samples weren't big enough to show it went colony. Ugly thing."

"You've started making moral judgments?" she choked. "That's news. Couldn't you tell the lover was intelligent?"

"But it isn't, baby," the ghost said, laughing. "That's the joke. It has a tropism for sentience, but it isn't sentient itself. That's what went wrong. Everything's sentient here, blame Hermes, they've been using the place to dump overactive sent-mechs and mutated symbs. I didn't figure it out till too late. Everything here's its natural food. A whole series of dumb mistakes."

"Which likely to be terminal, for everyone but you."

The ghost was smoking out, its outlines faint and shimmery with dust. Its voice drifted back as a vanishing rag. "You have to . . ."

It twinkled and evaporated, leaving a slight cold mist that held the spore-clouds back for a moment, and was gone. Desi gritted her teeth on a mouthful of powder. "That . . ."

{Don't lose it.}

"When I'm melting to bones, I get to lose it like everyone."

{But you aren't. I hold things together. I wouldn't have let you come without backup, you're *me*. I'm not full-grown but I'm developing. Trust me.}

"Where have I heard that?"

{The suit fell to pieces but we still have the sample-bottles. Collect some stem and a bit of tentacle. Then let's get back, it's hard work holding your body together. I'm getting tired.}

"What do I cut with?"

{Try your fingernails, the structure's loose. And bottle it quick before it finds I disagree with it.}

Desi fished a jar from the bog, held it near a boil and pricked with her nail. It burst poisonously in the neck and she screwed the lid down. The grove spasmed.

She snatched at a tentacle that tried to avoid her. The end ripped wetly against her fingers and went into the glass. She sealed the lid. The bowing stems swelled into barrels, fell in and burst. Stinking jelly rivered over her and she spat, clawing handfuls out of her hair.

The dirt had cleared in a circle around her that shrank from her touch. A last shred jerked away as she bent for her jars. The porridge was retreating, crawling pseudopods drawing back into jungle. She was the focus of a column of clear air, in the center of a vortex of dust.

"You saved the bottles and you couldn't save my faceplate?"

{The bottles are plain, your faceplate was nanoed ceroglass. *Windy*'s mistake, she gave you the best. Anyway, we do have samples.}

"Mistakes seem to be what we're best at."

{A racial characteristic. You have *me* with you now. When I woke up I didn't know my parameters, and now I do. I'm a holder. I held the dust away from your pickup over the ice. I'm holding spores off you now. And preserving your structure. Anything near us.}

"You mean this can't touch me."

{It isn't an option. This lifeform has a tropism against me. My touch destroys it. Let's go home.}

Desi turned, clutching her jars. Gray mold shrank away from her. "Don't suppose we could discorp?" she asked wistfully.

{Not while I'm holding you, it takes all my energy. I'll have more power when I grow older.}

"You're nearly grown now. What happens then?"

{If someone flowers on me? I just decide I'm not going to alter.}

"Can you be sure?"

{Yes. And I can do the same for your friend. You're both stable.}

"In that case," Desi said, "you can't grow up too fast."

She left her prints in wet mold, bottles clinking, and the melting forest shrank from her feet.

The road was where they'd left it, disfigured in patches and trying granite setts in place of cobbles where it still existed. Desi climbed wearily onto it. "Never knew walking could tire you out."

{You've never had to do it.}

She shifted bottles. "And if I survive, I'll never do it again."

{Exercise is good for you.}

"That's my line. *You* go improve yourself."

An urgent ghost materialized in front of her, striped pants fuzzy and gestures in syrup. "*Mee—ee—ee—zz Smee—ee—ee—ee—tt?*"

Its voice was a wispy bass vibration.

"Get fricky lost," Desi snarled, walking through it. "And if you've any writs spare, keep em for the restroom." She marched on.

The ghost looked as if it was still talking but its movements were too slow to tell. It waved its arms as they walked around the bend.

"Damn em," she concluded. "Suckers can't let me melt in peace."

"*Scr—oo—oo—oooo . . .*"

"Now what?" Not a ghost. It seemed to come from the air by her shoulder.

{Sounds like a badly-tuned carrier-wave.}

"Nah. Pitch too low. I really hate this place."

"*Whoo—oo—oo—oo—uuu—uum.*"

A jar slipped from her sweating fingers and headed for granite. Her symb caught it in midair and held it. Desi grabbed it and returned it to the pile. "If you can move jars, try me. Discorp-time."

{I'm still . . . }

She ignored the protest and gathered energy. They wavered on the edge of solidity, winked in and out and reappeared five yards up the road.

"Whoo-hoo. Knew we could if we tried."

Her symb groaned. {My mother had memories of finding you difficult. That jump strained me.}

"Not like walking's straining me. My feet are killing me. Ready? *Go.*"

They traveled into town in a series of disconnected hops like an intermittently visible kangaroo. The road bucked in protest but found them too fast. It writhed discontentedly and began to re-form as terrazzo.

Jones and Ed were sharing a bench and eating hotdogs when Desi discorped beside them. They both looked startled and Jones caught an armful of spilling bottles.

"These samples? Are they safe to touch?"

"Not if you drop one. But my partner tells me I'm insoluble."

"That's my own experience, though I thought I was your partner," he said, offering her a greasy bun. "It isn't as hot as it was, we've been waiting."

Ed obligingly closed it between his hands and directed a blast of his symb's microwave energy into the hollow. The mustard sizzled. Desi grabbed it.

"Ow. 'S hot. Who told you that?" she mumbled around a mouthful. "Is this dead?"

"Sure," Ed said. "We only eat cloned or it liable to talk back at you."

"Thank Jehoshua. Was starting to think everyone was unnatural." She sank on the bench and laid out struggling bottles. "We got Blinky?"

"Not yet," Jones said. "Want a soda?"

"Thanks, just mind where you put it, don't want to drink from the wrong bottle. Blinky?"

Blink. BLINK.

**We're here. Nice samples. We could use some of that.**

"No, you couldn't, kid. Not unless First has real good meltcontrol techniques, or you'll lose your continental plantlife. Not to mention your brains."

The question is irrelevant, **WE!** cannot ***touch* IT *physically***. **MY OTHER!** is misled by ***youthful* *enthusiasm***. **IT** may be worth examining for **OUR! *own* *experiments*** when **WE!** have ***time***.

"You know, Blinky, you almost lost the hic thing."

**I** understand better ***now***, with the help of **MY OTHER!**. There are ***still*** ***concepts*** that cause **ME** ***reflection***. ***Time*** is one. But **YOU** need **OUR!** powers of ***observation***. **WE!** can do **THAT**. **I** am ***relieved*** **YOU** have recovered **YOUR** ***protection***, but since **THE OTHERS** cannot ***yet*** ***share*** **IT** because of **YOUR PARTNER!**'s ***immaturity***, **I** suggest **YOU** enclose the ***samples*** with **YOUR** ***hands*** while **WE!** analyse **THEM.**

"Good idea. Stand back, guys." Desi stuffed the last of the hotdog in her mouth and wiped her hands on her pants. She remembered too late she hadn't any, and scowled. "Hope I can read my writing. Want to see em as we took em?"

**Great. We need a picture of how this stuff develops, and how it works on the material it converts.**

Would **YOU** gaze ***closely*** at each ***sample*** ***in*** ***turn***, telling **US!** exactly ***when*** and ***where*** **IT** was ***taken*?**

"No problem." Desi read off her labels. "Jungle edge behind Ed's place. This is mold, we got dust separate."

Good. **WE!** shall examine **EACH.**

She tipped sludge into her palm and cupped her hands. Her symb tensed and her arm-hair stood up.

"Are you okay?" Desi asked. "No holding problems?"

{I'm fine, but that stuff's dangerous. Had you noticed some's gone dusty, in spite of my stasis-field?}

**WE!** had ***observed*** **THAT. WE!** consider **YOUR** ***caution*** ***justified***. Please look at the ***sample*** with **CONCENTRATION.**

**Wow. Nasty.**

"Aint crazy about it myself," Desi muttered. The mold writhed and a few black grains roved the surface. She stared until her eyes teared. "You better tell me when you're finished, we've at least eight more."

**We won't take so long next time, we wanted a fix on its genetics.**

"Good idea."

"What you gonna to do with the goo when you finished?" Ed asked. "Look to me like it loose in your hands." He had an eye on his pickup, asleep on its wheels with his office-furniture dozing in the rear.

{I can discorp it right out of existence,} her symb said. {If there isn't too much at a time.}

"Into space?" Desi asked.

{Into bare nuclei. I don't ever want to see it again.}

"Neither do we. It's okay," Desi told him, "we'll fix it. My partner's tired of saving my butt."

"Already?" Jones said sourly. "She isn't much of a partner, I've been doing it geological eras and still haven't quit. I'm not sure why," he added.

"Natural imbecility?" Desi suggested.

That's **SATISFACTORY**. **I** approve both ***space*** and ***nuclei***. Would **YOUR PARTNER!** like ***help*?**

Bright sudden blink.

The sample evaporated, taking a layer of Desi's skin with it. She yelped. "Watch out, we've nine more to go. I could need my hands in future."

{We prefer safety. I'll repair you later.}

"Thanks, I'll remember that."

**It's interesting. We're noting the principles, we can use them. Without the side-effects.**

"That's a relief."

"*Zooo—eee—eee—oooo—uuu—uum.*"

"What's that?" Jones said.

"Don't listen, I think it's legal. We figured a carrier-wave."

"So do I. Who wants to speak to you?"

"Half the world's lawyers? Pass me a bottle."

He looked around, worried, but gave her the next. She voided more dust into her hand.

**Nasty but clever. We're filing the blueprints, First thinks we could use them for our own breeding-stock.**

"I hope you're taking care."

**WE!** are being most ***careful***.

"Well, keep your brains clean, I wouldn't like to see you turn gray and melt."

**It's okay, we're trying out mutations. When we've something that works, we'll use it ourselves on our continental shelf. The cellulose-transfer mechanism's nice, we think it would elevate the quality of our slime-molds.**

**WE!** have no ***intention*** of putting **OURSELVES!** at risk. **WE!** thank **YOU** for **YOUR *concern***. **WE!** are sorry **WE!** have so little ***experience*** of ***emotional* *states*.**

"I'm not sure Des is the best model," Jones said. "Her interpretations are rather individual."

**Sorry, we only wanted to help. We practice new knowledge where we can. Our examination of the samples is finished.**

"Great, Little Blink. What you come up with?" {They're alien, you meathead,} she added silently. {Trying to understand how we think. They're busting a gut here.}

{You weren't in a closed dimension ten feet across.}

{I'm starting to appreciate Blinky's instincts.}

Jones rubbed his shoulder. "Damn it, Des, my arthritis is killing me and I'm deaf as a post. You've regressed to sixteen. I haven't."

"I did? Pass me a mirror, I want green hair. Solved the mutation problem, Blink?"

**I** apologize for the ***closed* *dimension*, I** believe **I** was what **YOU** would describe as ***afraid*.**

"Buttdimple," Desi said. "You forgot she was a telepath again."

Jones flushed under the scraggly beard. "Don't mind me. We want any ideas you have for dealing with rot. If it can be dealt with, without an arc to create big genetic transformations. We need a really big change, this disease is planetary."

**I** do not think **I** can ***describe* OUR! *solution*** to **YOU.** But **WE!** will ***demonstrate*. WE!** have ***sounded* YOU** and **WE! *agree*** that **ED** is best ***suited*** to **OUR! *needs*.**

Ed looked unhappy. Desi nodded. "My choice too. He has a lot of power."

That is **OUR! *conclusion***. But **WE!** think **WE!** will have to work ***quickly*. HE** is due ***shortly*** for another ***change*.** **WE!** must use **HIS** powers ***while* HE** has **THEM.**

**We need Jonesy too. Ed can't do the change alone, not in the quantities you need. The whole planet has to be cleaned out fast, or what's left will re-infect the new bits.**

What **WE!** need is a ***chain***. A generalized ***effort*** all over the surface. **THEOTOKOPOLIS!** has the ***telepathic*** ability to ***sustain*** the ***joining!***, if **HE** can be fully ***awakened***.

Desi choked. ''*Who?*''

Jones reddened. ''Jones,'' he said tightly. ''Just *Jones*. Did I ever call you Blinky?''

Is something ***wrong*** with **BLINKY!?**

**No. It's our name. Jonesy's fine.**

The red under the beard brightened. ''Jonesy'll do.''

Then there is no ***problem***. **WE!** are ***sorry*** **WE!** ***upset*** **YOU. WE!** shall ***avoid*** **IT** ***in*** ***future***.

**But would you concentrate? We need your symb, and it's asleep.**

''That explains a lot,'' Desi said. ''On your feet, Theo.''

''*Jones*.''

''I was talking to your partner. If he gonna doze off when we need him, I'll learn to say all of it.''

Groan. {Haven't you stopped hurting?} his symb asked blurrily. {I was passing time until things improved.}

''They won't without you,'' Desi snarled. ''How's your TP capacity? Ed's due to change and we need help.''

The air crackled. {Testing.}

''I think I better go back check my place out,'' Ed said nervously. ''I'd like to help, but I aint the hero type. That trip to the Pole gave me stomach-cramps.''

''It gave us all stomach-cramps. All you have to do is what you did already, making dents in the fence. Blinky's working on it, you only need to stay around. If we can wake Theo.''

{I'm awake. And I'm not aware I'm a different person from my host.}

''You mean you're both useless.''

''We both hurt,'' Jones said.

''I've no skin on my hands and less on my feet. Symb's been too busy to fix it.'' A small inner guilt-reflex. Her bloody palms skinned over. ''How far can you reach?''

Stretched silence. {Quite a long way. Not out of the dimension yet, but into the city. And beyond. There are a lot of minds here.}

''Blinky needs a chain. Can you set one up for her?''

{To do what?}

Just ***act*** as a ***channel!***. **WE!** can give **ED** the ***pri-***

**mal!* *power!*** to ***transform***, but **HE** cannot ***direct!*** it **ALONE!**. There are ***many!* *minds!*** like **HIS** among **HIS PEOPLE!**, and **THEY** must **ALL!** do as **HE** does. **WE!!** can do the ***genetic!* *conversion!* TOGETHER!!**. In that way the ***rot*** can be ***mutated!*** into some ***harmless* *organism* *rapidly!*** enough to ***avoid* *reproduction***!*. Otherwise **WE!! *will*** face ***reinfection!*.**

"Blinky, you went back to hiccing."

**My First is excited at the idea of so many minds existing at once. There are only two of us. We're going to enjoy exploring, there's so much to find out. But we're anxious to get this done. We'll feel more correct when it's over.**

**WE!!** are ***conscious!*** of **OUR!! *isolation!*. WE!!** want to share **YOUR *vision!*** and ***feelings!*. WE!!** want to ***learn!***. If **WE!!** can help **YOU** now, **WE!!** shall feel ***part!*** of the ***universe!* OUTSIDE!!.**

**We want to belong**.

"You do that already. You guys ready? Ed?"

He looked at his feet. "I guess. If I have to."

**HE *should*** put **HIS *hands* *together!*** as **YOU** did, and ***open!* HIS *consciousness!*. I** am afraid **WE!!** cannot ***foretell!*** how **IT** may ***feel!*,** because **WE!! OURSELVES!!** have never tried anything like this ***before*. WE!!** will ***try*** not to ***cause* HIM *pain!*. WE!!** are sorry **WE!!** cannot be more ***definite*.**

"Great," Jones said. "Do I get the same guarantee?"

**We're really doing our best**.

"You'd rather turn into porridge?" Desi asked.

"You know I love suffering for your sake, Des, it's my masochistic side. Can I scream while I do it?"

"Can I stop you?" she asked, inspecting half-skinned palms. "Let's go."

A blurred ghost in repetitive striped pants half-materialized at her shoulder, slowly waving a muzzy paper. It dragged out a voice like frozen molasses.

"*I—i—i—i—i—f—f—f—f Ai—I—I—I—I m—m—m—m—i—i—i—i—gh—gh . . .*"

"**GO AWAY!**" Desi yelled, throwing a soda-bottle through its shirtfront. It blenched and winked out. "Shithouse thunderwater! Let's *start.*"

"Preferably soon," Jones said palely. "Before Theo passes out again from terror."

Ed cupped shaking hands and Jones shut his eyes. Desi put an arm around each and gazed at nothing, concentrating on building a link between them.

**Good. We're ready.**

A spark bloomed between Ed's palms, and flowered. Its light intensified until it burst through his fingers. His hand-bones were shadowed in brief X-ray, then the bright point flared out like a searchlight and blanked the park. Desi found trees written on her retinas in Japanese shadow. Jones was rigid, Ed's shoulders like stone. Her muscles tightened and everything dissolved in searing whiteness.

An unseen substance was forming in the cup, shaped from Ed's skin and flesh, a weightless mote that grew and grew. It overflowed and poured between his fingers, a change-gene tailored to mesh with plague-stuff. It rose on the wind and blew away. The currents carried it. Rising tendrils twined into the jetstream and circled the planet.

Jones stretched his mind and found others, shook them awake and pulled them with him. They merged and spread in a widening web that became a network. Ed, carried along on the beam, changed all he touched and gave them himself and his power with him. The light multiplied.

Metamorphic power grew between them, held together through Desi's linking hands, built a grid across latitudes and longitudes, filled in the gaps with genetic alteration and burst outward.

The atmosphere boiled with enormous mutation. The spill-over expanded, ran around the narrow curve of the bubble and pushed against its limits. The new patterns saturated the planet with transformation and reforged nuclei sifted down as plain jungle dirt.

Plague-colonies slumped, dried out and blew away. Old vegetation firmed back to solidity and new green shaped tentative mutations that were only vegetable. The polar ice melted in the wave of shaping warmth, gave up its black and instantly refroze into new crystal. The wind-patterns stumbled, paused and found old shapes again, and the crystal drifted over with snow. A few flakes fell on Desi's upturned face and she didn't notice.

The plague died and its scars healed over. It had taken, in realtime, maybe ninety seconds.

People wakened, turned over and wondered what they'd been dreaming. Others stopped in the middle of their work, wondered what had hit them, had a vague idea it was good and forgot it.

Everyone's skin itched with fallout and a thin layer of dust lay over the furniture. The population dusted and scratched and cursed do-gooders, since somebody must be to blame for this mess.

The fire in Ed's hands died. The bubble strained its compressed space, swollen with power, and began to expand. Life went back to normal and chaos took over again, as usual.

A pale invisible blink.

Ed slumped. Desi grabbed his collar as he fell. Jones sprawled with bench-slats digging in his back. The pickup choked on a sob in its radiator. Desi hauled on Ed, propped him upright and let go of both of them. She peered at her hands, and saw fading afterimages around her fingers. "Has it gone?"

Yes. **WE! *think*** so.

**Cancel that, we're sure. Every spore's now working for a living. You guys are clean.**

"Thanks," she said. "Nice show, good as a carnival and twice as useful. We don't know how to thank you. You any good at wakening the dead?"

Desi lay draped against the bench-back, practicing tan-levels without a mirror. She grew scarlet hair, reconsidered and thought it buttercup. It didn't suit her.

Ed beside her was flowering, slowly, quietly and in a small way. His energy levels were low. Jones slumped in his sweater, which was sweaty.

"*Zee—ouououou—ow,*" said the air.

Jones jerked and sat up. "What *is* that?"

Desi checked. "Still a carrier-wave," she said absently, looking him over. "Sounds like the same one. I guess I've seen worse. I'm not sure the beard goes with college-boy, too many overtones of Mrs. McGinty."

"Who?"

"I forget the details, but she owned some sinister prehistoric animal."

Jones examined the lilywhite pads of his hands and began making melanin. The beard waggled, and he absorbed it. "Didn't expect to end changed too, must be the spare power. Ed sure had plenty. How old do I look? That beard felt youthful."

"Exactly my thought. Maybe nineteen."

"Jeez. No-one takes you seriously at nineteen unless you're a hacker or a rockstar. Tell me when it looks right."

"Don't think you got the power yet," Desi opined. "Chain-teeping has to take it out of you."

"Thought I'd died. I'm used to touching mass minds, but I don't usually have to thread them. Learned a lot I didn't want to know. Hope I've forgotten it in the transition." He brightened. "Almost all. This the best I can do. What do you think?"

She weighed it. "Callow, but tasty. I liked you dark."

He concentrated some more and attained mid-brown. "That's it. I need food, my symb's in rebellion. How's Ed? I felt as if he'd maybe burned to a crisp."

The golden Hercules on the other side of her groaned, blew dust off his muscles and sat.

"Jeezle. Felt as if I'd maybe burned to a crisp."

"He made a better regrowth job than you did," Desi remarked. "Wouldn't mind a hotdog myself. We got any?"

"That's because I'm teeped out," Jones complained. "My changes depend on what I've strength for. His symb varies at random. There was a hotdog stand around the corner, unless it's something else now. Shall I go look?"

She stretched. "Go ahead. I need sustenance."

He stopped halfway up. "This place is empty."

"Looks crammed to me. Ed's gear, and yards of green stuff."

"I mean telepathically. We lost the Blinkies?"

"Went right out with the fireworks. I bet they're whacked."

Jones was stricken. "You don't think they—?"

"No, I don't. A planetary brain doesn't frizzle away just because it did a couple of minutes' hard broadcasting. This place is so small Blink couldn't fit her thoughts in, that's why she needed other people. Wouldn't worry about Junior, either, that sounds like a lusty baby. They're probably having a party."

"How do planetary brains have parties?"

"Medium-sized meditation on the state of the multiverse? Planning genetic variations in their slime-molds? They aint wearing funny hats and eating popcorn. I, on the other hand, wouldn't mind."

"*Skreee-ou-ooow,*" the air said decidedly. It modulated up and down several times and formed a holo-scientist three feet tall in matching white coat. Desi scowled at it.

"Go away. You're in the wrong era, you're the wrong size and this is definitely the wrong time."

The holo-scientist shimmered, pulsated and came back up nearer two meters. He was an obvious composite, with handsome tanned generic face and a Hermes Medical Center logo on his pocket. "*Miz Smeett.*"

"Present, though not willingly."

"*And Mr. Jones.*"

"Ditto."

"*Plus, I understand, a dependent sentient mechanism somewhere in orbit.*"

"You'll have to ask her about that, I think she made a declaration of independence. At any rate, she is having a SPASM. If it goes on I'll have to subdue her."

"You could set her free," the nineteen-year-old Jones suggested.

"You must be kidding. What's a sentient spaceship gonna do, wandering around the cosmos with no-one to nag? She's liable to turn pirate and kidnap guys to fall in love with. Wouldn't be moral. I am responsible for *Windy,* and I am gonna keep her occupied, before she goes crazy and starts eating people."

"*I'm glad you feel responsibility for something, Miz Smeett,*" the composite said coldly. "*Hermes is extremely concerned. We suspect you of being in contact with extracontinual intelligences.*"

"No!" Desi exclaimed, horrified.

"*Your levity has obliged us to remonstrate before. We distinctly detected an energy-surge from this dimension that wasn't explicable from local resources.*"

"You did?" she asked with admiration. "What detectives you guys would make! Don't suppose you detected the fungoid plague that was eating the citizens?"

The composite pinked. *"We'd begun to suspect untoward biological activity, but the local timescale's badly out of sync and it's cost some effort to localize the problem. You may have noticed it took us several seconds to mesh with you now . . ."*

"Whose fault was that?" Desi asked indignantly. "You made this bubble so small it had noplace to expand to. You might have metered it."

*"We did. But the timescale difference . . ."*

"Was a misdemeanor," she finished. "Or wouldn't you have minded if some rogue biological wiped your little problems right off the map?"

The composite pinked more deeply. *"That's a scandalous allegation."*

"The problem with scandalous allegations is they tend to be true."

They glared at each other.

*"In any case,"* he concluded, *"this dimension's currently in a state of rapid expansion for which we aren't responsible, but we suspect you are."*

"That would be Blink," Desi agreed. "She was cramped here. Probably means to come back later to check on the genetics of her slime-molds. Unlike you, she's thorough."

*"That's what I mean,"* the composite said warmly. *"Completely irresponsible. This continuum was rigorously compressed and monitored. Now we've lost control."*

"Well, that gives it a chance of returning to normal."

*"The timescale's narrowing,"* the composite admitted. *"It made contact easier. But really, Miz Smeett."* His tone became pleading. *"As an experienced medical operator, you must know the dangers of random change. This bubble exists to protect our populations. Your wild travels aren't authorized."*

"Authorize them," Desi suggested. "Then I'll be regular and you won't have to worry."

*"You're missing the point. We can't let people like you wander at will, inflicting Heaven knows what damage. It's a bad example."* He collected himself. *"We can't license your*

*departure from this dimension until we're satisfied you're carrying no infection in yourself or your possessions, and your activities elsewhere have had no ill consequences.*''

''But this is where we're likeliest to be infected,'' Jones protested. ''The locals can't control their genetics and they let off spores everywhere. Sooner or later we're bound to catch some.''

A shadow of satisfaction passed over the composite face. ''*We regret the inconvenience, but that's very true. It's a major reason for you to stay. We want to be safe.*''

Jones had reddened. ''Listen a fricky minute. I'm a member of the Press in good standing . . .''

''*So I understand,*'' the composite said politely. ''*And I'm sure you'll find plenty to occupy you here. Goodbye, Mr. Jones, Miz Smeett. Your cases will be reviewed in due time, when we've had the opportunity to consider them.*''

He faded gracefully away.

Jones glared. ''Occupy me! I'm an international network personality. They can't do this.''

''They seem to be trying,'' Desi said. Jones eyed her uneasily.

''The frick. Theo and I need to get together.''

{You don't need to label me,} his symb repeated patiently. {You and I are the same.}

''After how it's been lately, I'm waiting to be sure. Can they really keep us?''

''Dunno,'' Desi said, admiring the sky. ''I think they see it as discipline. Question being your attitude to same. I'm gonna have to discuss it with *Windy*. What about that hotdog? And maybe I ought to check on Ed.''

The car-dealer shook his head muzzily. ''Jeez, I'm snorkeled. If you buying dogs get me three, willya? And a coupla sodas. Changing shape always takes it outta me. Why we sitting in the park? Musta been one helluva party.''

''Tell you later,'' Desi said. ''Let's eat.''

''I've been waiting,'' *Windrunner* complained. ''Your friend stopped by.''

''Which one?''

They'd discorped up, the first major discorporation since their symbs reached adulthood, and they were out of breath.

They'd done it on hamburgers and coffee instead of hotdogs and soda since the cart had transformed, so they'd caloric surpluses and a nervous twitch each.

Ed had paid, insisting he owed them. He was vague about why but stuck on the conviction it was a hell of a party. He looked more like Adonis every minute and his newly blue pickup followed him like a puppy.

Desi and Jones looked fresh out of highschool, badly blown and unfitted to their clothes. Desi's had melted completely in the jungle so Jones's sweaty sweater came down to her thighs. His jeans were slipping off his hipbones. They sat on the deckplates, gasping. Wide spaces behind them gave generous glimpses of black-and-gold plumbing where the bulkheads had been.

"You look disgraceful," *Windrunner* said severely. "It was the little one, Other Blinky. He gave me directions."

"Little Blinky's a she, like her mama. Where to?"

"Out. They're both neuter, I was being polite."

"Of course they are. Be even politer and do it my way. Out where?"

"Just *out*. It—he—*she* showed me how to go *that* way. And suggested we go before this cosmos gets bigger, it's expanding fast toward infinity."

"That's big. Okay, let's avoid it. Power."

"I've been warming for three-quarters of an hour while you ate like pigs. *I* refuel faster."

"You weren't as low as we were," Desi said. She groaned over to the couch. "Heel, boy. And strap in, we need *big* power. *Windy,* have you a hole on your charts? Neutron star, maybe? A nice fast spinner?"

"No. I have directions *that* way. I think if I once got the habit we might be able to leave out the painful maneuvers you're so fond of and change dimensions quietly. I'd like that. My new symb's stronger than the last, I inherited good genes. Trust me."

"Been trusting a lot of people lately, not always wisely. Can be a bad habit. And stop smirking, them genes could be mine. Or even yours. Let's try. Heading *that* way."

Jones slumped, hauled on his jeans' band, and rubbed a hand across a wet forehead. "Can we try sleep one of these days? As an experiment?"

"Sure. Just not right now."

"You've said that every day for a week."

"Should be grateful we ate."

*Windrunner* was moving, acceleration thrusting them into the cushions. The planet receded, a clear bright marble on widening black, shrinking as if it was falling in the wrong end of a telescope. Her main drive caught and the engine-note swelled. The stubs of her bulkheads quivered.

"Hold on," she gasped.

A frantic pink face above a white labcoat came into reality in the middle of the holotank, waving its arms like a disordered traffic-cop.

*"Miz Smeett, you can't do this. You don't have clearance . . ."*

"Surprise me," Desi said. "Hit speed, *Windy*, I don't like it here."

"Neither do I," Jones squeezed from stretched lips.

The holotank shook itself and dislodged the composite, which vanished in a smear of pinkish fog.

"Good work, babe," Desi said with appreciation. But *Windrunner* was too busy to answer.

The drive thundered out of hearing to a persistent shudder of the floorplates and the airducts sucked in a sobbing breath. Whiteness gathered like smoke in the plates, obscuring the stars, an out-of-focus haze sequined with sparks.

Their bellies hollowed and the engine-note took a sidestep as if the ship had stumbled on a hole in the paving. An iris of darkness opened in the forward plate, small as the pupil of an eye.

*Windrunner* threw herself at it, ducts heaving. Emptiness tugged their bellies and everything loose rose into the air as gravity reversed. Then her gyros kicked in and they slammed back heavily to their seats. The plates showed spinning blackness.

The cabin distorted and they went out like a candle, drawn down the throat of a funnel of stars.

# TEN

# Mudbath

⌘

TP–TV

*the station of the multiverse*

* FLASH * FLASH * FLASH * FLASH* FLASH * FLASH * FLASH *

* THE LATEST BULLETIN FROM OUR UTTERMOST OUTSTATION *

* NEWS OF THE HOUR *

* BROUGHT TO YOU BY OUR OWN MAN OUT THERE *

* REMEMBER—TP-TV FOR ALL THE NEWS YOU NEED TO KNOW *

* HEAR THIS * HEAR THIS * HEAR THIS * HEAR THIS *

* A SPECIAL MESSAGE FROM OUR CORRESPONDENT, JONESY: *

❖

[*Dick's face is grim, a granite shine on his head-wide forehead, scalp-lock braided into a loop. His square jaw squares again to a cube:*]

This station prides itself on the quality of its news, bringing you the truth without fear or favor, unhindered by storm nor tempest nor dark of night, independent of all forms of governmental control. And today with sadness we find ourselves obliged to invoke our charter.

Over the eons we've loved and trusted our medical foundation, the Hermes Federal Center. But sometimes even those you love and trust can't be relied upon, and when that happens it becomes the duty of the honest citizen to denounce them openly and to seek, by all honest means, to bring them back to a sense of their public duty.

[*Roadhouse in the jungle. The vegetation writhes and the yellow brick road leading west heaves suddenly and turns to candy. Several Munchkins march east, singing. The road takes a bend and they find themselves walking back the way they came. They vanish around the turn and the singing gargles once and stops. The roadhouse shudders in a rain of plastic petals.*

*Interior. Chairs and tables in a gamesome ballet, with teapot-shaped people trying to make merry. The tableau freezes. The furniture crowds into a corner. A nine-foot person with cook's apron around an endless spine staggers from the rear and pitches over the bar, which turns to oatmeal. So does the cook. So does everyone. Skulls roll, grinning.*

*A slanted version of Windrunner's controlroom, where Desi, aged twelve and wearing bobbysox, sits demurely between missing bulkheads. She manages the controls from a piano-stool. A menacing scientist corps out in the holotank, up to the waist in five stars and a solar-system. He waves his fists.*]

SCIENTIST, SHOUTING : Miz Smeett! You're not authorized to leave this dimension!

*[He gestures widely, revealing a HERMES badge on his pocket. He rounds on Dick Tracy, who tries to look meek on the co-pilot's bar-stool:*]

SCIENTIST: Mr. Jones. You're condemned to stay too.

DICK TRACY (AS JONES): But we're bound to get infected, in spite of Miz Smeett's skill.

SCIENTIST, SIMPERING: That's why we want you here.

JONES: But I'm a member of the international Press.

SCIENTIST, POMPOUS: I'm above journalistic pretensions. The public interest isn't my business. I'm sure you'll find plenty to occupy you here.

DESI, AGED TWELVE (SLOWLY AND SADLY—IT'S AN INTERVIEW): I'm a Hermes agent, and I've served and respected them. But I'd be failing my civic responsibility if I didn't speak out.

Hermes used secret data on the multiverse to set up an experimental bubble universe, and our own mutated castoffs were dumped there as guinea pigs. Only, their science was defective, and the bubble came out too small. The difference in timescale caused by that badly calculated size-ratio was too great for the bubble to be properly monitored, and a natural disaster almost wiped out its population before Hermes noticed.

There's been careless construction and a defective followup, and now they'd like to see the whole unethical experiment buried. Their failure almost caused the deaths of millions, and they're in hiding. Instead of facing up to responsibility, they're trying a whitewash by imprisoning anyone who knows the truth. And that means trying to muzzle the Press . . .

DESI, IN THE BACKGROUND, THREE CENTURIES OLDER: Hey! Who the *beep*! said you could drag me into this? It's your *beep*! problem. I can settle my own *beep*! differences with the *beep*! agency if you'll just mind your own *beep*! business. All you *beep*! teeps are the same, no *beep*! consideration for other people. And what the *beep*! did you put on my feet? I've a *beep*! good mind to sue you for every *beep*! cent you've got. *Beep*! *Beep*! *Beep*!

[*The network switches hastily back to Dick Tracy, who looks as if he's about to cry:*]

This network sees itself as a responsible public service, here to inform you, fully and fearlessly, of all the news, no matter what it is, where it breaks or who may be implicated. We'll keep you up to date with all the developments in this scandalous case, as and how they happen. Thank you.

DESI, OFF: That'll be the day.

[*Dick Tracy (he sounds desperate):*]

And now, back to our regular coverage of Big Season Bagball, where your topranking slugger Mighty Mook Bigget's facing the baggy at the top of the ninety-third.

[*The holo fades on Mighty Mook in the act of winding up.*]

"Mightn't have minded seeing that," Desi grumbled. "Shithead. Can't you get anything right?" Her real voice was an ululating moan. She winced and rubbed her ear.

"Bobbysox were the network's idea," Jones piped. "I can't control their choice of visuals."

"Then why pretend the fricky broadcast's yours?"

"I give them the material . . ."

"You could lovin control it. Thought of renegotiating your contract, or is that too intelligent?"

*Windrunner* rushed through a tunnel of unlight that speeded and slowed. The cabin lightplates went up and down with it. Her breathing through the airducts was panicky. The outer plates were dark. Jones felt for Desi's hand.

"Dimplebutt," she brayed, sliding her molecules free and grabbing the drive-control.

The black throat slackened and light showed ahead. *Windrunner* rushed at it. It opened to a funnel, widening mists growing milky, freckled with sparkle. The plates blanked. She blasted out into normal space and their superposed hands came apart with a snap.

"Ow," Desi said, flexing her fingers. "Did I say you were a buttdimple?"

"Yes. This time you're too young for your vocabulary, you haven't grown into good taste."

"You mind your lovin vocabulary and I'll mind mine."

"I'm going to bed."

"Not until *Windy*'s nanned back the bulkheads. We could have breakfast, the toaster's working." She smiled like a watermelon. "Hermes gonna sue your ass from here to eternity."

"It was all true."

"That's why they gonna sue you."

"We'll settle out of court, we always do. It's a press-freedom issue, the network won't let go."

"Hope they don't let go of *you. Windy*, a system."

"Coming up in front of you."

"Jeezle," Desi said. "What the frick's *that*?"

The planet caught the light as a dimensionless flick. It swelled quickly to a silver teardrop and finally a globe that reflected sunlight so strongly it burned in the plates, even fully polarized. Desi manifested Ray-Bans and looked at it through them.

"Forcefield," *Windrunner* said. "Total."

"I can see that. Destructive?"

"Probably."

"They'd hardly have it there if it wasn't," Jones said. Desi glared. *Windrunner* shivered.

"Can you run it?"

Nervous pause. "I don't know. I can try."

"With your brave new symb."

"Didn't say I'd turned into Hercules," *Windrunner* said sulkily. "I've done so many dumb things lately, I suppose I can do another."

"Fine. Full speed on auxiliaries."

*Windrunner* pointed her nose-assembly at the mirror.

"Never seen anything like it," Desi said. "Complete reflectivity. Planetwide. You want to guess what kind of power it takes?"

"Um. Nothing to say it isn't mechanical."

"True. Thoughts on the mechanics? A controlled black hole the size of a fire-truck? Plus four more the same to provide power to control the first, plus . . . You don't think it might possibly be biological?"

"Could be nothing there at all but a little singularity."

"With artificial forcefield, growing like a daisy."

"I said physics wasn't my thing."

"Surprise me. Stuff like you proposing, universe is full of em. Not."

"What stuff?"

"Fascinating mysteries. That sucker's biological. It's a TP phenomenon. You know that really."

"Hoped I was wrong. I'd say it must also be advanced TK," Jones mumbled. "Sure as hell don't like it."

*Windrunner* abruptly sat on her tail and the batteries whined in complaint. "I won't get through there. It's impermeable to matter."

"Advanced TK," Jones confirmed gloomily.

"You sure?" Desi asked.

"My sensors are," *Windrunner* said.

"Shit."

"On the other hand . . ." *Windrunner* gathered herself and increased acceleration. Her big engines growled and the glittering sphere swelled suddenly. "Prepare to discorporate."

"What?" Jones yelped.

"She said 'discorporate'. Stand by your butt."

"She means 'warp'."

"No, she doesn't. She knows what 'warp' means, we do it all the time. She has an idea in her cute little meatlocker."

"Spaceships don't discorporate, their mass is too great for their symb's capacities. She can integrate her lighter at a pinch, and maybe her captain. Major discorporation's human."

"She has human genes, boy. Yours."

"The risk's unacceptable . . ."

"Who's the lovin captain?" {Can we cope?} she added silently to her symb.

{Don't ask. Maybe you'd better hold his hand, I'm busting a gut keeping your molecules together. Or hug him, that would put you closer.}

{What a sense of humor, your ma never giggled.} "Looks like we're taking it," she said aloud. "Okay, *Windy*, go."

*Windrunner* sucked her flanks in and a hot draft whooshed through her airducts. The surface rushed at them, a sky-sized mirror. A swelling blue speck was *Windrunner,* rushing in from vacuum with stars behind her. The reflection threw their shadow back at them.

"Discorporation."

They stuck for a moment, sphere and void exactly balanced, then the world went out in a silver splash and came back with a jolt, as if they'd dropped in an airpocket. The engines faltered, spat and caught their rhythm.

They were running into orbit above a flawless pink travertine marble, its spheroid surface veined white. A silver veil hung behind, neatly pricked with symmetrical stars in a regular pattern that could have been painted. This toy world's sunlight was diffused from everywhere, as even as a lightbulb.

"Jieronymus," Desi said.

"What is it?"

"A construct. And a damn nasty one, there's no way to tell when you're leaving whether or not you're headed into the sun."

"Does it have one?"

"Must have, light comes from somewhere. And the temp's about right for an E-type planet in near-Earth orbit."

"I'll know," *Windrunner* said huskily. "I've a working gravometer."

"Here?"

"Nothing works here, I register planet. I left a communicating probe outside. We have a link."

"Through the veil?"

She considered. "It could be illusion, the readings are irregular. But I'll reincorp it when I leave."

"If it isn't occulted," Desi said sourly. "Was a good idea, anyway. Who the hell's *doing* this?"

"That's the whole question," Jones said. "What do you bet you mean to find out?"

Desi grinned. "Not a cent. You want the lighter, or shall we just discorp into whatever?"

"Is that question serious?"

The controlroom emptied.

"Thank you, *Windy*," *Windrunner* muttered. "You just did what no ship ever did before, and it worked. Congratulations. Oh, thank you, don't mention it, I'm too modest to care, I didn't strain myself very badly. I'm sure we have a great future together. Think nothing of it, I love working with you, too."

She set herself to making great quantities of toast and

shooting it around the cabin while her nano-machines swarmed, spinning new bulkheads.

Desi recorped and levitated briefly to reconnoiter at fifty thousand feet, and again just far enough up to land without jarring her ankles. The sphere was pink marble from high up, the quartz glitter hurt her eyes halfway and it was still pink marble when she hit the ground. At ground-level it was also lumpy. Not at random, but in carefully chosen blocks and rectangular cutouts, like a solid-state puzzle that didn't quite fit. The silver outer glimmer was hazed blue with atmosphere but it was still mind-straining, even in Ray-Bans.

Someone was using a nearby precisely rectangular pit as a planter, to grow blue sugar hair that glistened. The air was hot and still, reflected light baking up from the ground, but the long silken strands waved gracefully. Desi regarded them with dislike.

"Blue sugar," she said to Jones, who'd finally located out at her side.

"Looks that way."

"Wiggles."

"Too many nans in the world," he said. He licked a finger, held it up and watched his spit dry. "Let's walk."

"If you insist. I'm getting a foot fetish, feet drive me crazy. That sugar aint nanoed, it don't smell right."

"But it wiggles. I want to walk on this surface."

"Watch your ankles. It all looks the same, you could fall down a hole before you saw it."

"That's what interests me."

Desi looked at him sidewise and started to hike, taking a loop around the sugar garden. The long blue hanks ignored her. They went on playing with themselves peaceably.

The odd thing about the terrain was they didn't break an ankle. The uneasy perspective of planes and cutouts dissolved before them and reformed behind them. The pavement underfoot stayed smooth, somehow never caught in the act. A square hole in front like the top of an elevator shaft would be plain pink marble when they got to it but there would be another hole behind, rectangular. The landscape went on being an ill-fitting three-dimensional puzzle. Only the eye-blistering light didn't change.

Desi stopped. "I'm missing something."

Jones stopped too. "It's an illusion," he said tiredly. "Want to use my eyes? I'm missing a lot, but I'm still a pro and my symb's grown up stronger."

Desi blanked her sight and got a view of the planet from fifty miles up. It stood on her retinas as an illuminated pool-ball, cut from pole to pole by a geometrical boundary. The western half was pink marble. The east was green-black with a soft wet sheen, lightly frosted.

"Is the black stuff mud?"

"I'd say so. Decided to land there. Wanted to look."

"And?"

"I landed here instead. And believe it or not, I've discorped before. I recall how it's done."

"I didn't see a black side at all. Just plain pink."

"It's illusion," he repeated. "Don't know if the mud's real but we should have seen it from orbit, it covers half the planet. Does what's under your feet feel like marble?"

"Yes, frankly. Nasty, shiny and very pink. But it keeps shifting when you aint looking."

Another planter filled with pale-green sugar had developed to their left and she looked at it evilly. The slinky hanks plaited around each other and fell silkily apart. Then they started again, widdershins. She scratched reflexively. "Telekinesis?"

"I think just illusion. The outer field could be telekinetic, since *Windy* thinks matter won't pass. This is illusion. I suspect we're standing on a grassplot, or something like it. Texture changed a few steps back. But I teep better than you. Try feeling, now you know."

Desi bent, eyes on him, and ran her fingers over the pavement. Hot, polished, fine-grained marble.

{I sense something too,} her symb said. {Don't be foxed by appearance. Use his mind.}

She ran her hands over it again, filtering heat and smoothness, the all-present pink. The slick surface faltered. She saw quartz but her fingers were deep in damp velvet. A second later it was back to marble. But Desi's eyes were closed. She rubbed her fingers.

They were wet. The material she'd touched was cool vegetation and a chlorophyll smell itched her nose. A shadow fell.

She opened her eyes on night, and recorped the Ray-Bans. The silver sky with its too-even stars had gone and the square was cloaked in midnight darkness. It looked square. They were in the middle, on the grassplot around a fountain that bubbled water scented with rosepetals. The walk and arcading that enclosed it were marble still, but black and shiny, with white lanterns slung between the pillars. Forms moved below, twining gracefully in careful disordered patterns. They glittered.

"Pretty," Desi said. "You any theories on how we arrived in an enclosed arcade without walking through walls?"

"We walked through walls."

She grunted. "Thought so too. Just checking."

"I mean, there are streets leading here. Remember how the pavement changed? Maybe it was we who shifted direction. So as to avoid solid structures."

"But an illusion, whatever."

"Yes."

"Still is. They kept marble, and rose-pink and white. They admitted grass and water cause you caught em at it."

Jones looked cautious. "The people are real. Why don't we talk to them?"

"Why don't they talk to us?" Desi countered. "We just appeared large as life in the middle of their grassplot."

"They knew we were here. They must have."

"And now they're waiting, see what the mice gonna do. Cute."

"What do you want to do?"

"Break something."

"Typical."

"Not quite," Desi said. "I'm interested see if this scenery breaks. Or if it just change again. To something else. Philosophical question? Whether this onion really have a center."

"All onions have centers."

"I'm wondering about this one."

But the formal pattern of movement was what broke. The figures turned slowly, in a single movement, and drifted toward them.

Their glitter came from feathers, metals and sparkly gauzes. A bird face with crystal eyes looked at them blankly, the patterns on its sequined mask catching the light. A long down-edged robe trailed on the grass. A hooked owl beak was at its shoulder, shaped in pearl shell with sharp silvered tip.

The owl wore a coronet fringed with beryls over a silver hood. The crane next to it, also hooded, was prolonged skyward by a fluted velvet cap that funneled out in a froth of ostrich-plume. The crane spoke first, in a deep male voice.

''Welcome.''

Desi saw a long shoe among the gauzes, rolled at the toe, cutout, pointed, but for a human foot.

''However uninvited,'' the owl added, an amused contralto. ''We love to meet strangers.''

''Especially those clever enough to find us.''

They both raised pale hands to their masks. A small ripple of laughter stirred the crowd. Wild beasts, birds and demons jostled on the marble pavement. The woman's face appeared first, mask, hood and crown coming off in one piece. Her smile was warm, outlined in sparkle.

The taller man was still tall without the cap. His lips were painted a deep red that glowed in the dark, and edged with gilt, but his smile was masculine-attractive. They had identical hollow cheeks, high cheekbones and dark-shaded eyes, brother and sister, but his hair was frost and hers was shadow. They laughed together.

''I do hope you aren't upset,'' the woman said. ''It was rather a silly joke.''

''But only a joke,'' her twin said earnestly. ''You must forgive us.''

''You see, sometimes bad people come.''

''They cause problems. We have to be careful.''

''Nothing to concern you, though,'' she said, catching Jones's hand. Her long fingers, thrust from a sequined gauze sleeve, were so frail they were almost transparent, the nails echoing the rosy sparkle of her mouth. ''We're happy to see you.''

The crowd was unmasking all around them, smiling painted faces shining beneath.

''We must look foolish,'' the woman said, shaking out long dark hair. ''Dressed up like this. But it's Carnival, and we love celebrations.''

''Whenever we can,'' her brother harmonized. They talked as if they were singing, a practiced aria shaped to their voices. The man took Desi's elbow. ''We were just going to eat. Please have dinner with us.''

The crowd stood back for them, young faces appliquéed with gold and silver, hair picked out with jeweled decorations. Their silks whispered on the polished marble, black striated with white, that reflected hanging lamps.

The man's hand was warm and strong with very long fingers, frail as his sister's, ending in gilded nails. He steered Desi with easy assurance through the ballet of robes that plaited graciously among the columns. Some seemed to flow backward against the current until she turned, and found they were all headed the same way, into an arch among the arcading.

Groups merged and separated, smiling and whispering. Their hair was black and red and gold in the lamplight, platinum and chestnut, blue and green and white, streaked with glass and metal to make it sparkle. Carnival. But the colors changed if you didn't quite look at them. And their jewels shifted.

''What's the big problem needs this protection?'' she asked, raising her face. She had to tip her head. He was even taller than she remembered. His eyes laughed, glowing in the shadow.

''It needn't worry you. We'll manage to protect our guests. Are you hungry?''

The word brought a rush of juices to Desi's mouth with the memory of burned toast and glutinous sandwich. Her throat was full of cheap, bitter coffee. She swallowed. Rich food smells tickled her nose. She was starving.

Jones ahead was bending over the woman, whose fragile hand lay on his arm. If her brother was taller than Desi remembered then she was smaller, tiny, stretching on tiptoe to hear him. Her glowing mouth breathed sparkly vapor into his face. Her brother's breath glittered too, and the columns and arches they passed were outlined with a twinkling haze that drew and defined them.

Carnival. Desi glanced back and saw the crowd pass through the doorway without somehow ever falling back or drawing together, into a hall lined with tables. Every one breathed out bright vapor that lighted their way and marked their footsteps. The black marble shone for a second behind before the footprints faded.

Then all of them were in the hall, chattering like birds in a melded scatter of liquid notes, taking their places around a hollow square where cups and plates were laid out for a banquet. The man handed Desi to a carved chair. Invisible hands drew it from the table and pushed it in behind her knees. She jerked, startled, and looked at empty air. He laughed.

"There's nothing to be afraid of. Wouldn't you like to wear something prettier?"

Desi glanced down at her saggy camouflage. "I'll make do. Wouldn't like the whatever to evaporate."

"I wouldn't," he protested, the painted lips glowing. "It would be bad mannered."

He bent, an intent profile under icy hair, and ran his fingernail down the back of her hand. His body had a heady sexuality, powerful as musk, that shivered her like the instant water that came to her mouth when he mentioned food.

Somewhere in the depths her symb was whispering.

{What?}

{Speak to me aloud. They can hear thoughts.}

"Then he'll hear me talking," Desi said, but she spoke aloud, clearly, her head turned away. Her host bent courteously toward her.

"I beg your pardon?"

"I'm thirsty."

"Forgive me." He snapped his fingers and a jeweled flask rose by itself from the middle of the table and poured wine in her cup. She flinched but tasted it. Her camouflage overall had become a rainbow gauze ballgown sprinkled with beads, with or without her permission. The stuff in the cup was wine, good, aged and very expensive. Carnival. The single sip made her head spin. If she swallowed the whole mug she was going to be horribly drunk.

{Control yourself,} her symb whispered in her blood. The world readjusted and turned sober. {It's only water. Talk, but don't think hard. They're physically deaf. He only hears thoughts. You needn't believe in anything you don't want to.}

''He'll hear me thinking at you.''

{No, he won't. I'm holding him out, he hears prattle. They aren't shapechangers, they're something different. Our organizations don't work the same way, it's how he'll trap you. He doesn't know I'm here. Keep it that way.}

''You mean if we don't shift he won't know we can?''

{Exactly. They know you can discorp. That's a pity, because now they may be able to stop you. So long as they don't know you can change too, we've a way out.}

''You think we'll need one?''

{Don't you?}

Desi looked at Jones. His face was blindly bent to the lady, his lips parted, his eyes blank.

''Maybe. What are they?''

{Something else, something other. I can't see clearly, they're strong. It's all I can do to keep them out of your mind.}

''What about Jonesy?''

{Leave him. I don't like it, but I've no spare energy.}

''Can't his own symb help?''

{We've different powers since we altered. They're telepathic, we're metamorphic. I only reach them if they're close. My link's scrambled. The atmosphere's bad.}

''How about I yell?''

{He won't hear you. He and his woman are too close together, she owns him already. Don't let yours get you to bed or I may not be able to hold him off. I can't fight you, and if you get in too deep I may have to try.}

''Pity.'' Desi looked her partner over. ''He looks beddable.''

{He's not. And if you drink like a fish, fake drunk or he'll suspect, you're supposed to be drooling.}

''On water?'' Desi reeled a little. She let the gauze dress

slip off a shoulder. It was back to feeling like a camouflage overall, though she still saw gauze. "Should have thought of this myself, the perfect mix of elegance and comfort."

{What do you think *he* sees?}

"What?"

{I can't see too clearly, but I know it's repulsive.}

"Shit," Desi said. She reeled some more, and fell lightly on the sinewy shoulder. A shock of sexual electricity paralyzed her to her toes.

{Don't *touch* him, I said he's too strong for me to help if you let him get sexual.}

Desi wrestled with her breathing and tried to control her loins. It took mental muscle, and it hurt. Like tearing the barb of an arrow through her belly. She gulped more wine, and saw double.

{It's water,} her symb said, far away. She couldn't grasp what it meant, or who'd said it, through the mists in her brain. She'd never been so drunk in her life.

{WATER.}

She sucked air, fogged with sparkle. "Water," she said slurrily.

Her table partner bent solicitously over her, their lips almost touching. "Did you speak?"

Desi gave him a slushy smile. "I'm drunk," she said with difficulty. "Will you carry me home when I'm flat on my back?"

"It'll be a pleasure," he whispered, his caressing voice stabbing like a sharpened barb. "Carry you home and take care of you. Personal care. I'll enjoy it deeply."

His breath brushed her cheek, her sight blurred with sleek muscles and long dark eyes and her nostrils with his musky scent, as sexually potent as a mating-call straight into her estrogen. She breathed, drowning, leaning on the pain in her womb. She wanted him. Needed, had to have him. Would—she knew it suddenly as if it was written on the wall in lights—die on his prick as soon as he entered her. What had he said? Not what she'd thought.

"*Take care,*" a small voice whispered. Not for the first time, she realized. The wine-flask lifted to refill her cup. A hand held it, like mist, like glass. "*Oh, take care. He'll really enjoy eating you, you've so much energy.*"

Desi came back to ground with a slap. The chair under her wasn't velvet-cushioned wood but something else, with a slick, slidy feel and an odd shape, too high, made for the inhuman.

Which sat beside her. Beside and around. The table was filled with alien faces, unhuman limbs, too long and too slender. They were dressed in vague draperies that masked their light, the glitter and glow integral to their flesh, a shining-through they couldn't control no matter how they tried to disguise it.

The table was a fungoid slab rooted in dirt, shaped by their will, condemned to be a plane. The chairs were luminous fungoid lumps. The slanted eyes showed nothing but dark, alien malignity.

{*Sidhe,*} said her mind.

The Lordly Ones. The huge-eyed faces had a remote resemblance to the human—some common root back in the dark. Possibly rogue Changes who'd escaped Hermes, in the beginning. Hermes, which wasn't always wrong. Their own race now. Not shapechangers, something else.

Her partner, smooth and hard as a steel arrow—that same arrow that plowed her womb—still bent over her. His gleaming lips weren't smiling. Perhaps they'd never smiled. His musky sexuality shadowed the fringes of her mind and ran through her nerves but it was not-human, the attraction of endless, ancient power.

Jones was slumped by the woman's side and her mouth was a long flat curve, her delicate hand with its pearl nails lying along his flushed cheek. Her lips were rich with sensual triumph. Her neighbors, long mobile faces shaped on the same lines, a following echo, looked as intently at her as she did at him. Desi's back crawled with a knowledge of danger.

Jones, on the woman's shoulder, was withering. His thin face grew thinner and shriveled. The bones of his hands showed through crêpey skin. His shirt hung loose. He'd started nineteen, he looked ninety.

"We've got to stop them."

{How?}

Desi glanced desperately around. All around the hollowed square table alien faces watched, impassive. Her neighbor's pearl-tipped fingers tightened on his cup, ready to mold her breast. Suspecting, perhaps. She was taking too long to succumb, she should be unconscious too.

The call of his pheromones ran in her blood, emptying her will, defining her hollowness, stabbing her. And it might be worth it for the climax, the ecstasy . . .

The peal came from outside, high and sweet like silver trumpets. It sliced her brain, squeezed her inner ears, pressed painfully behind her eyeballs. It echoed agonisingly in the roots of her teeth. A flight of twisted bats coiled through the archway and swung over the table, shedding cobwebs, their sonar cries shivering the lamps. Broken crystal tinkled in the dishes and iced diners' shoulders. The light, for some reason, didn't alter.

The flying creatures' wrinkled gray hides and clawed wings were shriveled as moldy leaves, a nauseous liquid dripping from their snouts. They had the stink of old, buried death, the death of libraries. Spinning ghosts of parchment fell away from them, layers peeled from their decaying skins or just the echoes of their dry decomposition.

They voided liquid excreta from mouths, wombs, anuses, changing as they flew. Dried bloodied bandage defiled the dishes, turning food to rot. Their screams were the last breath of meaningless agonies, not yet dead. Their stench filled the hall, dimming the lights. It blanched the living sparkle of the throned nobility.

The creature beside her had stiffened, listening. He snatched the wine-jug with his own hands and poured another cup. His dark touch rested softly, lingering, on Desi's cheek, but his eyes focused inward. ''Stay here, my love, sleep and wait. Suffer, need me. I shall come back.''

And, incredibly, he was gone. So were the others, gliding away. They'd risen as one, as if they shared a common mind. They all looked alike now, tall, splendid, expressionless as zombies. They turned to the arch with stately tread and filed through it. Their bronze skins glowed from within as if they were hot, their drab webs wavering slightly with refracted heat.

They stepped outside in an ordered column, and as she'd thought, they didn't hesitate or draw together at the doorway. The arch somehow let them pass, as if they had no real volume. Two or four or eight went through together, and it was exactly wide enough. Their meal lay abandoned behind them. The bats had gone, wheeling through the roof. The trumpets had died.

Desi lifted an unsteady hand and found thick liquid running down her face. The thought of bat-excreta clenched her stomach, but the drip was blood from her own nose. The exquisite delicacies on the golden platters were spattered with guano and furred with mold.

She touched her lips and sweated hair and her hands turned red. She was alone on her fungoid throne, except for Jones slumped over the table, his head slack among bloodstained water.

Her symb was right, the aliens weren't shapechangers. They'd walked around the table to pass that imaginary door. They couldn't discorp. They couldn't change form or contract their essence, only create perfect illusions.

The hall was a cave with dirt floor set with toadstools, lit by hanging fungus with a dull luminescence. The plates and goblets were rough pots, the food dun mash. There were no excreta, no drippings, no guano. The bats had been an illusion too, perhaps a signal, that stank with loathing.

She spat blood and reshaped.

{Not bad. You're too small but you may pass, they're too busy to notice.}

"Best I can do with my mass."

{You'll have to do him too, he's past it.}

Desi swallowed. "Dead?"

{Close to it, I can't get a response from him or his partner. Quickly, I don't know what's going on or how long it could last. Don't discorp until you mean it, they're sensitive to mental activity even when they're busy.}

Desi slid into trampled dirt. They were certainly corporeal, they'd left traces. The walls of the cave were running with moisture, glowing condensation beading every surface. She suddenly felt sick. It smelled of cellars, animals, blood. Some of it hers.

She touched Jones's shoulder. He was inert, a faint smear of breath stirring the water by his cheek, the bones under his shirt sharp and hollow as bundled sticks. There was no flesh on them, just pleated skin.

"Help me."

{I'm trying. It's the best I can do, he's out, they both are.}

"We've done better," Desi said. The resemblance was marginal, general etiolation and darkness. "He's hardly any mass left to change."

{Let's just go.}

"Where?"

{Anywhere. The mud half? There isn't much choice, we've lost too much energy to corp back to the ship and I didn't want their food. Alien protein.}

"My conclusion. Let's hope the people in the marshes are blind or vegetarian. Preferably both."

{If there are people, not more like these.}

"There are. Look."

Weakness and bloodloss had taken Desi's strength, though Jones's skeleton was almost weightless. Her first hop got her to the open, straight into confusion.

The dark people were in battle-order, separate groups of men and women. They looked more human from a distance. The taller, heavier males manned catapults, the lighter females knelt with bows. All pretense of beauty or carnival had gone and they were starkly bare; lean, predatory and stinking with the animal smell that clung to the hall. Beetle-wing plates covered them behind and they wore helmets but their limbs shone with inner fire, edged with pale light from above.

It was really night. A flight of spiked wings was outlined on the sky, leaf-tipped tails coiling as they banked. Threads of flame lanced down and showers of arrows flew up to meet them. Both sides were armored, for the arrows skittered back and the flashes reflected off the beetle backplates in random spurts.

An occasional fighter ducked smoothly as fire sizzled past. The fliers were more worried by their own weapons than the enemy's to date. The archers, moving as a single woman, right hands reaching to quivers, ignored both.

The battle went on in near-silence. The spiked wings flapped high up and flights of arrows left the strings in a muted whisper. There were no cries and no spoken orders, although both sides maneuvered with orderly efficiency. Deaf. Maybe it took the cutting vibration that had made Desi's ears bleed to give them warning.

The men worked methodically at arming the catapults while the women did the shooting, but she couldn't see what was in the cups. The long dark beams drew back one by one as the springs were wound. There was no order, but a volley of burning stuff arced up in fiery lumps, leaving after-trails of scattered flame.

"Yech," Desi said.

It smelled like rotten sulfur, brimstone mixed with putrescence. The spiked wings wheeled and shot upward out of range. Some of the missiles splashed the tailmarkers and lined them in phosphorus. The sky screamed, and a flaming shape pinwheeled out of sight. The arrows paused as the cups were reloaded and the beams pulled back for a second shot.

"Out of range?" Desi guessed.

{For the moment. They're re-forming for another run. My advice is keep moving, we're under everyone's stray fire. Don't know how long this kind of fight can last.}

The women refilled quivers as the fliers, dark specks on the stars, pulled their column together and spiraled around, maybe checking losses. They came down in a swish like a rising wind and another silver shower rainbowed to meet them.

Desi glanced down and saw saggy camouflage darkly stained. Jones's face was black with dried blood and her own lips and chin were sticky. "Jeez, I reverted without noticing. I've lost it."

{But the glamor's evaporated, too. They're busy. Corp out while they're in action. We'll need several jumps, depending how far from the border we are. If the fight ends before we reach it, they could catch us.}

"Or even after," Desi said grimly.

{I think not. That mud looked like dragon country. The

planet's divided, stands to reason the attackers are from elsewhere.}

"Uh-huh," Desi said. She reshaped a vague predator resemblance, left Jones as he was, and pointed her mind at the eastern horizon.

As she discorporated she caught a last glimpse of the arcades. They were crowded with shadowy figures, the figures of shrunken creatures bent and twisted like old tree-roots, whose hollow eyes looked wistfully at the sky. Shapeless webbing dragged behind them, the useless remnants of spiked wings. One still held a forgotten wine-flask. The nearest waved a skeleton paw in a violent gesture.

*Away.*

The land flowed and shifted as they jumped, a running together of pink and black, threaded with green and sliced with fire. A fish-hook struck in her gut, speared her belly and tugged her back, until it thinned to a filament and tore free. The terrain went in and out, grass and marble, damp, lamps like moons, mold, guano and glowing fungus. Hanks of blue and green hair twined around her legs and slid silkily away.

The city's roofs and arches fell back into night, its ordered squares breathing narcotic perfume. Sticky nets clung to her like honey and tore, taking skin and flesh with them. A tower rose like a threatening finger and dissolved. She never knew if it existed or not. Wheeling black shapes and threads of fire and silver cut her vision, faintly and distantly written on the sky.

The dawn washed them in pale gold as dirt spun under Desi's feet. She paused on each jump to snatch breath before drawing up her strength to fling them into the next. Her energies were failing, the hops getting shorter. She'd enough respect for the illusionists not to want to run out of juice in their territory.

Then her feet sank in mud and she was kneedeep in water, Jones's light frame of bones in her hands, daylight gleaming on wide pools among marshy islands frosted with graywhite angelhair tangles. The silver sky had developed a sun.

They were in dragon country.

# ELEVEN

## Hollows

Sun steamed off the water and high spears rose to a silver-blue sky. Green islands stood above the mere and clumps of yellow reeds rustled. The angelhair lay in drifts over them, spreading fine nets that shone with rainbows between tussocks. It stirred continuously with a faint, noiseless movement, though the air was still.

Clear water lapped Desi's knees, her feet buried in slime. Jones's body floated beside her with the shriveled hands rising and falling like paper boats. Her fingers on his collar kept his head above the surface. She was whacked, her knees shaking, an uncontrollable tremor in her arms. The collar slipped and she almost let go. She staggered and just missed a nosedive into mud. The green smell of river flowed around them.

"Can we make one more jump? Farther away?"

{I'm flat. When did we sleep last?}

"Can't hold him . . ." Desi jerked back from a vertical gulf behind her eyebrows and the collar slipped again. She twitched it feebly. "Jonesy, shake it. Wake up."

The skeleton went on peacefully floating.

{He's sucked dry. Hollow.}

"What *were* those things?"

{What you called them. *Sidhe.* Vampires. Soul-suckers,

they feed on vitality. We'd a lot between us, our kind attracts them. Yours would have had you if he could, if he'd gotten closer. You were more protected than Jones, I felt what they were. Maybe he's vulnerable because he's a telepath. I couldn't warn him without giving ourselves away, they're strong telepaths too.}

"Too like them. Poor Jonesy, he was bushed. Never did get to bed."

{None of us did. It could be too late to bring him back, I can't fill his energy-loss. We've nothing left.}

"Frick that." A tear ran past Desi's nose and dribbled over crusted blood. She licked it. "Where's the dragons?"

{I can't feel anyone, but that doesn't prove much. Most of my frequencies are dead. If we don't eat soon I'm going into stasis. You need more help than I can give you. I'm sorry.}

"Wasn't your fault your mama fruited."

{It wasn't hers either, but it killed her. This could disable me, possibly forever. And these people are dangerous.}

Desi snorted, a little nervous giggle. "If you go, so do I. You gonna lie around static for a million years like your great-grandma?"

{My ancestor hadn't a choice either.}

"Maybe you can change hosts."

{Not possible,} her symb said coldly. {If I'd energy I might reproduce first, but it wouldn't save me. As it happens, I haven't.} And it retired to a distant concentration.

A light touch brushed Desi's leg, and she jerked reflexively. Her pants fell open in a slash like a razor-cut and a line of blood opened on her thigh. It burned like a redhot wire.

A net of angelhair had drifted over the marsh on an invisible breeze, and a thread had touched her. The net brushed them and where it brushed it clung. Spider-light strands were tangled in her hair and Jones's shirt glistened with criss-crossed rainbows.

Water didn't stop it and where it lay it melded with skin and the flesh below. The slightest movement tore it loose, and when it tore it ripped off a strip of whatever was in contact, skin and the muscle-fiber under it. She looked wildly around. The air was in gentle, drifting motion. Fine threads blew in from every direction on invisible drafts, centered on them as if they were the poles of a living magnet.

The silk multiplied as it drifted, single threads opening to loose hanks of raveled line. Desi's hands and legs were scored with slashes, her coverall tattered, and the helpless quiver of her sagging knees drew more threads to her. Jones's shirt lay in slices on his back, the lumpy ridge of spine naked under bloodless skin. His cuts gaped open with long white lips, barely oozing. His failing arteries were too slow to bleed.

{This isn't good. His heart's failing already, bloodloss will finish him. }

"Can't hold," Desi mumbled. "Can't even stand, stopped feeling my legs. If I dumb enough to fall, this stuff will skin me. And I'm falling. Ouch! That hurt."

She was bleeding everywhere. The water darkened with spreading pink curls. Tears of pain squeezed from her eyes. "If we could get to *Windy,* she'd fight this. She's strong . . ."

{We think. I can't even raise her, there's too much interference. Static right up the spectrum. Too much mental activity, plus radiation from the forcefield. If I could have called I'd have done it ten jumps back.}

Desi's nails scraped on linen and Jones's head slid nearer the water. A red line opened across his ear. She tried to grip harder, and failed. He slipped a little more. She was drooping with pain and bloodloss piled on exhaustion. She tried to lift her head and thread tore her cheek.

{We're bleeding energy into him so long as you're in contact, it's like a temperature gradient, we can't help equalizing. We'll all end inert if you don't let him go . . . }

"Can't. Couldn't anyway, but he'll get shredded. Can we make that island, if we really try?"

{If I could move at all, I'd have shifted you out of this fiber. I'm burned out. If I'd been older and stronger . . . }

"You aint. Not your fault."

Desi stood under piling tangles of angelhair, water rippling at Jones's lips. The current lifted and ballooned his shirt and swayed his arms as if he were a corpse already.

"We shouldn't have come here. My dumb curiosity."

{It's true I can't feel a trail. This can't have been Blinky's choice of continuum, I think *Windrunner* made a mistake.

Perhaps the two Blinkies were occupied with specimens and she fell into a dimension at random. There's no . . . }

"I hate stupidity," Desi whispered. "Especially mine."

{ . . . ice.}

The inner voice was dying. She blinked, trying to pull herself together. Her symb was going into stasis, too short of energy to stay conscious. Leaving her alone. And her last shreds of strength were failing too.

{NO TRAIL.}

{OF IC—CCE.}

An inaudible hiss that echoed in her head and ruffled the threads. They blew as if a gust had lifted and slacked them.

Desi straightened a rubbery neck and saw reeds moving under the water, a circle of spears rising in clumps. Rings widened and ran together, splashing waves at the borders. A splashing circle of rising rings.

Not reeds. Spiky crests were growing from the slime, as if the marsh-bottom had created them. Rising like towers, taking color and form. Spiked horns shone dully in the sunlight, water running off blue and green scales on long horse-snouts whose nostrils blew vapor.

Saw-shaped teeth, long and sharp as carving-knives, fringed their jaws. Their huge eyes were vacant. Not blind or unintelligent, just empty, like holes in space. Their lifted forearms spread into paws pricked with hooked daggers, and elongated leaf-tipped tails whacked the surface like rising fish.

The marsh was birthing dragons.

{BURNED OUT . . . }

{ . . . DYING.}

{HE IS DYING.}

{SS—S—SHE IS DYING.}

{ . . . DYING,} the voices hissed. Inside. Outside. Half in and half out of being.

{S—SS—SSUCKED.}

{DRY.}

They stood eight feet to the shoulder, tails in balance with powerful haunches, dorsal spines rippling as if they sampled the atmosphere or had some other, incomprehensible, dragon purpose. Their wings were folded clear of the ground.

The ghosts in the arcade trailed dried-up rags. Desi shivered. The unfolded wingspan must be immense. The huge seahorse upper halves, stooped like pantomime masks over her diminished head, looked awkward, as if they must pull the whole structure off-balance. But the high-flying squadron that drew outlines on the stars had wheeled like dragonflies.

The masks bent lower with flaring nostrils, and the spines rippled.

{SS—SS—SUCKED.}

{DRY.}

The repetition decided them. They lifted their snouts to the sky like bugles and shrieked, a long bass hooting that splashed the water and made reeds and stems stoop. The tall fine pillars of vegetation leaned to dip the surface and the angelhair blackened and fell into shrunken loops, like melted plastic.

The sky blinked.

Smoke. Black plastic smoke, perhaps . . . But no smell, a graying-out of the sky. Green water-scents and earth-mold, dirt. Glass outlines formed and shimmered, blowing away.

The smoke was overhead, blue and thinning, making shadows, pale smoke-rings. Desi squeezed her eyes shut. The shadows changed, an echo maybe of her own vagueness, water clouding her eyes, a persistent haze of buzzing exhaustion.

"Help."

A real voice, human, a woman's contralto. She'd said something else, Desi didn't know what. She opened her eyes and tried to sit. The glass hands and faces had melted like icicles to an everyday world, and Jones lay face-down beside her on sunwarmed grass. The woman bent, long hair fanned on his back, with her fingers to his throat. Desi's mouth opened, and the woman looked at her.

"He needs help," she repeated. The echo was obliquely wrong, not quite a repetition. But the fingers were only on his pulse. "Sucked dry."

What the voices in the marsh had said. Desi looked at her doubtfully. "You got medical supplies? Blood? Anything?"

The woman straightened and sat beside her with unselfconscious ease. Her floral cotton skirt was from a vid starring farmgirls, businesslike white shirt, long bare legs tanned by sunlight. Her brown hair was a silky mane. {Good enough to eat.} Desi wasn't sure where the thought came from and didn't much like it. The woman tossed the hair.

"It was mine. They eat us, when they can. We fight them, you saw us."

"You?"

Seahorse masks and wings folded. Eight feet to the shoulder and a lot of head and neck above, leaf-shaped tip to the tail. The woman was her own size.

"We need to use frightening shapes. Like theirs." She smiled. "I run the . . ."

She'd said *newspaper*. Or it could have been *vidstation.* Desi's head swirled, and settled on a vision of colored holos. People were watching them, nice human people in jeans and cottons. *Good enough to eat.* They had real wood furniture, pale and grainy, with cheerful cotton cushions. She'd yet to see a tree anywhere.

An image of marsh-spears ran over her retinas and she rejected it. She saw them bending to dip the water at dragon-rising. In a pig's eye. A grove of oakwoods rustled behind her.

"You're kidding," she said roughly. "Kidding I met. I don't give a shit what you sit on, have you any plasma?"

"Sorry." The woman looked penitent, her fine brows drawn in a line of concern. "I'm a telepath, I run the—*vid-paper*—and I don't know how you see things. I have to search for pictures in your head."

"Don't trouble, for me. You could try the truth."

The fine brows drew deeper, in a wrinkle that suggested genuine confusion. "We have no—*plasma*—. I mean, even if we had, it wouldn't help you, he's —*glamored*—." She peered closer, a dark hollow that shadowed Desi's eyes. "Like you. You drank—*fairy wine*—."

"It was water."

The puzzled look deepened. "How could you know? You're not very telepathic. *He's* the telepath. You drank water, if you prefer. Water filled with—*dreams*—."

"I'd say nightmares. He needs help. Can you give it?"

*Withered dragons between the arches.*

Another moment of mental confusion.

{S—SS—SHE DID.}
{REALLY DID.}
{SS—SEE . . . }
The voices died.

"You saw their slave servants." It wasn't a question. Telepath. She knew.

{—?} Desi thought. A feeler. Last time she'd felt her symb it was fading. Jones was flat, almost melted in the turf, his skin transparent. It wouldn't take much for him to vanish too, he was evaporating.

"Steam," the woman said. "It's the sun. We can't cure, but we can hold him. For a time."

Desi nodded. It was getting lonely here. Her hand shifted, fumbling in the grass, and she glanced at it, startled.

{Still here. Can't talk or they'll know. These aren't deaf, I think they're blind. Took them time to find you because your signals were weak. Their guard-threads attracted them. They don't know about me.}

The letters formed and faded, glowing slightly. Desi moved her other hand uncertainly.

*How are you?* she scrawled. *Are they picking up our thoughts? Does it matter if they know?*

{I'm weak, but getting stronger. I'm keeping them out. It may not matter, but I feel cautious. I don't like my feelings but I haven't the same sense of immediate danger. They won't eat you. They've given you something back, some of themselves. It isn't a gift.}

*Is it ever? It's something they aren't hungry.*

The brown-haired woman was watching her closely, or her eyes were on Desi's face. "You're thinking."

"This is my partner."

"I'm aware of it."

"You can't help him at all?"

The woman's eyes squinted. "Perhaps we can—*trade*—."

"In his life?" Desi said.

The mane shook slowly. "It isn't so simple. We can't cure him, we can't cure ourselves. If we could, would we leave the—*dragons*—under the—*arches*—"

"Guess not," Desi admitted. "What's the problem?"

"You're from the—*outworld*—?." The woman had difficulty formulating the concept. It wavered in Desi's mind. "You may have knowledge we haven't."

"May," she said neutrally. "Is that it? I help you, you save him? Suppose I can't? You'd let him die?"

The woman scrawled on the turf herself. Her finger made no trace, glowing or otherwise.

"We wouldn't want it. We don't. But I said we can't help." She took a deep breath.

{TELL HER.}

{TELL.}

{HER.}

{PERHAPSS SS—SHE CAN DO—*it*—.}

{THEY TOO HAVE S—SS—UFFERED.}

{THEY HAVE NO CAUSE TO—*love*—THE—*fairies*—.}

{HE IS TRULY DYING.}

The woman shook her hair and fixed Desi's eyes. "The —*fairies*— are absorbers of essence. They swallow being. Some they swallow whole, like your friend, some in part if they can use them, like the—*people*—in the—"

"Arcade," Desi said. The rippling of consciousness wasn't doing her good.

"Arcade. Once an essence is swallowed, they have control of it. I don't know why they didn't swallow you." Again the narrow stare. "That's why we wonder if you can help. You've something we can't see."

{Hum,} Desi's left hand wrote in the grass.

"You're—*alien*—?" More trouble with the concept, her thought uncertain.

{Odd,} the symb observed. {Their difficulty with 'outside'. They get other details from your minds, but they can't scope that one.}

*Fascinating,* Desi scrawled. *They've worked out Jonesy's a journalist, which they got from his mind, and that's when he's dying. They can't know what it means, but they've managed to fake it. How do they see* Windy?

Pause.

{They don't. They're conscious of a drifting intelligence,

but they don't know what she is. They think you've a friend somewhere, different but like you. An outsider. They've no knowledge of mechanisms.}

*That's my* Windy. *It doesn't bother them?*

Another pause.

{No. She's just another alien mind.}

Desi gnawed a nail. *Weird,* she concluded. "What do you need from me?"

The disturbing fingertip scrawled turf without following its contours. Maybe she'd picked up the mannerism from Desi. It was sometimes above the grass, sometimes within. "We don't know. The—"

"*Sidhe,*" Desi said.

"Shee. They capture us, creeping in the marsh. The best and youngest. And if we get them back . . ."

{TELL HER.}

{TELL HER,} urged the voices.

"The part that's been swallowed remains with the—shee?—that drank it. If we can't identify the shee, we can't remake our people. And in time they digest them."

"That's why you can't help him?"

"His case is easier, because you know which one sucked him. If we caught her and brought her here, we could make her empty her—*power*—." Another hard word. The concept looked almost like *gut.*

Desi fastened on what she could. "You could make her spit him out."

"Perhaps. But we can't hold him very long. His essence is so low it's draining slowly to nothing. He's dying. If you want to save him, help us quickly."

*What does she really want?* Desi wrote on the grass, right hand to left hand.

{We have to talk. Say you need *Windrunner.*}

"I have to talk to my colleague" Desi said aloud. "In private. We'll think about how to help."

"We can help you get there," the woman said, her blue eyes innocent. "Where your friend is."

More upright citizens were forming in the trees. Desi watched them shape as smoky glass figures before they solidified. Men in plaid shirts and women in dresses. All dressed from the same old holovid.

*Don't admire my imagination,* her right hand scrawled.

{They think it shows them as normal,} her left replied.

*That's normal?* the right asked with incredulity.

{They found it deep down, maybe from something you saw as a baby. It must be your mind. Don't wave your hands, I don't exist.}

*Can we make it to* Windy?

{Yes. Barely.}

"We'll help you to go," the woman repeated. "My friends will lend you their power."

{They'd like to meet the colleague.}

*That's what I figured.* "Thanks, we can do it single-handed."

{WE?}

*Oops.* "I," Desi corrected hastily. "I can."

"You're not very telepathic," the woman said, with her narrowed brows. "You can't—*move things*—either."

{THEY ARE VERY—*alien*—.}

"We think you're weird, too," Desi said, and discorped out.

"Hi, guys," Desi said, slumping into her couch. It crunched. "What's *that*?"

{Crumbs. Pretend you don't notice.}

"Jonesy's dead," *Windrunner* sniveled. "You never loved him." Salt water ran out of her airducts and began to corrode the newly re-nanned paint.

"No, he's not," Desi snarled. "But if you keep on like this he soon will be. What can we do about him? What's going on here? Either of you have answers?"

{I think so,} her symb said, reflecting. {These are telekinetic. The *sidhe* are the telepaths.}

"I thought they both did both."

{They're overlapping races. I mean major talents. I assume the dragons maintain the field.}

"Yeah?" Desi asked, dubious. "What makes you sure?"

{It may not be completely voluntary, though I think they must want it. Self-protection. After all, they're blind. And strongly adapted to a specialized environment. The *sidhe* possibly put pressure on them.}

"Specialized lifeforms do have difficulties," *Windrunner* confirmed smugly. "I was very over-specialized myself at one time."

"And now you're under-," Desi said. "Go on, babe, I'm listening."

{I think the *sidhe* keep power-sources under their houses. I could feel them surging while you were at table. And they aren't mechanical.}

Desi shivered. "Captured dragons?"

{Could be. Their people want them back badly.}

"Don't blame em. Being slowly eaten alive by *sidhe* isn't exactly a major career-choice."

{Clearly. But there's desperation in their thinking too, a worry about survival. If the *sidhe* capture too many . . . }

"They could end too strong for the survivors. Particularly if they've a breeding-program in hand. Raising little slaves in captivity. Yeah, figures." Desi stared into space. "Run me up a sandwich, *Windy?* Steak. You know, babe, we recovered very fast."

{Something in the water. Dragon water.}

"Thanks." Desi absently accepted the sandwich from the serving-claw of a passing mouse and bit it. "Not bad," still thinking. "They're very biological."

{That's my opinion.}

"But we don't have to play things their way."

{We do have the option. I was thinking so too.}

"Well, you would," Desi said. "We're the same." She chewed and swallowed. "So," she concluded. "We got a solution. Or we can try. If *Windy* gets off her under-specialized butt."

*Windrunner* made rattling noises in her mouseholes.

"For Jonesy," Desi said.

The noises stopped and everything listened.

The globe was still pink travertine, but practice helped Desi see the black-green waver under the illusion. She recorped in the middle, avoided angelhair and landed on the largest of a chain of islands. She thought it was roughly where she'd come from.

It was dark. That fitted the timescale but took her by surprise, since the planet still looked evenly bright from above. The brownhaired woman materialized at her shoulder, and a deeper shadow signaled the arrival of the oak-grove.

The woman brought a mental picture of healthy, happy people in velvet smoking-jackets or satin lounging pyjamas sitting cozily in front of roaring logfires behind drawn drapes. A different vid, from the styles. The real night was mild. She turned one narrow look on Desi and another on the canisters piled at her side.

"Was your colleague helpful?"

"She aint Einstein, but she keeps trying. Is the guy still alive?"

"Barely. He's in danger of going out." She narrowed on the canisters. "You need these metals?"

"You do," Desi said. She didn't see any need to go into detail on how much energy she, her symb and *Windrunner* had used to shift the mass, brake it out of orbit and guide it to a landing. The turf didn't *look* dented, but it likely wasn't there. She chewed glucose unobtrusively while her symb groaned the length of their muscles. "How are dragons at lifting weight?"

"We—" The woman checked. "They can transport mass. You want them to carry—metal?"

"Right over *sidhe* territory. Is it dark their side too?"

"It's a little before dawn in——*squeedle*—City. Where yours is, who sucked your partner. You want us to drop metal? Remember we need her alive."

The city name was untranslatable, between a taste and a color. It was either yellow and tasted of muffin or lemon-flavored with a doughy texture. Both smelled of spoiled organics.

"I understood that. Not on them, someplace near."

"If we're to do it, we must start now. Their defenses will be ready after last night's raid, and we need darkness." The woman's eyes were black and hollow. "If we must, we can prolong night by two hours or more. But we pay heavily, and it grows harder with day."

"So find me a dragon and let's do it."

The woman's face was still innocent but it had drawn out in the echo of a snout and her smooth head was shadowed by a phantom crest. "You want to come? It'll be dangerous. The fighters can drop the metal alone."

"They don't know what to do with it after it's down. I'll do that. Find me someone to sit on."

The woman didn't argue. She flicked her mane and melted in the trees. Literally. Two steps inside the grove her outline thinned. The leaves sucked her up.

Desi waited.

*You think it'll work?* her right hand wrote on the darkness.

{It must, I can barely feel Jones or my brother. That much was true. They're clear as water. They may really fade away, they've lost so much energy they're on the verge of discorping to nothing.}

The glowing traces were faint and misty. The hand trembled.

*Hang in,* Desi sketched. *We'll do it.*

The sky was black with dragons before she noticed the trees had vanished. Outline and shadow mingled above her and seahorse heads stooped against the stars.

{THESE?}

"One each, you'll find them heavy. And somebody gotta carry me."

{YOU WILL PUT YOURSS-SELF IN DANGER.}

{WE}

{CANNOT HOLD YOU}

{IN THE MIDDLE OF BATTLE.}

{WE}

{MUSS—ST MOVE TOGETHER.}

"Understood," Desi said. "You think you can stay level long enough to get me there? Once you're fighting I'm on my own. I need these dropped where I say."

{YOU}

{WILL FALL.}

"No, I won't. Look after yourselves. I've done this. More or less," she added in honesty.

{More or less,} her left hand wrote sardonically.

*Shut up,* the right replied.

{WHY}
{DO YOU}
{GESS—STURE}
{TO YOURSS—SELF}
{WITH YOUR HANDS—SS?}

Desi blushed slightly. "Religious ritual," she said rapidly. "Preparation for battle."

Silence.

{YOU}
{ARE NOT}
{LIKE US—SS.}

"No," she agreed. "I'm something different."

A long black neck leveled toward her and she grabbed the crest. It was sharp and bony, in diminishing spikes from the ears to the base of the tail like a polished horn knife. She found a smooth patch aft the skull and wedged in her knee.

"I hope my weight won't drag you down."

{?}

Plain incomprehension.

{They're telekinetic,} her symb repeated. {Your weight makes no difference. I'm not sure they even really fly. It doesn't understand.}

*They're sure not like us. Totally biological. Weren't they using lasers?*

{They wouldn't know how. It was a directed plasma-beam created out of their own energy. It's why they can't protect you when they're fighting, their strength goes elsewhere.}

*Let's not let the Federal Government come across them, imagine that capacity in the hands of the Navy.*

{Keeping you out of the hands of the Government was my mother's life's work. Shall we think about survival?}

The canisters snapped out of existence and Desi found space below her. The spread wings blacked out half the sky. Spread, but not flapping. The dragons glided on invisible winds, air unreeling under them. A path of shining water streaked below as they headed into blackness faintly lit by a dying moon.

{IF YOU NEED}
{MORE DARKNESS—SS}
{YOU MUSS—ST TELL US—SS.}

{IT WILL COSS—ST US—SS PAIN.}
{BUT THAT IS NOT IMPORTANT.}

Impatient, two different voices. Both huge echoes. The night swallowed them.

Scattered lights lay below, lines and squares like ranked stars, and the ear-slicing cry of *sidhe* trumpets cut her head. They were high up, the ground beneath them small and shrunken. The dragons banked and wheeled away.

Reddened moonlight reflected off scales like dull coins. A powerful slash of tail rippled the spine and nearly threw her off. She slipped, recorped and held on.

"Open country on the edge of town," she gasped, the thin air cold in her lungs. "Marsh, dirt, forest, whatever, long's there basic carby-hydro and maybe silicates. Drop me, then engage em. Give me fifteen minutes. It'll take that long, so don't get cut to pieces before I catch you."

The dragon laughed. Its bass bugling shivered the sky. The formation swung against the moon and circled down. The planet had no moon, alone within its forcefield. It was nevertheless falling toward the horizon, broad as a shield, pomegranate color, its curtailed disk fading in mist. Rushing winds almost tore her from her seat.

{DOES THIS—SS COUNTRY}
{SS—SUIT YOUR NEEDS—SS?}
{WE DO NOT}
{UNDERSS—STAND}
{—*squeedle*—.}

"Carby-hydro," Desi shouted into the slipstream. "Dirt, fungus, stuff you could eat."

Ripple of disgust.

{WE WOULD NOT}
{EAT}
{ANYTHING HERE.}

"That's understandable," she muttered.

{BUT WE HAVE}
{FOUND}
{WHAT YOU WANT.}

{We hope,} her left hand sketched.

*We all fricky hope*, the right replied. *Or we're in the Jieronymus shit.*

* * *

She stood ankle-deep in mud with canisters piled around her while the column streamed away in high outline against the stars. Fading moonlight touched vegetation.

She sniffed, detecting the universal *sidhe* odor of decay, and poked her fingers in a porous trunk. It gave easily, too easily, like old styrofoam. When she broke a piece off she found the reasons were the same, its inside was air. A loose cellulose skeleton held it up.

{Fine,} her symb said. {We're in business.}

"Great." She wiped the hand on her pants. "Let's break out the mothers."

The canisters were full of leaking glue that smelled of dope. When she poured the contents on the ground it was just viscous enough to run, and programmed to do so under its own power. The sticky streams crawled away, spread and separated. She watched tentacles of nano-material writhe into brush and sat, sighing.

"Jeezle. I don't think I've slept in a month."

{Then don't. We start in just under ten minutes.}

"The story of my life."

The vegetation was crumbling, corky trunks falling in as the mother-nans reduced them to component elements. The dissolution was rapid and efficient. New shapes rose up as the molecular machinery started to rebuild.

"Our-guy magic," Desi said, chewing more glucose.

The moon went down.

The battle at the city was in full cry, random plasma-lines slashing the foliage and spent arrows pattering among the branches. The nans had created machinery from basic elements, drawing metals, glass and cellulose from soil and trees, building armor and control-circuits to the blueprints they were designed to follow, creating the semi-organic computers and shaping their fighting-principles.

The mothers were replicators, a swarm of daughter-molecules cloned from their nuclei rising out of the basic materials to follow the same orders, cloning and replicating in their turn. They built fast and strong, and a line of heavy tank-shapes grew out of the ground. The finished machines impressed even Desi who'd been expecting them, twelve feet high from tracks to turret with limited but effective functional intelligence.

She ducked involuntarily as she guided the leading tractor into the open, a splash of phosphorus filling the woods with light and a choking smell of decomposition. The rest swung into formation behind. The glare reflected off their viewplates.

"Clear on your orders?" she asked. The guide-unit was capable of understanding, but she hadn't thought a voice-function necessary. It clicked in acquiescence.

The trunks thinned as they approached the buildings, shrinking to fields of pallid fungus. She looked across at the *sidhe* town that tasted of spoiled lemon. Seen in the open without glamor, it was neither a marble puzzle nor an arrangement of scented arcades. A huddle of flattened molehills, loosely laid in staggering rows, was lit here and there by pale lamps too dim to touch the ground. Their glow pulsated. Bioluminescence.

The town was the color of the dirt it stood in, its tracks trodden mud. The fungus-fields shone with the pallor of decay. Scrubby outliers of brush reached out and died on the edges. It was almost pathetic.

Another shower of arrows hailed down and Desi called up her tractor's force-shield, hoping the hastily-charged batteries would last. Darts spanged off nearby canopies and the squad grew blue veils. "Then you're on your own."

She waited for the volley to peter out, then slid down and headed for scrubland. The tanks rolled forward. A glowing sulfurous blob rose out of the mounds, trailing fire. Dragons scattered, and their squadron circled and re-formed. The phosphorus spent itself again in the forest and flame licked up. The trees were hazed with smoke. Not that pathetic.

The tractors had formed a classic fighting crescent, horns widened to circle the town as the strengthened center advanced straight upon it. Their tracks crushed the fungus into shapeless blobs. Their modified-fusion engines were noiseless and their air-cushions made to glide over obstacles. The *sidhe* were busy anyway.

Desi had set clearance at three feet to allow for boulders but the terrain was smooth. The horns of the crescent closed together in ghostly silence. The huts were three to five meters high and the *sidhe* were deaf. ''Fish in a barrel,'' she sighed.

The crescent had narrowed to half a circle, and the flanks drew together around the huts and rolled inward. The death was quiet and not at all spectacular. Desi had expected a crash, or at least a rumble. The town's destruction was the creaky scrunch of a trodden toadstool.

The mounds gave, bent and folded. Chunks of porous material rolled, puffing dust that smelled of dryrot. The air filled with a sour woody haze. Fallen lamps spilled luminosity that sank slowly into the ground. The city could have been made of cardboard. The tanks rolled through as though it was scarcely there.

Floating dust thickened rapidly to unbreathable. Desi'd remembered the stink and brought a recycler. She put it on now, pulling up her collar. The stuff itched. She'd end with a rash again, her symb's attention was fully occupied in guiding the fighting-line.

The pale ghosts of withered dragons rose out of the earth as the halls fell above them. They raised blind snouts, silent, their dried-up rags of wings trailing. Unidentifiable smaller things scuttered squeaking from under their haunches. Desi extended a hand to pull them to safety, but she could have been transparent herself. They seemed too dazed and helpless to react.

The *sidhe* attack had faltered. Their telepathy couldn't warn them of programmed machine minds, the concept itself was too alien to be thinkable. Perhaps it was the vibration of falling houses that told them the unthinkable was upon them. The arrows fell off to a sporadic scatter as the archers turned.

They couldn't know what was happening. The town was filled with shadow and the metal hulls ran in silence, dully shining. Maybe the *sidhe* received second-hand thoughts from withered dragons. If they understood. Desi wasn't sure the slaves understood anything. Nobody on the planet had seen machinery. When the roofs opened the gray ghosts drifted out on the wind, mindless as leaves. The one that had warned her away had possibly been newer and less drained than the mass. Ragged shreds of webbing trailed in the dirt and the shambling haunches scuffed the mud of broken streets.

The catapults went on firing, at a dragon-column so high it must be out of range. The dragons were aware of chaos and had drawn off to reconnoiter, but they didn't understand what was happening either. Their jangled thoughts rustled in Desi's skull.

{WHAT}

{IS HAPPENING}

{BELOW?}

{THE—*fairies*—ARE FALLING BACK.}

{WHY?}

{WE FEEL}

{NOTHING.}

{ARE THEY FRIGHTENED}

{OF DREAMS—SS?}

"No," Desi said, sadly. "Of the only thing they never met. Reality."

The dragons went on circling, so high they were darker speckles on night. Their minds were confused. On the ground the *sidhe* had reorganized, for the next shower of arrows tinkled off tractor-canopies.

The tanks kept rolling. The last mounds crunched under their treads. Fractured lumps of fungus sagged in open domes and ghost-dragons rose like slow smoke from the ground, the skittering things that squeaked and jabbered fleeing before them.

"Steer your people to the woods if you can," Desi thought upwards. "There's shelter. It's going to get hot here."

Chunks of wreckage sprouted spikes under the arrow-shower and slave-dragons stood listlessly with silver rods growing out of withered hides. They had no reactions, vacant.

{WE CANNOT.}

{THEY ARE DIGESS—STED, LOSS—ST TO US—SS.}

{LOSS—ST TO EVERYONE.}

{WHAT HAVE YOU DONE?}

A frozen silence numbed Desi's ears. The dragons, blind, got their information from *sidhe* minds and the *sidhe* were trying to comprehend ruined halls with relentless tanks advancing over them. Dust was thick on every surface, but the tanks' force-shields haloed them in sparkle like roman candles.

The dried-up dragon slaves drifted in circles and wandered at random, driven by tanks, by arrows, by clouds of dust. Some stumbled among the fields and others headed into the forest which gave a semblance of a roof. They might roam there forever, or until they died. Now they were loose, their kind had turned its back on them, no longer recognizing them as their own. The *sidhe* had no farther interest. Desi looked wildly around.

*What's the matter with these guys?*

{I'm afraid the slaves have stopped being people. No-one wants them anymore.}

*They'll die there.*

{Perhaps it's the best thing that could happen.}

*Did I free them for that?*

{Apparently. At least we may have saved future generations.}

*Let's lovin hope so, because I wouldn't have done it for this.*

The first splotch of phosphorus came over the mounds, a flaming ball as big as a haystack. The *sidhe* artillery had the luck or talent to engulf a leading tank in viscous combustion. Its shield died. Desi watched calmly.

The tank melted to a spreading pool. The gunners had the range now and the next shots were good. The crescent's center broke into molten lumps that ran in liquid streams from under the fireballs. The arrows picked up as the catapults reloaded.

The fire sank into earth and died. Out of the burned furrows gleaming shapes humped back toward the sky, twelve feet of rising metallic solidity. The arrows spanged off them. They recharged their batteries on the ambient heat and generated shields. The new tanks speeded to rejoin the line, leaving rubble-heaps diminished by the amount of material it took them to rebuild. The crescent rolled forward without slackening speed.

"My tractors are about to be under their guns," Desi said to the sky. "You can't depress a catapult far, beam needs to swing."

Pause. The echoes were frightened.

{WHAT ARE}

{THESE THINGS—SS YOU HAVE MADE?}
{WHAT HAVE YOU DONE?}

"They're only machines. Like the *sidhe* catapults, but more complex. They'll flatten them for you, so you needn't keep your heads down. You just took the city."

{WHY}
{DO THEY NOT}
{BURN?}
{THEY RISE AGAIN}
{OUT OF THE EARTH.}

"They can go on doing that so long's they got mother-nans to carry out replication. They won't last forever, because the structures break down in a day or two, then the daughters begin to make imperfect copies. You'll probably have moving lumps for a while, but they'll die. They last max ten days, in battle conditions. That'll do us. You coming for the bitch ate Jonesy?"

Bass bugles rang through the sky, descending. Their note was exultant. The last splotch of phosphorus fell short and spattered broken hills, its path twisted as if the catapult was falling. The fire burned sullenly out. The fields were stark with dragon scarecrows whose rags blew thinly on burning drafts. The skittering things had melted.

The dragon squadron swung low to land, claws spread. High shrieks and low bellows echoed above the rhythmic crunch of nanoid tractors flattening molehills.

The *sidhe* were in flight.

Dawn came with a sudden jerk like the raising of a blind. The sun was already high and the shadows diminishing. The broken hills had blown away in dust and the fungus-fields were in liquefaction. The tractors rolled westward to work on the next town with a triumphant dragon crew spiraling above them.

A lot of *sidhe* had fled into the woods. The prisoners were huddled in the muddy clearing that had been a city, the brother and sister among them, bleached and shrunken.

They stood in a circle facing outward and in the dawn light their faces, hair and clothes were a uniform gray. Desi pointed her prisoner and a dragon jerked her out. She came spiritlessly. Her brother took a step and stood still, beaten. His eyes were on Desi's face, curious, considering. But she couldn't read them.

The ghost-dragons had gone, dead or drifting in the forest, but a squad of fliers was rounding up the skittery things that had run out from the cellars with them. Their tactics were simple and drastic. The huge hind legs rose and fell like pistons. Desi watched, nauseated.

{WE MUSS—ST}
{DESS—STROY THEM ALL.}
{THEY ARE}
{AN ABOMINATION.}
{THE BASS—STARD DWARVES OF}
{—*fairy*—AND—*dragon*—UNIONS—SS}
{WITH THE—*power*—OF BOTH}
{AND THE SS—SHAPE}
{OF NEITHER.}
{THEY ARE THE—*fairy*—}
{—*powerhouses*—.}

*And that's why we really came,* Desi said. *So they could destroy their corpses' freaks. They didn't care for the ghost-slaves at all.*

{It looks as if it was. I suppose the originals were really dead already? Well, she proposed a trade. You can't deal in other people's politics.}

*You can dislike them. Let's hope at least the trade was honest.*

She had seen the hybrids before the executioners caught up and they sickened her too. They were deformed lumps that squeaked pitifully. The knobs of undeveloped wings grew on their backs.

They spun brief bright illusions of twisted beauty and tried to lift themselves out of their holes, but they didn't seem able to use their abilities without direction and their old masters had no farther use for them. Perhaps they'd never been much use for anything but building pretty pictures.

Whatever their powers, they were deaf and blind. Their stamped corpses blew on the wind.

{WE SS—SHALL GO BACK NOW,} Desi's dragon boomed. It put a feral claw around the *sidhe* woman.

{THERE IS NOTHING LEFT HERE. YOUR PARTNER IS WEAK.}

Desi climbed wearily onto its neck, her head buzzing with vertigo compounded of hunger, exhaustion and nausea.

{GLUCOSE,} her symb advised urgently, writing big capitals across the scaled hide. She limply fished out a tablet and sucked. Her stomach settled but she lay astride the neck with her forehead on the scales, relying on the dragon to keep her from falling.

She felt an instinctive revulsion for the *sidhe* woman, but the dragon picked the captive up in its claw like a log of wood and its immense wings opened like sails. The sunlight lit it with shifting color as they headed back over marsh and water.

A last glance showed gray, fleshy-leaved woodland bearded in moss, with a burned swathe where the machines had crossed it. From high thin altitude she caught the flashes from other shining wings, small and far away, darting and wheeling above an invisible city which was already reduced to greasy brown smoke.

Silver, fire and phosphorus were paled by sunlight but this battle was joyfully noisy. The deep buglings of dragon triumph rang out, borne on the wind.

{WE SS-SHALL DEFEAT THEM EVERYWHERE,} her dragon said.

"As long as the nans hold," Desi mumbled. "Ten days max."

{THE MACHINES WILL NOT TURN ON US—SS?}

"Shouldn't, I programmed em for *sidhe*. They just go flat. But don't get overconfident."

"They'll last long enough," the fairy woman said from below. Her voice was still musical but subtly grayed, as if touched with decay. "Long enough to kill a thousand years of civilization."

{THEN THEY WILL LASS—T LONG ENOUGH,} said the dragon.

Desi let her head fall. She'd run out of glucose, and she still felt sick.

* * *

She slumped on grass beside the brownhaired woman, whose brows were still wrinkled. "I brought you water."

Desi heard the dragon-boom behind the voice, but she took the glass. The liquid was clear and the taste had a mellow solidity, almost a texture. It put tendons in her legs. She swallowed and her vision cleared.

The dragon-woman gazed steadily. "What will you do? Stay?"

Desi shook her head. "Just long enough to cure my teep. Appreciate the hospitality, but I need to space."

The woman's brow cleared. "We're grateful to you, but you frighten us."

"I frighten myself," Desi muttered. "Couldn't do that twice. And not in a hurry, it takes my ship time to recharge her nans."

"We don't understand you," the woman said. But she was almost smiling. "You're much too strange for us. I'll send for the—" she searched. "—The shee."

Jones's outline formed at her side, faint and glassy, and slowly solidified. His head was slack, lank hair stuck to his forehead. His eyelids were lead-colored and his lips corpse-white. The morning sun carved his features in angles and hollows and his outline had a disquieting uncertainty.

The *sidhe* woman blotched the fresh landscape, her long limbs gangling, sharp teeth bared in a sardonic grin.

"My last meal," she sang. "My, he was delicious! What a pity I had no time to digest him. Such power!"

Desi looked at her with a grudging admiration for courage. She wasn't going to bend her head. But there was fear in the defiance, and a subtle glance backward. Her brother stood on the edge of the trees, half in shadow, his back bowed. Their eyes met. The woman knelt over Jones's body. "This is for *him,* and for no other."

{GIVE,} said the dragon boom.

{FOR WHATEVER REASON.}

She stooped, sucked air, and expelled it in a fit of coughing. Then her mouth drew together, widened and her face flared out in a trumpet that swallowed Jones's head whole. Desi shuddered. The brownhaired woman gripped her arm. "She'll do it."

As the *sidhe* exhaled, her own body crumbled. Her flanks hollowed and her bones thinned and grew brittle. Her thick hair faded and shriveled into sparsely floating spider-strands scattering a mottled skull.

She rose an old woman, her monkey face puckered into gullies. But her eyes still glittered, dark and ironic. Her brother cried out, a piercing howl that hurt Desi's ears. Jones stirred.

The *sidhe* prodded him with her foot. "He'll live," she said in a thin ancient creak. "If anyone cares."

"I do," Desi said.

The shrunken lips parted on vampire teeth. "Then, since you say so, I'll give you a gift. I know what you want and where you can find it."

"In exchange for what?" Desi asked with suspicion.

"My gift is free." The smile widened, like a knife-cut. "Your intelligence above has the way, she can't miss it. Take the man and go, you've done enough. Cursed the day we met you. But my knowledge is good, my word on it."

Desi gazed into inscrutable eyes between lids like wrinkled paper.

"Her word's good," the brownhaired woman said. "They have their honor." She looked at Desi. "But I've a piece of advice. Be careful. Their gifts are poisonous."

"Perhaps I admire her," the *sidhe* said. It was impossible to make anything from her whispering voice. "She did what you couldn't."

And she limped away, a hooked claw on her brother's arm. Jones groaned and clutched his head.

"I must have *really* hung one on last night. My symb's still out."

—? Desi sketched.

{He's recovered enough for us to finish the job ourselves. My brother's waking. I don't trust any of them, they find you too dangerous. Let's go.}

"Yes, go, and quickly," the *sidhe* man sang. "Before we change our minds."

He pressed his cheek to his sister's. Desi had a sudden memory of her symb talking about temperature-gradients. Substance ran from the one into the other, the man shrinking while the woman straightened. They were both diminished to shrunken homunculi. As they turned, away, the light rags that veiled them caught on a breath of air from the water and lifted, exposing their backs.

They were hollow, the empty molds of people, refracted light shining through the eyeholes in spectral rainbows.

Desi snatched a whooping breath, grabbed Jones and corped out.

"I have a course," *Windrunner* said. "It isn't what I'd have chosen but we can try it. It *feels* safe."

Her panel tentatively touched Jones's knee. He patted her vaguely and sprawled in his couch. He was in charge of himself, but pale.

"Was that Lou-Beth? Can't be, haven't seen her since college. My first great never-ending love. Married a guy with a provincial hard-rag. Must be decades. She hasn't changed a day." He sounded wistful. "Ugly dreams. Can we go to bed now? I'll die without sleep."

"Not yet, boy," Desi said. "She and I want you out of here. Don't teep anyone until we're clear, huh? Especially the love of your life."

He yawned. "If I can't have passion or sleep, how about food?"

"*Windy,* make the guy some dinner."

"Steak sandwich, one," *Windrunner* said absently. "And coffee?"

"Okay. But I was hoping for napery and crystal. Seeing a civilized woman suddenly gave me immortal longings. For something like decency, just once."

A mouse scuttled in with a plastic tray and disposable mug. He took them sadly.

"She's checking her engines," Desi said. "You can't expect her to do everything. We'll have napery later."

*Windrunner* sent another mouse with a red paper napkin. He sighed as he took it.

"She loves you."

"I know. It's a comfort." He pushed the panel firmly away. "Engines?"

It was *Windrunner*'s turn to sigh.

The planet lay naked below, one big landmass in an ocean like a glaucous eye. It looked ancient, as though the continents had drifted around the globe several times already and were back for the moment in a single lump.

The land showed forest, plains and marshes and each pole was frosted with an icecap. A white sun lit it, its blinding corona spreading on black, and the blue terminator wavered over sea and mountains. A bright crescent of atmosphere outlined the limb. It definitely had no moon.

There was no green-black, no pink marble. The sky beyond was a clear orb of stars, the milky streak of the galactic plane veiled with a trace of silver mist.

"Ready," *Windrunner* reported. "All systems clear."

"Take us out."

"I've my probe to pick up, we can't go too fast until we're past the old field-line."

"It's only a probe. Make another."

"It's mine," *Windrunner* said primly. "And I'm short of nans. You nearly cleaned me out of mothers."

Desi groaned. *Windrunner* switched in engines and picked speed up gently. The orb receded and the galaxy beckoned, studded with diamonds. The big main engines rumbled, warming, and their speed increased.

"*Ooop!*" *Windrunner* screeched. They jerked violently in their harnesses and Jones spilled coffee in his lap. He choked on his sandwich. The braking-jets were screaming like banshees.

"It's impermeable to matter!"

"Not again," Desi said.

"Prepare for discorporation."

"Jeez," Jones whimpered, rubbing his leg. The universe went out, the sandwich rose to the ceiling and fell back on the deckplates with a dispiriting slap. The stars came back. "What was *that* for?"

Desi gazed upon a dwindling witchball centered in the aft plate. "Somebody foxed us again. The field hadn't changed, only the illusion. And if *Windy* wasn't a mean-minded bitch we'd have splatted. A *smart* mean-minded bitch," she amended, as a snivel began in the airducts. "You're improving, babe. You'll soon stop being a learner."

"It turned impervious without warning," *Windrunner* whined. "But I got my probe back," she concluded smugly.

{You know,} Desi's symb said softly in her head, {the dragon people weren't so very different. I sensed underground slaves in their half, too.}

"Don't tell me. Shrunken vampires."

{It wouldn't surprise me if the two races are symbiotic. They share their talents. An old, jealous, enclosed society.}

"Which would like to kill us."

Desi leaned back. She had two visions. One was her last glimpse of the dragon-woman as she and Jones were in the act of discorporation. The brownhaired innocent had turned to lead her prisoners into the grove. And her back view was the same as theirs, the hollow mold of a human form with refracted sunlight glittering through the holes of her eyes.

But while their shapes were shrunken and empty, hers was filled with rosy light. A rich red glow like a ripe yewberry, the diffused color of fresh blood.

The other was the probe's recorder, which had been running while they were below. The aft plate still showed the shining droplet, shrinking rapidly as *Windrunner* accelerated. But the probe's holo beside it ran through unchanged from beginning to end. Black starred space with a close white sun, a couple of distant ringed gas-giants and some asteroidal stones. The rest was blank, an empty orbit full of vacuum. The probe had detected no planet at all, past, present or future.

"Coming up to warp," *Windrunner* said.

"Okay, honey, get us out."

"Sleep at last," Jones said with contentment.

"Great," Desi agreed. "Let's hope we wake up elsewhere."

*Windrunner* launched herself into the void.

# TWELVE

## Pack-Ice

Desi woke up with a stiff throat and gummy mouth, and found Jones passed out beside her. He lay on his face whiffling gently. She swallowed painfully and sat. There was no reason why that bastard should sleep on her bed and she made a note to nag him. If she wakened him now he'd probably nag her.

*"Miz Smeett?"*

She turned. Pinstripes and briefcase, faintly translucent. "Oh, Jeezle. Piss off, I'm sleeping."

*"Miz Smeett, I must talk to you. My client . . ."*

The ghost rustled papers. Desi straightened with righteous fury. "Your client's copping a harassment suit, you non-existent bedbug. Go away!"

The blast of her rage blew the ghost out of the cabin to whatever electronic wilderness it had come out of. She lay down, simmering. Jones grunted.

"What is it? Breakfast?"

"No," Desi snarled, closing her eyes.

The cabin shook with a loud clear chord and a piercing whine. She sat with resignation. "Not again."

⌘

## TP–TV

### *the station of the multiverse*

WAKING YOU UP TO A BRAVE NEW MORNING WITH NEWS, VIEWS AND REVIEWS FROM OUR CORRESPONDENTS ALL OVER THE CONTINUUM. AND, TO START YOU OFF ON ANOTHER PERFECT DAY, HERE'S YOUR ALL-TIME BEST MAN—PUT THE SPOONS DOWN AND LEND YOUR EARS TO JONESY!

❖

[*Fade-in on Dick, even squarer than usual. The scalp-lock is green glass with spangles and hangs to his waist. The grin is as wide as a watermelon. The voice-over, contrariwise, has risen an octave and makes neat little cuts on the eardrums:*]

Hi there again. Continuing our coverage of major intergalactic errers, Hermes, this station announces its refusal to be intimidated by finicking multibillion-credit lawsuits. We shall continue to search out the truth, the whole truth, the half-truth and the faintest fraction of truth wherever we find it, and nail pernicious lies and their pernicious liars to whatever counters we have at hand. For the continuing adventures of our fearless correspondent and his incomparable companion, let's take another look at a day in the life of Delicious Desdemona!

[*The temptress is seven feet tall and magenta. Her hair is hallmarked platinum tinted blue and her bosom remarkable even by Miss Multiversal Sexlife standards. She pouts with lips as fat as tractor-tires. Her teeny little eyes are natural star sapphire, but possibly the network ran overbudget before they got to size. The landscape is wildly waltzing forest melting to oatmeal. She undulates up against an embarrassed Apollo in a red pickup:*]

APOLLO, WRITHING: Well, some guys asked us ta go to the Arctic and we didn't wanta, accounta the good relation I got with my truck, but the broad insisted, an something funny happened and it went away. That's it, sorta.

THE SIREN, STERNLY: Tell the truth. This planet was suffering a plague.

APOLLO, SWEATING UNDER HIS MUSCLES: Well, yeah, but this planet always got some plague or other.

THE SIREN: The whole truth, please. This plague was unusual.

APOLLO, EVEN MORE EMBARRASSED: I guess so. Don't remember too well.

THE SIREN, ACCUSINGLY: And it was caused by Hermes.

APOLLO, REDDENING: Hell, no. They was kinda slow noticing but they wouldn't do that. Dammit, they fixed it.

THE SIREN, INCREDULOUS: Fixed it?

APOLLO, ANNOYED: Sure, lady was a Hermes agent.

THE SIREN, HAUGHTY: The lady was I.

APOLLO, WITH CERTAINTY: No, she wasn't. Whole lot cuter. Is them tits real? You thoughtta plastic surgery?

[*Consternation. The network switches back to Dick, whose jaw has sagged to a triangle. He pulls it to something like shape and fakes a brave smile.*]

Ignoring the famous unreliability of casual eyewitnesses, this network announces its devotion to the search for truth, and its resolution never to cave in in the face of intimidation. And now, back to our early-morning sports coverage.

"Hey," Desi said, kicking the body on her blanket.

"Huh?" Jones asked, half-waking.

"What do you call *that*?"

"Huh-what?" He knuckled his eyes. "Was having a good dream, it had you in it."

"Then it didn't have a license," Desi said rudely. "My name aint fricky Dismalmona, it's Desi. That's spelled D—A—I—S—Y. Desi. S-M-I-T-H. Smeett. Desi Smeett. That a problem?"

"Well, yeah, actually," Jones said sleepily. "That's pronounced Daisy."

"No, it aint. Dazie? Sounds like an insult. What do you mean, defaming me all over the network?"

"Me? Aint talked to them in days. You've been too busy to look, but I was out of commission."

"Well, someone did. You didn't make this broadcast?"

"*What* loving broadcast?"

"*Windy*, run the man the holo. In private, I'm taking a bath."

Echoes of rage penetrated the shower. Jones thrust an angry face in on her. "They used my byline. That wasn't me, couldn't you see that?"

"No. Wasn't *me*, could see that."

"I wasn't there, so some guy used my name. I'm going to sue them."

"Looked just the same to me."

"I *told* you the anchor was a station artefact. If you see the sim, doesn't mean I'm behind it."

"Then you could do like I say and take responsibility for your own material."

"How do you suggest I do that?"

"Put your face on it. Use your voice. Make your own holos. Try truth. Whose show is it, yours or the network's?"

He sat on the edge of the shower-tub. "Theirs. I just work there."

"Teeping across dimensional boundaries?"

"Okay, not many people can. I'm well paid for it."

"To take the heat. Who pays if they slander Hermes using your name?"

He looked dejected. "It's the best-paid work around, except top independent. Do you know anyone who'd pay to look at my face?"

Desi considered it. "Okay, you're ugly, but don't fool yourself, you aren't that much uglier than anyone else."

"I don't look like Dick Tracy."

"You have that advantage."

"But he's what people want. It's why they pay channel-fees."

"You tried?" Desi asked, shoving her head out of the stream. Lotus-scented water dripped on his toast. He wrung it out absently, noticed and discarded it.

"No . . ."

"Then maybe you should. You could tell the truth. The *real* truth. Someone would have to listen."

"Hermes' lawyers?" he said gloomily.

Desi withdrew her head. "They listened already." He went on sitting sadly with spray running down his back. "And shut the door."

"I'm sorry to interrupt your philosophical discussions," *Windrunner* said coldly, "but I've a problem. A real one, half a lightyear ahead."

Desi shot out, naked and dripping. "What?"

*Windrunner* highlighted the holotank. "That. It's where my course goes."

Desi poked her nose in the projection. "What is it? Looks about the size of a watermelon seed."

"The projection's magnified, but it's still the size of a small asteroid. As far as I can compute. It doesn't exactly offer a surface."

"What's happening?" Jones asked, following her with sagging toast and water in his hair.

"Looks like an invisible attractor," Desi said resentfully. "I hate em. A smallish reality-flaw."

He looked in at the gaseous smear. "I'd say a gas-cloud."

"Cause you don't know any physics. You never get a gas-cloud that small or that focused. It's material agglomerated around a singularity. A small one."

"Very small," *Windrunner* confirmed. "Not much more than planetary mass."

"Slightly bigger, with that agglomeration. Maybe the size of a single system, or a collapsed giant star. Aint an ordinary black hole, too little gas, too much distortion. That is a naked singularity, recent from the small amount of quanta it's gathered, which says to me another bubble continuum. Did Her Bloodiness tell you what you were looking for?"

"No, only where to find it. Here."

"Another trap?" Jones asked unhappily.

"Maybe," Desi muttered, toweling.

He looked at her. "You're going to walk into it, aren't you?" She looked back, innocent. He ruffled his spray-soaked hair. "How did I know?"

"We'll put you off someplace," she suggested. "Aint your business anyhow."

"No," he said. "Where you go, I go."

"That's my boy. The world champion of really alien corn. Any way you want it. *Windy*, take us in."

"In there? It's going to tear me apart. Again."

"If it's where we're looking for, you'll have no trouble at all. Just pull in your belly. Getting out could be another problem," she added. "But we'll look at that when we get there."

"It's more Boy Blue, isn't it?" Jones asked.

"It's not your business. I said we'd let you off. The offer stands."

"Let's go."

"Warp?" *Windrunner* asked.

"Sure, take a run. But I don't expect problems. Gimme the speed to cross the boundary."

*Windrunner* sighed and accelerated. The smear grew to a cloud the size of a man's hand, and didn't get much bigger. Clotted gases lit the plates, hardly thicker than vacuum, and ran off *Windrunner*'s sides. The spinning knot opened, and swallowed them whole.

Filtered light came from all around, iceberg color. An immense architecture filled the holo, an eye-baffling crisscross of pillars and arches high as solar prominences, frozen to immobility.

Genuinely frozen. *Windrunner's* hullplates were flaking and the soaring vaults had a glassy solidity. Desi, naked in the pilot's couch, found her bathwater crystallizing on her skin.

"Careful, *Windy*, I don't want to hit anything. It might be as real as it looks."

"It can't be," Jones protested.

The lattice, if it was one, could have swallowed giant planets among its arches. Shapes in the distance were shadows of columns, lost in a maze of sparkle and refraction.

''You rather find out the hard way? Pass me a sweater or something, I'm freezing.''

She struggled into pants and rollneck through her straps, *Windrunner* throttled back to cruising-speed. The vaults passed overhead like the mockery of a cathedral.

''Vessel approaching,'' *Windrunner* said. ''From above . . .'' She flinched.

''And another behind,'' Jones said. Desi held course with her mouth shut. ''Watch it!''

The shapes hurtled at them, nose-arrays directed straight at the controlroom. *Windrunner* speeded to pass under an arch and both intruders vanished. Shadows stirred among the pillars, through the vault below them, among more inverted arches ahead.

''You gone fulltime crazy?'' Jones shouted. ''What were those?''

''Nothing,'' Desi said. ''Sensors didn't register. They were ghosts.''

''The tank holo's changed completely,'' *Windrunner* reported shakily. Desi nodded.

''Check. Sensors likewise.''

''Ghosts?'' Jones repeated.

''Sure.'' Desi's hands locked on the controls as the ship drifted by another archway and blue-shifted darts solidified from nowhere, homing in on her from all directions. ''Still nothing on the sensors. You don't recognize their configurations?''

He cowered instinctively. Crossing shadows accelerated into *Windrunner*'s tail and belly. Another pair screamed in at right-angles behind. The archway passed in a dazzle of ice and all the angles of the lattice shifted. ''Should I?''

''Uh-huh.'' She kept steering. ''You're looking at *Windy*.''

''What?''

''You're seeing multiple ghosts of ourselves. Coming at us. They're all blue, I'd know that snoot-foliage anywhere, and every time we pass a node they evaporate and double.''

*Windrunner* let out a small sob. ''Yes, I know them. They're me.''

''Look,'' Desi said. She headed into another set of vaults and an increasing fleet of long-nosed blue ships arrowed at them from all around the compass. The angles shifted as they passed and the fleet evaporated. "Images double every pass, and they change direction whenever we do."

"But they can't be reflections, they're coming from all over. We're on a straight course and we haven't covered any of those pathways."

"I'm not sure straight means much here," Desi said. "See how the lattice keeps altering? This is a bubble, a very small one, and the lover's curved. Looks to me like the lattice fills it, and every time we pass a node we change location. Warp, if you like. And create ghosts."

"Too many. We can't have been to all those places, we haven't passed that many arches."

"Multiple projections. A continuum's time-space. I'd say we set up a time-ripple when we entered. Or something did. You're seeing images of where we've been and where we're about to be, and maybe anyplace we ever could have been. The images are virtual, all possible realities at once. Function of the space being too small."

"This is another artificial dimension?"

"Wouldn't surprise me. If it wasn't, damn thing should have disappeared up its orifice, it's too small to be sustainable. Must be unstable. Gravity's peculiar, too, those arches shouldn't survive. They ought to fall in."

"Hermes getting nasty?"

"No. My employers make dumb mistakes, but they never did anything really spitefully illegal. It's against their charter. But I know who could have, she did under pressure once before. You met her."

He paled. "Blinky?"

"We weren't her first contacts," Desi reminded him. "She's very innocent and naturally helpful. And I don't think she quite always exactly knows what guys mean to do with things that she gives em."

"Like who?"

"You already named him," Desi said. "You know who I'm looking for, and Blink's been taking me on a tour of the multiverse dutifully following everywhere he went. Guess he must have been back since we saw her, unless he's displaced this lover himself. After all, when we met her she didn't understand Outside. And she'd have told me if she'd known, she'd got it I was looking for Ice.''

''Unless she believes in Magical Mystery Tours.''

''Not Blink, she's sweet and smart when not led astray by the over-clever. Your vampiric friend teeped this dimension and offered it to me as a gift, probably poisoned. Where I wanted to go. With her best hopes it killed me. Didn't know what it would be, but I expected something weird. Guy has a talent.''

''Boy Blue.''

''Ice.''

''Our family ghost.''

''My ex-husband.''

''Goodlooking guy. If you like the color.''

''I have done,'' Desi said. ''Where's the light coming from?''

{It's being refracted throughout the dimension,} her symb said. {From one node to another. The gravity's so restricted.}

''It is, but there must be a source. Trick's finding it, the way we bouncing around . . . He likes boys too,'' she added over her shoulder. ''Like the kid whose daddy's suing me, if your memory goes that far back. But you need to watch, he has this funny sense of humor.''

They passed under another vault and a hundred blue shadows converged on *Windrunner*. ''There must be a gravity point here somewhere, I'm bored with scooting around like a tennis ball.''

''I like boys, not,'' Jones said with simple bitterness. ''I take affairs straight. Maybe if I froze myself I'd look more impressive.''

''No, you wouldn't. But do it, if it's what your psyche calls for. Free the molecules.''

''I'm a topclass teep. That's my psyche.''

''Then your looks are your problem. No-one's stopping you from changing. You religious or something?''

{Why don't we just fall inwards?}

''Cause we change position when we pass through an archway. It's this damned built-in bounce.''

{The ship's under power, so you're passing archways with a package of energy. If you cut the engines and bled acceleration, she should fall toward the gravitational center.}

{In a curved continuum?} her counterpart asked, suddenly waking.

"Jeezle, he's as bad as his boss," Desi said. "The architecture's impressive, Blinky's a smart little genius. But since there *is* a light-source, which means a star, it's likely to be the most massive thing around. Consequently, we should gravitate toward it."

{I'd deduce the arches are either virtual or some kind of very rarified plasma. Something almost massless. Or the space would expand and break them up.}

"I think all this is a clever game, Ice's, or Blink's at his request. Don't underestimate the boy's unidealism. Whatever they are, I don't care to run into them."

"I don't either," *Windrunner* said. "Am I allowed to just fall, or would you rather discorporate?"

"I'd prefer to circulate," Desi said. "For once you and I are in agreement. However, it seems possible my partner's got something. Let's make like a stone."

"I'm glad you've a long lifetime, the gravity's so low we could fall for a century. Gin rummy, anyone?"

"Try your sensors," Desi said. "I've a grav-source to starboard. Poke your snoot that way, and bleed off more speed. I think we may be finally falling."

A giant column passed endlessly as *Windrunner* braked. Its crystal volutes looked like the result of eras of accretion. The light broke up in it in fountains of rainbows. They were headed for a blue-white flare, a blowtorch through diamond. The center of the labyrinth.

"You think the Minotaur's home?" Jones asked.

Desi grinned without amusement. "You can bet on it."

*Windrunner* navigated into the open. A neat small solar system hung in the shadow of the columns, which reflected it in streaks like interlaced nebulae. Bright starry sparkles lit the sky, a regular pattern of receding white globes that wavered a little with rotational movement and diminished into infinite distance.

"Really small dimension," Desi said. "You can see the

same star over and over, then reflections of reflections. Pretty. Blink got some real esthetics here.''

The sun was clear and alone, its single planet crusted with ice. A huge moon, also crusted, lit up the nightside almost as brightly as day. The darkness beyond the terminator looked phosphorescent.

''I bet it's cute down there,'' Desi said. ''Maybe you guys better stay clear. To quote, I may be some time, and if you don't hear from me in say thirty hours, standard galactic, don't land, leave. *Windy,* stand off. If you hear distress-calls, don't answer. Won't be from me.''

''Where are we heading?'' Jones asked.

''You weren't listening. You are a guy. In fact, you're two.''

He folded his arms. ''You were blaming me for not taking charge of my life. Well, I just did.''

''If taking charge of your life means following me around, you been doing it for millennia. Or it feels that way.''

''I'm just getting used to collecting toes and fingers. Lead on.''

''I can practically guarantee there gonna be some. Probably yours.''

''I'll chance it.''

Desi looked as if she was about to say something, then changed her mind. ''It's your skin. Take central heating, you'll need it.''

''Even I can deduce that,'' he said, growing a parka. ''Look, fur.''

''Jeremiah. You don't know Ice. Nan it up separate, or he'll freeze your balls off.''

*Windrunner* sighed gustily, but provided thermal clothing. ''I'm standing off. I will point out I'll have to play rummy with my central mouse-brain.''

''Great,'' said Desi. ''You've a chance of winning.''

They landed on frost surrounded by rocks and furred-over trees under icy armatures. The temperature was low enough for the clothing. Nothing moved.

''You sure he's here?'' Jones asked.

''Yes.''

"What's this ice thing with him?"

Desi shrugged. "Affectation? Boy's a genius, he feels he has to use it. Likes the look. Setting's decor. He should be on TV, he has a natural sense of the dramatic."

"Then why isn't he? Everyone else is."

Desi looked at him with new eyes. "Oh. That's it."

"What's what?"

"Your sense of the dramatic runs to not doing what everyone else does. I must have a big personality-flaw, I collect freaks."

Jones scowled. "I'm a professional teep, not a ham actor."

"Fine, teep me where the guy's hiding. Why does it stop you doing something with your hair?"

"I did," Jones said, hurt. "I like it like this."

"Oh," Desi said. She scratched hers, but left it brown. She was spending her energy on not shivering.

A plain lay in front of them, rugged ground without relief except jagged trees and a scatter of boulders. It *looked* like decor. White peaks marked the horizon. The big moon peeked over them and cut bright crescents in the icy armatures under the frost-fur. Last time they'd seen it, it had been the other side of the planet. Now it was rising like a searchlight, brightening the glare that refracted through everything.

Jones turned slowly, his mind tracking. There was something. A wary intelligence that watched and listened. He groped for a boulder, meaning to sit, and found it ten feet away. He'd been standing right by it, looking at the frost-growths on the granite. And wondering how this world was old enough to have weathered igneous rock.

The frost had become a transparent sheath and the rock was too lumpy for sitting. It was limestone. The fossil of a trilobite lay under the ice-ferns. The shape next to it looked like a bone from the far end of a tyrannosaur.

"Joky guy."

He walked over to a glass-plated tree and touched it. It melted instantly to milky sludge that slobbered on his legs, glued his feet to the ground and re-froze to glass. Its skeleton extended dagger arms upward, a wicked spiked-steel candelabra that looked like a caltrop. He called up warmth to melt himself free and the sludge flowed off under its own power and turned the ground into a skating-rink.

"Don't waste your energy," Desi said. "It's part of the trick. If you let the landscape make the rules, you'll burn out before you get anywhere."

The tree's steel skeleton splintered to shards with a tinkle, but a spiky stump remained just above ground level. After a moment the stump grew spikes that lengthened into sword-blades and began to rebuild, its glass skin growing around it until the tree stood exactly as it had before. It began to acquire frosty fur. The rising moon lit it.

"Tasty," Desi said. "I'd say mechanical. Place is programmed."

"So would I. Dangerous, but clockwork. There's lifesign that way."

She looked across a sheer crystal lake whose rocky sides vanished in amethystine darkness. An irregular island rose in the middle, quartz cliffs shining in the growing moonlight.

"Just where I'd expect it. I think I'll discorp, apart from my blisters the guy has a habit of manipulating temperature. If that water melted for just thirty seconds, you could burn all your calories swimming out."

"I'd noticed."

{Assuming it doesn't go right through the planet,} his symb remarked.

"Excuse?"

{Like a wormhole. I can't detect bottom. But don't let igneous rock worry you, there's active vulcanism. Hot center and magma near the surface. You could stop needing thermals fast if you fell. It's the sedimentaries that are artefacts.}

"Thanks, I love useless information."

They recorped on rock glazed with ice, overgrown with a scatter of crystalline lenses exactly placed to catch sunlight and throw it blindingly back, and a delicate architecture of ice-thorns forming a thicket as tangled as razor-wire that protected the cliff-face.

"Does this feel right?"

"I guess," Desi said. "If you mean it feels wrong."

"Looks like a fortress."

"I imagine it is. Don't discorp here, it would be dangerous.

This is his place. You could find you've come out in the thorn-hedge, or the rock, or the magma. In fact, don't move. Stand still."

"Impractical. I'm freezing to the ground already."

A chilly ghost in dark pinstripes shivered out beside them, a flaking envelope in its phantom hand.

*"Miz Smeett, it's essential I should talk to you . . ."*

It broke up in a small shower of hail that pattered to the ground and scattered their feet. Desi threw her arms up. "You can't get away from em."

"I think it was discouraged," Jones said.

The rock opened.

Ice stood his usual six inches off the surface, his blue-white brows raised in amusement. On his home ground, his hair stood up in fresh crystal spikes and a powder of glitter over his cheekbones highlighted a smooth bluish skin. A careless wave dispatched Jones to the heart of the thorns and he and Desi were left alone, face to face at last.

"Hi, Des, glad you could make it. I worried about you for a few minutes there in that Hermes dimension. Dissolving into soup? I'd hate you to finish as a dumpling. But I knew you'd escape, I trust you. My smart little wifey."

"Still the same shithead," Desi noted. "If my friend's seriously hung up on those spines, I am really gonna kill you permanent."

"Your teep." Ice glanced back. "I'd think he could look after himself. That much, anyway." A shrug dismissed him. "He can't be important, you haven't slept with him."

"I been too damn busy following a paper-trail. Can't say I see many signs of your sexlife."

"In my case I'm seriously cultivating celibacy. You should try, it does wonderful things for your energy." His blue eyes glittered with lively entertainment. "Leaving you free to make interesting creative maneuvers."

"So I noticed. I'm interested to death. I also came to get back my property. Once I have it, you can be celibate at leisure."

"Of course you did. Wasn't that the point of the game?" He slanted a brow. "I suppose one must expect vampires to be spoilsport bitches, but you don't know the fascinating problems you've missed. I didn't tell our little planet quite all my thoughts and it's rather naïve, it thinks it's doing us both a favor. True love, you know. You wouldn't like to go back and finish the run?''

''No,'' Desi said.

''Too bad. What's also too bad is I don't feel like giving. Your property, I mean. If it counts as property. Perhaps what I want's an intact family unit. Oldfashioned values, like the pioneers? Little woman in the kitchen, cooking up remedies to free the world from everything exciting, while the head of the family stays out front inventing exciting things for her to free it from? We were the perfect team, until you got nasty.''

He paused for a moment to choke with laughter. ''Not to mention the war of the cradle. Wouldn't you like to reconsider? Look how creative we could be together. We've a positive duty to make copies, with our total IQ. Come on, Des, don't be grumpy. Let's begin again. I can trash the teep, you don't really want him.''

Desi raised her brows under her fur hood. ''With not so much as a quid pro quo?''

''Okay, I *won't* trash the teep. He can take your pet ship and they can both go home. I'll even show him the way, and give them both a kick to get them started. Human and conscious, if you convince me I really want to. But you'll have to work at convincing me, baby, I've spent so long celibate I've started to like it. Up here in the castle, looking down. You can get so all-hell creative.'' He sounded wistful. ''Guess we could try marriage again and see. I've a strong sense of duty.''

''I hadn't noticed. Thought your ideas were all-hell childish. Thought you'd maybe caught a shrink-bug, the sort eats your brains. Is one reason I came, you've gotten me worried. If you keep regressing you'll end back in diapers and if you've damaged our common problem, I'll kill you. I mean it.''

Ice grinned. ''That's my Desi. Really knows how to fascinate a man. You'd better come in, before your friend freezes. If he goes cryo in the middle of a thornbush even you may have trouble putting him together, especially if he falls on his face. This place is unstable. We did what we could, Jelly-Brain and I, but the continuum tends to revert to singularity. Every so often it takes a jerk and there's a quake. Sometimes it's even disagreeably volcanic. People can get hurt.''

Jones stood still in the middle of the thicket, crystal razor-blades against his skin, long icy swordblades crossing around him. A gentle frost-fur spread on his exposed face and hands, stiffened his clothes, lensed his eyes with ice. Desi glanced back at him, and at her husband. Their eyes locked.

''Give me what belongs to me.''

''Take it if you can. I'll fight you to the death for it, Des, I warn you.''

''So will I, be warned.''

''Pity.'' His white teeth glittered. A wave of cold crackled off him and the ambient temperature dropped ten degrees.

''For you,'' Desi said, and discorped out of her thermal suit.

She touched ground in a pillar of flame, her naked toes melting the dirt, her burning peak of hair streaming smoke, the bubble of heated air she stood in reducing the ice-trees to metal fingers that trailed waterdrops. She'd known she could use the China House madam and her fiery hairstyle, it was right in the files. Ice's grin widened as he changed too.

His body metamorphosed to pure water that ran through his parka, leaving it stiff. Clear blood pulsed in his arteries, pumped by a transparent heart. The lines of his skull and brain were ghostly echoes under spikes of glass hair. His breath plumed out of crystal nostrils. He stretched a wet finger to Desi's hand.

A jet of steam hissed between them, covering the landscape in falling snow. Their ghostly forms loomed menacingly through it. When the shower cleared her hand was still extended but dark solidity was spreading through her.

Wooden fingers long and sharp as oak-twigs poked at his surface tension, looking for a hole to let his heart out. He discorped and vanished. A storm-wind whipped up ice-flakes and snapped off branches. The crystal lenses tinkled together in a burst of reflections and the Desi-tree's bark began to smolder.

She swayed under the hurricane, an anxious eye turned on

Jones in the thicket as thrashing spikes cut through his clothing. His furs opened on naked skin and a bloody line slashed his cheek. She evaporated rapidly, to corp out on the plain with the wind following, trying to blast her molecules into air.

She pulled herself into a vortex that twined her streams with Ice's and their united being skated over the planetary surface, on rising air-currents generated by its own energy.

An immense anvil cloud rose to the stratosphere, covering lakes and mountains with shadow. Freezing rain started high and ran in liquid lines in front of it, the warmed water thawing snow to slush as Ice diverted his energies to saving his skin. The cloud drew him up with it, shearing winds giving it a horizontal spin that generated suction in its center. The black spout of a twister felt for the earth and sucked up the debris of broken vegetation, swaying as it vacuumed across the country.

"Careful," Ice said, out of the tempest. "Don't forget the boyfriend."

"I'm not," Desi said. But he'd used her lapse of attention to disengage. The tornado died and its load scattered, in random droppings into re-freezing water. She fell to the ground in a shower of raindrops and pulled herself together to reorient.

{You should be careful,} her symb said grimly. {I said I can hold you together, but I wasn't counting on being a weather-system. If you get too rarified we'll both discorporate, and see how you like being an algorithm.}

"True for him too," Desi said. "It was his idea."

{And a damned bad one.}

"They all are. Where is the lover?"

{Behind you. Will you stay corporeal while I try to recharge?}

Desi swung. She'd heard the grumble of disintegrating rock and she was half-prepared for the burning ash-shower that geysered up from a newly-formed fumerole. A gout of lava spurted after it and fell in fiery spray. The ground shook. She discorped again.

"Shit. He knows the planet's systems, he can manipulate them. It must cost power, unless he's using mechanical aids."

{He has to, his will's reinforced with fusion-cells. Nobody's symb can do this stuff alone, even his. He's just directing their energy. Your mistake is playing his way.}

Desi spread her sensors, looking for lifesign. She detected Jones, faint but still breathing, back in the thornbushes, and another, stronger force near him. She sighed. "Haven't had this kind of fight since the last time. Guess that's why we finished divorced, it was just too wearing. I'm out of practice."

She directed her mind back to the plateau, where the lake was boiling and rivers of magma welled from below, solidifying in weird shapes in the middle. The displaced liquid condensed and overflowed, flooding the plain.

The planet was a mess of wreckage, trees half-melted, refrozen slush lumped on the rocks, scattered with mounded detritus. The searchlight moon glared down on it, cutting the ruins into black and white shadows. The seismic interference had awakened its latent volcanic activity and a mountain on the skyline was in full eruption, spouting fire and smoke.

"Hi," Ice said. The plateau was knobby with frozen snow and a head-high thorn-cage closed Jones in with dagger-pointed prickles. Most of the reflecting lenses had melted, but staring moonlight whitened the rock. "You know, Des, we're a great couple. You wouldn't like to reconsider?"

"No," she said stonily, small, brown and warily balanced.

"Ah, well. Back to work."

"Time out!" Desi yelled.

"Okay," he said equably.

His clothes thawed, flowed and shaped around him. Desi recorped hers. They finished facing, but with her looking down at him. He smiled, restructured himself, materialized studio chrome chairs and sat.

"So, leetle Meessy, what may I do?"

He crossed one neatly-trousered knee over the other, his voice fatherly, Germanic, richly patronizing. The suiting, expensive conservative navy, was finely striped in a lighter shade and set off by a shirt the color of lettuce with a brown-and-pale-blue handpainted tie. A lettuce-leaf handkerchief in three neat points completed his left breast. Black wingtips at one end matched creamy hair at the other. His fingernails were polished.

Desi giggled from six-feet-six of coltish grace. She didn't sit, but bent her neck toward him like a beautiful giraffe. Her micro-miniskirt was thick enough to stop her freezing but her waist was so tiny the broad waistband was a handspan around. Yards of leg in black gauze stockings separated it from high buckskin boots. Her breasts, roughly the size of walnuts, made little bumps under black jersey. The dagger fingernail she tapped on her teeth was blood-colored to match her lips. She pouted. "Please tell me . . . ?"

"Yes?" Herr Professor flicked imaginary lint off a lapel for his imaginary audience. His hair glazed over, recollected itself and turned back to cream.

Desi picked at her teeth with the nail. She switched a blond ponytail. "What do stars dream?" she blurted. Central Europe with American overlay. And giggled again.

The professor frowned. "The stars have destinies outside human comprehension," he said. "They are alien and unknowable, especially those featured on TP—TV."

Offstage applause. The professor bowed slightly. Desi wriggled, hitched the jersey on her walnut breasts and tinily bit her nail some more. If she made him hesitate, she'd have an opening to attack through. "If a dog has Buddha nature, what has a sponge or an avocado?"

The professor turned the question over. "The lines of life lead upward and downward. An avocado-tree is certainly natural, though one is less sure of its fruit, which tends these days to genetic improvement. Buddha, however, to the best of my knowledge, sat under the bô variety, whose nature and fruit are doubtful. As for the habits of dogs, they're repulsive. Ask your begging friend in the thornbush, should he melt."

More applause. Desi giggled.

"Can you do what you think right, by doing wrong?"

"Everyone does wrong every day," the professor said rapidly. "Some choose to, some are chosen and some have the choice imposed upon them. Most of them probably end up all right, if the husband or wife in the case doesn't catch up with them. Others have undoubtedly been wronged badly, particularly the overweight and slow runners. This is right, since they were clearly in the wrong."

Light distant patter, with some hoots of laughter. Desi cocked her left hipbone with an air of not knowing how she looked. "What is the nature of a good lie?"

"On or off the golf-course? One should always define his terms."

"Her."

"Pardon?"

"Her. The term was mine."

"Pardon."

"Granted. Off."

"A good lie needs to be believable. If it's truly believable it can do incredible damage, however glaringly inauthentic its antecedents, to the point of becoming the truth. Those who attempt to comfort their friends with lies, however true, do wrong, since the friends usually see right through them."

Clap. Nibble.

"What is the quality of a just war?"

"The quality of a just war is naturally the most expensive, though materials issued to the combatants do not have to be up to the same standard and indeed, usually aren't. This must clearly be so, since they come out of taxpayers' money. The qualities of an unjust war are identical, especially from the point of view of the wounded."

Silence. Desi cocked her hipbone the other way and bit her nail simultaneously. "We know what the black thoughts of a white man are. What are the white thoughts of a black man?"

"The white thoughts of a black man are completely out of order, as you will find both communities entirely agree, and will be persecuted with the full rigor of the law by the right-minded wherever they are. The left-minded, being by definition red, have no part in this discussion. It is, on the contrary, normal for white men, or even blue men, to have black thoughts. I often have them myself."

"If laughter is yellow, what color is grief?"

"Yellow laughter is the laughter of chagrin, which is in many ways identical to grief. Grief therefore must by definition be yellow also, though possibly in some cases shaded toward orange, depending on the terms of the will. Those communities whose grief is white may purchase harmless coldwater dyes at their local hypermarket, whose address they will find in the Yellow Pages.''

''What is the theft of honesty?''

''The theft of honesty is carried out, to the best of my knowledge, by jealous horticulturists, who should presumably be punished with ten years of couch-grass. The untruthful and defamatory, on the other hand, may be pursued in law, but the effort's unlikely to buy you more than poor man's pence.''

''What is the honesty of a thief?''

''An honest thief should turn in his brother-thieves with all just speed whenever he can cop a plea by doing so. This will improve his chances of disappearing with the takings, and so keep his pence from becoming a poor man's. If he's both dumb and honest he doesn't have to, but may then have a plea copped against him, which is okay in paradise but less useful on earth.''

''What do you see when I see purple?''

''That's difficult to answer. When you see red, what I see is the shortest way to the exit, this being the course dictated by experience.''

''What can you see in your own eye?''

''My own eye,'' the professor said thoughtfully, plucking out the nearest and holding it to the light. ''Damned little, actually. Naked eyes have no expression, gaining their character from brows and lashes, which are therefore worth painting to fool other people. My own personality otherwise is no business of anyone's, and I refuse absolutely to know it myself.''

He put the eye back in, blinked once, and looked haughty.

''What color is a rainbow in the dark?''

''A blind man can't see a rainbow even in the light, and no-one at all can unless it's raining. Here it only snows. Your telepathic friend may know the color of radio rainbows, but if he does his lips seem to be sealed.''

''What does fruit taste like that's rotted into the ground?''

''Fruit that's rotted into the ground wasn't worth tasting, or it would have gathered less moss. You can't go around tasting everything whenever you want to. Greed is a tasteless activity, particularly in public."

"If I have the whole argument in my grasp, what's escaped me?" Desi asked, crooking a becoming knee.

"I have," Ice said, changing hastily to himself and remaking his clothes.

"And that represents the quality of your thought pretty accurately," Desi said, getting back into her own furs. "Which is about what I'd have expected of you. If you'd understood my questions, you'd have given me what's mine. I said you were losing your grip."

"Not necessarily. If you'd understood my answers, you wouldn't have kept on asking."

He grew long hair and developed a helmet. The segmented battle-armor was basically leather but his curved sword was steel, nicely damascened and aimed at her neck. She discorped six feet and ducked it.

"Style's a bit retro for you, don't you think? I always saw you as modern."

He grinned under the skull-shaped faceplate. "I'm an old-fashioned guy, that's what I was explaining. We could cut this short if you agreed to my proposal. Before I have to cut *you* short, which would be a pity. I mean, I expect we can reconstitute, but it could be inconvenient. Especially with the boyfriend turning to glass while we wait for you to be in shape to seduce me."

"No need," Desi cooed. She drew in her cheeks to *sidhe* hollows, spired her hair to complex braids hung with silver bells and grew eight inches. Her space-black eyes slanted to her temples and her canines lengthened over her lip. "I'm in shape right now. Where shall we start? I'm incredibly hypnotic, goes with the territory. You don't want to kill me, baby, look what you're losing. Like my teeth in your neck. Put the dumb sword down. That could have hurt."

Her voice sang in overlapping harmonics and jeweled nails as long as daggers wove hypnotic arabesques in front of his face. Her huge eyes were as deep as infinity, sucking in his psyche. "Your future's in my arms. Come closer. I long to kiss your throat and show you eternity."

"I don't doubt it," Ice said, avoiding her stare and discorping sideways. "Excuse me if I have a previous appointment." His backhand ought to have severed her at the waist. It didn't. Her *sidhe* copy was intangible. "Bitch!"

"Dickhead," Desi sang. She undulated snakily and blood dripped from her nails. Her tongue was pink and pointed and it licked lasciviously around red lips. "Let me love you. You lust for my touch, under your ear where the skin's softest, the friction of my caressing mouth . . ."

"Which is full of extremely visible teeth."

"Look closer. Come to me, let us unite and be one forever. Let me consecrate you to me with the holy blood-tie that will join us vein to vein . . ."

Ice was drawn in slowly, against his will, caught the edge of her eye, and went limp. His sword fell, but not on her neck. His arm slackened and dropped to his side. She drew him to her and her nail gently traced the line of his cheek. "Closer," she purred. "We'll make beautiful music together. Just give in. You have no will left . . ."

Ice, his lips almost touching hers, exerted himself with an effort that cracked his leather armor. He'd lost enough control for its molecules to stiffen and a flaking split grew down his breastplate.

"Now that, baby, is where you're mistaken," he said, with lingering wistfulness. Desi was panting, her lips parted, her tongue still reaching for his jugular. He pulled himself together and the leather melted back into thermals. The sword shrank and solidified to a stake, its point dark with dried blood. He materialized a wreath of garlic and threw it around her neck.

"Wrong period," she jeered. "I'm a *sidhe*. I'm not sure there's a cure for them."

Ice looked thoughtful. "Are you sure? You found one. I think a dragon, they seem uniquely fitted for survival."

Desi didn't wait for him to change, she melted through him, hissing viciously. Her symb stopped a few yards farther on to drive roots into the rock, which kept them both immobile while it sucked up minerals. There was a shortage of metallic ores and they had to spend energy on transmutation before it could start plating her with copper. It had the foresight to start at the breast, and the stake glanced off with a dull clunk.

"Ouch," she said. The dent had bruised her sternum. "You haven't gotten any better at anatomy, that aint where my heart is."

Her symb powered up for a rapid finish and they swung to meet him, scaled in copper from head to toe. Her eyes burned redhot between copper wires.

"No," Ice agreed, surveying the eyes. "But I've learned caution. Do you really want hand-to-hand combat? That's nice, you care. You want to touch me."

"With a barge-pole. You may find me hot to handle."

"I find your effects a little diminished, I preferred the weather-stuff. It showed largeness of mind. One of the things I've always liked about you is your vision. It's why I'm disappointed." He jerked his head backwards. "Des, Des, how could you fall? Does the guy have *anything,* apart from a bad case of frostbite?"

"Sure. But you wouldn't understand it. He's nice."

"Nice?" Ice burst into open laughter. "And that's what attracts you, after years with me? Come on, Des, you've a bad memory. What's nice got for someone like you? You've better taste than that."

"I used to think so," Desi agreed. "Maybe I grew up. Shall we finish?"

"I think we'd better, Mr. Nice is solidifying. How about really getting to basics?"

His shape changed, shrank to abstraction and darkened to negative. A complex emptiness hung in the air, a spiked core of blackness that multiplied outward in endless copies. The replication briefly mimicked sketched limbs before expanding outward. Fresh images branched from the first in leaf-shaped whorls that replicated in turn. The edges of the manifestation blurred as its growth extended beyond sight.

{Uh-oh.} Desi's symb retracted its roots and snapped back to their mutual center.

"What in hell's *that?*"

{The ginger-man stage of a Mandelbrot progression, with Julia sets extending out of it. Theoretical, of course, but nasty in practice since it reflects his thinking and this entire bubble's built around his brain-patterns. The continuum's fractal throughout, I should have noticed. Everything in it's himself.

A trick of Blinky's, I imagine. If he keeps it up long we've serious problems, they're all infinite and the Julias can be multidimensional.}

"We have problems," Desi concurred. The replicating shapes had taken over the reality of the plateau center in an overlapping dazzle that spread like cancer. "They're working through quaternaries and into the structure of the multiverse itself, hots knows where they could end. But the energy's coming from the continuum, and it's unstable. The bubble's breaking up."

Air and rock quivered, their molecular lattices losing structure in fractal echoes. Fresh volcanoes opened and began to spout lava as the crust destabilized and the water of the lake disappeared, hissing, into the hole Jones's symb had detected. Steam fountained.

The landscape was disintegrating, the icy architecture falling apart and the sword-trees splintering. Reality pulsed erratically, its forms blurring and reassembling at random. The air rarified and emptied Desi's lungs, and came back thickened with sulfur-fumes. She pulled her templates inward. A stronger and more threatening shudder shook the ground and the pulsation intensified.

"Shit!"

{Agreed. It's settling into an attractor with chaotic variation. The strain's shaking the planet to pieces. And you're right about the bubble, it can't stand this. It's collapsing.}

"Or turning into something completely different."

{It's more likely to revert to a black hole.}

"A micro. Dumb bastard. You could be wrong, I don't think he'd endanger the baby. It can't be with him."

{It was recently. You can all discorp elsewhere, Ice must mean to take the child with him. He must have a way to a safer dimension. It would make sense to have safeguards with this chronic instability.}

"He's fond of his butt. You and I can probably escape, but Jones and *Windy* can't. They haven't the time or energy. Shed metal, I'm incorporating in."

{Wait, you don't know what dimensions he's gotten to . . . }

The copper plating dissolved just in time. Desi discorped

into the void, her molecules open to mesh with whatever. The bubble paused, quivering, as the two came together.

The merging shook the roots of the continuum in a sexual shock like chain-lightning. Ice, water, rock and trees dissolved in chaotic patterns, shifting at random between extremes of possibility. The dimension hesitated among latencies, shook itself and resettled to the frozen archetypes of its original materials.

Jones blinked ice off his eyelids, let go of his reassembled molecules once he was sure they meant to stay in place, and melted his way out of the thicket.

The confounded essences of Ice and Desi rematerialized slowly, sprawled across each other in the snow. It melted in their excess heat and their wet clothes paused to decide whom they belonged to.

Desi on top was the first to move. ''Ouch,'' she said, sitting up with a groan. Ice was spreadeagled, his eyes closed and his lips slack in a goofy grin.

''You laid him out,'' Jones said.

''You didn't freeze to death or anything, finally,'' Desi said. ''Thank hotshot, was afraid we'd need an arc to remake you and I'd have had to crawl to Hermes. I aint in the mood.'' She scratched, and paused. Her eyes filled slowly and icy drops ran down her cheeks. ''I won. I guess that makes me real happy.''

''Mmn,'' Jones said. ''I can see it does. Would you call that fight fair?''

''You're kidding, Ice never fought fair in his life. I won kind of accidentally, hadn't changed out of vampire-mode when we merged, then forgot in the heat of the moment. I seem to have absorbed his energy. Never really thought I'd make it. Not that the lover didn't deserve it, but I'm taking time to feel victorious.''

''Accidental.'' Jones looked at the corpse with a certain envy. ''He doesn't look as if he'd suffered too badly, anyhow.''

''He's liable to wake up with one hell of an appetite. Well, this is where I collect my winnings. You know it's a letdown? Expected somehow to feel happier.'' She snuffled and wiped her nose on her sleeve. ''Let's look around the old homestead.'' She stood and brushed herself down, rearranging her fur collar.

''If you must,'' Jones said doubtfully. ''Wouldn't bet on it not being boobytrapped, from what I've seen. Would you mind telling me exactly what the quarrel was?''

Desi looked at him in astonishment. ''I thought you knew. We used to be married, but the guy's a control-freak. So things got more and more violent, and finally we separated. Then . . .''

The moon went out and the plain refroze solidly in darkness. An ultraviolet sun blinded them through blackish-brown mists.

The cliff-wall had parted on a square opening and a small blond boy stood in it, clearly visible in the UVs. He might have been six and looked albino. His hair was glass-fiber, his red eyes glowed like paired furnaces and his toes and fingers were too long and too many. His lips were white over feral teeth.

''What did you do to my father?'' he demanded, in a voice like the whine of a distant mosquito that drilled the eardrums. Maybe he didn't really speak at all.

''What's *that?*'' Jones asked, startled.

''What the fight's about,'' Desi said. ''The kid. Our son. When the guy left, he took the baby with him. Naturally, he didn't ask me if I cared. I had custody, dammit, court judged I was a responsible person, and I'm his mother. That's why I been risking my skin following him around, I wanted my kid back. Shit, I loved Ice. He's never loved anyone except himself. He didn't love the baby, what did he care? All he wanted to do was hurt me.'' She dripped salt icedrops onto the fur.

{And you didn't want to hurt him,} her symb said.

''Sure I did,'' Desi sobbed savagely. ''He deserved it. My baby's mine.''

Jones looked at the child's teeth. ''Does he know that?''

Reality flipped again, and turned inside-out.

# THIRTEEN

## Sword and Stone

The space they fell into was dark. Glassy arches winked with random light-patterns and the nodes sparked with an ozone smell. The flashes lit it fitfully.

It was a minor repeat of the dimension's gas architecture, a miniature cathedral. Where the outer vaults were high as solar prominences, these were just big enough for a tank-corps. The running sparkles that joined them sketched an interlinked structure. Repeating shadows and rhythmed static suggested that this space too was four-dimensional. The child had vanished.

Jones gulped. They were hanging in void, and a flare of blue-yellow lightning had just shot along a pillar and exploded in the node above his head. The space brightened, and quieted to darkness. A redder bolt climbed another column to mate with the first and the joining hazed them with bitter-smelling smoke. ''Where are we?''

''My symb thinks the whole dimension's a blueprint of Ice's brain,'' Desi said, looking around. ''So either we're in his head, which is unlikely, or we got moved to some construct inside the rock. If it's actually anywhere. Images are physical, but I can't believe his skull's filled with smoke really.''

''I don't suppose you brought us here yourself?''

"Who, me? I fell in here on my butt, like you. I said Ice was jinky, watch for tanktraps."

{We may be somewhere physical,} her symb said. {But it makes no difference, *it's* a virtual image and the electrical effects represent physical states. His brain's quiescent, in non-dreaming sleep. It won't last, the regular flashes are alpha-wave activity. As soon as he wakens, or even starts to dream, you'll have fireworks here like the Fourth of July.}

"What a place to live."

{I'll be surprised if he lives in it. I think your son imaged it to confuse you. Even Ice must relax sometime, or why does he have a planet?}

"Don't ask," Desi said. She craned her neck around.

"What's the matter with this kid?" Jones asked, baffled. "Apart from the custody-fight?"

Desi sighed. "He's another mutant genius, but severely mutated. Ice and I quarreled about having a baby. I wanted a gene-check, it's even mandatory. He said it would deprive our sex-lives of spontaneity, or something, and we were okay anyhow. Being in love, I let him overrule me. It's a side-effect of sex on the female brain, they lose their judgment, I told the ape so. For some reason it doesn't seem to happen to men. Or maybe we just don't talk the same language and don't realize it. I say red and he hears green."

"I wouldn't know. Men's brains can get messed up too," Jones muttered.

"They do? You must show me one, I'll eat him alive."

"The last woman I loved did that exactly. Lou-Beth, the pretty one with the long hair I kept seeing with the dragons? I don't think she meant to, but she digested me without noticing then didn't like me liquidized. So she married a real guy, who slapped her around."

"Can't understand that," Desi said. "Your natural state's so liquid, you'd think she'd have heard you gurgle as she swallowed."

"What you see is what's left."

"Of course," Desi said. "It's the standard male excuse, it was all *her* fault. As this was mine. It turned out our genes didn't match after all."

He looked at her sharply. "You wouldn't know so much

about Hermes and their multiverse experiments, maybe, because they should have heard of this kid, and didn't?''

''What do *you* think?'' she said. ''He's eighteen months old, realtime. Bite that and taste it. Ice latched on fast, like the day the kid was born. So fast, I wondered later if he'd expected it. When the problem became so obvious even I saw it, he and the baby were archives. I'd no trouble with custody, the lad has differences with the Federal Government he kind of didn't mention when we got married. Found out when he'd gone. I've been on his tail ever since.''

''He should have known his genome was unstable, you can't get a license unless you test clear. Are you sure you're legal?''

''Were, past tense.'' Desi sighed. ''I was tested for med-school, so I know I'm standard. It must be him. Now, I wonder if the wedding was legal too. I loved the guy, so he had to be honest. Break for laughter.''

''He *must* have known, if he lied.''

''He's a genius, maybe instability's part of it. Nobody can say now. His Central AI records are someone else's. It's unhackable, of course. Guess no-one told him.''

''What did the cops have on him?''

She grinned without amusement. ''Apart from hacking the CAI? Thought you'd seen some. Piracy. Abduction of a minor child. Crossing dimensional boundaries without a license. Illegal creation of artificial universes. Seducing Blinky, if anybody knows that. Cheating Hermes by concealing his son's birth-records, in which I'm an accomplice, because I faked them too. As you guessed. Impersonating some guy with an intact genome. Probably faking a wedding, plus begetting a gene-damaged baby through criminal carelessness or evil intent. All of which turns out to be my fault. I'm a woman, therefore should have a higher standard of morality. I am not supposed to be into stupidity, and being in love aint accepted as a reason. I'm supposed to have used my brains, exactly as if I'd had any.''

''Oh.''

''Yes.'' Desi turned an implacable face. ''And if you're thinking of interfering, don't. This is my problem and I'm trying to fix it.''

"Um," he said.

The missile came blazing out of darkness, where a recent neural firing had left smoke and red and yellow reflections. It was a late-model naval torpedo, narrow-beam sentient, with long-range flamethrowers as well as contact explosive. Its nose-cone was homed on Desi and feelers of adhesive skin-sensitive gel reached out for her. Jones it ignored, though a tendril sniffed him in passing. Its wake was burning.

{I'd a suspicion this could turn violent. We've mineral reserves in hand, luckily, I was still converting when we fell in here.}

Desi discorped reflexively. The torpedo second-guessed her and recorped at her side with its throwers still throwing. Burning glue turned her to a pillar of fire. Her symb's reflexes were well-judged and fast, because the skin it stuck to was plated in anti-flammable ceramic.

The fire consumed itself slowly and Desi evaporated. She reappeared on the far side of a node and a swarm of virtual fireflies spread around the lens. The torpedo hesitated, nose swiveling, and was foxed by its own fire. The echoing gravity sent waves of sensation back from everywhere. Desi rematerialized on its tailpipe with a foam-projector.

"Don't be dumb, if this image is two-way you'll damage your Papa." She hosed the shell down from the tail forward and its throwers died. "You trying to give the guy a stroke? Even I never wished that on him."

The architecture strobed as a series of junctions suddenly came to life, light streaming in urgent distress-signals from neuron to neuron. Reflected surges ran among the arches and set the space glowing. The vaults quivered. The glow took a long time to die, until final calm washed the crystal to shadow. The torpedo was frozen in its foam coating, the muffled outline stiff with tension. It relaxed in the dark and began to slough plastic.

"Listen," Desi said, lowering the nozzle. "You have to think things through, or someone'll end by getting hurt. If you want rough games, let's play em outside like your Pop and I did, before you do damage. You aren't trying to kill him. Cool down."

The torpedo shook off the last of the foam and sucked it

in, maybe to replace mass it had lost in throwing gel. It reshaped briefly to a glowering small boy whose skinny legs and arms were in continual, unending regeneration. His hair was long, then short and straight, then it fell in corkscrew ringlets. It had started black. It cleared to glassy and brightened to red. His features switched around in a perpetual *tic douloureux*. His hands writhed with splitting and melding fingers, three, seven, four.

His face was screwed in a sneer that might have been pain or loathing or just a childish grin. The effects of metamorphosis were hideously inhuman. Possibly emotional disturbance made him worse, or perhaps he lost control when his attention was distracted. He looked at his mother with eyes like coals, his pointed teeth shining.

"*You* hurt my father. I'm like this because of *you*. It's *your* fault we had to run away. If *you* weren't here, I wouldn't make mistakes. That's what girls do, they *mess up* real people. Ugly, dumb, stupid old ***girl***. You aren't even the right *shape*. I'm gonna ***KILL*** you."

"Okay," Desi said peaceably. "But let's not take your Dad along by accident. That would *really* be stupid."

The child didn't listen. He was into a fresh transformation, a multiplex war robot with jointed firing-arms and wraparound vizor. His head spun on its axis, looking for shooting-angles, and the insect arms lifted and clicked their weapons.

The emptiness was disorienting, masking the fact that his forms were miniature, reduced copies like deadly toys. He hadn't the mass for fullscale reproduction. But the redbanded armorpiercers aimed at Desi's middle were close enough and big enough to do the job.

Desi hung waiting, arms and legs spread like a starfish. She didn't try to move, and the bot followed the volley with another on the same heading, no doubt to pulverize what was left when the first had reduced her to pulp.

The shells scored direct hits on her ribcage, and passed on through as if she were mist. The robot shrieked, in the voice of a small boy having a tantrum. It loosed another double volley after the first, through Desi's ribs and out behind. She stayed where she was, arms and legs hanging.

"Let's be reasonable. I'm a full-grown Change with molecular dispersion capacity, girl or not. You think I'm going to stand still and be blended? You have to be smart even if you don't like people. Your Daddy uses his intelligence. You—'' She focused into the distance beyond him. ''Don't. Maybe you'd better, soon.''

The spatial circumference of the labyrinth was restricted. The vanishing missiles, their paths marked by dwindling threads of flame, were vanishing to points one way, and a swarm of specks swam over the gravitational horizon behind. They were coming up fast. Their pointed noses swelled to darts as they screamed around the curve of the continuum.

The child was too busy shrieking with fury to look where her eyes were. Maybe he wasn't being fooled by so transparent an old girl-trick. He didn't react until the darts were on top of him.

He swung at the last moment, saw them and panicked. The robot fell apart to a frightened small boy swimming in space, four flights of plastic destruction accelerating into his breastbone.

Desi didn't discorp until the last moment, giving him the chance to put things right. But he was too really terrified to know how to do it. She detonated them herself a thousand yards off and they blossomed in angry sparks. The vaults twinkled with a shower of fireworks.

The boy's insect shriek quivered the structure. He'd lost form completely, dissolved to a spinning pillar of blood and flame with two red eyes glaring near the top. Pseudopods slightly like toes and fingers poked from the edges, and drew back in. Coils of gut unwrapped from its belly to stream like obscene garlands, and were sucked back into the mess of organs. His mouth opened to a fire-spouting nozzle that spewed phosphoric saliva around the columns.

The glass blackened, turned red, began to glow and melted away to burning icicles. They'd no reason to form spear-tipped shafts and fall, out there in open space, but they did, and their coagulating points were aimed at Desi's head. Her mouse-brown shag was lightly stuck with sweat and ruffled with shifting.

She felt rather than saw them coming, busy watching her son, and discorped as they reached her. They speared the space she'd just vacated and passed into the maze, cooling as they went. A faraway sparkle suggested they'd crashed into a pillar and probably accreted with it. Their fire went out and they didn't come back.

Desi's smile had gone, a deepening furrow in her sweaty brow. She flung out her arm as if throwing a fishing-net and a fine seine of neural threads spread from her fingertips. They caught the boy and tightened around him. She reeled him in, her symb-reinforced nerve material resisting his efforts to flame or explode free, and held him neutralized.

The boy fought like a captured shark, ripping at the meshes. His body was trapped in its most recent shape, distorted and not remotely human. Desi untangled him, her mind directing the strands, and rearranged cells and organs back to something like a child.

"That's enough. I'm your mother, half of yourself. What did I do? I carried and gave birth to you, I'm responsible for how you act. You're human, and you've got to behave that way."

The child glowered. He had another try at breaking the net but it was fine as monofil and just as strong.

"You're worried for your Daddy and you got the right, I know you love him. I don't want to keep you away from him. But I've rights too. It isn't good for you to grow up alone, away from everyone, never learning how to be a person. You need other kids, you have to grow up and go to school. You've got to take control. You're too young to understand, but it's true. Why don't we go talk to your Dad? Let's try to *act* like people."

The boy's eyes glinted. He'd given up struggling and reverted to a spindly pale child, probably albino, with hair like spun glass and eyes as red as embers. He'd currently six fingers and they twitched nervously.

He looked as if he desperately wanted to change, maybe had difficulty keeping one shape. His child's face had an unbaby tension. He still looked six. He'd either grown uncommonly fast, or Ice had spent more time in strange continuums than Desi believed. He was too alien to judge. He lowered his eyelids over red irises. "Will you let me out if I say maybe?"

"If you'll talk for a minute without trying to kill me."

"Okay," he said sullenly. "But no promises."

"Fine," Desi agreed. "Talk, and no promises. Let's find your Daddy. He ought to be in on this."

She dissolved the net. The boy's change was total and instantaneous. "I'm gonna kill you because you are a filthy break-it-all-up *slimy old* **GIRL**," he shrieked. "Girls are *dumb*. They *stink*. They think you can fool around and tell-a-man-what-to-*do*. They are ***NOT HUMAN***. I'm gonna ***kill*** you, because you are *dumber* and more *stinking* than any of them, and they all ought to be ***dead***. When I grow up I'm going to track them down and *kill* ***ALL OF THEM***. You ***stupid slimy old BITCH!***"

He didn't waste energy on refinements but flexed straight into a crude semi-shapeless killing-machine, a spiked cylinder that rolled for her face.

{And that *is* enough,} Jones said. His telepathic anger was cold enough to freeze the neural connections. They stuttered, half died, and restarted sluggishly.

Desi and her symb were both shaking, quivering with exhaustion, over-extension and misery. Her hands were raised against the roller but her guard was down.

Jones tensed, felt his way through unaccustomed cells and took hold of his molecules. The light-filled shape had some of the qualities and the extended shape of a manta ray, with a flexible tail that snapped like a whip around the roller. The impact spun it off-course and it lost its form. The boy came back to a rough resemblance of humanity with the beaked head poised menacingly over him.

{I ought to kill this, now. You've made a mistake, Des. This thing isn't human and it never will be. I think I even sympathize with Ice, there's no way you're going to civilize it and make it go to school. It isn't a child, it's a monster, and probably too dangerous even for Hermes. They couldn't put it in the same dimension with people like Ed, it would kill all of them. It means to destroy you, and nothing's going to stop it. Could be Ice is the only one can handle it, and you're not allowing that. I suspect the real solution's euthanasia. It isn't your fault it was born defective, but it's too badly damaged to fix. Our wild genes do these things sometimes, it's a price we pay for being what we are. You've kept hoping you could make it love you. But you can't, babe. It's truly incapable of being human.}

Rivers of tears ran down Desi's nose. "He's only a baby. All little kids hate their mothers sometimes, we're stronger than they are and we have control of them. I think a lot really would like to kill us from time to time, if they had his abilities. Or believe they would. Ordinary kids can't, so it doesn't matter, and they grow out of it later. He's never had the chance."

{And you don't know all of it,} she added silently. Her eyes went on weeping. {He's so badly damaged he won't live beyond childhood. He'll be old at ten, if he lasts that long. He isn't likely to. Ice and I quarreled about what to do. I wanted to love him, give him some normality, no matter what it cost. I'd have gone along with hiding him from Hermes. But Ice was like you, he wanted to shut him up someplace and just let him play. That's why they're here. Of course he likes it better than trying to be serious.}

She folded up in a disconsolate ball and wept into her thighs, tears running down her face and soaking her coverall.

"Ice is to blame for how he thinks," she said aloud, small and pale. "He gets ideas from his daddy. A lot of men make stupid ugly jokes, and they can sound okay from a cute adult. Grown-up people don't take them seriously, but he believes in his father."

{I've no sense of humor,} the ray said stonily.

"I'll bet you do it too. It's everyday guy-talk. How's a baby supposed to know what people really mean, when they don't know themselves?"

The Jones-manta hissed. {I happen to disagree, but I won't argue now. This insane thing can't be let loose, even if its father makes bad jokes. It isn't safe.}

Desi wiped her nose on her sleeve. "Of course not. I wasn't going to. But you can see for yourself, he's not afraid of you even in that shape. You're a guy, he trusts you. It's me he wants to kill. It's why I wanted to humanize him. It's what mothers are supposed to do with kids."

The child, exhausted by the fight too, had simply curled up in the ray's wing and gone to sleep. His unconscious mouth was sweetly slack as if he was dreaming. His loosened fingers changed slowly, three-five-nine, and his hair shaded quietly from red into coal. If you could overlook the alterations, he was any sleeping child.

Jones sighed and coiled his tail. {So what do we do about him?}

"There's only one thing left, and I'd have said I'd rather die first." Desi pulled herself together, her eyes red. "I just gotta let his father have him. If I'd had him when he was a baby it might have been different, but it's too late now. I suppose he'd the right to choose his parent, and I guess he did. I can't help. I've lived so long wanting him, I hadn't ever thought he wouldn't want me." She choked. "So Ice won after all. That bastard always does. I'm clearing out, I'll leave them in peace, I don't care anymore."

{That's why you're crying.}

"Have I a choice?"

{No, I don't think so. But will Ice leave you in peace? He's been leading you on.}

"He will if he really thinks I mean it."

"How do you convince him?"

Their eyes met, hers red and wet, his still hard. He reflected, and they softened. {Well, I guess there are ways of putting it to him. Are you sure he can manage the kid?}

She nodded. "I think so. I suppose I've got to believe he loves him, he's given himself trouble. That isn't exactly vintage Ice. I have to think he's one thing Ice *does* love."

{Apart from himself.}

"Maybe a little better," she said gravely.

{What about his defective attention-span? Is Ice going to get bored before this dies naturally? It won't get too strong for him as it grows older?}

Desi's eyes looked into distance. "I've got to believe so. He's strong. And he's been fairly constant about annoying me. We'd better hope he can, I don't know what else to do. It seems to be out of my hands anyway. I did say we shouldn't underrate the guy."

The columns around were beginning to sparkle with awakening color and the flashes between nodes multiplied. A rattle of sparks ran around the continuum like artillery. A rapid throbbing grew in the matrix and spread until the space was buzzing with electricity.

The manta undulated its wings. {Looks like he's waking up. Maybe we'd better leave.}

Ice was lying on a fur couch in a kozykorner decorated in cloned zebra. A perfumed towel over his forehead drifted curling vapors and a large logfire, probably holo, snapped in the fireplace. The couch made cradling motions and cooed softly. A chromed domestic of charmingly archaic design stood beside him holding an icebucket. He groaned when he heard them materialize, lifted a corner of towel to check, and let it drop again.

"Wow, Des, that was an orgy. Didn't know we still could. Warn me next time and I'll dream up some chemical padding. Though the headache's too wholesale just to be you, why do I think my kid's been clanking in climbing-boots around my inner scenery?"

{Really?} the manta appreciated, in a sinister screech. Ice winced.

"Charming getup, love the light-effects, but turn down the sound, huh? I'm feeling fragile. What's that?"

{Yours,} Jones said grimly, passing over the inert bundle. {Desi's decided to renounce her interest, she thinks you go together.}

Ice smiled, waving the domestic to take the child away. It put down the icebucket and carried him silently out of the room. "How right of her, finally."

{It's my opinion too. You deserve each other.}

Ice raised his eyebrows. "I think he blames her for making him exist. Being alive makes him suffer. He's in pain all the time."

{He gives that impression. I'd supposed it was partly because he knows he isn't normal.}

"He does, but the physical changes are agonizing. I've trouble distracting him sometimes, he cries."

{Why does he blame it all on Desi?}

Ice yawned. "I may have referred to her as a dumb bimbo sometimes. He has a literal mind. I cope any way I can."

{I guess so,} Jones admitted. {But must you give him war-toys?}

Ice almost sat up in indignation but thought better of it, wincing. "I deny it absolutely. Nothing but the best educational constructors, or he'd take the bloody planet apart." He looked reproachful. "What's Des been saying? It's probably only nine-tenths true. Oh, by the way, thanks, Des, appreciate your spirit of renunciation. Womanly of you. You've a large mind, I always said so. Among other attributes. You must call again."

He focused blearily on the ray. "I suppose he may have gotten into the film-library, I do come across small metallic buzzing things in the bathroom occasionally. Inconvenient, I keep having to swat them."

{Fit an anti-kid prog,} Jones advised tersely. {If he keeps messing in your head you could end with an aneurism.}

"Wouldn't help, he's a genius. Besides," Ice protested, "he doesn't play killer-games with me."

But Jones had discorped, his light-display strobing with bad temper.

"Nice wings," Ice noted absently. "Your taste in guys is improving, Des. What happened to the over-intellectual teep?" And he vanished likewise, taking the kozykorner with him.

Desi stood alone on the darkling plain. She stared at it, and it darkled back. The moon hung more or less where it should be, roughly the right size. Night temperatures crackled the air. She scraped salty ice from her cheeks and discorped too.

"You don't quite seem to have carried out your Quest," *Windrunner* said nastily. "But you've upset *him,* I've never seen him shapechange. Wasn't sure he could." She sounded impressed.

Desi dropped in her couch, crunched, and got up again. "This place still fulla *crumbs*," she said accusingly. *Windrunner* called a mouse without farther explanation. She'd belatedly noticed the salty traces.

"Did you kill the dragon?" she asked appeasingly when it had finished.

"No," Desi said. "Get any sleep while we were gone?"

"I'm only a ship, ships don't *need* sleep," *Windrunner* muttered to herself. "Yes. That is, as much as I was able with weird gravitational pulses and stuff. I was slightly worried once, when the scenery went blurry. Wondered if I ought to come down and look for you."

"Kind thought, bad idea," Desi mumbled. "Told you not to. Any ideas about getting us outta here?"

*Windrunner* paused to master astonishment. "The arches are a construct," she said finally. "But they haven't real mass."

"My symb thinks the same."

"That's reasonable, we're sisters."

Desi hadn't the energy to explode. "So you are," she said, deeply discouraged.

"So they're too fragile to mess with. That leaves us with the center of gravity."

Desi sighed. "I was afraid so. Oh, well, who's captain? Haven't tried a sun lately. We'll go for the core. Does that give me time for a hamburger?"

"Several," *Windrunner* said reassuringly. "I'll get us there, if you'll give orders at interface." She sighed too. "I'm getting over-familiar with unfamiliar temperatures."

"I know what you mean," Desi said. She wandered through and switched in the galley.

"I'm not sure," *Windrunner* said cautiously over the intercom.

"Uh?"

"That this life's good for him. That manta makeup's *scary*. And he's gone to bed in it."

"Don't worry," Desi said, munching. "If he's like me, he'll revert in the night and find the bed doesn't fit. He had an attack of paternity."

"What's that?"

"A guy thing they get at his age. Gimme a buzz when we're in range."

*Windrunner* sent another mouse to clean the crumbs around the grill, without saying a thing.

* * *

"A million miles and closing," *Windrunner* reported. "Temperature rising seriously. Do you want to come and help?"

"That's a dangerous question," Desi muttered, choking on a soda. She was still rocked by sporadic wet hiccups. "On my way, babe."

The vidplates, polarized, were filled by the star's immense corona, occluding the sky. Cooler yellow prominences rose up out of it, and collapsed slowly. The white combustion went on in silence. Patterns of roiling gases moved on the surface as currents welled up from the depths.

"My symb recommended it," *Windrunner* said, her voice shaky. "But it looks hot."

"Fairly." Desi wiped her nose. "Hang onto your shield, and remember you're a person so you can always corp out of it."

They were falling fast through the stellar atmosphere, *Windrunner*'s skin laboring to hold against the blast of solar particles and a temperature that wanted to melt her into it.

"Strong wind, I'm blowing off-course. That's why I called." She sounded pleading. Wanting to be told to turn and go back before she broke up.

"Great," Desi said strongly. "We're doing fine. Hang together and keep trucking. You could burn a little, but it won't be for long. You warming main engines?"

"Warming?" *Windrunner* said, her voice fading in and out as she tried to keep her course in the teeth of the gale. "I'm trying to *cool* them before they explode."

"Just so long as you're prepared for warp."

"I'm prepared," *Windrunner* assured her.

A soaring wall of flame wiped out the view and burned the plates blank. Jones staggered in in his underpants, hair in his eyes. He was human again, if half-awake.

"Something happening? You might have told me, your refrigeration's shaky—" He took the flare full in the face and raised a hand to his eyes. The bones shone through. "Jeezle!"

"Siddown and shuddup," Desi said rapidly over her panel. "Use straps. Okay, *Windy,* warp for center. On my mark, and get us full thrust as fast as you can or we're cooked. Ten. Nine."

"Not again," Jones complained, dropping in the couch and groping for his harness. "It's hot."

"Happens when you heat things," Desi said from the computer. "Four. Three. Two. One. Mark, and lean on it."

*Windrunner* turned her nose to the flux and switched in reactors. The big engines burped, overheating in spite of their refrigeration, and took in mass at the second swallow. The cabin faltered, oscillated and lost phase for transition. The photosphere rushed past them, an inferno of gases, and burned itself away.

■
■
■
▪

The plates were black, filled with imaginary shimmers. *Windrunner* flipped out of nowhere like a skipped stone, sliced herself a groove and fled, shrieking, for a soothing gas-cloud. She slowed once she was in it and rolled over, bathing her scorched skin in healing hydrogen. She took a sobbing breath, closed down her batteries and started hungrily to suck mass. After a while she tuned her functions to autorepair and started rebuilding.

The cabin temperature was still uncomfortable and wounded mice buzzed on the ends of their feed-cables, half in and half out their holes. The repaired vidplates slowly began to register images. The holotank blinked and brought up a cosmos. Desi panted. "Whew!"

"Whew?"

"Wasn't sure we could do that. Aint my favorite way to exit a system."

"So why do it?" Jones asked, exasperated.

"Cause the bubble was so small. Knew we'd have a problem leaving. You liable to exit with too little energy, being minuscule, and implode all over the scenery. Consequent agreement among our symbs we needed all the grav we could get, and that was in the star-core. Limited our options. Nice work, baby."

*Windrunner* stopped whimpering to give a snuffle of recognition. ''It still hurts but I'm improving, the gas is cool here.''

''Take a good bath,'' Desi said. ''We stopped being in a hurry.''

''We did?'' Jones asked. ''I didn't know sloth was part of your lifestyle.''

''It depends on where I'm going. What I have waiting now's a seventy zillion credit lawsuit and the rest of my life in jail. You might care to rethink your own future. If we ever get back where we came from.''

**You could come and live with us.**

**WE**! should ***like*** to have **YOU**. **WE**! are ***working*** on **OUR! *population***. Of **OUR!** continental shelf.

**You'd like them. We're trying to make them more like you.**

A brief vision of stalking ghost-stars robed in organic gel that shone like a complex crystal, passed through their brains. The stars were gathered into a colony and were trying to erect buildings out of digested rock. A small public garden in sculpted slime-mold was arranged in the middle.

''Nice,'' Desi said. ''Esthetic. I particularly like the exo-skeletal brains, though you might find it practical to put the skull outside. Stops em getting dented.''

**THEY** have no ***combative* *instincts*. WE!** therefore ***hope*** the ***problem*** will ***turn* *out*** to be **SELF-*regulating***.

**And they regenerate very quickly. We hope they'll evolve well.**

''In case of accident,'' Desi explained. ''I don't know our combativity's linked to the existence of skeletons. It seems more an evolutionary adaptation to limited living-space. If there aint enough room, you kick the other guy. You maybe ought to think about that before you expand your future generations.''

''I wouldn't follow the human model at all,'' Jones contributed. ''Give the poor suckers a chance.''

**WE!** have ***been* *impressed*** by some ***human*** models.

**And less so by others.**

**WE! *hope*** to let **OUR! *community*** develop for **IT-SELF**, as **YOU *originally* *counseled***.

**They're long-lived and slow to reproduce, we hope that'll give them the best chances. Their environment isn't threatening, there's only us here.**

And **WE!** hardly ***want*** to ***hurt* THEM. THEY *are* OUR *offspring***, in a ***sense***.

**We enjoy seeing them grow.**

"Okay, guys, don't let me lean on you. Do what you think's right. But if any human explorers show up in the distance, get your little guys hardhats. Fast."

**WE!** have ***been* *attentively*** watching **YOUR *progress***. **WE!** have learned ***many* *fascinating*** things.

**Including, it can be wise to protect yourself.**

**WE! *mean*** to use **OUR! *new* *knowledge***.

**So if people come, they may not see us. We watched the methods of the illusionists carefully**.

Desi laughed. "You're great learners."

**It's what we do best**.

The ***multiverse* *is*** a wonderful ***place***. **WE! *hope*** to learn **MANY! *more* *new*** things in ***time*** to ***come*.**

**But we really want to get them right**.

**WE!** have ***understood* *at* *last*** why it ***is*** so ***important***.

**My first feels shame. We did wrong without meaning to.**

"I don't see that," Desi said firmly.

"Unless they're thinking about putting me in a bubble," Jones mumbled. "And I forgave them for that. I think."

"Don't be dumb. That wasn't Little Blink's fault, she wasn't even there. You weren't hurt anyway."

"Only in my pride."

"The one great masculine invention. Which even they thereupon declared a deadly sin, though it's never stopped em." She rolled up her eyes.

**WE! *were*** talking about the ***bubble* *universe*** that contains **YOUR SECOND!!**. The small ***changer*** that came from **YOUR *body*. WE! *are*** to ***blame***. **WE!** had not ***understood*** that **ITS *construction* *might* *hurt* YOU.**

**It very nearly did hurt you. Physically, I mean. We're afraid it may have hurt you mentally even more. And** *Windrunner* **was hurt too. We're sorry.**

Though **WE!** ***learned*** very much from **OUR!** ***observation***. **WE!** ***feel*** that **WE!** ***understand*** the ***operations*** of what is ***correct*** ***now*** much ***better***. **WE!** ***are*** ***listening*** with ***attention*** to **YOUR** advice on how to ***raise*** **OUR!** ***offspring***. **WE!** ***see*** that **WE!** ***still*** have a ***great*** ***deal*** to ***learn***.

**We'd have liked to help you. It hurt us to be shut out when you needed assistance.**

But **WE!** ***constructed*** the ***bubble*** to the ***directions*** of **YOUR OTHER!**. **WE!** ***believed*** **WE!** ***saw*** the ***necessity***.

"You were right, Blink," Desi said wanly. "It was a necessity. You've done most good by doing as he asked. Don't let it worry you, I'll survive and so will he. Sometimes people have to stand by their imbecilities. Nobody's to blame."

**THAT** does not ***seem*** to **US!** to ***be*** the ***case***. **WE!** ***should*** have ***preferred*** to ***help*** **YOU**.

**You were right, you see, the bubble was too small. We couldn't get in to affect what went on there. We could only watch.**

***Watching*** was ***painful***. **WE!** ***regret*** ***now*** **OUR!** ***inability*** to ***intervene***.

"Jonesy helped," Desi said, showing him her teeth. "Ice is okay if you stand well clear of him. Only advice I got is, if the boy offers useful suggestions on developing your people, tell him no thanks. He likes to play games."

Jones said nothing, but his brows drew together.

"You in pain?"

He shook his head. "No. I'm regretting their inability to intervene, too."

"Our problem now is how to get home. We've been drifting in circles. Damned if I know where we finally got to. Any ideas?"

"Shoot," Jones said, before either of them could answer. "You could've asked me. How d'you think I get my reports to the TV station?"

"By some kinda nasty submolecular whatsitsname?"

"Don't be obtuse. Yes, the message goes through substations. Who are generally human. A few are AIs, but it's much the same thing. What makes you think I can't follow my own signal?''

''Why didn't you say so?''

''You never gave me a chance. Gentlemen—I don't see why you should get away with perpetually labeling this neuter entity female, it should have a free right to choose, like everyone—I believe I can get this dumb bimbo home. To quote her ex-husband, who's undeniably a shit but also possibly had provocation. What I wouldn't mind's a little help with navigation. As she keeps telling me, physics aint my strong point.''

Desi burst into exhausted tears. ''You're all the fricky same, give you an inch and you call me names. No wonder my kid got confused about women. I'm going to a monastery.''

''You won't be welcome, babe. It'll take you around five minutes to subvert the inmates, who'll necessarily be men. Then they'll call you names too.''

''A women's monastery, frickhead.''

''That's a nunnery. I concede men are apes. I'm being tactfully silent about women.''

''Don't flatter yourself. You're still swinging by your tails.''

''But we do love you, baby.''

''I know. And we're supposed to be so tickled by the news, we can't wait to run in the kitchen and start scrubbing. Thanks, I been there. Have you ever asked yourselves if we love you?''

''Repeatedly,'' Jones said mournfully. ''Answer seems to be universally no. But I'll take you home anyway. If you persons can help?''

**WE! *perceive*** no ***problem***.

**Just show us the way, bub.**

**WE! *will* *show*** *Windrunner* the ***path***.

**What's the difference between he and she?**

''Now look what you've done,'' Desi sobbed disgustedly. ''You've confused them, too. Around five million years of moral evolution.''

''There isn't one,'' Jones said simultaneously. They both paused. ''Weren't you in favor of equality?''

"I've changed my mind."

"Well, I haven't. Allow me to wrap my tail around you in sign of solidarity and let's present a united front, it confuses the enemy. Call yourselves what you want, guys, I was giving you the choice."

"Anybody mind if I put my skin back on first?" *Windrunner* asked, muffled, from her ducts. Her vidplates had come completely online and were showing a bright array of galaxies. "Or even sleep a little?"

"Anything you like, kid," Desi said hastily. "We owe you several."

"Thank you," *Windrunner* said with dignity, and began to integrate her mice in their mouseholes. She even lowered the cabin temperature as a sign of goodwill, leaving Jones with frost in his armpits. He went for a sweater, sighing.

"Thank you, ladies," Desi said politely. She too was semiskinned and needed leisure for growing. She went to bed.

"Okay," *Windrunner* said, sending a regenerated mouse to clear the breakfast. She was frisky and in full running order. "Course, please? You don't have to roast me or compress me to neutrons, just point. I'm a big ship, I can get there myself."

"We should put you out to stud when we get back," Desi grumbled. She'd found a last residue of carbonized toastcrumbs down the back of her seat.

"I'd like that," *Windrunner* said. "If the guys are cute." She sent a vacuum-mouse without being asked. It coughed as it sucked, to Desi's satisfaction.

"We could make our fortunes," Jones said, optimistic. "Smeett-Jones Industries? We could retire."

"Smeett-Jones-***Windrunner*** Industries," *Windrunner* corrected. "And I want real antennae, cosmetic's humiliating. Other ships look down on me."

"When the lawyers are through with us, retirement may be our only option," Desi said. "Apart from a nervous breakdown, which I'm about due for. Okay, make waves, I'm along for the ride."

**We're ready when you are. Just give us a heading.**

We! are *looking* *forward* to *this*. IT *will* be *new*.

Jones closed his eyes. "Try *that* way."

*Windrunner* pulled herself out of her gas-cloud, sniffed at vacuum and chose herself an orbit. She built speed and grooved. The engines hiccuped, roared and steadied. She tensed for jump.

**Just stay with us, we'll help you with the power.**

*LOOP.*

Through blue-shifted gases and dense young star-clouds. A crackle of quantum communication lifted their hair and deformed the furniture. What it said was beyond understanding, but Jones smiled. The gases tickled, smelling of geranium.

*LOOP.*

Rare distant radio static and the hiss of shrinking singularities. A sweet millenial female voice spoke out of it. "Well, hello, sailor. Wondered when you meant to call in person. Next time, why don't you stay to breakfast?" Her amber perfume stretched in a thought-ray like the beam of a lighthouse that led to a

*LOOP*

through something infinitely mathematical that could have been the hexdump for a universe, with no feel or smell but width, constriction and the indefinite smoke of burning dust.

*LOOP.*

A strengthening pull spired them down through ghosts of possibilities to increasing probability. "Hey," a male voice yelled through cycling galaxies. "Willya shut the goddamn door?"

*SLAM.*

WE! *believe* that THIS is *home!*.

**See you guys again, right? We're counting on you.**

*Be* *careful* of YOURSELVES. WE! *value* YOUR *acquaintance*.

**Give us a call. We don't mind if you say he or she.**

Circles of light digested them and left them gasping on familiar shores that solidified from mirage to commonplace reality. The holochart steadied to a pattern of well-known stars.

Desi sniffed, and shed more salt. It was becoming a habit. "Home," she said. "Jeezle, how I hate it."

⌘

TP–TV

*the station of the multiverse*

HERE AGAIN WITH A SPECIAL EDITION, AIMED AT ALL YOU BOYS AND GIRLS OUT THERE WITH YOUR BIG, BIG SOCIAL CONSCIENCES RIGHT AT THE READY, WITH ANOTHER HOT FLASH FROM OUR OUTRIM RANGERIDER—HERE'S JONESY!

❖

[*Fade-in on Dick Tracy, scalp-lock in ringlets. The grin stretches elbow to elbow. He opens his mouth, closes it and looks confused. His face balloons in and out, collapses to a sizzle and re-forms as a skinny drink with trainwreck hair and an oversized sweater covering the rips in his jeans. It doesn't cover his bony knees. He's tired, determined and has better teeth than you'd have expected. His voice is pale and clear, like tidewater:*]

Hi, we've met, though you won't remember since you haven't seen me. I'm Jones, and I teep for this duck. First time for a while I've been in close enough range to quarrel with what they do to my material. And this is my partner Desi, the Hermes agent who makes all the headlines, and you can hear her for yourselves.

[*Desi, small, brown and unwashed, is sprawling sideways in her couch eating French toast, which drips syrup over her coverall. She wakes up suddenly, in a rage.*]

DESI, VERY MAD INDEED: What the hell is this? You mighta let me change. You think I want to appear on public vid the way I got born?

JONES: Well, yes, actually. I thought you were accusing us of distorting facts.

DESI, DARKLY: There's facts and facts. This aint a fact, it's an infringement of my civil liberties.

[*A moment of flux while she tints her skin gold, grows emerald eyes, stretches a foot and has the Tailormaid nan her an eau-de-nil gauze bibfront with one strap hanging. She rethinks it to include strategic spangles. The toast evaporates. A scrabble of mice can be heard in the background over* Windrunner *complaining. Desi reappears with cocked pinkie, holding a champagne-flute:*]

DESI, SMUG: Okay, interview me.

JONES, WITH APPRECIATION: Oh. I hadn't understood what you meant by truth to reality.

DESI, HUFFED: You want this interview, or what?

[*She sips daintily. A pinstriped ghost with a legal envelope materializes behind her and looks around, confused. Desi grabs its throat, folds it very small and stuffs it in the recycler without altering her smile. She re-cocks her pinkie. The flute almost turns Coke-color, but catches itself in time:*]

JONES: Can you tell us what really happened on the disputed occasion of the fungoid plague?

DESI: Hermes fouled up. Course, they got work to do, but they still built that fricky bubble too small. I aint saying it wasn't needed, even Ed thought so. But they let their alarm system fail. There was also sabotage, but a serious public utility ought to be able to face that.

JONES: What about their effort to muzzle the Press?

DESI: In your case, it's understandable.

JONES, CONTROLLING EMOTION: That isn't what you said then.

DESI: Well, I was pissed off then.

JONES, DISBELIEVING: And now you aren't?

DESI, SWEETLY: Perhaps I got older. My memory's failing.

JONES, GRIM: Let's hope theirs is.

DESI, ANGELIC: I'm sure it must be. Look how inconvenient it would be if I remembered.

JONES, GENUINELY SADDENED: You're throwing me to the wolves?

DESI, ASTONISHED: Me? I wouldn't. They completely forgot about you, too. How else can we keep things level?

[*She grabs him by the ears and kisses him passionately. His stool falls over amid muffled gulping. The network tries to cut them off and doesn't make it, they fade and reappear. Distant cheering from off-camera. The station techs may be feeling put-upon:*]

DESI, COMING UP FOR AIR: Didn't you want to make an announcement?

JONES, DAZED: Uh—sure. From now on I'm presenting hard news on my own as an independent, with control of my byline. That's Jones, J-O-N-E-S, of Smeet-Jones-*Windrunner* Enterprises, care of me on *Windrunner.* Who's available for brain-to-brain breeding with the latest symbiotic improvements, stud-fees by arrangement, consult *Windy.* I believe they depend on cuteness, ship's or owner's not yet specified.

*WINDRUNNER,* OFF: Either, I get to decide.

JONES: Thanks. If anyone wants authentic on-the-spot pictures of the plague, exclusive, we're open for business. Fees will be decided by me, and depend on your bank-balance. And now, I suppose the station would like a word from their sponsor.

[*They spire out and vanish.*]

"Not bad," Desi said. "Didn't think you'd the guts."

"Been feeling downtrodden, does bad things to my temperament. You really think Hermes could forget the suit?"

"They've got to. Was their fault and they know it. They're

not getting off free, I want proof they've fixed their mess or I really go public."

"Won't they stay mad?"

"May. If they do, I guess I start over as a country practitioner. *Back* country."

"That bother you?"

"No," Desi said. She stared at the panel, tracing patterns with her finger, and more salt filtered down her cheek. She'd reverted to unwashed brown. "That isn't what's wrong. I feel bad about the kid, I should have fought harder. Before, not after. After was too late. I deserved to lose him, and I guess you were right there was nothing left to save. He's still my baby, though, and I don't feel right about him. It's true he suffers. A long, short painful life I could have prevented."

"Didn't you tell Blinky that people can't be held responsible for everything that goes wrong?"

"It's easier to say than to practice."

"Always, babe. Is that a reason to throw yourself away? You've been on my case on the subject long enough."

A tear dripped off the tip of her chin. "It was my ability to like guys that died too, really. I loved Ice and he screwed me. I kinda thought fighting him might put things right again, so long as I won."

"And it didn't."

"No. It put them wronger. I ended totally convinced I don't love even him."

"Then that's got to help. You're free."

"I don't feel free. I just feel broken, like a fricky beerbottle."

"Uh." Jones looked down. "I know that one. You remember the late great love of my life, Lou-Beth, as represented in holo by dragons?"

"I remember, country-style, long brown hair. You'd a pretty clear picture of the original. Thought she dated back to college and married an editor."

"She did. I've devoted my life to not recovering."

"Now that," Desi said, "is just plain dumb."

"Yeah, isn't it? Just concluded so myself. So, since you think that, why are you so anxious to do the same?"

"I'm not," Desi said, sitting up with indignation.

"Got the impression you were. Now, I was once a shapechanger."

"You still are."

"Uh-uh. I mean like you. A different person every day in a different skin, with different wisecracks. Ran a multimedia performance-group. Don't think I looked human once a week. Was never off the vidshows. Lou-Beth didn't like it, was why she picked up with an editor who was plain too busy to change shape ever, except maybe when he'd a problem with his copy, and then he turned into a Yakuza and beat her."

"Sounds like you picked the wrong girl."

"Sounds like you picked the wrong guy. Anyhow, I thought Lou-Beth held the real me together. Found there wasn't one, when she went I didn't know who I was myself. So I dissolved the group, went back to me and became a correspondent. Reverse revenge, it's completely useless. It's so long since I shapechanged, my molecules hurt with the exercise."

"That manta wasn't bad for a creaky old guy. Even Ice admired it."

"I lost my temper."

"You ought to do it oftener. Did you have a name when you ran a vidgroup?"

"Shiloh."

"I remember him," Desi said. "Sent me crazy a couple hundred years back. That was you? How could you spoil it?"

He smiled thinly. "Same as you. Decided I was liquidized."

"You were wrong. But if you had to pick a face, why that one?"

"I was born with it?"

"If you don't like it, change it. You could try Shiloh."

"I can't guarantee to be the same. I'm older."

"So'm I. I aged a thousand years yesterday."

"I know, I saw. That was a mistake, too. It won't alter anything that matters. I, however, am a reasonably well-behaved ape, I've a particularly long tail and an intact genome, and we've recently acquired a new young symb each who may have new perspectives. We also just became partners. Shouldn't we celebrate?" He narrowed his eyes, compacted his mass to a blue steel blade, grew oxidized titanium inlays on his cheekbones and draped parts of the result in platinum mesh.

"You think it's too young for me?" he hummed, in a bronze bass with contrapuntal silver fingerings. It resonated in the walls. Desi considered.

"No, just kinda vidstar, take some living up to. If you do a lot of manta-stuff, you may make it. Your newscasts'll slay them."

"I'm sticking to doing those as myself," he sang. "This is go-out-and-get-drunk-in. You don't work in cocktail."

"I kinda forget as soon as I get occupied," Desi admitted.

"So go take a shower. If the liquid ape may take the cracked beerbottle out."

"Refreshments gonna be liquid too?"

"You can bet on it. I was figuring to appear on the newscasts as a guest-star, under the table."

"Not with me," Desi said. "Especially if I'm gonna have to practice in the country."

"Okay, on top of."

"Exhaustion's going to your head."

"I was hoping something would. With a couple of other wishes."

"Oh?"

"Don't ask now. Get a little drunker and I'll explain. Get a lot drunker and I won't have to."

"Haven't been propositioned since I was a hundred," Desi said. "You must be *really* out of practice."

"You want a single rose in a plastic wrapper, and your hand kissed?"

"I didn't say so. Hang around and I'll shower. It may stop me crying."

"If it doesn't at least temporarily, I'm going back to Jones."

"Hots forbid," Desi said. And blushed.

The hotel was midtown and multidimensional. Blue steel and green bronze drifted through, six inches above the floor. They both remembered blisters. Desi's eight-inch heels and gown of bone beads framed in wire would have stopped her walking even if she'd wanted to. They'd had cocktails, attracted looks and gotten the giggles. They drifted, giggling, not quite straight.

"Miz Smeett?"

She rotated. "You're dreaming, there's no such person."

"Miz Desi Smeett." Immaculate pinstripes and a legal envelope. Desi halted.

"Shit. I put you down the toilet once today."

"That was my ghost." Pinstripes smiled slightly. "You haven't been kind to it. But as it happens, Miz Smeett, I really must speak to you. I apologize if I'm spoiling your evening."

"Accepted. Now go away and spoil someone else's. I'll give you my lawyer's address, spoil his. Jonesy, tell me the address of a lawyer whose evening he can spoil."

"I'm behind on the subject, no-one's sued me since yesterday."

Desi opened her mouth on an explosion.

"Please," Pinstripes said. "Do listen, I beg you. I believe there's a misunderstanding between you and my client. He was under the impression you'd injured his son. Now he's had time to actually talk to the young man . . ." He coughed into his hand, embarrassed.

"You mean after you chased me all over the multiverse, the lover changed his mind?"

"Something like that."

"Now, just you listen . . ."

Jones cut the knot with a steel blade persona and toning voice. "Miz Smeett has suffered grave inconvenience."

The lawyer swung, grateful for the kind of man he understood. "Obviously."

"Her feelings were injured and her reputation damaged."

"My client's aware of it. He's anxious to make amends . . ."

"Which will not be cheap," Jones sang. "We've several businesses to get started."

"But most evidently, my dear sir. If we could perhaps go into the bar and discuss it?"

"Tomorrow," Desi cut in. "Tonight he's drunk."

"I negotiate best when I'm drunk," Jones protested.

"That's what I mean. As your granddaddy told you, alky increases confidence while diminishing performance. I'm luckily not taking you to bed, so you won't have to fail me in greater detail."

His hatchet jaw cracked with disappointment. "You're not?"

"Not if you talk my affairs guy-fashion, like if I weren't here. Why don't you and me go consider your performance, and *he* can call tomorrow at SJ*W*'s offices to sort out the money?"

Jones looked hurt. "Thought we were dancing."

"Okay, we're dancing. But not too long or you'll be flat on your face, and it won't matter if I take you to bed or not."

"Fine," he said, with returning cheerfulness. "SJ*W* offices, first thing tomorrow. Where's that?" he added, parenthetically.

"*Windy*'s controlroom, got noplace else till we've the takings. And better make it second thing, you'll be starting with a hangover."

"Shall we say ten?" Pinstripes proposed with diplomacy.

"Better say twelve, you don't know him." Jones and Desi grinned at each other.

"How's the bottle?"

"Rolling. How's the liquid?"

"Shaking."

"So let's rock, rattle and roll."

A mechanical messenger stopped Desi during a no-feet waltz to hand her a candy-cane. She bit the end off, chewed, and passed it on. Jones achieved their spin-turn and took the second bite.

*Smith*—**Windrunner**—*Outer Orbital—Blackmail acknowledged, incident rectified, report for duty with or without partner—Hermes.* In pink and white sugar.

"With or without?" Desi said, reversing.

"Don't be dumb. I can teep from anywhere."

"Yeah, but will you have spare energy?"

They spun thoughtfully.

"We could leave a mouse in charge of the office."

"If we paint it like a target, customers maybe even see it."

"How about a manager?"

"Now, there you're talking. My brother-in-law . . ."

"No," Desi yelled. And lost control of her beads.

*Windrunner,* in orbit, played through a catalog of electrical wingdings and chose impressive useful gadgets she could add to her nose. She imaged them from several angles and emailed an order. That inspired her to catch the eye of a high-class spun-ceramic yacht in the next bay and wink at it lewdly. They slid closer, touched noses and giggled.

"My owner'll pay," the yacht teeped later. "Let's not tell him till morning."

"Let's not," *Windrunner* said. "They do such dumb things."

"You can say that again," the yacht agreed. They waltzed lightly and went back to rubbing noses. The giggling became very expensive.

**They forgave us.**

But **IT** was **MY! *fault*.**

**Sometimes Jonesy understands better.**

**HE *was*** not ***blinded*** by ***LOVE!*.**

**Not for Desi's Other or her Second. He would have killed for her.**

**HE *would*** have ***KILLED!* THEM *both*.**

**For her.**

For **HER.** There is ***still*** a ***great* *deal* I!** do not ***understand*.**

**They aren't like us.**

But **WE! *owe* THEM** so ***much*.**

**We owe them ourselves. What would you do if someone tried to destroy me?**

**THAT *is*** a very ***big* *question*.** The ***biggest*** of ***all*. I!** must ***reflect*** upon **IT. I! *see*** that to be ***correct*** is not ***easy*.**

**I think that's its virtue.**

***Virtue*** is ***one*** of the ***new* *ideas* YOU! *grasp*** more ***quickly*** than **I!.**

What if she's wrong about her Second, the small changer?

*WRONG!* is *another* *idea* that *causes* ME! *difficulty*.

It means more than one thing. She might honestly believe what isn't true. We did, when we built Ice's bubble. From ignorance.

THAT *is* *true*. *What* if SHE *is* *WRONG!*?

What if the Changer doesn't die? What if the father isn't strong enough? It's a genius. It hates the mother who made it. Suppose it learns to hate the father who shuts it in? It could find its way through the dimensional labyrinth, anywhere. Even here. It wants to destroy everything.

IT *could* *inflict* great *damage* on *ALL* of US!.

Because it's human. Hate's one of their qualities. As love is. They're powerful forces. We don't really understand them. What could we do? What should we?

WE! must *reflect*. WE! must *reflect* *most* *seriously*.

Yes. We must know the dreams of the stars, to understand the nature of things.

WE! must *know* if *even* this *THING* *may* have *Buddha?* in ITS *nature*.

If we must, we may have to do right by doing wrong.

*If* such a *proposition* is *possible*.

We must think.

WE! have *already* told a *good* *lie*, by *concealing* the *Changer* to *save* ITS *life*.

Must we now carry out a just war, to destroy them all before they kill us? Change is their quality. It may happen again and again.

The *white* MAN has had *black* *thoughts*. May WE! *hope* the *black* MAN *will* have *white* thoughts*?

The laughter has been very yellow. How dark may the grief be?

Are WE! not *stealing* *honesty* when WE! do not tell* what WE! *know*?

**Can we trust the honesty of a thief?**

What is *purple* when *seen* by the *incomprehensible*? Can WE! *ever* *understand*?

**What expression shall we see in our own eyes, if we see evil and do nothing, or do evil and see ourselves?**

What *color* is *goodness* when IT is *lost* in *darkness*?

**What will our innocence taste like, if we let it rot away?**

The *argument* may be in MY! *grasp*, but IT *is* the *answer* THAT *escapes* ME!.

**The universe is full of hard questions.**

WE! must *think*.

**Yes. We must think.**

We! have Our! *own* to *protect* *too*.

OUR OWN.

*TOO*.

Silence.